The Wittenbergs

The Wittenbergs

a novel by
Sarah Klassen

TURNSTONE PRESS

The Wittenbergs
copyright © Sarah Klassen 2013

Turnstone Press
Artspace Building
206-100 Arthur Street
Winnipeg, MB
R3B 1H3 Canada
www.TurnstonePress.com

Turnstone Press gratefully acknowledges the assistance of the Canada Council for the Arts, the Manitoba Arts Council, the Government of Canada through the Canada Book Fund, and the Province of Manitoba through the Book Publishing Tax Credit and the Book Publisher Marketing Assistance Program.

Printed and bound in Canada by Friesens for Turnstone Press.

Library and Archives Canada Cataloguing in Publication

Klassen, Sarah, 1932–, author
    The Wittenbergs / Sarah Klassen.

ISBN 978-0-88801-446-7 (pbk.)

    I. Title.

PS8571.L386W58 2013   C813'.54   C2013-905181-3

In memory of Johann P. Froese (1878–1949)
and Katherina Dueck Froese (1887–1919)

This story is for their descendants, among whom are:
Joan, Robert, Lois, Sarah-lynn and Gerald.

The only safe place is inside the story.
—Athol Fugard

Lord, you have been our dwelling place throughout all generations.
—Psalm 90:1

The Wittenbergs

Wind

A girl sits astride a fallen tree trunk halfway down the bank of the Red River. The weathered trunk lies angled diagonally across the steep slope, its root end pointing to the top of the bank, what's left of its branches almost at the water's edge. The girl, who should be at school, has taken a book from her backpack and alternates between reading and staring out across the water. When she reads she is completely engrossed: her brown hair falls forward concealing her face, her mouth is slightly open, both hands grasp the book. A novel. She is oblivious to the roar of motorboats racing north to the lake or south through the city. When she lifts her face from the page to the river traffic, she sees the large *Paddlewheel Princess* rounding the bend on its way downriver, its flag whipped by a stiff wind, its railing crowded with seniors enjoying a pleasant autumn cruise. When they wave, the girl waves back and watches the paddlewheeler continue north. It's late afternoon and already the sun is still

well above the trees and buildings on the opposite bank. Grey
gulls circle above the water.

The girl slides farther down the tree trunk as if intending to
get close to the water so she can dangle her feet in it. Below her,
half-embedded rocks protrude invitingly from the riverbank
and she inches down lower on her tree until she is even with
one of them, gets up, pulls herself onto the rock, manoeuvres
her body into a squatting position, then straightens cautiously,
until she is upright, a figure on a pedestal. The rock is smooth
and she is tense. But after standing still for a few minutes, her
limbs relax, she breathes deeply, gazes out over the water and
raising both arms shouts across the river:

My name is Ozymandias, King of Kings.
Look on my Works, ye Mighty, and despair!

She laughs out loud, perhaps with pleasure at the words. Or
at the audacity of Ozymandias. Or her own.

She glances down and sees that the book she left balanced
precariously on the tree trunk has fallen and is wedged between
two stones further down from where she was sitting. She jumps
from her rock and lands too hard on the sloped stony ground,
jarring her body. Her hand reaches down for balance, finds the
tree trunk. She grabs it, moves her hand along the bare, rough
wood and a splinter drives deep into her palm. She gasps and
lets go.

Moments pass before she can bear to look down at the inch
of splinter protruding from her hand. Horrified, she sits down
beside the trunk, brings her hand close to her face so she can
clamp her teeth around the stub of the splinter. She squeezes her
eyes shut, pulls hard until the whole thing grinds out accompanied by searing pain. There is blood on her hand. The girl
sits frozen, staring at the blood, not much more than a dribble,

but as the pain flares a sickening sensation settles in her stomach. She lets herself slump against the tree trunk. She is on the steepest part of the slope and must guard against sliding further down. She tries to dig her heels into the hard ground.

The book, a novel by Jane Austen, lies below her, beyond reach. Slowly, like a turtle coming to life, her body moves forward, still in sitting position. Gritting her teeth, she begins to wiggle herself down in the direction of the book.

At the top of the riverbank voices become audible. A gang of boys has arrived, AWOL from school like the girl. They are riding their bikes on the bumpy trail that runs through the trees along the river. Their shouts and raucous laughter roll down the riverbank.

Unwilling to place her injured hand on wood or stone, the girl makes slow progress on her mission to retrieve her book. She is afraid to stand up, but grasping whatever she can get hold of with her good hand, she brings herself to her knees. Her awkward position causes her to fall forward and she braces with both hands. The pain in her injured one triggers an unstoppable cry.

Her cry summons the raucous boys, who leave their bikes and storm down, a ragtag army that halts when they are still well above the girl.

Hey!

It's a sucky girl!

Hey, sucky girl, you sick down there?

She's freaking out.

Whatcha doin'?

You friggin' hiding down there?

She's crying.

Hey, you. Hey, crybaby!

The girl, handicapped as she is, appears frightened at first, but as if galvanized by the rowdy boys she tries again to get up on her knees, succeeds, and moving forward that way, retrieves the book and shoves it into the waistband of her shorts. Then, using both hands for support, she turns herself around and with clenched lips scrambles on all fours slowly up the rough riverbank. Her action is cause for derisive laughter.

Hey, crybaby! Better learn to walk.

Looks like a water rat.

Nah, she's a friggin' pig.

When the girl reaches the waiting boys, the slope less steep here, she stands up to face them. They are younger than she is, but have the advantage of numbers as they form a ragged semicircle around her, a barrier they are daring her to breach. Pulling herself tall, shoulders back, she narrows her eyes and glares at the boys. A gust of wind whips her hair into a wild halo.

Her voice a feral growl, she says, Let's just see who's a crybaby. Let's see who's the pig here. She fists her good hand, holds the bleeding one close to her chest, and lowering her head charges forward, shoulders a boy to her left, then one to her right. Every impact a solid, satisfying thud. Forcing her way through the barrier, she reaches the abandoned bikes and stomping on spokes and tires makes her way up the riverbank.

Whether it's the blood on her hand or the fierceness in her eyes or the tears running down her cheeks, no one touches her, no one gives chase. Crowding around the damaged bikes, the boys untangle their own, lead them toward the path that disappears among the trees.

When the girl reaches the park at the top of the riverbank, she stops to brush the twigs and mud from her clothes, examines the book for damage, her hand for blood, then following a gravel path she starts walking slowly, gains speed and by the time she gets to Kildonan Drive she is running.

~

Sunlight pours through the window, depositing a slatted square of light on the beige carpet. An old woman, cocooned in the warmth of a duvet, keeps her eyes closed, reluctant to face the light. She forgot to close the venetians last night. A bedside radio, muted, murmurs words that sound like *desert storm*. Music swells and fades. She remains motionless, a curled shell. She could, if she wanted to, name the days of the week, recite the names of her children and grandchildren. Give her a minute and she'll pluck the name of her great-grandson from the tip of her tongue. Another birth is expected in the family but that child is, so far, nameless.

Her body uncurls slightly from its foetal position and the sharp, immediate pain, dormant until this moment, reminds her: she must take her medicine. Some days she thinks if she could manage to play dead at least until noon there would be no pain. But there would be no life either. Her eyes blink open. Light stabs them like a knife and the lids fall shut again. Give her a few more minutes and she'll move the swollen fingers of her right hand tentatively: open, shut; open, shut. She'll test the swollen wrist, bend the stiff elbow, and so on. The left hand will be next. She'll urge a foot forward cautiously until it pokes out in exploratory fashion from the duvet and finds the sunlit room, always cool after the warmth of her bed. It will take the combined effort of flesh and will to get her sitting upright, a skinny, angular creature, feet reaching for the carpet. Fully awake, she'll look around as she does every morning but, please God, not too many more until the day she dies. She'll turn up the radio.

Today the slightest movement is intensely painful and she delays the ritual needed to get mobile. Lying still, she might take stock of what was done or left undone yesterday, if anything was. Or review plans for today, if any plans exist. She might try to retrieve last night's dreams. Were there dreams?

Lately she's been taking a mental inventory of her

possessions. On the oak dressing table a collection of photos, the eyes—mostly blue like hers—follow her every movement. The closet door conceals a rack of shoes and an array of dark skirts and floral blouses—rayon, Fortrel, polyester. In the small sitting room the padded rocking chair her son bought for her waits to receive her and an ivy vines tirelessly on top of the glass cabinet filled with china too good for a dishwasher. She has no dishwasher. Which of her grandchildren will want a dozen settings of Royal Doulton when she is gone? A short shelf of books: three Jane Austen novels (only three? shouldn't there be four?), a two-volume history of the Mennonites, two versions of the Bible—Luther's German and the King James. When has she last taken down a book, turned its pages and read even one short paragraph?

Next to her small collection of books, a solid row of photo albums.

The enumeration of her possessions weighs her down. She wants to be rid of them, travel unencumbered on this last leg of the journey. It must be possible to divest oneself of all unnecessary baggage, if not of pain, and enjoy the scenery. And the few travelling companions left. And the light, new every morning.

While her mind wanders, her eyes open and her body begins to move in spite of pain. An arm reaches out. Hands open and close. Open and close. A foot inches toward the edge of the mattress. When she finally hoists herself to an upright position, pain shoots to the tips of her fingers, down to her ankles and up along her narrow back to the base of her neck.

A final, enormous effort and she is on her feet. She makes her way bravely, slowly to the kitchen where a cluster of pills waits with the promise of relief. There is the stove and on it the kettle. She will make tea. Another day has begun.

~

Mia Wittenberg shoves a worn copy of *Pride and Prejudice* into her backpack, eyes the bowl of apples on the kitchen table, picks a shining red one, holds it for a moment in her hand, then changes her mind and returns it to the bowl. She calls a quick "Bye" in the direction of her mother's room—closed—and hurries out the door as if she's executing an escape. Wind from the west blows debris along the sidewalk and, pushing against it, she breaks into a jog, not just because she's running late for afternoon classes but because jogging has become her favourite way of moving, whether what she's moving toward promises pleasure or not. Right now she'd rather be heading south along Kildonan Drive toward Bur Oak Park, where a shaded path snakes along the bank of the Red River. She could stare all afternoon at the ripples of light teasing the sluggish brown current. Or sit on the riverbank reading *Pride and Prejudice*. She borrowed the book from GranMarie and read her way well into it one afternoon when she skipped school. Her hand still smarts from the splinter she caught that day on the riverbank.

Several houses down from the Wittenberg bungalow the front door flies open and a tall boy hurtles down the stairs of the weathered two-storey. He races along the sidewalk ahead of Mia, his long legs establishing a sure rhythm. The sun halos his black hair. The house from which the boy emerged has stood empty for months, but just before the start of the school year a family moved in. Mia has seen this boy, tall and tanned, in the hallways of George Sutton Collegiate. Already Angela has discovered his name: Kurt. Kurt Brady.

Looks like a Greek god, Angela claims.

Greek? Bev says. He's obviously aboriginal.

Angela is set on Greece. Anything the girls know about that country comes from their history teacher, Peter McBride, who has already begun recruiting students for a trip to Greece in spring. He likes to slide a Greek myth in between explorers and fur traders. Yesterday he told them the story of Pygmalion, a sculptor who hated women, then fell in love with the beautiful statue of a woman he had fashioned, a woman who came to life, the marble transformed into flesh and bone and blood.

Cool! was Angela's response. Angela is totally in favour of love. And beauty.

Bev is thoughtful. The creator falling in love with his creation? she mused.

Bev, you're always thinking about God, Mia said.

But the story playing out in Mia's head today as she crosses Henderson Highway is not about Pygmalion or any other creation narrative. It's about her sister's pregnancy—Alice is scheduled to give birth for the second time. Another boy. A brother for Lucas. The latest ultrasound clearly showed a small penis. Female genitalia would have had everyone breathing a surreptitious sigh of gratitude, and not because they don't like boys. They all love Lucas, and Taylor too, although they don't know very much about him.

The baby will not arrive until November, but already there's consternation. What will his coming mean? Will his liabilities outweigh his assets? The doctors speak in generalities. They are vague, hinting obliquely that certain conditions are more likely to appear in a boy.

Alice is not the one concerned. Alice is euphoric. God will make it all good, she says. He'll see us through. Alice's euphoria is a shield, a protective buffering she needs right now. Will need for a long time. When Mia thinks of her sister, her forehead wrinkles, not so much with worry as with concentration. There must be some reason for the existence of children like Lucas and Taylor. But what is it?

Science has not been Mia's favourite subject, but this September she added biology as an extra course. Because of Alice's

The Wittenbergs

pregnancy. Because of what they know now about Lucas. And her cousin Taylor.

Bio's good, Angela says. They don't make you write essays. Angela doesn't like essays: too time-consuming, too solitary. And it's not that she isn't capable. Mia knows her friend's social life simply doesn't allow for much school work. Bev, who is going to be a nurse, has always liked biology. Great, she says. We'll all be together in the same class. But they are already together in English. And history. And math. Mia hasn't told her friends why she's chosen biology. They don't know about the ultrasounds.

When Mia reaches the row of aspen that marks the start of school property, she slows her pace, comes to a stop. All week the trees have gloried in their autumn yellow, but today, lit by the afternoon sun, they possess a translucence unlike anything she has ever seen. Startled, she looks away, then turns again to stare. She wants to stay here, the afternoon breeze in her hair, the scent of burning leaves wafting toward her from somewhere. The beauty of the aspen trees sends a shaft of joy shivering through every bone and muscle; it sends sparks to her scalp and to her toes. She stands still, savouring the sensation, holding on to it, willing it to last. But like a gradual change of light, a longing replaces the joy. A longing she can't define or describe. What is it she wants? Her sister wants another baby, a healthy one. Her father wants to be principal of George Sutton Collegiate. Her melancholy mother wants to be left alone. GranMarie wants her tea and her pills. But what does she want?

Two squirrels chase each other furiously up a twisted oak. A wind springs up and rattles the yellow aspen leaves. The September sun shines warmly as Mia turns and walks slowly the rest of the way to school.

Because it's early in September everyone in Mia's grade twelve English class has read the assigned story by Leo Tolstoy: "How

13

Much Land Does a Man Need?" A hopeful land-buyer races against the sun to mark the outline of the real estate he is determined to own. His legs pump furiously, his arms swing at his side like pendulums until he is exhausted and must slow to a walk, stumbling forward, frequently changing his course to include the most fertile portions as he draws the boundary around a large acreage. All will be his if he hurries. The Asian tribesmen who own the land stand silently by, waiting to see if their client will slide into home plate (so to speak) before the sun slips below the horizon, ending the race.

Could of told you he wouldn't make it, someone mutters. It's that kinda story.

Dumb story if you ask me, adds someone else.

Ir-rel-e-vant. A smart alec.

Mia wonders what Kurt would think of the story, but Kurt is not in any of her classes

Boring, someone is saying. Boring, boring, boring.

Undaunted, the new English teacher, Hedie Lodge, nudges her crew into a discussion of the existential questions the story raises. What gives meaning to life? What's really important? That sort of thing. Mia, the copy of *Pride and Prejudice* concealed beneath the desktop, remembers words about gaining the world and losing your soul. It must have been Pastor Heese on a Sunday. She half-raises her hand to offer those words, but it's Friday afternoon, the class poised for the weekend, wired as if it's spring and the school year ending instead of just beginning. The discussion is already floundering. Land acquisition is not something the class cares about. Neither, it seems, is a well-lived life. Mia lets her hand drop to the desktop. She watches Hedie Lodge. Will the teacher try to hold her students to the task? Will she insist on pursuing this faltering lesson? The teacher is tall, willowy. She has thick brown hair and warm eyes that attract Mia. She thinks she'll like Miss Lodge and wants her to do something to redeem this Friday afternoon. Bring it to a good conclusion.

And the teacher tries. Listen up, she says. On Monday I'll give you the guidelines for a major assignment that will be ongoing for the year.

A groan greets this announcement, but at least all heads are up and turned toward the teacher.

It's a group assignment, Miss Lodge continues, and here's step one: you will form groups of four, at the most five, and you'll select a short story to work on. I'm going to let you choose your group mates.

The students like this and the bustling that ensues has energy. Heads turn, eyes meet in a general sorting out—whom to group with? Whom to shut out?

It's Mia's turn to groan. Angela and Bev are looking at her, she can feel it. And Danny too, if he's aware of what's going on. Mia has had her fill of group projects. She hates them. They bore her.

Any further instructions Hedie Lodge might want to give are sabotaged by the buzzer that marks the end of the school day. There's a scraping of feet, a gathering of books and backpacks, a swarming into the aisles, a mass migration toward the door. A palpable ending to this class. This school week. Mia watches her classmates take flight and when the last one has gone she collects her books.

Hedie Lodge has stepped to the window and is looking down onto the street that runs past the school. It's beautiful out there, she says. Come, look.

Mia joins her teacher at the window. The street below is lined with school buses and cars, the impatient blare of horns surges in through the open window. And the acrid smell of exhaust. Light glints from glass and paint. It's all familiar. Ordinary. Noisy. But beyond the vehicles and exhaust and milling of homebound students Mia can see yellow aspen leaves trembling in the wind. And above all tumult, the lightly clouded sky.

This group assignment, when's it due? she asks.

This first part, the short story part, will be finished end of the month. But the groups are ongoing for the year. For poetry, and then novel …

All year! Mia's eyes widen with alarm.

Are you okay with that? Miss Lodge turns from the window to face her student.

Oh, well … yes. I guess so. *All year?*

Hedie Lodge laughs. You look as if you're trapped, Mia.

How accurately this teacher has gauged her. Mia notices for the first time that she and Miss Lodge are the same height.

Groups are okay, I guess.

But you don't like them.

It's not that I think group projects are stupid, I'm sure they aren't. But I'm always appalled, I mean, do you realize …

Mia stops short when she realizes what she is about to tell the teacher: the time wasted when students start discussing an assigned topic. The pooling of ignorance, the incredible detours, like complaints about the hopeless math teacher, say, or graffiti in the washrooms, details so gross and disgusting it makes you want to puke, and always who did what with who last weekend, where to get drugs, that sort of thing. Relieved that she's prevented a stupid outpouring, Mia looks guardedly at her teacher. Hedie Lodge's grey-green eyes, fixed on her, do not reflect annoyance. Or impatience. Thoughtfulness, maybe.

When do we read *Hamlet*? Mia tries again, taking a new tack.

In spring.

In spring! Mia's horror is only partly fabricated. Everyone will be thinking of grad and exams. Nobody will take *Hamlet* seriously in spring.

Hedie Lodge smiles. You talk as if you're the teacher. And then she says, I'll bet you've already read *Hamlet*.

Mia reddens but admits nothing. Sorry, she says. I'm ranting, and I didn't mean to criticize the group project. Have a good weekend, Miss Lodge.

The halls are empty, no one left at the lockers. Buoyed with the prospect of a weekend, Mia breaks into a jog and when she reaches the stairs dances all the way down and out the door where Angela and Bev are waiting.

~

A glossy photo of a frosted chocolate cake on a crystal plate stares up at Millicent from a page in *Canadian Living*. The way the camera has caught the shine on the chocolate frosting distracts her from the recipe below. Too much concentration on that photo could undermine her determination to overcome inertia. To overcome sadness. With her husband and her daughter at school, she has spent most of the day in bed. Dozing. Shutting out the world. The sun. Shutting out the circumstances that constitute life.

One circumstance cannot be shut out. Alice will deliver a boy in November. Millicent suspects her daughter is withholding from her what the doctors say about the latest ultrasound. Alice thinks it would overwhelm her mother. Everyone thinks that. They always do. Always have. As if she, Millicent, is not to be counted on. Or counted in. As if she is out of the picture, less vital even than her elderly mother-in-law. And maybe they are right.

The imminent birth is a concern, and today that concern has given her a rare spurt of energy. She means to harness it for the project of baking a cake for supper, a dessert to follow the pizza Joseph will order in when he comes home after visiting his mother as he does every Friday after school. When the pizza arrives, he'll pour a glass of wine for her, one for Mia, a beer for himself. The cake will be a surprise. Joseph will make a big deal of it and cut himself a generous slice. Mia will ask for a skinny slice, please, and when she's eaten it Joseph will coax her to join him in a second, but instead she'll leave to meet her friends. Angela and Bev. And that boy, Danny.

A crease appears on Millicent's brow. Joseph. What is Joseph doing this very moment? Where is he? In his office or at the school board office? He's always in some office, always busy in an important way. Nothing in her life is that important.

A knife on the kitchen counter catches her eye. She reaches for it, runs a finger lightly along its cutting edge as if testing for sharpness, then holds the edge against the soft flesh of her inner arm. She shudders and drops the knife.

She turns on the radio for music to background her effort and finds the voice of an announcer. Something about the possibility of war in the Gulf. What Gulf? Kuwait, the announcer says. Saudi Arabia. Iraq. It has nothing to do with her. She fiddles until there's music. Somebody's going to Graceland.

A mother shouldn't have to worry the way she worries about her daughter's second pregnancy. She should be free to anticipate a normal birth. A happy baby. But just this week she's detected signs of uneasiness beneath Alice's determined exuberance. Signs of a possible lack of courage.

It will be all right, Millicent tells herself with as much conviction as she can scrape together. Lucas, after all, is walking and talking, if not exactly like other children, at least in his own fashion. Doesn't that make him unique? And doesn't the world value uniqueness?

Graceland, Graceland, the radio repeats.

Again the knife catches her eye.

Alice has aligned herself with some curious church where they play drums and raise their hands or clap when they sing. Millicent doesn't want to imagine the comedy enacted every Sunday in that sanctuary, if you can call that box-like building a sanctuary. She would be uncomfortable in such a church. She wouldn't be caught dead in it. Not that she attends church of any kind. Hasn't for years.

Alice has never considered abortion. Millicent has. Twice she has pondered that medical possibility and twice rejected it. Was that courage or lack of it? Her two daughters have never been told, of course. Millicent wonders if Alice should be more worried, not about the unborn child, but about Brian, her husband, a man given to dissatisfaction. A man whose state of mind, as far as she can see, is more often sullen than hopeful. Brian is not easily pleased. Not with his work as a cameraman with a local TV station, not with his wife's church, and not always with his firstborn, Lucas.

Millicent loves Lucas, who is struggling to wrap his child-brain—a special brain, apparently—around the imminent arrival of a baby brother. Whenever she reminds him that his mother will be going to the hospital to stay overnight, maybe more than one night, his eyes become enormous and he is bereft of what limited speech he masters.

You'll come and stay with Oma, Millicent says, knowing that such an arrangement would tax her beyond endurance, not because Lucas has too much energy, but because she has not enough.

No, Lucas always says, cringing away from her. 'Opsital. Me and Mom. 'Opsital.

Millicent has never had to worry about Mia, her younger daughter, for whom nothing seems impossible. Who heads into each day with the composure of a queen. She possesses a poise that astonishes Millicent.

She finds a mixing bowl, locates the tin of cocoa, two eggs, butter, the bottle of vanilla, and feels her resolve draining away. She does her best to rally. She will make this cake and it will be praised. Some of it will be eaten, some of it relegated to the freezer, some thrown in the garbage. But the whole project is suddenly without point. Useless. Terribly boring. It has settled its weight on her shoulders and the heaviness is creeping into her arms.

Later she will be convinced that in spite of this lassitude the cake would have been mixed, baked and iced in time for supper if the phone hadn't just then interrupted everything:

Mrs. Wittenberg?

Yes. What?

Your daughter Alice asked us to call you. She's here at the Women's Pavilion.

Millicent's free hand flies to her throat. She must call Joseph.

~

Joseph Wittenberg is seated at his desk in the vice principal's office in front of a pile of paper work from which he is allowing himself a reprieve: a quick mental detour to the weathered bench in his garden. From this bench he can see an unruly tangle of shrivelling vines and stubborn weeds, bent gladiola stalks, petunias and impatiens gone limp. Just weeks ago the garden was a lush kaleidoscope of colour, but now there's only the blaze of zinnias, yellow, orange, and pink—a new variety he found last spring at a local greenhouse. They'll brighten the dying garden briefly, then the sedum and chrysanthemum will take over and bloom late into fall. This year's cucumber crop was prolific, but now it's time to pull out the dried vines. The last tomatoes should be picked. The carrots can be left in the ground until

October. After visiting his mother Joseph will pick up a large pizza on his way home to supper. Afterwards he'll sip his coffee on the wooden bench, pull out whatever's dead and begin digging, exercising muscles that all day have been unused.

Still on the garden bench he pictures Millicent, fortressed against life, wrapped in that shroud of sadness he cannot understand. If she's up to it, she'll watch him from the window.

The three-thirty buzzer sounds its alarm, summoning Joseph from his garden bench back to his office. Back to the stack of paperwork. The year has barely begun and already there's an accumulation of it. But he won't neglect his garden.

The shrill signal, anticipated by more than a thousand students and five dozen teachers at George Sutton Collegiate, shatters the stillness—or restlessness or boredom—prevailing in the classrooms. It overrides lectures, last-minute homework instructions and group discussions that have become quarrels or stalemates and in some cases near-brawls. All classroom activities stop instantly when the buzzer sounds.

The hallways are Joseph's domain. He should be out there in the maelstrom, not in his office. He is expected to control noise levels in all common areas. When he appears in the halls—his stride deliberate, his chin jutting slightly, his gaze sweeping the territory like a searchlight—noise decreases, brawls are prevented or cut short and crass language reduced to muttering. He knows that some students fear him and while he doesn't discourage this fear, he's learned when it's best to smile and ease tensions. He also knows that he is hated by a handful of students, but takes that as part of his job. Mostly he is respected.

Over lunch today he phoned the maintenance department about the new custodian and spoke to the assistant superintendent about a missing shipment of revised biology texts. He spent half an hour closeted with principal Ab Solinsky and a police officer to hammer out a strategy to combat drugs at GSC. After that he dealt with two mouthy students and now he is determined to write at least three of the many references for students who are already applying for post–high school bursaries or weekend jobs.

By the time the buzzer stops—exactly seven seconds after it started—classrooms have disgorged their occupants and the halls resound with a babel of newly found baritone, high-pitched soprano, raucous laughter, shrieks of joy, imperious announcements, questions, invitations to parties—my parents will be out of town, my old man has this stash of booze like you wouldn't believe. The rude clanging of lockers is deafening. Amid the alarming crescendo of a Friday afternoon, the school week is ending.

The secretaries in the front office will brace themselves against the volatile energy that flows from the student horde surging toward the exits. A small stream of that energy will veer off to invade their territory before it recedes and drains from the building.

Joseph considers going out into the halls to monitor the exodus, but instead turns to his work.

Alyssa Schwabb: a so-so student, second daughter of four, is determined to enter university in fall. Science. Hopes to become a vet. Hmm.

Bertram Weston: Wants to study law. Well, he should. He's a first-rate student.

Danny Haarsma: Danny's asking for a reference for a job at Kmart. Joseph hopes he gets it. Maybe then he won't hang out with Mia so much. Their friendship doesn't alarm him. Doesn't delight him either.

Joseph Wittenberg, if anyone asks, loves his work. But he is restless. More than ready to exchange his office for the roomier, more elegant principal's office.

A sharp knock at the door. Which teacher is sending him a

recalcitrant student on a Friday afternoon? As the week draws to its close, the heady promise of freedom zings like an electric current through the classrooms. Joseph knows which ones are likely to become zoos, which harried teachers' nerves have the greatest tendency to tighten and snap. His mandate includes dealing with discipline, truancy and absenteeism, beside the mundane maintenance of textbook inventories.

The knock signals that at best he will be delayed, at worst his schedule will be rearranged.

Come in.

A girl in a brown jacket and cropped hair enters, strides toward his desk, confident and casual. How did she get past the secretaries?

Hi, Mr. W. A half-smile plays across the girl's face, a slack backpack hangs from one shoulder, obviously not crammed with homework. Joseph recognizes her, but what's her name? She's not one of his frequent callers, but once or twice last year she made involuntary visits to his office. Was it for smoking in the girls' washroom? Truancy? He's not aware that she's a particular thorn in a particular teacher's flesh so early in the term. Is this girl in the new English teacher's class?

Joseph has spoken once or twice with Hedie Lodge and noticed the easy grace of her movements. The unselfconscious candour that suggests she's already at home in her new position.

I came by to say have a great weekend. The girl's half-smile has become a wide grin.

Joseph Wittenberg is not taken in. He knows he is being provoked. Motions her to a chair. The girl sits without speaking and her eyes sweep the room, curious. The grins slips from her face as she shifts her gaze to the single narrow window in the office, then to a point directly above the vice principal's head.

Looks ferocious, she says. That ... that ... coyote? She sends the vice principal a questioning look.

Wolf, Joseph says. You're looking at a wolf.

Students often fix their eyes on the framed Robert Bateman print hanging above Joseph's head. In circumstances of guilt or fear they find it easier to face a painted creature of the wilds than Joseph Wittenberg's lake-blue eyes.

So what is it I can help you with? He is impatient with this girl. What is her name? He will not deign to ask. Her visit is trivial. He should not have let her sit down. I'm not anxious to hang around on a Friday, he says, and I can't imagine you are. Let's get on with it, shall we?

The girl swings her gaze round to face the vice principal, who is a handsome man, and she has the air of a girl who has learned to appreciate handsome men. What's the matter? Don't like a friendly visit from a friendly student? The attempted innocence of tone joined with brazen flirtatiousness annoys Joseph. It's a tactic other female students have tried even though he's old enough to have fathered them, though not, like Ab Solinsky, old enough to be their grandfather.

Joseph Wittenberg is about to become a grandfather for the second time. Alice is due in six weeks. His spine tightens whenever he remembers this, as he does now. And now he also remembers that last year he had the annoyance of this girl's company in connection with her defiance of the history teacher, Peter McBride, who accused her of plagiarism.

Could a grade eleven student spout such advanced vocabulary? Peter stormed.

Joseph didn't doubt that she could, with effort. Certainly Mia's wealth of words constantly surprises him. And now he remembers his visitor's name—Jane. Jane somebody. He will not use her name.

Oh, I do indeed appreciate your wish for a pleasant weekend, he says. And I wish you the same.

The plagiarism charge was verified by McBride's fortuitous

consultation of a reference book found in the school's library. Joseph rises from his chair and gestures toward the door.

Jane makes no move to rise. Once again her attitude undergoes a shift and her voice and demeanour become earnest. If I'm determined, she says, I mean totally, seriously determined to change, I mean like even in the last year of high school, what are the chances I'll get into university, do you think, Mr. W? Should I be doing something about it? Can you advise me?

Joseph, still standing, is not amused. No matter how dense, a student in the last year of high school knows enough to take such enquiries to the guidance department. Jane's gall is wasting his time and he is about to say so when she rises abruptly. Surprising how tall she is. Strong too: played volleyball last winter, Joseph remembers, before the second smoking-in-the-washroom incident. Really, she looks promising. Joseph has learned not to write off a student too quickly. He has seen too many misfits, academic Cs and Ds, loudmouths and even suspected drug pushers leave the school for the wider world and succeed. He has seen the last become the first.

Out! Joseph says and the girl, with a toss of her cropped head, moves toward the door, pauses, turns, wiggles her fingers in farewell and is gone.

Joseph sits down again, and writes that Alyssa Schwabb has been a stellar student at GSC and will continue to excel as she enters her first year of university. He states that Bertram Weston has impressed his teachers with his intelligence and creativity, and "we support his choice of law as his future area of study." He vouches for Danny, "a determined young man, sure to apply himself to details of work at Kmart as he does to his school subjects."

Joseph has no idea whether Danny has begun applying himself to anything this term. Maybe the boy thinks he has an in with the vice principal because he's known his daughter since elementary school.

Leaving the rest of the paper pile, Joseph takes his briefcase, pulls his jacket from the closet, locks his office door and wishes the secretaries a good weekend. When he leaves the building and steps into the mild September afternoon, he is greeted by a refreshing autumn wind. He stops to inhale the fresh air. Leaves are turning brown and yellow, the sun is low but still warm. There's a whole other world out here, he thinks, as he often does when he emerges from a day, or a week, spent mostly indoors, in the temperature-controlled confines of his office with its one narrow window or in the hallways reeking with adolescent smells or in the windowless textbook room. He deliberately slows his gait as he walks to the almost empty parking lot.

Joseph's brain, allowed to decelerate on the short walk to his car, revs instantly when he approaches the driver's side and sees the ugly wound gouged into the shiny door of his immaculate black Camaro. A red message adorns the hood—GESS-WHO-WUZ-HEAR. His key falters at the lock. He tries again. It refuses to slip in.

Damn! Jane's visit clicks into place. She was the decoy, the instrument of detainment while the job was being done. Or was she simply establishing an alibi?

At once Joseph reorders his schedule. He'll be late visiting his mother, an obligation he likes to get over with before the week-end begins. He'll have to inform Millicent that he'll be delayed. He'll ask her to order in the pizza.

Furious, Joseph does not panic. He is accustomed to entering crisis mode, and this is hardly a crisis. When things get seriously out of hand, Joseph closes in around himself, enters a deep and steady calm. He can't say whether it's inborn or whether it comes from years of practice, this ability to divest himself of anxiety. Millicent, he's learned, considers this ability a strength. And sometimes a cause for resentment.

Tom Gibbs is still in the automotive shop with students who

love the inner workings of vehicles so much they can't disengage, even on a Friday. Before he can remove the foreign substance plugging the lock he must complete his supervision of a student who is midway through his first try at an oil change.

Joseph returns to his office. He calls Millicent, who answers after the first ring, breathless. Thank God it's you, Joseph. I was just going to—

Anything wrong, Millie?

Alice is in labour. I have to get to the Women's Pavilion. Right now. I have to be there.

When Joseph leaves his office for the second time, he has no words for the secretaries who looked up when he returned and again now as he leaves. The new English teacher is leaning across the desk of one of them, chatting. She is wearing grey-green, the colour of her eyes. She too looks up, looks his way and when their eyes meet, Joseph finds in hers a warm neutrality. His steps falter as her gaze holds him. Something stirs inside him, something with enough force to nudge aside for a moment his anger at the gouged Camaro.

Gibbs dismisses his student and grabs tools; Joseph, a handful of rags. They run to the parking lot where Tom works at the lock while Joseph rubs at the lipsticked message. No need to distress Millicent. With luck she won't notice the scratch keyed into the driver's side.

A ripple has disturbed the surface of his calm. Alice's boy was to make his appearance in November, after the first report cards and parent-teacher visits. After the carrots were harvested.

~

Marie Wittenberg has passed the hours in solitude until now it's afternoon, the sun low in the sky. At four o'clock she rallies because it's Friday. She finds a floral blouse to go with the dark skirt she's wearing—no sweatpants-and-shirt outfits for her. She must be *salonfähig*, as her mother always said, because she's expecting Joseph. She fills the kettle, sets out cups and cookies, the usual ritual that takes more time, more energy each Friday. It suits her that Joseph likes to fulfill his obligation right after school: it's when her arthritis pain is least severe. She is an agenda item to be conscientiously completed and then checked off. Perhaps with relief. Let it be.

Still, given a choice, she'd want Joseph to be less hurried when he comes. Not glance so often at his wristwatch. He should tell her about his day at work. She can't imagine an entire life spent at school. Her own years in the classroom were few. And long ago. She'd like him to ask her questions. Not about what she's done today because what would there be to tell, but about her life when she had a real life. When her limbs were strong and blood rushed hotly through her veins. He should enquire about her life before he was born. Her life before Canada. He should ask her to write it down. Or, better, he should offer to write it down himself. But Joseph has never shown interest when she told him stories about the past. Her past. He preferred stories about big trucks and hockey and everything had to happen in Canada, not in some far-off, backward country.

Russia? he'd say when he was a teenager and a master of scorn. What's Russia got to do with me? But recently, on a day when she forgot herself in reminiscence, he leaned in to listen. Well, he was only being polite. Indulging his old mother whom he is obliged to visit.

Marie likes the way Mia pulls up a chair, breathless from bounding up the five flights and says, You look great, GranMarie, and tells her about the new English teacher or a story she's read.

Marie is fond of Alice too, sailing into her apartment like a refreshing breeze. She's not impressed, though, with her grand-daughter's recent association with the Church of Abundant Joy. Joseph speaks jokingly of it and Millicent is convinced it's a temporary aberration. Brian, Alice's husband, is not part of this new thing. He hasn't got the temperament for it, he says. Although she no longer attends church, Marie has always assumed that her children and grandchildren would associate themselves with one, one that held to sound traditions, sober preaching and solemn chorales. What kind of a name is "Church of Abundant Joy"?

Time is running out for Marie. She doesn't fear the running out, but she knows she's drawing her daily allotment of energy and concentration from a diminishing store. By noon she has depleted the supply, but after a nap there's a fresh spurt that lasts for most of the evening. She is only mildly alarmed at the signs of loss—her memory less reliable, her courage in limited supply. And she has learned to live with pain.

The phone rings and it's Joseph. Hello, Mother.

I'll buzz you in, Marie says, her finger fumbling for the right button.

No, wait, I'm not here, Mother. Not in your building.

Not here? Where are you then, Joseph? What do you mean, not here? When are you coming?

As it happens, not today.

What? What happens?

Something's come up, Mother.

Where?

At … at school.

You're at school?

No, no. I'm. I'm at … Well, something has come up, I mean, I won't be able to drop in. Not today.

I see, his mother says, confused.

Sorry, Mother.

Marie hangs up. Disappointment is nothing new and of course she understands. She should have said, It's okay, Joseph, you're busy. She knows her son has withheld from her the essence of what there was to tell.

Solitude is a companion as constant as arthritic pain. As familiar as disappointment. She settles herself, resigned, into the rocker. But what to do with the space that's opened up in her afternoon? She looks around.

Among her possessions is the seashell on her oak dresser. A spiralled shell with spiky extrusions, pink inside. It comes from Yalta. Her father brought it to her mother, who lay on a white bed in a white room, breathing in the sea air. Resting. Always resting. When Marie considers getting rid of things, she doesn't mean this shell. Nor, so far, the perfume bottle beside it. The delicate glass catches the sunlight reflected back from the dresser's mirror. Where is the card that came with it? The card that read, "With all my love, Ronald." Well, maybe she's thrown it out. About time, too. She rises, takes the pretty bottle from the dresser, turns it in her hand, admires the faceted glass, the rose-shaped stopper, then makes her slow way to the kitchen and shoves it behind a stack of plates above the sink.

Uncertain, she walks to the shelf of photo albums. There's one devoted to Alice, one to Mia and one to Taylor, her other grandchild. How old is he now—eight? Ten? Older? She lets her fingers run along the spine of one album, then the next. And here's that brown velvet one, her oldest album. Definitely not up for grabs. It contains the whole past. Her forebears, buried in another country, are gathered in this book. Marie has reached an age none of them managed to achieve: she is eighty-nine.

She lifts the brown book from its place and, avoiding the rocker, carries it to the wing-backed chair that best supports her fragile spine. She opens the book at random, and there's that faded sepia photo of a man with a rugged face, eyes intent on the camera. She knows they are blue because that's what her mother always said: blue as the sky. His hands, resting on his knees, are the hands of a working man. Marie has never seen this man who was her grandfather. He died in the prime of his life. Mysteriously.

She closes her eyes. Finds herself in the village Wassilyevka, where three children are posed for a picture. The photographer's head has just disappeared behind a black cloth. Two of the children stand up straight. She is one of those two, the taller one. She is looking down into the sleeping face of the recumbent child. Her mother did not want to be in the picture. As clearly as if it happened last week she remembers her mother saying, I don't want to be in another picture with a dead child. And her father, helpless and baffled, said, Well then, just the children.

Marie opens her eyes, slips out of the memory and finds herself in her own small apartment on her wing-back chair.

Last week Mia said, Your memory's like the hard drive of a computer, GranMarie. It's getting full.

They were sitting on the small balcony off the sitting room with cookies and tea. Below them the intermittent traffic noise reminded Marie of a time when she too had places to go and deadlines to meet.

Computer?

Dad bought it for me, Mia explained. For my last year of high school. And I'll need it for university. But don't worry, GranMarie. You don't have to learn about computers.

Marie closes her eyes again. She is walking along the village street lined with white picket fences behind which apricot and pear trees have burst into blossom almost overnight. Once she lived in that village, a young girl opening like a bud, coming alive to the world. Now, the memory of it is dim and tinged with sadness. She remembers leaving the village. And returning to it. And leaving again. She remembers there was a revolution. And a man named Lenin. But today the past confuses her and suddenly she feels strangely empty of emotion. She should get up and make tea, but she doesn't move. The open album is heavy on her lap.

~

The wind has picked up and Mia keeps her head down as she runs into it. When she turns onto Kildonan Drive, there's Danny, hands in his pocket. Waiting. For her. His face is sombre. What are you doing here, Danny?

He doesn't speak at first, and when she resumes walking, he follows her.

I couldn't handle school if my old man was the vice, he says.

Mia pauses, as if to consider Danny's words, then says, Well guess what, it's actually an advantage. If I need money for the cafeteria, I just go to his office. Or he'll write a permission for a dental appointment I forgot to ask for at home. I like it when he comes into a class I'm in. He'll smile at me from the door when he leaves. I like that.

Her father doesn't actually smile at her from the door.

Yeah, but then he reams us out for not clearing the halls fast enough, Danny says. Or he blames us because textbooks are disappearing or he wants to embarrass somebody by personally dragging them out of class into his office. And there's his voice over the intercom. Like, DANNY HAARSMA, REPORT IMMEDIATELY TO THE OFFICE.

I've never heard him say that. Not your name.

Not yet, you haven't.

Are you in trouble, Danny?

Might be.

What?

But Danny won't say.

Mia has known Danny Haarsma since grade three, when he arrived at school, a small, straw-haired boy, son of Dutch immigrants who moved into a small house on Edison Avenue. The teacher sat him next to Mia: You'll look after him, won't you, Mia? Show him where things are and everything? Mia accepted this task proudly, seriously, like a mother hen looking after a less than promising chick. He was a reluctant student, apparently without curiosity for learning. But he loved to draw. Good teachers praised his talent, others ignored or never discovered it.

As they made their way up the ladder of grades, Danny haphazardly, Mia easily, the obligation placed upon her by the teacher never left her. One year Danny told her, as if reporting a routine matter, My dad's not here now. We're not all together. He drew a picture of himself and a thin woman. She's my mom, he said. Mia, who was always making up stories, composed one about a small boy lost in a thick, dark jungle and terrified until he was discovered by a brave girl who had torn her way through malevolent vines and confronted wild boars and serpents to reach him.

That's very nice, Mia, her teacher said, the praise tentative, as if she suspected that one of Mia's parents had written the story.

They have continued walking and Danny says, Everybody connects you with the vice, you know.

Do they?

Yeah. They do.

You can come in if you want, Mia says when they reach her house and she looks for her key. My mom won't mind. Dad's at my grandmother's. Mia would like it if he said no; she wants to read *Pride and Prejudice*.

Danny glances uneasily at the empty driveway, then, as if this requires bravado, follows Mia boldly up the steps.

In the kitchen, Mia notices the food mixer and bowl on the counter, ingredients for baking, the magazine open to an enticing photo of a chocolate cake, but when she calls, I'm home, is it okay if Danny stays for pizza? Mo-om?—there's no answer. Surprised, she checks her mother's room. Empty. Maybe Alice has persuaded her mother to come to the park to watch Lucas lumber up to the top of the slide, pull back and refuse to slide down. Mia wants to be there too, in the park, pushing Lucas on a swing. She gets two Cokes from the fridge, hands one to Danny and heads for her room. He follows, sits on the bed while she selects a tape. Do you like Paula Abdul? she asks, knowing he probably doesn't. She starts the tape and Paula sings about dreams. And being lost in them. Lost. Mia doesn't think she has ever actually been lost, although she hasn't always known which way to go.

I'm thinking of quitting school, Danny says.

That's a really dumb idea.

Why?

It's the last year, why not just hang in there? Mia wants to tell him he's a fool, but his blank face and dejected form remind her of the boy who once clung to her. He has grown tall and remained skinny and his mood troubles her. Mia wants to protect him as if he is still her project, a project she has neglected and must now return to.

Why do you still hang out with him? Angela keeps asking. You know it's keeping you from something better, don't you? I mean, aren't you afraid of getting stuck with him? He's not exactly cute, know what I mean? Everyone's going to think you two are an item. Get rid of him already.

Bev thinks otherwise, encouraging Mia to bring Danny along. She's always ready to make room for him. If you ask me, she says, the guy needs all the boosting he can get.

Sometimes Mia is tired of being a booster. She never thinks

of Danny in a romantic way. They are simply friends and not until this year has his oddness, if it is oddness, troubled her. Some days his nervousness borders on frantic. Other days his eyes are clouded. Or distant. She doesn't mind his rumpled appearance, that's just Danny, and she's never compared him with other boys. The brains. The show-offs. The muscled, self-assured jocks Angela would give her right arm to hang out with. Or the guys whose access to any kind of vehicle makes them automatically irresistible.

I'm going to be an aunt, Mia says.

Oh. Danny's voice, flat, comes from the bed where he lies stretched out like a corpse.

For the second time, Mia says, and tells him about Alice's ultrasounds, the last one showing that she's carrying a boy. Her father said maybe just keep that detail in the family for now, but today she needs something extraordinary to snap Danny out of his despondency.

Danny doesn't move.

We were hoping for a girl, Mia says and immediately regrets it.

Yeah? Would that be better?

Actually, Mia doesn't think a girl would be better. Two boys would be just fine for Alice. Two nephews for her. Two grandsons for her parents. But this conversation is heading into a corner of Wittenberg territory that's become clouded. She should steer away from it. In any case, Danny doesn't take biology and wouldn't be entertained by what she's learned recently about chromosomes. She wonders if she should call her father at school and ask if he's staying late, should she order the pizza.

Paula Abdul continues her mournful song. Danny is still stretched out on the bed, eyes closed, legs hanging awkwardly over the edge, so motionless he might be asleep. Mia grabs him by the shoulder and shakes him. Hey, Danny, why don't you draw something? I want you to draw me. She finds paper and a pencil. Clears a space next to her computer. Here, she says, and Danny gets up from the bed.

She wishes her mother would show up. Or call. She looks around, then steps into the doorway and strikes the pose of an oriental dancer, her face dead serious, her arms raised, bent at the elbows, wrists bent and fingers held like petals of a lotus. She feels ridiculous, won't be able to hold the pose for long. She'll burst out laughing. Danny sits down at the desk, scrutinizes his model for several seconds and begins drawing. Mia is relieved when she sees Danny become purposeful, focused on his work, his eyes alert to every detail of her body, his hand steady, the tension in his jaw softening, his face less frightening.

He has finished the outline of her torso and is sketching her raised right arm when the telephone rings in the kitchen, startling Mia out of her pose. The laugh she's been holding back escapes, a brief outburst. She runs for the telephone.

Hello?

We're here at the hospital. Your mother and me.

Mia swallows. Everything okay?

Alice had a boy.

Everything okay?

Her father's voice is hearty. Fine, he says. We'll be all right. We'll all of us be all right.

Mia hangs up the phone. Turns to Danny, who is sitting at her desk, still holding the pencil in his hand, scrutinizing the headless sketch in front of him. The baby is here, she says. Alice had a boy.

Danny puts down his pencil. Wow, he says.

Mia looks up and laughs, as though "Wow" is stupid or strange. Danny rises from his chair. The drawing session is over. Mia suddenly wants him to put an arm around her, hold her, but he is moving toward the door, removing his silent presence, his inability to offer even words.

When he's gone, she sits down at the kitchen table. The curtains are gauzy white sheers dotted with green flecks. They have been there as long as she can remember. The floral wallpaper is faded. Garish red and gold zinnias her father brought in yesterday from the garden strut in a ceramic vase on the table. There's a glass pitcher half-filled with water on the counter. She sees the way the light strikes the surface of the water. The fridge hums as it always does.

In the bedroom Paula is singing about love.

What will her sister name the baby?

I've got a name, Alice has said. But it's a secret.

Mia gets up, changes into sweats, laces her running shoes and pelts out of the house and down the street. She quickly gains momentum, feels energy surging through her limbs. When she passes Kurt's house she stops and cupping her hands around her mouth hollers, Kurt! Kurt! Come on out! Run with me! The wind has picked up and whisks her words away. She runs into the gusty evening chanting, We'll be all right, we'll be all right.

She needs a destination. Doesn't want to run to the empty park and return to an empty house. But where to go? GranMarie. She heads in the direction of Wild Oak Estates and bounds up to the sixth floor. Her grandmother comes to the door and Mia bursts in as if she has escaped great danger.

GranMarie's free arm cradles a photo album.

Spending a little time with the past, GranMarie? Mia says, breathless from the stairs.

Look. Her grandmother opens the album to reveal the faded photograph of a man with work-worn hands. Did I ever show you this?

Mia is pretty sure she's seen the picture. Yes, she says. You said it's my ancestor. She takes the album from her grandmother and stares at the man. He is seated, but she can tell he must be tall. And strong. In the prime of his life. His forehead is broad, dark hair combed back, jaw almost square, eyes looking boldly ahead as if staring down the future. He has large hands and wears the sturdy boots of a farmer.

He died young, GranMarie says. It's quite a story.

A story I've heard before, Mia thinks. Something about a journey undertaken. Something about buying land. She studies the photo with a critical eye, as if seeing it for the first time. Will you tell me his story, GranMarie? she says and follows the old woman to the sitting room. The light is thin and the air too close. Mia wants to open a window, but the gusting wind might be too harsh for her grandmother.

Quite a story, the old woman says again, settling into the rocking chair. And maybe even true. She closes her eyes and looks as if she is about to doze off.

I've got a story for you, GranMarie. Mia, still holding the album, leans forward. This one's true. Alice had her baby. A boy. Congratulations, you're a great-grandmother. Twice over.

The old woman's eyes open. That's … good news, she says uncertainly. Isn't it good? She looks up for assurance.

It's the start of a new story, Mia says, thinking, We'll just see how good it is.

When her grandmother doesn't respond she goes to the small kitchen, finds packaged soup and a block of cheese only slightly mouldy. While the soup simmers she pares away the mould and makes sandwiches. She sets the small table, places the container with pills near her grandmother's bowl.

Refreshed by her nap, GranMarie eats with pleasure and tells Mia, You're a good cook.

And about that ancestor, Mia prompts, the one who …

Your great-great-grandfather, the old woman interrupts, spooning soup.

You said it's quite a story.

Well, but there's not that much to it. Or maybe I've forgotten. GranMarie reaches for her sandwich.

How did he die? Mia wants to keep the conversation going.

He died of fear. He was terrified to death.

Really?

Well, that's what they say. That's what they've always said. She puts down her unfinished sandwich. Her eyes lose focus. She stares vaguely at the opposite wall.

You're tired, Mia says. I'll come again and then you can tell me. Everything. Okay, GranMarie?

Everything? You want me to tell you everything? Do you have any idea what you're asking? The old woman's eyes refocus. They become wary, as if she is facing a test that she might fail.

You could start with the man in this picture, Mia says. What's his name? She is sure she's been told. Many times.

Johann Bartsch.

I'll come on Saturday morning. When you're rested. You can tell me on Saturday.

Yes, of course. The old woman speaks dismissively, as if she doubts Mia will come. Doubts she'll feel rested.

Jogging home, the wind even stronger now, Mia holds in her mind the picture of that man cut down in the prime of life. Has she ever really looked at that picture before today? How could she not have been impressed by that rugged face? A face that speaks of courage. And faith. Didn't all the ancestors have courage and faith? She is determined to remember his name: Johann Bartsch.

She wonders what Alice has named the baby.

~

SARAH KLASSEN

Because of the premature birth Alice stays longer than usual at the hospital and when she brings the baby home she has named him Jeremy. Brian has made no other suggestion, and simply said, Okay, fine with me. She calls the pastor at the Church of Abundant Joy and he is as eager as she to arrange a service of anointing for the new boy.

He's a very special baby, Alice tells him. Dropping her voice to a whisper, she adds, He might have Fragile X. Like Lucas.

We'll pray you through this, Alice, the pastor promises. We are with you. You are not alone. He recommends including Jeremy's entire family in the service, and Alice's friends too. Bring them, he urges. I'll announce it to the congregation. We'll pray for you. We'll surround you.

The doctor has told Alice it's too early to be certain that her second boy will be slow to thrive, like her first. He has not spoken the words "Fragile X Syndrome," but even Alice believes he will. Soon.

Will he live? she had asked.

Of course.

His words leave room for hope and that is enough for now.

Mia agrees to come to the service, not just for Alice's sake, but because she wants to. She does not invite Bev or Angela or Danny, although Alice has insisted her friends should come too. Angela and Danny would jump at a chance to miss classes. Bev would come because she believes in prayer. What exactly will they pray for at this service? Is the prayer intended as a preventative, since a diagnosis has not been confirmed? Will it be a plea for a miracle? A request for endurance?

Millicent volunteers to stay home with Lucas, but Alice says, no, Lucas has to be there too with his new brother. Joseph's presence is taken for granted, and he comes as much out of duty to Millicent as for his daughter's sake. Brian, who has so far avoided stepping inside the Church of Abundant Joy, has no choice. He has felt the heaviness of fatherhood ever since Lucas was born and now he feels it more than ever. He takes a day off work.

Bring your camera, Brian, Alice says. But he leaves it at home.

Marie Wittenberg declines to come. More and more she finds old age a convenient excuse for avoiding unwelcome obligations. She does not wish to enter the Church of Abundant Joy. I don't think you need me there, she says, sitting in her favourite chair, Mia beside her. Mia has brought Lucas, whom she's babysitting; she keeps a watchful eye on him. There has been no mention of ancestors.

Aren't you excited about the baby? Mia asks, determined to stir up in the old woman some trace of enthusiasm.

GranMarie shrugs. Who needs excitement? Not good for my heart. She smiles at Lucas, who chants, No good, no good, in a monotonous voice. Mia is unsure how much she should tell her grandmother about the family's concern for Jeremy. Will the information be too much for her?

It's Lucas who spills the beans: Grammerie, he mutters, Grammerie, my ... my ... Jeremy—he's, he's speshul, very speshul. Mom says. Like me. Mom says. As if this is good news. As if everybody will just love the baby to pieces like he does. He looks at Mia for approval. But Mia is not looking his way.

Of course he's special, GranMarie says.

The family is ushered to the front of the church, a cavernous space equipped with a good sound system and an overhead projector. The large screen is filled with an image of a rainbow in a sky from which the clouds have receded. A woman at an electric keyboard begins to play a sombre melody, almost fune-real except that it sounds tinny. Millicent sits between Mia and Joseph. Brian, in a clean blue shirt and new jeans, is holding Lucas. Out of the corner of his eye he watches Alice, who sits beside him. She's humming beneath her breath, cradling the baby. She's wrapped him in a pastel blue blanket. Lucas has never sat so far forward. He is nervous, agitated, looking around for children from his Sunday school, but there are none to be seen.

In the time allowed for stragglers to be seated, the Witten-bergs have time to ponder the birth of Jeremy, how it has already begun to take over. At mealtime, in conversations, the boy's birth hunkers with them. For Joseph it's still a secret to be kept from everyone at GSC. Millicent has been jolted awake, as if the premature birth has caught her by surprise. Mia, when she's jogging, moves in the company of the fact of Jeremy's arrival on planet Earth. She watches her sister. Thrust into the limelight, Alice's face, wreathed by a mop of dark unruly hair, glows.

The service begins. A woman steps forward to read from the Gospels, a story describing how Jesus heals a paralyzed man by saying, *Get up, take your mat and go home.*

When she's done, the congregation sings:

O healing river, send down your waters,
Send down your waters upon this land …

Alice's clear soprano rises above the congregation's feeble singing and carries the melody on which the words rest. Mia listens for her father's baritone, but Joseph isn't singing.

Let's try that again, the pastor says. Instead of "land" we'll sing "child."

After the song, the pastor invites Alice to bring the baby for-ward to the pulpit. When Brian remains seated, he says, You too, Brian. And Lucas. And the rest of the family. Come. He motions with both arms, a gesture meant to be welcoming. Brian hesitates before grasping Lucas's hand. Father and son walk forward to stand beside Alice and the baby. Alice's face continues to shine. Jeremy is passive. Mia thinks of the Madonna-and-child paintings she's seen in art books, the baby's eyes looking out from a strangely old and wise face.

No one else comes forward and the pastor does not repeat his summons but dabs his finger in a vial of ointment and draws a cross on Jeremy's forehead. He repeats the anointing. Twice.

Daddy. Lucas cranes his neck. His voice is a hoarse whisper. Daddy, what? What? What? Brian shushes him. Baffled, the boy repeats the question, louder this time. His father places a large hand across the boy's mouth, whereupon the child yanks away from him and mumbling Oma, Oma, stumbles his way down to sit with Millicent.

The pastor places his right hand on the baby's head and prays, addressing God with confidence, as if he is personally acquainted with the deity and sure of being heard, sure that God wants Jeremy to live a normal, healthy, fulfilled, productive, happy, devout life. The prayer ends with an expression of gratitude, as if all requests have already been granted.

When the Amen is spoken, Alice raises her bowed head, smiles at the congregation, then steps down from the platform and returns to her place. Brian follows, head bowed, eyes downcast. Lucas shifts over to sit between them. He pats the exposed hand of his baby brother.

Stillness falls over the people scattered in the pews. Mia breathes it in, wanting the silence that enfolds them to last. Joseph looks at his watch. Lucas begins squirming. The pastor speaks a benediction and then, accompanied by another tinny keyboard hymn, the family leaves the sanctuary.

In the foyer Alice stops and looks back to where the people are rising. She waits to let them come to her, and her family waits with her. Everyone wants to see the baby. How sweet he is, someone says while someone else calls him a darling, darling boy. There are hugs and tears and someone says, There's nothing on earth wrong with that child. As if they have all been taken in, fooled by a false alarm. Or as if the pastor's prayer has been answered before their eyes.

~

A week after the service Mia holds Jeremy in her arms while Alice watches and Lucas presses against her for attention. She's pretending she's the baby's mother. She looks into his still unfocused eyes and wiggles his thin arm. When he falls asleep, she studies his dark lashes and his tiny fingers. She holds him perfectly still, then begins rocking him cautiously.

Alice is looking for a support group and is collecting books and pamphlets on Fragile X Syndrome. She writes or phones medical experts, scours the library and recruits Mia. You're my research assistant, she says, unfailingly cheerful.

Mia is relieved that Alice is taking initiative, not sitting back while her church prays for Jeremy. Not that Mia hasn't prayed too. Not that she hasn't wondered why the Lord's Prayer does not mention healing. Or what it means to pray: *Your will be done.* And how in the world could anyone *pray without ceasing*? But Mia is wary of becoming her sister's assistant.

With Jeremy in his crib, the sisters sit down to compose a letter to their aunt in Toronto.

You're good with words, Mia, Alice says.

Unwilling to be seconded, Mia says, I think you can find a few of your own. In the end you'll write it your own way, she adds. Aunt Sue likes you better than me anyway.

Alice ignores the edge in her sister's voice and writes.

Dear Aunt Sue:

How is Taylor coming along? I'm hoping you'll be willing to write and tell me everything you know about this affliction that seems to have chosen our family. (So far the jury's still more or less out concerning our newborn, Jeremy, but Lucas, as you might have heard, has been confirmed.) How have you managed to live with it? How do you cope? What help have you found for Taylor? And for yourself? What books do you recommend?

You and me have so much in common, don't we, and I believe you've got lots to teach me and I'm totally eager to learn. Please write me soon. I need all the help I can get. And will be VERY grateful.

Alice.

P.S. Please don't think that I'm dismayed. I am NOT dismayed.

Neither Mia nor Alice knows very much about their cousin Taylor. Their father has not visited his Toronto brother in years and when Aunt Sue and Uncle Phil last brought Taylor for a visit they spent most of it with Aunt Sue's family. Mia remembers her cousin's spindly, frail arms and his unclear speech, his ears so large they must surely attract teasing. She didn't pay much attention to him then and neither did Alice, but all that has changed.

Other things have changed too, Mia has noticed. Her mother spends more time than usual out of bed, as if now she has a reason to rise. She'll ask Joseph to drive her to Alice's in the morning and some days she spends more time there than at home. She cooks soups and casseroles in Alice's kitchen, entertains Lucas with games she buys at Kmart, walks with Jeremy when he's cranky, and tells Alice, Don't worry. He'll be just fine. You'll see. When Millicent comes home she's exhausted.

Joseph, of course, carries on. It's not easy to say how the birth of this grandson has affected him, except that it has. Deeply. Sometimes at school when Mia sees him walking toward her down the hall, she thinks his gait has altered, or his administrative confidence has lost some of its muscle. At such times she wants to avoid him, but when he catches sight of her he rallies instantly, as if he has taken himself in hand. Twice he has given her a high five. That's more attention than he usually allows her at school.

And Brian? His TV station has assigned him to a journalist who is covering rural stories—unusual crops, genetic engineering, pollution of Lake Winnipeg. This takes him out of the city. Away from home.

~

Mia leaves early for school and when she arrives sees a forlorn figure on the steps, hands shoved into pockets, shoulders hunched. Danny. She's been avoiding him ever since she learned he vandalized her father's car. DANNY HAARSMA, REPORT IMMEDIATELY TO THE OFFICE. The intercom had crackled to life as her father's voice boomed out, invading Peter McBride's history class. She has not spoken to Danny since and doesn't want to now.

Hey, Mia.

She sets her face to frown. Hey, Danny.

Guess you're not happy to see me.

You guess right.

You mad at me? he asks.

Shouldn't I be?

Yeah. You're his kid.

Mia has come early to school for a reason. She is on a mission and can't let Danny derail it.

Vandalizing someone's car—that's dumb, she says. That's totally brainless. She shoulders him aside and leaves him shivering, his thin jacket slight protection against the stiff autumn wind.

When Mia reaches her English classroom, the door is open, the teacher standing at her desk. She is wearing high-heeled shoes. Navy. Mia walks in and finds herself suddenly at a loss, as if the encounter with Danny has stolen her energy.

In her navy heels Hedie Lodge is taller than Mia. She smiles at her student, then turns to write on the chalkboard. She asks, What can I do for you this bright morning?

It is a bright morning. On the way to school Mia watched the sun scale the treetops and transform windows along the street into squares of gold.

Good morning, Miss Lodge. I have an idea. A request, actually.

And that is?

About the group assignment. I blabbered on about how I don't like group assignments. I'm sorry. But I have this idea. My grandmother's old and I think—*I know*—she's got lots of stories. And nobody's really listening to them. To her. Me, for instance, I'm guilty. But I think they should be written down. For her grandkids. And she's got great-grandkids too. Mia pauses, wonders if Lucas and Jeremy will ever care about those stories, or even be able to read them.

And so … ?

Well, and so I'm thinking I could be the one to write them down.

You'd be the scribe?

Yes.

And what has that got to do with the assignment?

Mia hesitates. No wheedling, she's promised herself. No presumption. And no abject begging. Miss Lodge, she says. I'm wondering if you'd consider letting me do an independent assignment? Instead of the group project. I really want to do this. It would be a sort of creative writing project. Instead of analyzing literature I'd be composing stories. She pauses. She is being too anxious. Is about to promise she'll work hard, harder than she would in the group.

Are you planning to be a writer, Mia? Is that what this is about?

Mia is embarrassed. She imagines Miss Lodge weighing the situation: Can a new teacher take a risk of making an exception for the daughter of an administrator? I'm putting her on the spot, Mia thinks. It's not fair. This plan won't fly.

Hedie Lodge does not say yes, does not say no. Let me just mull this over.

Thanks. Oh, thanks. Mia sends her teacher a smile infused with hope and leaves the room.

That afternoon Mia's English class discusses a new story, "The Lottery," in which the villager who wins the annual lottery gets stoned by the neighbours. Both Mia and Bev have read the story.

It's horrible, Bev tells Angela, who forgot about the assignment. People get stoned. I was totally shocked.

Stoned! Angela says. That's so cool.

Mia bites her tongue.

Real stones, Bev goes on. Rocks. The winner gets killed.

The class discussion is animated. Explanations for such extreme and therefore fascinating behaviour fly across the room: blood lust, ignorance, prejudice, jealousy, tradition, fate. Someone trots out the predictable, *Man's inhumanity to man,* and someone else says, Violence is entertainment. Lots of people get off on that. I do. The speaker looks around as if this is a brave confession and deserves applause. The story is a hit. Even the most reluctant students will read all of it when they get home tonight.

Is the story true? Danny asks, rousing himself near the end of class. To squelch the snickering Miss Lodge quickly says, In what way can fiction be more true than fact?

It can't, someone said.

Mia has said nothing about "The Lottery," though if Danny hadn't defaced her father's car she would speak up now, to detract from his naïveté. She understands that the story can be read as a parable, but that doesn't make her like it. The woman who wins the lottery doesn't deserve to die, obviously. Neither does the Wittenberg family deserve three afflicted boys. Mia resents her classmates' fascination with the story.

When the others have no more to say, she raises her hand. Is everything random? she asks. Does chance rule? She has to raise her voice because all eyes are on the clock, the class is nearly over and everyone is listening for the buzzer.

When the class leaves Miss Lodge motions Mia to her desk. About that independent assignment, she says. Go ahead. I want you to try it. I'll put together some guidelines.

Mia beams her gratitude. It will be a research assignment too, she promises her teacher. Not just interviewing my grand-mother—I'll find books in the library …

Good. Miss Lodge smiles.

Still in a rush of gratitude, Mia says, I told my grandmother that story. The Tolstoy story about the man who wants land.

Did she like it? What did she say?

She right away started telling *me* a story.

About?

About a man who wanted land.

Walking along Kildonan Drive, Mia begins a story that has begun stirring in her mind. *A traveller sets out early one morning on a journey. A journey that may end in success or failure. The sky is ...*

Mia looks up. A jet has left a long white trail across the azure sky.

~

Joseph is expecting a knock on his office door. Just a routine meeting with a new staff member, he tells himself, though his preparations belie that argument. He has stacked his paperwork in tidy piles on his desk, shoved the wastepaper basket out of sight and wiped away with his handkerchief the dust accumulated on the bookshelves and brought vividly to light by the sun. He has opened the window to let fresh air in—air conditioning has been shut off for the year. He has given his shoes a polish, although of course they will remain unseen. This tidying and fussing has left him self-conscious.

The knock finds him in front of a mirror fastened to the inside of the closet door, looking himself in the eyes—his are sky blue. His thick bran-coloured thatch of hair has a mind of its own. He has smoothed it down with one large hand and flicked lint from his jacket lapel with the other. His hands are farmer's hands. Built for labour. He has sometimes wondered what it would be like to have to earn his living that way, as his ancestors did. But today his mind is far from farming. One last glance at the mirror shows him that a rush of blood has made his face ruddier than usual. His throat feels dry. He closes the closet door and hurries to let his visitor in.

Hedie Lodge is not wearing perfume but it seems to Joseph that her presence fills the room with a heady aroma. He holds the chair for her, then goes around the desk and sits opposite. Her eyes are warm. Smiling. An amused smile. Levelled at him. She leans back in her chair and tilts her head slightly. How unlike Millicent she is. Joseph stops himself. He is not in the habit of comparing women, on his staff or not, with his wife. But it's true. Her eyes hold—what is it they hold? The sheen of happiness? A glow of contentment? Millicent's as a rule are melancholy.

Hedie is waiting for him to begin the conversation.

How are you finding everything at George Sutton Collegiate? he asks. The students. The staff. Is your classroom satisfactory? Any supplies you need? Are we all right to work with? Are you surviving? Joseph knows that one of her English classes, the one his daughter is in, has already acquired a reputation for unruliness. Don't hesitate to ask for help, he says. Let us know if there's anything at all. He is speaking too urgently, had better stop before he offers her the moon. He intended to be business-like. Calm. To listen and let Miss Lodge speak. Instead he finds himself rattling on, agitated in the presence of this new teacher whose quiet demeanour has touched something inside him. Something that has lain dormant. From the day he set eyes on her it's as if he is able to sense her presence in this building, even when she is not actually within sight. And when she is, he has had to resist seeking her out with his eyes.

So far, Hedie says, I'm surviving. Her voice is pleasant. I mean, I haven't been pelted with spit bombs and my car hasn't been vandalized. She stops. Looks at Joseph. Looks away.

Joseph is about to say his car has been repaired, but instead he tells her that this meeting is just informal. Later in the year you'll be subjected to the real thing, he adds. Either the principal or myself will do the grilling for that round. He grins to let her know he's joking. He should have said "either the principal or I." Mia would laugh at him.

Hedie meets his eyes steadily, as if she is looking for

something to learn. Or remember. Her gaze is not intrusive but she is paying careful attention to him. Will he be found wanting? And then she turns away and looks around the room. The painting of a wolf above Joseph's head, the bookshelves, the light fixtures on the wall—everything comes under scrutiny. She is less pretty than Millicent. More robust. Except for her hands— they are small and delicate. She has the air of a woman who knows what she wants and is not impatient. Or perhaps she has everything she wants and needs nothing.

Your daughter is in one of my classes.

Yes. Joseph knows this.

I'm letting her do an independent assignment.

Joseph looks up quizzically.

I think she wants to be a writer, Hedie says.

A writer? Joseph looks puzzled. A near-stranger is telling him what his daughter wants to do. He doesn't ask what Mia wants to write about.

From what I've seen so far—and it's not that much—she has talent, Hedie says.

Joseph is embarrassed that he's unable to comment on this talent. Mia has always done well in school. Brought home stories he didn't bother to read. I'm proud of Mia, he says quickly. She's a good daughter.

Yes, Hedie says. I'm sure she is. And before Joseph can respond she adds, You're busy. She indicates the stacks of paper on his desk, and, as if she is now directing the agenda of this informal meeting, rises to go. I don't want to take your time.

Joseph gets up quickly to open the door for her, but she is already reaching for the knob and their hands touch, his large hand against her small one. She leaves the office and he is alone. And disappointed that the interview is over so soon. He is sure that he has failed.

He returns to his desk, where his work is waiting. Work that buffers him against Millicent's sadness. Against Alice's unrealistic hope for her boys. Against temptation. *Work, for the night is coming,* they used to sing in church. Hard work will pave the path to his goal: one day, soon, he will be the principal of this school. He turns resolutely to the work before him.

~

Mia is in the kitchen with her mother, who is at the counter going through the motions of preparing a salad. Exhausted after a day spent helping Alice with the boys, Millicent moves her hands slowly and methodically, as if the task requires too much of her. Mia presides over a pot of bubbling pasta sauce. Its spicy aroma fills the house, greets Joseph at the door and hovers like a savoury blessing over the trio as they sit down at the table.

Joseph attempts a small flourish as he pours wine for his two table companions and Mia acknowledges this hint of ceremony by raising her glass. Millicent follows suit. Joseph pours his beer into a glass and then there is silence as they fill their plates and begin eating.

Mia goes to the fridge and returns, triumphantly holding aloft the salad. Tada! she says. Look what someone forgot.

Millicent's face registers dismay and Joseph sends his daughter a chastising look. Repentant, Mia offers the salad first to her mother, who waves it away, then to her father, who helps himself to a large portion.

If there is to be conversation it must start somewhere. Mia is about to speak but Millicent beats her to it.

I have to go back to Alice's right after supper, she says. I'll need a ride.

I'll drop you off on the way to choir, Joseph says.

Wednesday night choir practice at church has marked the

middle of the week for the Wittenberg family as long as Mia can remember. Joseph rarely misses. At one time his baritone filled the house with anthems: "Holy God, we praise your name" or "Joyful, joyful, we adore thee" as he warmed up his voice. He no longer sings at home, Mia has noticed. As if the need for praise is no longer there. Or he gets enough of it at choir practice.

How's our little prince? he asks. How's Jeremy?

He slept most of the day, Millicent says, but Alice thinks Lucas is coming down with something, she wants me bring him a treat. Can we stop at Safeway for the chocolate cookies he likes?

Mia has finished her pasta and is stabbing with her fork at the remaining bits of salad. She puts down the fork. I've asked my new English teacher to let me do an independent assignment, she says and looks for a reaction. Not from her mother but from her father.

Joseph looks up. What sort of assignment? he asks.

I'm going to interview GranMarie. She'll tell me stories and I'll write them down. She's got lots of stories about her life.

Yes, Joseph says. I suppose she has.

Millicent rises from the table and leaves the kitchen. Mia folds and refolds her napkin.

Joseph is putting on his jacket when Millicent comes out of the bedroom carrying a small suitcase. Both Joseph and Mia are startled and stop what they are doing.

What's with the suitcase, Mom?

Moving out? Joseph asks. Leaving us? No one smiles. He takes Millicent's coat from the closet.

It's just in case Alice wants me to stay overnight.

Mom! Mia objects. You've already been there all day. You're not going to cure the baby. Or save Alice from herself. Face it, Mom, Fragile bloody X is here to stay. Get used to it.

Millicent recoils from her daughter's words and Mia is

remorseful. When her parents leave she feels oddly abandoned, the empty house enclosing her like a shell. She's not afraid of solitude—she's used to it. Her father is often away evenings, her mother in her bedroom with a book, pretending to read, dozing. And that leaves Mia free to do whatever she wants. But the way her parents walked out with the suitcase has left her feeling she's as disadvantaged and pathetic as all those homeless people the city is known for. And as rootless as Danny with his hopeless mother.

Mia walks slowly through the house, room after room, entering the modest spaces she and her parents occupy. A family. Are they a happy family? Of what stuff is a happy family made? Silly question.

When Alice married and moved out, Joseph claimed Alice's room for an office. Every administrator needs a room of his own, he said, and equipped his with a new desk and a couch. Once in a while he sleeps on that couch. Mia assumes her mother's sadness has something to do with that.

She ignores the uncleared table, the unwashed pots in the sink, and walks out of the house. On the front steps she pauses, clears her throat and yells: *To be or not to be, that is the question,* then runs laughing down the steps. Dusk is settling on the empty driveway, on the front lawn and on her father's garden. But there is enough light still for a quick run to the park. Above the roofs the yellow moon floats like a pale Frisbee stopped short in its arcing path across the heavens.

Mia imagines the same moon looking down on a village from where her great-great-grandfather once set out, maybe before daybreak, maybe charged with hope. He returned to the village with a stone in his heart.

What was God thinking? GranMarie said, shaking her head after she had told the story to which Mia listened with complete attention.

Running along Kildonan Drive she allows the companionship of the moon and that distant ancestor to move with her
through the deepening dusk.

Land
(Assignment #1)

Johann Bartsch set out on a June day with the purpose of
buying a parcel of land rumoured to be availabe a day's
journey east of his village The travellers who brought the
rumour to his door assured him the land was rich and fertile and the owner a decent man. Bartsch, who had two
sons, wanted land, and he told his wife this opportunity to
add to his present holdings was a gift from the Almighty.
He hired a Russian driver with a droshky and sturdy horses,
tucked a wad of roubles under his shirt and started out just
as the rising sun's first rays shimmered on the roofs of barns
and houses. The villagers were just beginning to stir. Smoke
from breakfast fires rose lazily, spread out, thinned and dissipated against the sky's deepening blue. His wife Judith had
packed food for the journey: a length of smoked pork sausage, dark bread baked the day before and a bottle of tea.
As the men headed north, the yellow steppe fell away on
either side of the vehicle and Johann Bartsch felt buoyed by
a sense of well-being.

He may not have been thinking of Leo Tolstoy's story
"How Much Land Does a Man Need?" His descendants
would read that story one day, not in Russian, not on this
steppe, but in a different language, on a distant continent,
seated at Arborite desks in public schools. They would
imagine the legendary land-buyer racing against the sun,
legs pumping furiously until he was exhausted, then walking and finally stumbling forward, changing his course

56

when necessary to include the richest portions, drawing a boundary around the largest acreage possible. All would be his if he hurried. The Asian tribesmen who owned the land stood silently by, waiting to see if their hopeful client would manage to close the circle around his desired land before the sun slipped below the horizon, ending the race.

That sobering story, as native to the fertile steppes as the two travellers themselves, may have been unknown to Johann Bartsch—he couldn't read. His illiteracy was not generally known in the village where he lived and near which he already owned 150 **desjatin** of land. It's often possible to camouflage one's shortcomings, whatever they are. Even glaring ones.

Picture this: The villagers arrive before sunrise on a crisp October morning at the yard of Johann and Judith Bartsch for the annual pig slaughtering. **Schwienskjast**, they call it—pig's wedding. Breakfast is waiting. Bartsch takes the head of the table, where a Bible has been placed, open to Psalm103. He lets his arms rest on the table, his large hands clenched on either side of the open book. He intones with a firm voice:

> Bless the Lord, O my soul,
> and all that is within me
> bless his holy name.
> Bless the Lord, O my soul,
> and do not forget his benefits.
> Who forgives all your iniquity,
> who heals all your diseases.

He is reciting the words, but almost everyone believes he is reading them. His wife Judith knows for sure. Johann stops after the last line he has memorized, closes the Bible and speaks a prayer. Everyone eats heartily and then the men rise from the table, fuelled and ready to get on with the killing.

This communal event is not a ritual, although the annual autumn slaughter of pigs marks the cyclical nature of life on the Russian steppes. For the most part the seasonal cycles bring blessings to the fruitful land where the Bartsches live in community with others of their kind, separated by distance or time from the several populations that arrived there before them: Nogai. Tatar. Cossack. Ukrainian.

Bartsch and his Russian driver continued their silent journey. The driver's ink-black hair strayed from underneath his cap and he let his dark gaze sweep the landscape from right to left. Sometimes he turned to study the man beside him. Bartsch did not speak much Russian; the driver knew only a few words of the Low German spoken in Mennonite villages. Neither man spoke Ukrainian. Birds swooped down, as if in hope of finding kernels of grain around the travellers' conveyance. They dodged the wheels of the droshky, rose in a cloud of dust and emerged from it into blue sky, then swooped again. Storks brooded in huge, ungainly nests built on roofs or treetops. It was an ordinary day.

When they saw that the sun had reached its zenith the men stopped for the noon meal. Johann unpacked the bread and sausage, set the bottle of tea on the grass. When his silent driver pulled out a knife, broad-bladed, shiny and obviously sharp, Johann became alarmed at this previously concealed travel companion. But perhaps the man was only being helpful. Taking a firm grasp on the knife, he cut the pork sausage into generous slabs. He didn't cut the bread, which was still fresh and best torn into chunks. The

men took turns drinking from the bottle of tea, still lukewarm. The driver reached into his pocket for a stronger
liquid, offered it to Johann, who tipped the bottle to drink.
Afterwards the driver spread out his coat, lowered himself
onto it, closed his dark eyes and slept. Normally Johann
would have joined him in the **Mittagsschlaf**, but the way
the sun had glinted off the steel blade of the knife troubled
him and he decided to forego the customary afternoon
nap. Instead, he tried to reflect with gratitude on the land
he would buy.

For Johann Bartsch, living at the end of the nineteenth
century, it was impossible, and unnecessary, he believed,
to envision a future—his or his descendants'—without
land: the wind-blown steppes, the green fields in spring,
the gold of harvest. It did not occur to him that his people
might one day choose to live in cities located on a part of
the Earth's surface he'd never bothered to think about .

The journey was resumed when the driver, whose name
was Pavel, woke up. They made good progress, during
which Johann remained acutely conscious of the wad of
roubles tucked close to his heart, where they formed a
small bulge. Had Pavel noticed it? The driver glanced occasionally at his passenger, a glance that might be harmless.
Or not. Under his shirt, Johann's heart beat harder than it
had in the morning. Although the sun was now streaming
down its heat, he wished he had not removed his coat,
which had concealed the bulge.

Occasionally they passed through a village, the inhabitants at work in their gardens or in adjacent fields. Children played beside the road that led straight through the
village. Here and there old people sat in the sun. A yap-
ping rush of dogs followed them for a distance beyond the
village before giving up and falling back. Bartsch became

drowsy and dozed off for a good many verst before he was abruptly awakened by the jostling of the droshky over uneven ground. The road they'd been travelling on had vanished and the steppe spread like a rough brown sea all around them. How small the droshky seemed, its two human passengers insignificant.

Johann looked about anxiously. He turned to Pavel. "Where are we?" he asked, and his hand moved to his chest. Pavel stared straight ahead as he urged his horse left for a while, then veered right. "Where are we going?" Johann demanded, a wave of panic tightening his throat as he became convinced he was being driven into alien territory. When Pavel said nothing he yelled at him: "Stop! Stop! Where is our road?"

Although Pavel may not have understood his passenger's every word, he understood his alarm. He reined in his horses, fixed Johann with his dark eyes, shrugged and, using gestures, admitted he couldn't be absolutely sure which direction to take on this trackless expanse, but he would find his way eventually, he promised, and with that he whipped the animals on. After a further stretch of uncertainty he gestured with his whip toward the distant horizon where clumps of trees and a low-lying cluster of buildings indicated human habitation. A small village that took on shape and substance as the travellers neared it. The driver grinned at Johann and made reassuring gestures to indicate that, yes, this was the place.

The sun was not far from setting when they arrived at Wassilyevka, their destination. Johann was relieved to climb down from the droshky, stretch his legs and meet the farmer who had land to sell. The man invited him into his home for a meal. Pavel looked to the horses and found a farmhand for company. Johann's heart still pounded much too rapidly, whether in fear or anticipation, but his nervousness gradually subsided in the warmth of his host's geniality.

After the meal of potatoes and eggs the two men went out to inspect the rich soil of the plowed field. Johann employed his limited Russian, added gestures and glances. Figures were signalled by means of splayed fingers and soon an understanding was reached. Johann took the roubles from their hiding place next to his heart, counted out the agreed number and transferred them, with huge relief, to his host, who wrote on a piece of paper and handed the paper to Johann, who had learned to sign his name. It was too late to make the return journey. Seller and buyer shared several glasses of wine and the former offered the latter a bed for the night.

The next morning Johann Bartsch and Pavel set out for home. The wind was brisk, a thin layer of cloud mitigated the sun's strong rays, and from time to time they passed fields that shone with the promise of an abundant harvest. Relieved to be unburdened of the wad of money and pleased with his land deal, Johann made a determined effort to converse with his Russian driver. He learned that Pavel had three children, two sons and one daughter, with the hope of more to come. He used his fingers to inform Pavel that he also had two sons, but didn't say that his wife was pregnant again. Time might have passed agreeably, with Johann exhilarated, glad to be bringing good news of the land purchase to his family. Instead, a nagging sense of unease settled in his chest and would not abate, not even when the journey neared its end .

Johann Bartsch arrived home safely. He had not been harmed or even threatened by the driver with his black gaze and his large knife. But though Pavel had not harmed him, the terror that had gripped Johann Bartsch remained embedded in his mind and soul and haunted his dreams at night. "Like an unconfessed sin," he told Judith, who tried to comfort him.

Several weeks after the purchase of land Johann remained uncharacteristically in bed one morning and stayed there until his death not many weeks later. He died, his family believed, as a result of the ill-fated journey.

And who is to contradict this belief?

Judith Bartsch was a spunky woman. She could read, sew, cook, manage the servants and admonish her children. When she had completed her grieving for a man who was enterprising, energetic and good, though illiterate, she would proceed to run the farm with hired help and the assistance of neighbours.

But first she prepared to give birth. The village midwife was called to help Judith Bartsch deliver a girl, tiny but healthy. Though her oldest boy was named Johann—everyone called him Hans—Judith named her daughter Johanna, in memory of her unfortunate husband.

~

Mia is at her desk in her east-facing room watching her first twelfth-grade English assignment for the new teacher roll out from the printer. When the last page emerges, she separates the sheets, tears off the edging and rereads the essay. Her blue-jeaned legs are crossed at the knees, one of them swinging rhythmically as she reads. Her brown hair falls straight down to her white turtleneck sweater. She lifts each page with care and bends attentively over the reading.

When she's put down the final page, she straightens the stack of papers and before she looks around for a paper clip, lingers over the details. Maybe the droshky driver didn't really spread out his coat—she thinks of it as a drab khaki colour—and maybe he didn't take a nap after lunch while Johann Bartsch sat erect and nervous nearby. And Judith Bartsch may not have opened the Bible for her husband at Psalm 103. It may have been Psalm 21 or 23. There may not have been a Bible at all. Mia, who has read whole chunks of the Bible, smiles at these inventions; she thinks they add a nice touch to the narrative.

What can I tell you? GranMarie asked, when Mia sat down with her pen and notebook for the first interview. What do you want to hear?

About that man—my ancestor. Mia gestured toward the brown album on the shelf. She didn't say great-great-grandfather—Johann Bartsch seemed more like a stranger.

You want to know about your ancestors.

Yes.

They're Mennonites. You are a Mennonite.

Mia has ancestors that aren't Mennonite. Her mother's family is from England. She is a hybrid. Rooted in the soil of two foreign countries.

What GranMarie told her over several Saturday mornings was a bare-bones story, sparse details that were offered, retracted, replaced by other details. What Mia received could be summarized in a few paragraphs, not a proper story at all. Two men going on a journey to buy land. One of them dies shortly after, seemingly for no reason. How likely is that? She has had to fill in the gaps. She has laboured over this assignment. There was joy in the labour and the joy has left her exhilarated. Still, she doesn't believe her characters actually "leap off the page," as Hedie Lodge said they should in a good story. Her teacher will find fault, most likely. But the assignment is due today, the noon hour slipping by and she doesn't want to be late for afternoon classes. Nor will she risk asking for more time so early in the school year.

She wonders if Miss Lodge will be impressed with the allusion to the Tolstoy story, the story her class read the first week of school.

Mia decides she'll write a letter to accompany the assignment. Not an apology for possible errors. Not a plea for kindness. Perhaps an acknowledgement of the agreement she's made with her teacher. Or perhaps she just can't stop composing, arranging and rearranging words until they satisfy her. Or maybe she's thrilled over the novelty of the new computer, her own. She's one of the few students at GSC to own one.

Dear Miss Lodge:

Here is the first instalment of my major English project for the school year. The characters Johann and Judith Bartsch are my great-great-grandparents. My main source of information is my grandmother and I sure hope she'll survive the year. As I worked on this piece, I wondered what my ancestors might have thought if they'd known I'd one day be poking around in their lives. Would Johann Bartsch be disappointed if he knew his descendants live in a city? On property with barely enough space for a garden? And that they don't speak German, high or low? Would Judith Bartsch eat the pepperoni pizza we'll most likely order in for supper tonight? Would she like it?

I'm keeping in mind what you said about writing creatively. I'm not sure I know what that means exactly, but isn't that what I'm going to find out as I write?

I like this assignment a lot. Thank you for allowing me to do an individual project.

Mia stops to reread the letter. A smile breaks out on her face and a wry chuckle forms in her throat and becomes audible by the time she reaches the end. She deletes the entire letter except the first and last sentence, prints off what's left and signs her name.

~

Mia watches as the biology teacher shows slides of chromosomes: XX, XY. The images are familiar: Alice has gathered mountains of material about genetics and expects Mia to be interested in every detail. As if by her frantic action a baby's flaws can be erased. You're so gullible, Alice, she told her sister last week. There is no silver bullet. Get that into your thick skull. When Alice flinched and her eyes filled with tears, Mia felt instantly guilty. But her sister had choked back the tears and stubbornly continued her pursuit of healing for Jeremy.

Bev, the first student to whom Mia speaks about Jeremy's now officially confirmed condition, looks across the lab at Mia. She sends a note: Let's do genetics for our project. You and me and Angela. After class she says, This is relevant. For you, Mia. For your family. And I'm interested, too. And so is Angela.

Angela is scribbling in her notebook, possibly revising her list of the school's top ten males.

Mia would prefer to work alone. Or, since no one is excused from this project, join other students. Though it's her last year of high school, she has made few friends besides Bev and Angela. And Danny. But Bev assumes they will group together and volunteers to get started on the research during her spare. Mia doesn't say that her sister has corralled her into amassing more information than she can absorb.

We'll get the ball rolling, Bev says. Let's meet after supper. In the park, Mia, you like the park. She elbows Angela, who looks up from her list and nods a vague assent.

Mia is irritated by Bev's transparent efforts to show sympathy, but knows it's the best her friend can do.

Lately Mia has felt she is teetering between two paths—one taking her beyond her small circle into a wider world, the other leading inward, to a private solitude. She is puzzled and wonders whether other teenagers like to be alone. Danny, maybe. But in his case it's a strategy to deal with being always pushed aside. Left out.

After supper Mia dons sweats and running shoes, and imagining Jeremy bouncing in her arms, lowers her head against the west wind and races down Kildonan Drive to Bur Oak Park. Wind and sun have lapped up the rain that moistened the sidewalks this morning and running is a pleasure. A solitary pleasure—Bev and Angela don't jog. When she arrives at the park they are waiting as promised. Bev is spreading books, pamphlets and charts on a picnic table, securing them against the wind with stones she picked up along the path. Her hands are gloved against the cold. She is businesslike and begins, energetically:

Fragile X Syndrome is all about sperm and eggs. It's about your DNA. That's like everyone's trademark, she explains earnestly, as if she's discovered something completely new. It contains genetic information, the key to a person's entire body composition. And maybe even the soul.

Mia thinks Bev made up that last bit.

Angela feigns interest.

Fragile X is genetic, Bev continues. It's passed on by your parents. You inherit it. Whether you're a guy or a girl depends on your father. Every girl has two X chromosomes. A boy has one X chromosome and one Y chromosome. This is important. She looks at Angela, whose attention has strayed from the subject and is fixed on a squirrel scooting up an oak tree trunk. These X chromosomes can be fragile, Bev goes on. They mutate, and that gets to be a problem. It's not good. If a girl has a mutated X chromosome, well, she's still got another, healthy one, right? But guys, they've only got one. So they're more likely to get it.

Get what? Angela asks.

Fragile X Syndrome.

Bev looks up, pleased with what she's brought to the project. She looks to Mia for approval. Mia doesn't point out that Bev's information is simplistic; Fragile X is far more complicated than this. That's weird, Angela says, leaning forward, her interest genuine now, her long blonde hair brushing her low-cut pink top, new for September. Imagine, she says. All this stuff getting passed on while you're having sex.

The girls are alone in the park. Oak leaves, brown and weightless, let go of branches and are whirled away by the wind. Mia looks away from the picnic table with its diagrams, away from her friends. Bev senses her withdrawing and sits up like a question mark. She would be astonished to know that this project, which sparks her interest and Angela's reluctant cooperation, looms like a burden for Mia.

I wish we could just dissect some little pig or something, Mia mutters, her eyes following a path that winds through a growth of stunted bur oaks. Every muscle in her body suddenly yearns to be in motion.

Bev recoils, as if she's been slapped. She begins slowly folding up a large sheet of paper on which she has drawn a chart.

C'mon, you guys. As if she's been zapped by a passing whim, Mia climbs nimbly onto the picnic table and, avoiding Bev's hands, the spread-out information and the stones, begins dancing from foot to foot, swaying, moving her hips, waving her arms and whooping. Bev and Angela are stunned. Mia jumps down from the table. C'mon, you lazy lumps! she yells and, swinging her fisted hands, runs around the table, kicks aside a trash can and races around a shrub with red and yellow leaves. Bev and

Angela stare, speechless. Angela is first to get up, Bev follows sheepishly and they fall into step behind Mia. Faster! she yells, running in wider and wider circles and they chase each other in and out of the oak trees, around a shrivelled chokecherry bush, whooping like children on a playground.

The girls have jumped onto the table again, on what's left of Bev's research, when a vehicle comes roaring down Kildonan Drive past the girls. A screech of brakes and the battered grey car stops, reverses with mad speed until it is even with the girls. The driver wears shades though the sky is cloud-covered. The youth beside him has wild hair and in the back seat a third figure leans nonchalantly out the window and lights a cigarette.

Hey, man, one for each, he says and stares up at the girls, his face bold and insolent.

Mia expects Angela to scream. She thinks *she* will scream. But all three have frozen and become a mute tableau mounted on the picnic table. The driver gets out, hitches up his jeans, flexes his muscles and strides casually toward the girls. With the advantage of elevation Mia towers over those dark shades looking up at her.

What d'ya say? the driver calls back to his buddies, who have remained in the car with their cigarettes. Not bad, eh? And scared shitless, all three. What you couldn't do with them, eh, Jem?

Jem, from the back seat, laughs, sucks on his smoke and leers at the girls.

Angela emits a pathetic whimper. Bev is breathing audibly. Dusk is settling in.

That one in the pink shirt? She's mine. The youth in the passenger seat gets out and lets the car door slam shut to clinch his claim.

Angela whimpers again.

Don't, Angela, Mia orders.

Yeah, Angela, the guy says. Don't.

C'mon, Mia says. Jump! She kicks the stones away, then scrambles down from the table and the other two follow like witless sheep. She strides past the shades and his passenger, past Jem still in the car. Bev and Angela keep close to her. She is angry at her cowed friends and at the intruders. The driver has come up behind her, grabs her arm, yanks her around so she's face to face with his wide leer. His other hand holds up a can of beer, as if offering it.

You gutless creep! she spits out through gritted teeth. She grabs the can from his upheld hand, tears herself free and yells at him, Dirty scum! She swings with the hand holding the can. He ducks and she misses. Despicable loser, she barks out. Bev and Angela back away from Mia, who glares at the driver with devastating fury.

You were brave, Bev will say later.

Angela will claim that Jem grabbed at her breasts, but Mia knows he never left the car.

You were brave, Bev will insist.

But it is another vehicle, a sedate white sedan stopping just then behind the other vehicle that saves them, if they are indeed in danger. The driver asks Jem for directions.

The girls fly down Kildonan Drive as if wind-driven and given wings to outdistance a whole horde of hoodlums at their heels. Mia could easily be far ahead but she slows down for her friends. By the time they arrive at the Wittenberg bungalow they are gasping for air. And laughing, or maybe crying. Hysterically.

Just don't tell my dad, Mia warns in a sharp whisper as they huddle on the driveway, regaining breath and composure. She gets out her key. And not my mother for sure. They tumble into the kitchen where, wound tight as springs, they talk non-stop and all three at once, and Mia takes a litre of ginger ale from the fridge and finds a bag of pretzels. When Angela and Bev climb into Joseph's Camaro to be driven home, Angela in front, Mia mouths once more, Don't tell.

That night she has trouble sleeping. The scene in the park plays and replays non-stop in her head. Her life has been sheltered. Free of violence. She shivers under the covers, then dozes lightly, wakes, sinks back into a light sleep, then deeper, and dreams that Bev's papers and charts tear away from the anchoring stones and dance eerily like wild, white spectres on the weathered surface of the picnic table. The spectres grow bigger, become black and solid and a vicious wind flings them at Mia's face. She wakes up screaming.

~

Joseph Wittenberg brings his Big Mac into the staff room. A voice calls: Joseph, you'll be delighted to hear I'm planning to send you a visitor. She's got a mouth on her, and it ain't pretty.

Make that two visitors, says Joan Gustav, the art teacher. Danny Haarsma has failed to bless me with his presence. Twice. And it's a pity, she says to her table companions. Danny, would you believe, can actually draw.

I'm predicting the first GSC pregnancy of the season. This tidbit comes from a table where four phys-ed instructors sit hunched over a card game.

And I'm predicting there'll be bombs over Iraq, Peter McBride pronounces from the coffee machine lineup.

The staff room at noon is a zoo, and Joseph, looking around at its denizens, can't help grinning. Things are normal and normal is good.

Hey, Peter shouts. Hey, Grandpa Wittenberg. Over there. He points to a table with empty chairs and gestures that he's bringing coffee.

All the staff knows now about Joseph's new grandson. There's been an outpouring of congratulations and cards, Peter's a funny one. Flowers have been sent to the house. What they don't know is the worry attending the boy's birth. They haven't heard that this grandchild is afflicted. The name of that affliction has not yet been leaked to the staff, as Joseph has feared. But it will be. Not by Ab Solinsky, who had to be informed when his vice principal took a few hours off for the prayer service, but by one of the secretaries who attends the Church of Abundant Joy. Joseph is surprised that she hasn't already spread the news.

Peter sits down beside Claudette Avery, head of guidance, and Joseph takes the chair across from them. Claudette is staring at the salad in front of her as if examining it for defects. She is one of the few in the room not determined to get a word in, not interrupting. Her silence is not passive. Her mind is at work, Joseph knows, and it's a mind to be reckoned with. Claudette, like Joseph, is ambitious. She's got her eye on my job, he has frequently told himself. Worse, she may have her eye, as he has his, on Ab Solinsky's job.

Claudette, what's your pretty brain churning up? Peter says.

Claudette smiles.

Claudette the sphinx, Peter teases.

Ever been Myers-Briggsed? she asks.

What's that? Is it fatal?

Joseph leans in to hear. And so do others. Claudette's is a resonant voice that commands attention. A singer's voice. Contralto.

It's a personality measurement instrument, she says. It measures the ways people prefer to tackle problems.

What problems? Fixing the world?

Try the Blue Jays' losing streak. This from the phys-ed card table, where now the World Series is being analyzed with passion and precision.

Try the upcoming war in the Gulf, Peter McBride says.

What war? When? Where? What did I miss? Joan Gustav is not one of GSC's news junkies.

It's more like how you choose to solve everyday problems, Claudette says, ignoring the war.

Aha, like the best method to tame rangy kids.

And they're getting stupider every year. (A jaded voice, fraught with cynicism.)

But sexier. (Someone else.) I'm betting that our first pregnancy of the year will be Jane what's-her-name. She's been glued to what's-his-face since day one of the school year.

So long as no one present here turns out to be the putative.

This hits below the belt and there's a palpable bristling. Everyone remembers that last year a favourite math teacher left GSC in a cloud of rumours.

Is Jane Kerr doing serious drugs? someone asks.

So, Claudette, were you ever Myers-whatever? Peter is deliberately changing direction.

Most teachers are extroverts, she says, evading the specifics of the question. They've got a taste for action. They tend to analyze. Make judgments.

Is that good or bad?

Neither. But most teachers are in this category. That's why they're always ready to swing on Friday afternoon. After being with kids all week. They gain energy from others. From their students. Their colleagues. They go out for beers after work. They party. VPs are definitely in this group. She indicates Joseph and there's laughter around the table.

Joseph doesn't usually join the staff for beers on Friday night, and they believe it's not because he's a certain personality type, but because Principal Solinsky sets limits on fraternizing between staff and administration. Joseph lets them believe what they wish. Why should they know about his Friday visits to

Wild Oak Estates or his family's pizza suppers? Both have lately become irregular.

But then there's Hedie Lodge, Claudette says. Our new staff. She definitely gets her energy from inside herself. She needs to retreat, to withdraw. Needs time to replenish.

Joseph looks around, but can't see Hedie.

Not many teachers are in this category, Claudette continues. Hedie is intuitive, perceptive.

Everyone but Joseph has lost interest. I'm skeptical about such measuring of personality, he says. Such classifying. Such slotting into cubbyholes. People are inconsistent. Unpredictable.

Claudette smiles, gets up and makes her way to the coffee machine.

The heart is deceitful above all things, and desperately corrupt; who can understand it? The words float unbidden into Joseph's mind, surprising him. They aren't true, surely. Not of Peter across from him, not of any of the other teachers in the room. Certainly not of Claudette, who is trying to figure him out. She wants to unsettle me, Joseph thinks. Wants to make me uneasy. But she's not corrupt. Not deceitful. And she never appears desperate.

Joseph often skips lunch to deal with pressing matters related to textbooks or student behaviour. "Urgencies and Emergencies" he calls them. Sometimes he and Ab Solinsky postpone lunch until classes have resumed, the noon-hour noise has died down and the halls are more or less empty. Then they head for the Highway Diner.

This year Ab is focused on a major undertaking—the renovation of the gym, the home of the George Sutton Saints. He wants it done in time for spring commencement. The refurbished gym is to be given its own name. Baptized, so to speak. Joseph suspects that Ab thinks of this project as a legacy he'll leave to GSC when he retires. Soon, Joseph dares to hope. He is doing everything he can to make himself useful, even indispensible, to the fulfillment of Ab Solinsky's dream.

Ab is no longer young. The ground for a possible regime change must be prepared for. As part of his strategy, an unobtrusive-as-possible paving of the way, Joseph makes sure to eat with the teachers several times a week, unlike Ab, who rarely enters the staff room. Most of the teachers like Joseph well enough. He knows they also like the equally ambitious Claudette Avery, who has returned with a fresh cup of coffee.

Hedie Lodge has stepped into the staff room. Joseph can feel her gaze as it sweeps the room, searching for a place. As if summoned, his eyes meet hers, more grey than green today because she is wearing a grey sweater. Her quiet self-sufficiency leaves Joseph weak inside. He forces himself to look away.

A sharp rap at the staff room door. Everyone looks up and a phys-ed teacher rises, ready to turn away any petty requests.

It's for you, Joseph, he announces. Want to speak to your fan club?

Joseph takes the shortest route, squeezing between chairs. He brushes against Hedie's shoulder at the crowded table where someone has made room for her.

It's Jane Kerr at the door. Hi Mr. W, she says. Joseph sees the thin boy who stands slightly behind her as if he hopes he won't be noticed. His hand clutches a folder. Danny, Mia's friend. Danny, who keyed his car. When he was tracked down, easily, he hinted he'd been pressured. "They" had persuaded him and "they" had ways to make him "cooperate."

Joseph knows the school is not immune to gangs. Or free of drugs. He looks at Jane. And thinks of Mia, who has always brought home an assortment of odd friends. Wounded birds, he's called them. Danny, for instance. But Jane—Jane looks as if she wouldn't be easily wounded.

He can think of two reasons why Jane would come to the staff room to champion Danny. One, she's fatally attracted to trouble. Or, two, she needs an excuse to get a glimpse into the staff room where she might see and be seen by male teachers, and even better, by administrators. Joseph doesn't think she's motivated by sheer malice. She's probably doing drugs, but hopefully not yet a pusher.

Danny's vandalism is beginning to bore him, as he is bored with the attention of adolescent girls.

He's done it, Jane says. On time. Speaking as if she's an appointed mediator, Jane takes the folder from Danny and pulls out a water colour of a car, the side view. Voila, she says.

Joseph keeps his face from breaking into a grin. He was pleased when he devised the punishment, a punishment that did not so much fit the crime as it fit the criminal. Learning that Danny was taking art, he ordered him to complete a series of watercolours of his vandalized-and-recently-repaired black Camaro. This first instalment, he can tell, is good. Good enough to frame and hang on his office wall. The idea amuses him. However, he's not amused that Jane is handling this as if she's part parole officer and part mother duck. Taking the painting from her, he turns to the boy. Remember what's next?

He remembers, Jane says. Next week he'll ...

Jane, you're behaving as if you're in charge here, Joseph interrupts. You're not in charge. And your friend here is not a deaf mute.

Jane tosses her head, steps back as if offended and shoves Danny forward. Tell him, she says.

Next week I paint a front view of your car. And the week after, the car's gotta be in the middle of traffic.

And?

And I clean the art room for Miss Gustav every day after school. His voice is not quite sullen, not quite the voice of a martyr.

Right. And one more thing. You will from now on attend art class. *Every* art class. Joseph closes the door. On the way back to his hamburger he keeps the painting close and inconspicuous, but once seated he can't help spreading it out for display. Everyone leans in to look. Joan Gustav cranes to see.

He's one of my best, she says. If only he'd show up for class. He's got a future. I'm planning an art exhibit for our first parents' night. This painting, she points, definitely has to be in it. Can I have it?

Joseph rolls up the painting possessively and Joan returns to her lunch, boasting that where math and science and sports fail, art can succeed.

Joseph has learned that Danny's mother has a temporary job at Kmart and that Danny works there too, sporadically, stocking shelves. He thinks that by the time the snow falls and stays, a trio of watercolours featuring his Camaro will be completed, framed and hanging above his desk, replacing Robert Bateman's ominous wolf.

Joseph does not return to his office after lunch but goes directly to the textbook room, where the shipment of revised biology texts has arrived. He picks one up, riffles the pages, and stops when he comes to diagrams of genes and chromosomes. When Joseph discovered that Mia had added biology to her full grade twelve load, he understood why. He stares at those diagrams that represent someone's blueprint of a human being. That illustrate the difference between male and female. Between healthy and misformed. The words that want to surface in Joseph's thinking are not Shakespeare's *Oh what a piece of work is man*. He hasn't read much Shakespeare since his school days. The words pushing up are something about being *fearfully and wonderfully made*. Lucas and Jeremy are not fearfully and wonderfully made, Joseph thinks, and neither is his brother's boy, Taylor.

They are imperfect. They are flawed children. What in heaven's name was God thinking, allowing such a mistake? He closes the textbook, holds it clenched in his hand, then hurls it against a wall. It thuds loudly and lands on the floor, its spine broken.

There are voices outside the door. Two healthy, well-formed teenage boys enter, grinning. Hi, Mr. Wittenberg. Our bio teacher wants those new texts. Are they here?

All here. Joseph gestures toward the pile.

The boys fill their arms with books and carry them off as if they are feather light. Joseph stares after them, then picks up the broken biology text, shoves it between books on a top shelf and walks briskly back to his office. He has no meeting scheduled for after school. There will be time for the garden.

~

In spite of the scare at Bur Oak Park, Mia regularly laces up her Nikes after supper and heads in that direction. Today she wears gloves and a headband that holds her brown hair back so it fans out behind her. Her breath emerges white and a north wind whisks it away. The cold air enters her nostrils, mouth, lungs. In the chilly quiet between rush-hour traffic and the after-supper stream of cars, Mia's brain, cleared of the day's noise, sharpens. Her arms, bent at the elbows, move like pistons, her feet hit the ground easily, the spring in her step sends her flying forward through the evening. Already the sparrows have found shelter.

I should drop in on GranMarie. Mia's body responds instantly to the brain's nudge, veering into a detour that brings her to Wild Oak Estates, where she finds GranMarie dishevelled, uncertain, her hands submerged in a sink full of dishwater, her best teacups and saucers stacked on the counter.

Am I surprising you, GranMarie? I should have called.

The old woman says nothing at first, simply stares at her visitor. Then, recovering, she wipes her wet hands on a towel and beckons Mia to a chair in the sitting room. Well then, she says. Where were we?

Oh no, GranMarie, I'm not here to interview you. I just dropped in. To see you.

GranMarie looks baffled.

We do stories on Saturday, remember? After you've got your bones and brain moving, like you always tell me.

When her grandmother still has nothing to say, Mia says, I've got such good news, GranMarie. Yesterday Jeremy looked straight at me when I held him. His eyes sparkled like little stars. And he curled his fingers around my thumb. Tightly.

It's not true. The baby's eyes didn't really sparkle like stars and his little fingers didn't grab her thumb and hold on, no matter how much she wished it.

Alice is so proud of him, Mia continues. And so am I. We all are. She stops for GranMarie to say she is proud too, but the only response is a faint twitching at the corners of her wrinkled mouth.

After a while the old woman says, There was a boy in our village. We called him Petya. He wasn't quite right. She touches a finger to her forehead. We all teased him. After school one day some boys dared him to cut the tail off a kitten they caught in the street. It was a grey one. A stray. So tiny. GranMarie uses her hands to outline the kitten's tininess. They were cruel, she says. We were all cruel. She shudders, then continues. He got confused, poor Petya, but we didn't have any pity. Those boys kept at him and at him and at him until he ran to the house for a knife. And he hacked and hacked at the animal's tail while the boys held it and yelled, Hard, Petya! Harder! There was blood running and that poor cat struggled and howled and Petya screamed. He screamed and screamed and screamed.

The old woman's voice rises with each repetition of the word.

Her hands flutter like trapped birds and fly to cover her ears against her own voice. Her eyes brim with agony. It wasn't right, she says, her voice a strange wailing. We shouldn't have.

Mia has never seen her grandmother so distraught. Has never heard her cry like this. She reaches for the frantic hands and holds them tight. Come, GranMarie, she says. The dishes. She leads her grandmother back to the kitchen, positions her at the sink, hands her a tea towel and prepares to make short shrift of the cups and saucers. The old woman wipes her eyes and stands beside her granddaughter, docile and obedient.

The cups, Mia has noticed, are clean. Who used all these dishes? she asks. Did you have company?

The old woman's hands stop their meticulous towelling. She stares ahead as if she's trying to recall for whom she brought out her good china. Well, weren't you here? she asks after a long while. And there was—she hesitates again—our neighbour from our village, you know, the one who sometimes was the midwife. And the mother of that boy, that Petya—did I ever tell you about Petya? Her voice falters with the name. She turns, looks straight at Mia, her blue eyes dark. Clouded.

Shocked, Mia continues washing the clean dishes. She attempts to bring her grandmother back, back to this world, this small kitchen. To distract her, she offers the other good news, the news she'd intended to save for another day. This news is true.

We're going to Greece, she says. Our history teacher is organizing it. Angela and Bev too. In spring. Imagine, GranMarie. Greece. The Acropolis. The islands. I'll see the Aegean Sea. I'll swim in it.

GranMarie's eyes focus and grow alert. I always wanted to see the Dnieper River, she says wistfully. I wanted to swim in it. But I never did. And after a pause she says How will you get there? To, to … Where did you say you're going?

Greece. We'll fly across the ocean. Like birds, GranMarie.

Greece, the old woman muses. Why not Russia? Why don't you fly to Russia?

Yes, Mia says. You're right. It seems suddenly ludicrous that she is going to Greece instead of the country from where her grandmother emigrated. I will, she promises. Some day I'll go there.

Be careful, the old woman warns. Not all travelling is safe. Not everyone arrives. I could tell you stories.

Not tonight, Mia says.

When the dishes are put away—their presence on the counter never explained—Mia makes tea and sits with her grandmother as the clock ticks its way toward sundown. When she leaves Wild Oak Estates the sun has slipped behind the houses and she should really cut short her run, no jogging after dark, she has promised herself. She would have had to make this promise to her father if she'd told him about the night three hoodlums terrified three teenaged girls. But she continues toward the park, her brain humming with the details of the day: Jeremy's tiny, limp fingers; the anticipated trip to Greece; Danny's embarrassing stumble when he walked into English class late and everyone laughed. His eyes were still glazed over in math class.

And uppermost, her grandmother's confusion. Is she losing her marbles? She'll ask her father if he's noticed, though he's been too busy to visit her.

Was it a party of long-forgotten friends conjured from her grandmother's memory who sat with her this afternoon and lifted those teacups with ghostly hands to ghostly lips?

GranMarie said "we" when she told the story about Petya and the cat. Mia doesn't believe for a minute that her grandmother could have been anything but a horrified bystander to such cruelty.

The slap of footsteps coming up behind her is not imaginary.

Her muscles tense, her speed increases as she nears Bur Oak Park. She pictures the pursuer, a sinister, hulking figure coming closer, catching up. She feels the quickening of her pulse. When the runner with the strong stride is right behind her, she stops and turns abruptly, fists raised, and the pursuer crashes into her. It's Kurt, the new boy on her street. He's holding on to her for balance, and she drops her fists. She wants to lean against him but he pulls away.

You stalking me? Mia, breathing hard, tries to control her voice, embarrassed to show how near she was to panic.

Who better to stalk?

They both laugh, not too self-consciously. They resume running, side by side now, and Kurt slows down.

You do this every day? he asks

Yes. Well, no. Not *every* day. Is Kurt fishing for her schedule? That possibility is not unpleasant. She finds it unaccustomed but also companionable to be running with someone beside her. She increases her speed as if to prove she can match any pace he cares to set. She could keep on running all night. Kurt doesn't surge ahead but remains shoulder to shoulder with her. She sees his breath in the chill air. Hears the impact of his feet on the path, heavier than hers. They jog along every path in the small park, repeating the route several times without speaking and then head back. Kurt says he's trying out for the basketball team—the George Sutton Saints—and he must exercise regularly. Like every day. Mia already knows he's trying out for the team, Angela has informed her. Angela knows more than Mia about Kurt. She knows everything about any good-looking male at school, student or teacher. Your dad's one luscious hunk, she'll say.

When they get to Kurt's two-storey he doesn't stop but stays with Mia until they reach the Wittenbergs' white bungalow. Both are breathing rapidly and Mia waits for him to say something about running together again, but he only says, See you at school, and is gone.

Running up the steps, Mia doesn't look back. That night she falls into a dreamless sleep and wakes to a dark room, the clock telling her it's two a.m. She is instantly and fully alert and the first thing that comes to mind is running past shadowy oak trees with Kurt beside her. She wonders if her parents are asleep or awake. Are they in separate rooms tonight? Are they worried about Jeremy? She hears the hum of the fridge and is unable to fall back to sleep. Into her sleeplessness drifts the figure of GranMarie, the dishwater in the sink, the clean teacups on the counter. The way those gnarled hands towelled the dishes. The way the old woman's mind stumbled into another place, another time. I'll have to get on with the stories, Mia thinks, before GranMarie goes completely bonkers.

Finally drowsiness comes and Mia falls asleep cradling the hope of running into Kurt at school in the morning. And the hope that Lucas and Jeremy will never know the cruelty that drove Petya to violence.

The Prophecy
(Assignment #2)

A caravan of gypsies entered the village, three rattling, horse-drawn wagons spilling over with babies and black cooking pots, mothers and grandmothers in red and yellow shawls. The wagons were pulled by black horses, the horses controlled by black-haired men and the entire parade escorted by a ragtag entourage of children as wild and colourful as field flowers. A passel of dogs followed, a challenge to the village dogs, whose fur and growl rose ominously to greet the invasion. Wind snatched up the dust flung up by horses' hoofs and wagon wheels, whirling it aloft until the air was filled with it.

The Wittenbergs

The villagers referred to the visit as "That nuisance" and kept a wary eye on their chickens, horses and especially their excited children. They called in their dogs. They hoped the intruders were just passing through on their way to another village and would not be camped for days on the outskirts of theirs. The carefree transience of people who took no discernible care for tomorrow baffled the villagers, who claimed to be aliens and wanderers, a searching **Völklein**, a peculiar people. They claimed to be looking for an eternal city, but in the meantime they had planted themselves firmly on the fertile steppes. Dependent on land, they were suspicious of people who owned none, yet claimed the privilege of camping on fields that were spoken for. Fields that belonged to the diligent farmers who plowed the land, sowed the seed and prayed for a good harvest.

Unlike their parents, the village children welcomed the caravan. They tumbled out of doorways and stood at the gates of the picket fences, the bolder ones running into the street to trail the wagons, enthralled by the exotic spectacle that had invaded their ordered lives with a burst of excitement. They envied the gypsy children who wandered barefoot and unrestricted across the land and didn't have to go to school.

"Katya, Yusta, Netchen, Kolya, Yasch!" The voices of mothers calling their children home mingled with the noisy laughter and foreign chatter of the gaudily dressed intruders. Men called to the horses. Dogs snarled and barked. It was carnival time. A wild new spirit electrified the village and dust filled the air.

The Widow Bartsch did not close her door to the gypsies the way many of her neighbours did. "They are **Menschen** too," she told Hanna, who stood in the open doorway. "We can give them a piece of bread. If they ask."

Hanna was fifteen, no longer a child, but when the noise came closer she too ran to the gate and waited. She remembered dimly an earlier visit of the gypsies. She had just learned to read and had been holding a book in her hand when a swarthy man appeared in the doorway of their house strumming a balalaika and singing a song with a rhythm and melody nothing like the German hymns her mother sang. Nor like the minor harmonies the Russian maid intoned in the afternoons to lull Hanna to sleep. Her mother's eyes had filled with tears as the man sang and played. It was the first time she had seen her mother cry. And also the last.

Today a short, squat woman with round metal hoops in her ears so large her floral kerchief could not cover them detached herself from the others and walked toward Hanna. Her eyes were dark as night and their bold gaze commanded attention. When she had looked her fill, the woman's face broadened into a sly, conspiratorial grin.

"The mama—where she is?" she asked.

Hanna turned and led the woman into the house where Judith was chopping onions and cabbage for soup. Uninhibited, the gypsy stepped closer to the table. "Garlic?" she asked. "Garlic in the soup?"

Judith Bartsch shook her head. "No garlic. This is borscht."

"Borscht!" The gypsy laughed. She pulled from her skirts a packet of seasoning and handed it to Judith, who opened it, sniffed it and dropped it on the table. She went to the pantry to get one of the loaves of bread she had baked that morning.

The woman turned to Hanna. "I say your future," she said and reached out to grasp Hanna's head between her hands, turned it this way and that. Her short fingers traced the features of the girl's face. She lifted Hanna's brown hair to examine the ears and then gazed again into the flax-blue eyes. Murmurs and grunts of approval accompanied the scrutiny. She let go of the girl's head and grasped her hands, turning them palms up.

"Ah," she said. "Ah-h-h," as if she was left breathless by what she could see in the lines etched in Hanna's smooth palms.

"No!" Judith Bartsch had returned to the room, a fresh loaf in her hand. Her voice was stern, anxious. "No, NO! We don't want that."

But the gypsy had already begun speaking and kept on as if she couldn't stop: "I see this one shining, shining like a star," she said. "This one, she scatter pearls like bread crumbs where she go. Yes. Yes. She find love, such big love. And, aaah! O what I see! Don't be afraid, my child, don't be afraid. Be content. I see also sadness. Such great and terrible sadness. So. So. Every life has sadness, no?" The woman shrugged but when she raised her eyes Hanna saw in them the shadow of alarm.

"Get the broom, Hanna," the widow ordered and when the girl stood transfixed by the fortune teller's eyes, Judith strode to the corner herself, grabbed the broom and raised it as if to strike. The gypsy let go of Hanna's hands, turned and fled.

"Shameless." The widow held the loaf of bread in one hand, the broom in the other.

Her daughter watched the short, wide figure move through the gate toward the street and pause a moment, the large round earrings glinting in the sun. Before hurrying after her tribe she turned to look back.

"We don't believe it!" Judith shouted at her. "It's all super-stition. You people are so superstitious." Then, turning to

Hanna she said, "Did you see how the broom scared her? Don't even listen to them. Don't believe a word they say."

"Of course I don't believe them," Hanna laughed. "'Such big love,'" she mimicked.

"'Such great sadness,'" Judith shot back. "Now they will camp at the end of the village and pester us for days." She watched as her daughter ran once more toward the gate so she could stare after the parade. Judith set the broom back into the corner, the bread on the table. She picked up the packet of seasoning the woman had left, took a pinch of it and dropped it into the soup. She called the Ukrainian kitchen girl, who had vanished at the first sign of gypsies: "Set the table, quick now."

Hanna had often heard the story of her father's fateful journey to buy land. How her brothers Hans and Peter had stood at the gate, gazing down the village street waiting for their father. "When's he coming home? Did he get lost?" They had plagued their mother all day until, exasperated, she had told them their father had gone to the Promised Land, and when a man travels to the Promised Land, there's no telling when he might return. The boys should be patient.

After their father's death, Hanna's brothers had always referred to the new property in Wassilyevka as "The Promised Land." Years would pass before their mother would consent to inspect it, declaring the price paid for it much too high. But she would never agree to sell it. She hired neighbours to work the fields until Hans and Peter were old enough to do the work.

By the time Hanna was ten, her brothers had built a small shed on the land and stayed there in summer except when they were needed on the fields of their mother's village. Sometimes when Hanna begged to go with them to The Promised Land, they condescended to take her. "But don't make a nuisance of yourself." She loved running on the wide steppe, the wind in her hair. The distance from home thrilled her. She imagined herself a carefree gypsy.

Hanna had been told how her mother came out of the house that day to meet her husband when he returned after buying the land. She had watched him climb down from the droshky like an old man, his body bereft of confidence, his eyes fearful and guarded. "I knew I had lost him," Judith always said. A few weeks later Johann Bartsch was lowered into the hard ground and clods of earth thudded down on the coffin. The widow had already stopped crying. Dry-eyed, she brought her sons home and made supper.

"And then I had you," Judith would tell her daughter. "I felt such joy when I first held you. You were sent to be my comfort. You were my future."

~

Sitting beside Bev Plett on Sunday, listening as the choir sings *You, God, are my firmament*, Mia is still thinking about the gypsy fortune teller. Her father is in the choir hidden behind the altos, she can see only the top of his head and his one hand, holding the sheet music.

I heard that story so often, GranMarie said. My mother told it, over and over.

GranMarie had been unusually alert when Mia arrived that Saturday, ready to speak about her people, the Mennonites, as peculiar people who were always on the move in search for a better place. But gradually the alertness waned and her telling became fragmented. Mia, remembering her promise to Miss Lodge, visited the city's library, where she discovered that the two volumes of *The Mennonite Encyclopedia* would help her fill in the gaps.

Today she wonders whether Johann Bartsch's death might have been foretold by a gypsy similar to the one in her grandmother's latest story. She wishes she had thought to invent such a prophecy in her first instalment for Miss Lodge. Too late for that.

The choir has stopped singing and Pastor Heese reads from the book of Isaiah, something the prophet said about beauty instead of ashes, the oil of gladness instead of mourning. A garment of praise. The words flow around and through Mia and she shivers with pleasure. But what do they mean, those beautiful words? What did the prophets know? What was it that fed their vision? How did they decide when to thunder doom and when to speak comfort? How much was given to them to say? How much did they pull from their own imagination? Their own desires?

The gypsy's prophecy—was that meant just for Hanna or did the prophecy extend to future generations? Will I find great love? Mia wonders. Will I have children? Boys like Lucas and Jeremy? And Taylor? What's waiting for me? She longs to see into the future.

When the children are dismissed for Sunday school, Mia watches them leave, helter-skelter, a colourful parade, rosy-cheeked, bright-eyed youngsters hurrying along the aisle in a rush of joy. What Mia feels is not joy, but a longing for joy.

After the service she and Bev go to McDonald's, order hot dogs and pop, and Bev says, I felt like Pastor Heese's sermon was just so full of hope, hope for the whole world. Didn't you feel that, Mia? She is about to say more, but there's Kurt Brady, holding his tray and looking around for a place. Bev motions him to their table. We were at church, she tells Kurt. We're talking about the sermon.

Oh, yeah? Kurt says.

Mia looks down, embarrassed.

Kurt's dark hair is damp. He's been running and Mia feels a pang: she would have liked to be running with Kurt, his shoulder brushing hers, their strides matched. Instead, she's been sitting in church with Bev.

It was beautiful, Bev says. The sermon. Wasn't it beautiful, Mia?

Absolutely stupendous, Mia says, and because it's ridiculous to be embarrassed, she adds, It was all about wearing the garment of praise. She looks at Kurt, mischief in her eyes.

Kurt is working on his cheeseburger; he is not looking at her. Weird, he says.

It was about joy, Bev says. It was …

The oil of joy, Mia interrupts. What do you think of that, Kurt?

Kurt looks up from his cheeseburger, puzzled. That's cool, isn't it? he says. I mean the joy part.

Well, I'm thinking of the Middle East, Mia says and turns to Bev as if now she wants to needle her. You know, all that talk about war in Iraq? Can't you just imagine how joyful they are over there?

Bev is caught off guard. She takes a sip of her pop.

The battle I'm looking forward to, that'll be basketball, Kurt says with a full mouth. I can't wait for the season to begin. That Iraq thing—yeah, that's all the talk these day. But it might as well be on Mars.

Mia is quiet. Disappointed. Basketball will swallow Kurt up. She wants him to talk to her. About other things besides basketball.

About literature. About Iraq. She wants to run with him in Bur Oak Park. Wants his arms around her. She wants him to kiss her.

We're so sheltered here, Bev says, recovered. Because if you think of the total picture, I mean if we think globally, there's so much violence and kids younger than us get caught in it. Her face, characteristically earnest, has taken on an even deeper gravity.

I seem to remember you said something about hope, Mia resumes her teasing. Hope for the whole world. Hmm? How about a little oil of joy poured on Iraq?

Bev is baffled.

Kurt laughs awkwardly, picks up his tray. Thanks for the company, he says, and looking at Mia, smiles as he leaves.

Bev piles debris on the tray and walks in silence to the trash can. Mia follows, humming, *You, God, are my guiding light,* into the ear of her best friend.

~

After the Sunday service Joseph parks his car in the garage and instead of going straight into the house walks around to the back yard. Leaves have fallen, yellow and crisp. This afternoon he will rake and bag them. He has long intended to repair the fence with its broken pickets and peeling white paint. In the perennial bed the pink sedum is in full bloom. Autumn Joy, it's called. And the chrysanthemums have become small bushes that will bloom a deep maroon through the first snow if the temperature doesn't drop too soon, too abruptly. Around the splotches of colour the rest of the perennial bed is a sad sight and the impatiens and petunias are dead or dying.

As he turns to where the last tomatoes are rotting on the vine, Joseph sings, *You, God, are my tower of strength.* The beets, his annual pride and joy, have this year failed to thrive. One of these days he will dig up the carrots.

Every spring he surveys his garden plot with anticipation and hope. And with the resolve to nurture and tend it, even though the harvesting of carrots and beets, the pleasure of late-blooming flowers, overlaps with the start of the school year—new students to be slotted into appropriate courses, new teachers to be welcomed and oriented, new texts to be stamped and stacked on shelves. And in spring, the season for planting and sowing, making the rounds of greenhouses for bedding plants, garden soil and fertilizer, coincides with the end of the school year, the season for final exams and reports, graduation exercises, caps and gowns, all of which he is responsible for. Still, he has always found time for his garden.

But his family? Alice's pregnancy and Jeremy's birth have been overshadowed by the demands of school. I can do better, Joseph vows. When winter comes I'll go skating with Lucas. I'll learn how to smile at the baby.

He bends to spread a large hand on the hard earth, resolved to care for it more faithfully in the future. He thinks of Hedie Lodge. He can't help it. Her small hands. The sheen of her dark hair. He wants to sit a while on the garden bench, but inside the house Millicent will be waiting.

Late in the afternoon Joseph can be seen raking the fallen leaves into huge brown piles for Mia to bag. Father and daughter working together as if they are bringing in a harvest.

~

Marie Wittenberg no longer knows for sure whether her son will come to her on a Friday afternoon. Things are not as they used to be and what could once be counted on is now too often in doubt. But though her son's Friday visits are uncertain, she knows Mia will come again. She suspects her granddaughter is not motivated by a hunger for an old story stored in the memory of an old woman but by a strict teacher's assignment deadline. Well, thank goodness someone is setting rules for the young. But never mind the motives; at her age Marie has learned to be grateful for the small mercy of a visit. Grateful that her mind works as well as it does. As often as it does.

Today it's Alice who comes, bringing Lucas and Jeremy. She places the baby in the old woman's lap to be stroked and petted. Like a little lamb. A helpless little lamb. Lucas, today more dervish than lamb, scuttles around the small apartment. Grammerie, he mutters. Toys, Grammerie? Need toys.

Easy, Lucas, Alice cautions, and turns to her grandmother. We'll come every week, GranMarie, she promises and the old woman smiles as if she knows this will not happen.

Marie's mind strays from the children and Alice. It settles on her mother, whose face comes more often to mind than that of her own husband, the man who gave her two sons—Joseph and Philip. That man's face is blurred, but she can clearly see her mother's sad eyes and thin shoulders as she stirs soup in a large pot on the stove, steam rising from it. When she wants to move the heavy pot, Marie steps forward to lift it for her. "No, Maria," her mother says. "You shouldn't. Your back is young, it's still growing. We have to protect it. My back is strong. It's my lungs that are sick." Her eyes are brimming with sorrow and she says, "My life was predicted. It was foretold. By a gypsy."

The baby's whimpering calls Marie back to the present. She sits up straight, pulls her narrow shoulders back as far as possible. "Don't slouch," her mother used to say. "Your shoulders are narrow, like mine. They cramp the lungs. You have to make space for the lungs."

Alice has been bending over the baby, soothing, cooing as

she changes his diaper, but now she straightens and turns to embrace the old woman with her free arm. She kisses each creped cheek. I love you, GranMarie.

Marie wants to raise her arms, enclose mother and baby in them. Instead she says, How's our little man coming along? And remembering his name, How's our Jeremy doing?

Oh, GranMarie, Alice says. Her tears come in quick spurts, she can't stop them, can't keep from sobbing. Oh, GranMarie. What are we going to do?

Seeing his mother's tears, Lucas howls and Alice takes him by the arm. Time for hugs, Lucas, she says and dabs her face with a sleeve before pulling the boy toward GranMarie. Lucas, frightened, kicks and screams and refuses to hug the old woman. Alice gathers her children and leaves. When the door closes behind them Marie can hear Alice scolding and her children crying. She raises a hand to touch her cheeks. Dry. She has no tears left to shed. They are all used up. She can't comfort anyone. She has no advice to give. She is of no use at all.

You're one big memory bank, someone told her recently. Mia, it must have been, listening to that old story about gypsies. I couldn't write the stories without you, GranMarie.

What if the bank fails? Sometimes her memories run rampant, clamouring for attention, but how quickly and without warning they become blurred and faint. Marie is afraid that one day she won't remember a single thing. Right now she can't remember if she's ever told her granddaughters in so many words: I love you, Alice. I love you, Mia.

Snow

On the day of the first snow—a harmless scattering of wet flakes—the after-school staff meeting at GSC is finally adjourned just past five-thirty. Joseph stays to begin an inventory of usable *Hamlet* and *Macbeth* texts. After that he'll head out to Future Shop to look at new computers for the school's growing business department. He's told Mia to warn Millicent not to expect him for supper. When he leaves the school grounds he sees a lone figure waiting at the bus stop, a slender silhouette against the snow. It's Hedie Lodge.

My car has a date with Tom Gibbs, she says when Joseph stops his Camaro and she gets in. Snow has turned the streets slick and Joseph drives cautiously, not only because an accident with Hedie in the car would be a disaster. He drives slowly for the simple pleasure of finding himself so near this woman who has snow on her thick brown hair and on her navy coat. Computers are suddenly unimportant.

Where do you live? he asks. I'll drive you home. He knows where she lives; he's looked it up.

Hedie does not refuse his offer.

Later he will wonder whether all this happened by chance or whether Hedie's staying late—marking papers, she says—was planned. The possibility of such intention will trouble him then, but now he is grateful to be beside her in a world that is quietly welcoming winter. The Disraeli Bridge is slick and slushy, Main Street dusted with snow. On Portage Avenue the first Christmas lights have been strung up, not yet lit.

Come up and see my place, Hedie says when they have reached her street, no trace of self-consciousness or coyness.

Joseph can think of no reason to say no. He parks the car and follows her up the narrow staircase to the third floor of the old brick building and into a small apartment with wide windows.

A room with a view, he says, standing beside her, looking down on cars crawling along the street, their beams ghostly in the snow. Beyond the traffic, the frozen Assiniboine, the city's other river.

I never close the blinds, Hedie says. Who would see me up here?

Joseph chuckles and they both look down in silence. He steps away from the window, away from Hedie. Shelves tightly packed with books line one wall. Along another, a floral chesterfield and above it a watercolour landscape. He studies it, then picks up a photograph of a young man on a side table and looks quizzically at Hedie.

My brother, she says.

I should go. Joseph says, relieved. I'm heading for Future Shop.

But you haven't had supper. I'll make something quick.

She takes two TV dinners from her freezer, heats them in the microwave—roast chicken, mashed potatoes, peas, gravy—and they eat in the small living area from lap trays, shut off from the snow-covered world. Thoughts of Millicent and Jeremy and Mia linger on the periphery of Joseph's consciousness but they do not impose themselves. Circumstances are graciously allowing him this interlude, this escape from routine, from anxieties and pressures that for the vice principal have become considerable by late fall. The energy required by the new gym. The unexpected resignation of the custodian. Truancy. Vandalism. Drugs.

Here he has no duties. He is free to watch as Hedie offers wine, puts the kettle on as naturally as if she has often done this for him. As if he belongs here. The intimacy of eating and drinking together becomes a communion, and this unfamiliar place is suddenly familiar. His eyes follow the quiet movement of Hedie's hands. He feels consoled and welcomed. And completely unsettled. He is curious about the woman who has welcomed him. Whose life before coming to GSC he knows nothing about.

Is Lodge your maiden name? he asks, meaning: Were you ever married?

She hesitates before telling him that she once went by the name of Hedie Belvedere. She watches for his reaction.

Joseph tries to imagine the students calling her Miss Belvedere and the idea brings a smile to his face. He looks up and she is smiling too. Their smiles turn to laughter and then Hedie tells him about her parents.

Her mother came from Australia, a teacher, a restless woman who emigrated because she needed adventure and hoped for love. In Canada she married a Russian, Jacov Bilovetz, whose family had come to Canada with the intention of becoming rich. The family had farmed in southern Ontario near Lake Erie but failed in their ambition to acquire wealth. The youngest son, Jacov, had found employment in the construction industry when he met Imogene Fogg, a young teacher with an accent that struck him as refined and elegant. When he asked her to marry him, she agreed, but on the condition that he change his name. She had no desire to be Mrs. Jacov Bilovetz. Well, then they would take her name, Jacov had suggested. But she didn't care for Fogg either and had wanted to be rid of it for some time. What then? Jacov, deeply in love, asked. After thinking it over she came up with Belvedere, a name she'd read in a novel.

A year after they married, Imogene quit teaching and started a family: two boys within two years. The first one died young of meningitis. The second became an engineer and left to work for an oil company in Saudi Arabia, was transferred to Australia, then to Kuala Lumpur, from where he wrote brief Christmas letters. It's his picture on the table. Jacov believed his son had simply disappeared into his career and surely must have found the prosperity his grandfather had craved.

And where do you come into the picture, Hedie? Her name is soft and unaccustomed on Joseph's tongue.

Hedie hesitates again, then continues her story, skipping over Joseph's question. My father was injured in a construction accident, she says. His back was broken and he became a paraplegic. When he died it was rumoured that Mother had supplied him with the necessary means, you know, to end his suffering.

Hedie looks up to make sure Joseph hasn't missed the point. No one could say just how severe the suffering had been, she says, but Dad thought he just couldn't live like that, so dependent on others. And those suspicious about the circumstances of his death were also willing to keep quiet.

Joseph lets this information—it seems a bit like a confession—sit with them in the room a good while before he presses for more. And you? What about you?

I was an afterthought. My mother was pregnant with me when my father fell. Hedie grows silent and Joseph does not break the silence.

When Hedie speaks again she says, Apparently I look like my father. He was tall and had grey eyes. My mother was rather small. I've got her hands.

These physical details appear to conclude what Hedie wants to tell him, but Joseph needs more. Your name ... , he says.

Hedie's smile has a touch of mischief. Oh, she says, Belvedere. That name always seemed pretentious. Insincere, somehow. So I took the name of my maternal grandmother—Lodge. And, no, I was never married. She is still smiling.

But the time for storytelling has come to a close and he must go. He really must go, leave the comfort of this home. He rises. But Hedie reaches with her small hand for his large one. You haven't told me anything about yourself, she says.

Joseph shrugs awkwardly and looks away. Not much to tell, he says, trying to detach himself from this evening, this warm place. Her hand. But Hedie won't let him. She leads him away from the empty plates and glasses back to the window, where it has stopped snowing and the traffic is sparse. They look down to where the river winds its ghostly way through the neighbourhood.

It's okay, she says. You don't have to tell me anything.

Hedie, he says, removing his hand from hers. Hedie Lodge. He picks up his coat and moves toward the door. She follows him down the stairs and out onto the sidewalk, where he bends to kiss her on the forehead, then heads for his snow-covered car.

~

Mia jogs home after school and goes straight to her father's garden patch, where the last small drifts of white lie wedged along the fence, all that's left of the first early snow. She tries to pull a carrot, but the ground is hard and she is left with a handful of limp greens. She tries for another with as little success. She steps to the middle of the brown lawn with her fistful of carrot greens and imagines herself standing in the wings of a huge theatre, waiting for the cue that will summon her onto the stage and into the spotlight. It's not applause she craves, but the drama itself. The prospect is exhilarating. And, for a moment, with the late sun's rays warming her, she is unafraid. Next fall she will begin the real business of life. She will study history and languages and art—everything. And then the world will open up and there will be a place in it for her. There must be.

And Kurt. What's his role? Will he share with her a scene in this drama?

And sudden as a breeze fear creeps in. What if life will prove more complex than she believes? She will listen for cues and miss them. The play itself will be unfamiliar, the lines she is given to speak difficult to learn, or else not meant for her.

Mia isn't expecting to see her father in the garden. He's at a meeting planning a teachers' retreat. And she'd be astonished to see her mother here, bending to pull a carrot from the rows that should have been harvested by now. Or even just sitting on the half-rotten bench. Her mother is in the house somewhere and Mia is alone in the garden. She wanders over to the bench, sits down and tilts her face to catch the sun. Its low rays cast long shadows on the dying garden.

Her ancestors, it seems to Mia, lived always close to death. GranMarie's brown photo album has pictures of small children with closed eyes, their dark lashes and soft round cheeks, the toes of their tiny shoes pointing to the sky. They didn't suffer long, GranMarie says. And think of what they didn't have to go through.

Mia doesn't believe that the dead could ever be better off than the living.

Sparrows flit among the shrivelled stalks and stems. There's a sudden icy breeze. Winter's breath. Defying wind and all thoughts of death, Mia fetches a spade and a pail from the tool shed and begins digging the carrots.

~

Millicent has stepped to the kitchen window from where she can see her daughter digging carrots with quick and vigorous movements as if she commands a source of strength that can't be depleted. Mia has inherited this from Joseph, Millicent believes. And has received nothing from her mother to match it.

Millicent doesn't know that her daughter is sometimes terrified of stepping into the stage lights. That sometimes she wants nothing more than to slink away to a seat in the audience, somewhere near the back in the shadows where she is allowed to be an observer, unseen and safe. Millicent herself has been an observer more than a participant. She would understand the girl's fear. She knows that fear. And would be surprised to learn that her daughter knows it too.

Millicent moves away from the window.

She has sometimes believed the dead are better off than the living. But now Jeremy has come, and everything has changed. Even she is being pulled into this new thing. This opportunity. At last she can do something for her family.

Millicent grew up in the southwest of Winnipeg near the Assiniboine River, in a community far across the city from where she lives now. She was an only child and her childhood was blessed with love and encouragement.

You didn't just move when you learned to walk, Millie, her

mother often told her. You danced. You were such a natural. So graceful. And joyful. Our little dancing flower.

Her parents gladly paid for dance classes, where instructors gushed praise over this talented girl, her sense of rhythm, the sheer music of her movements.

The way Millie moves, she heard her father tell her mother, it looks so … so oriental.

But though she was blessed, she was also burdened. It was during her early teen years that she first sensed a tendency toward joylessness. It began gradually. Perhaps it happened in tenth grade, when everyone expected her to win the dance competition she'd been training for, but the prize was given to an immigrant student, a Latin American girl who could dance the rumba and the cha-cha-cha with more passion and verve than anyone. Millicent, shocked, believed this was a mistake that would be quickly corrected. When no one apologized for the error, or even suggested that one had occurred, a sudden sorrow took hold of her and life acquired the grey colour of defeat. Simply getting dressed for the day felt futile. She brooded. Her hands lay idle in her lap. Her parents were beside themselves. Weeks passed.

Then one morning she felt a fountain opening up inside her, shooting up small spurts of gladness that gained force and height and brought a return of joy. The world reclaimed its bright colours; it was waiting for her. Her class was scheduled to see *The Pirates of Penzance* at the Playhouse Theatre. A new dance class was about to begin. Her best friend was planning a weekend party. She would get her first manicure.

The next bout of melancholy may have occurred when she had to miss a camping trip with friends to Birds Hill Park because her aunt and cousins were visiting and her mother, uncharacteristically, insisted: No, Millie, you don't leave when they've taken the trouble to drive from Edmonton. What would that look like? Or it may have been not getting the summer job at the law office. The simple filing position was given to a stupid girl with large breasts. Or it may have been losing her favourite opal earrings. The grey weight grew heavier and the fountain of joy, though it bubbled up intermittently, faltered too quickly.

That fountain shot straight up to the sky when she met Joseph during her first year of university.

Mennonite, she said. What's that?

You don't really want to know, Joseph teased, tracing the outline of her hand with a strong finger, over and over as if he meant to memorize it. It would take all night for me to explain that kettle of fish, he said, his large hands continuing their exploration, moving along her arm, making their slow, purposeful way toward her breasts.

Your hands, they're so big, Millicent said. Like a farmer's.

I think my grandfather might have been a farmer.

But Millicent wasn't interested in his grandfather's hands. She was content with Joseph's.

Before university Joseph had worked as a bricklayer. He was older than his classmates. And wiser and handsomer, Millicent thought. In the presence of his masculinity, his confidence, she was stirred to imagine herself walking up a church aisle with this solid-shouldered student with blue eyes, a rich voice and a slow smile. She had imagined a honeymoon. She had never felt this way about any boy she'd known in high school. At night she wrapped herself in newfound exhilaration, slept soundly and woke, rested. And deliriously happy.

Why a Mennonite? her father asked, as if the word denoted a particularly weird species. But the sheer marvel of his daughter's attracting any boyfriend at all outweighed his reservations.

Look how happy she is, her mother said.

Joseph's mother looked Millicent over, not warmly, but courteously. She offered tea, seldom anything more. Then she retreated to her favourite chair with a book, as if to avoid the challenge of a conversation. As if she had completed her assessment of this petite, dark-haired English girl and was willing to let things take their course.

Do you love your mother? Millicent wanted to ask Joseph. She assumed his mother loved him—who wouldn't love Joseph?

Much easier to bring Joseph into her own home, despite her still dubious parents. She helped her mother prepare roast beef and Yorkshire pudding and gravy and for dessert she baked a sponge cake. Joseph's praise set her on a domestic detour—she discovered that she loved to cook.

She had never felt that she belonged in university and after her second year, about the time her family became cautiously excited about a wedding, she dropped out of the arts program.

Mennonites, Millicent discovered, were peculiar people. They seemed preoccupied with finding out who was related to whom. They made quilts and gardens and plum jam. Most of them—though not Marie Wittenberg—expected their children home for Sunday dinner, served at noon, right after church.

They abhorred war. They wanted to fix the world. They shopped at thrift stores. They always sang in four-part harmony. She loved watching Joseph in the church choir, in the baritone section, singing anthems that filled the sanctuary. *Holy God, we praise your name.*

We used to sing in German, Joseph told her. The whole church service was German.

Well, thank God that's changed, Millicent laughed. She felt strange enough in an English service with Joseph's people. After the service they might be invited to someone's home for dinner where everyone eyed Joseph's English girlfriend with unmasked curiosity.

Mennonites were also like everyone else, she discovered. They got jobs, they fell in love, married and built houses, went on vacation with their families, played baseball and volleyball, quarrelled and made enemies, started businesses that sometimes succeeded, sometimes failed, they were gossipy and could be alarmingly competitive. Mennonites liked to travel to faraway places cursed with poverty, drought, disease or illiteracy, places where their blankets and skills and money were needed and they came home feeling satisfied with themselves. Another preferred destination was the Soviet Union, the country they had come from. Fled from, they always insisted.

After they married, Millicent continued to accompany Joseph into the Mennonite life, but she never stopped feeling she was stepping on alien ground. It wasn't because in many families there was as much Low German spoken as English. Or because an occasional German hymn might be sung during a church service, or someone might quote scripture in German. And it wasn't the food. Joseph never expected her to learn Mennonite cooking: cabbage borscht, vereneki with rich cream sauce and fried sausage, piroshki, plum platz. She wasn't wild about any of these, but if he'd asked early in their marriage, when she still loved cooking, or if her mother-in-law had offered to show her how, she would have been glad to learn to make these dishes. She might have been able to enter into that women's world of cooking, sewing, gardening. Didn't her own mother live in an Anglo-Saxon version of that world?

It was something about the stories these people told. They were not uninteresting, these narratives of escape and loss, but they were not *her* stories. The genealogies they were so endlessly preoccupied with were not *hers*, and that difference, she concluded, was significant. No one asked for her story, not that she had anything to tell. She knew little of her family background and assumed it was not particularly interesting.

If Millicent had been inclined to be nostalgic about the past, she might have recalled the way her limbs once moved to the rhythm of music as she danced, the lightness of her body, the heady pleasure of performance. But Millicent had become stuck in the present, and the present did not include dancing. Joseph did not dance.

When Millicent became pregnant Joseph was ecstatic. And she too became excited. At first. And curious. But gradually, she couldn't quite say how, childbirth began to loom as a challenge so huge it would destroy her. She became terrified. Wanted out. She would want out of her second pregnancy too, but neither her parents nor Joseph took her fear seriously. No one came to her rescue and she lacked the courage to act on her own.

It was Marie Wittenberg who one day, unexpectedly, said, Don't be afraid, Millicent. You'll survive. We always do. Her voice was blunt and the attention she gave her daughter-in-law, although brief, was so startling it couldn't be ignored.

After Alice was born, Millicent and Joseph brought her to church, where Millicent sat with her in the cry room while Joseph sang in the choir. The service was piped into the cry room, where young mothers breastfed their babies, changed diapers, cooed and sang along with the hymns. During the sermon they exchanged whispered reports. One had sewn or knitted every stitch her baby wore. Another spoke German to her child—We've decided she'll learn her mother tongue before she learns English. Those with toddlers vied to keep their own quiet.

When Alice was old enough for Sunday school, she was expected to sit through the church service too, and Millicent was expected to keep her quiet. That was when Millicent began to resent Sunday mornings and the ridiculous—in her opinion—ordeal of sitting with a squirming child for an hour and a half.

Mia was different. Mia sat alert and curious, following the hymns, prayers, even the sermons with great seriousness, as if she understood every word. Both girls enjoyed the youth group and would eventually have sung in the choir as their father did if they'd been encouraged, Millicent thinks.

In time she stopped accompanying Joseph and her daughters to church and stayed home to read magazines or stare out the window or sleep. Her former sadness, familiar and periodic, returned and she gave in to it. When her family came home from church they brought hamburgers and french fries from McDonald's.

It wasn't only within the culture and religion of the Mennonites that Millicent felt like a stranger. The whole vast world was scary. Bit by bit, as her children grew, darkness closed in on her and wanted to claim her completely.

Today she believes it will be possible to take up once again the struggle against that darkness. For Alice's sake. For Lucas and Jeremy.

~

It's Friday and the teachers at George Sutton Collegiate are going on a retreat and have given their students what students crave most—release from the classroom in the form of early dismissal.

Teachers and administrators, carrying the hand luggage they brought with them this morning, crowd into the chartered bus that takes them to the Agassiz Retreat Center where, after a light supper, they will convene their first session. Ab Solinsky and his vice principal left early in Joseph's car. No idle chatter along the way. No comment on the bleak autumn landscape. Their conversation is focused on school matters.

At the retreat centre, testing and curriculum top the evening's agenda, and when the discussion is brought to a close just after ten—they will reconvene next morning to discuss the gym renovation project—there is still time and energy to party. They retire to the lounge, where they act much like the teenagers they set free for the weekend. Agendas are forgotten, hair let down.

Joseph observes them from his corner table, a copy of the weekend schedule in one hand, his drink in the other. There is Claudette Avery, who chaired the retreat planning committee, joking with Peter McBride. Two phys-ed teachers have recruited Joan Gustav and Tom Gibbs for a card game. Ab Solinsky is at the bar with the math teachers.

Put that away, Hedie Lodge says as she seats herself next to Joseph and tugs the agenda from his hand. In the dim light of the lounge she glows, as if lit from within. She wears a black V-neck sweater and the skin of her throat is warm and creamy.

She's brimming with life, Joseph thinks. Overflowing with it. He retrieves his agenda. What do you think? he says, waving the printed sheet in front of her.

I'm looking for free time on the program, she says. Not enough of it. What were they thinking, the planning committee? She is teasing, knows very well that Joseph was on that committee.

He takes his ballpoint pen and draws small blue stars beside coffee breaks and time slots where he has no obligations. She takes out a red pen and circles the times she has free. One of her red circles overlaps Joseph's blue star. They notice this simultaneously and turn to each other. Their eyes meet.

The auspicious time slot falls on Saturday afternoon after the gym project will have been discussed. After Hedie has met with the guest speaker, an import from south of the border who for an alarming fee delivers motivation to any audience who will hire him. Hedie has been asked to introduce him at the banquet on Saturday evening. By Saturday afternoon Joseph will have met with Ab Solinsky to rehash the staff's response to the gym renovations. Basketball season is about to begin and Ab had wanted a renovated, state-of-the-art gym for the George Sutton

Saints. Joseph helped draft the arguments favouring the project.
The superintendent was impressed and so was the entire school
board and the plan received the approval of the minister of education. Chances that Joseph Wittenberg will get the top job look
good. He has said nothing about this to Millicent.

In the days and weeks that follow the Agassiz retreat, Joseph
will not remember the details of his meeting with Ab, but he
will mull over the convergence of time and place, how they con-
spired to create opportunity, and how this became an invitation
to which desire, overriding all reservations, all better judgement, said: Yes.

~

Joseph is in his room waiting for Hedie Lodge. The school's
professional development budget has been stretched to allow
administrators the luxury of private rooms. Hedie, like the rest
of the staff, must share. Joseph's is a fairly standard room—bed,
desk, a door leading to the bathroom, a south-facing window,
two upholstered chairs, noticeably worn. Above the desk there's
a picture of a sailing vessel in rough water, the first thing he saw
when he woke this morning. He's hung up the jacket he flung
on a chair, tidied the papers spread on the desk and is prepared
for her knock.

Waiting, Joseph thinks of that evening when he followed
Hedie for the first time up the stairs to her apartment and she
welcomed him with food, the warmth of her home, a bestowal
of gifts he had not expected. But was it the gift of her story that
held most value? Even though it was far from complete, it seems
to him now that it's more than he possesses of his own story.
More than he knows of Millicent's. But that evening he wasn't
thinking of Millicent. And he mustn't now.

Waiting for Hedie, Joseph knows he should be content with her story. He should not want more.

Hedie is late and when she finally knocks he hurries to let her in.

Notice how prompt I am? Hedie says, out of breath.

Her attempt at lightheartedness leaves Joseph strangely sad. Good girl, he says, as if she is a student. He doesn't ask why she's late. He is not in a playful mood. Not really a playful man. He takes her by the hand and leads her to the bed. They sit together on the edge of it, on the red and purple geometric design of the spread that one of them will soon pull back. Both are solemn now and for a moment Joseph wishes himself elsewhere even though he has urgently wanted—and still urgently wants—to be here, right now, together with this woman, for as long as possible. At least as long as prudent.

What are you thinking? Hedie asks shyly, as if this is a risky question. Joseph might be thinking of his family. Of his wife, whom she's never met. Who has never been mentioned between them. Of Mia, who is easily the brightest student in her ragtag grade twelve English class.

Joseph wants time to stand still, but time never does and Joseph too must move. He moves closer to Hedie, lets his fingers trace the contours of her face. He nuzzles her thick brown hair. His mouth, hungry, finds hers.

Sunlight streams in through the south-facing window. Joseph has not closed the heavy drapes. He spends so much of his days in offices and in the windowless textbook room, that now it seems wrong to shut out the light. And anyway, no one can see into the fourth-storey window except the gulls he has seen swooping down to check out the hotel's dumpsters in the parking lot below.

~

Saturday morning Mia wakes to the doorbell ringing somewhere in the distance and her mother's footsteps heading down
the hall.

Danny's here, Millicent says, knocking at Mia's door. Ready
to rise and shine?

Warm under the covers, Mia would prefer not to. It's Saturday. It's early. What in the world is Danny doing here? She closes
her eyes as if that will make him go away, but curiosity overrules
and she rises, pulls on a robe and comes to the door, dishevelled.

Hey, Danny. What's up?

Clearly Danny is no more capable of shining than she is,
although he has more or less risen. His unkempt hair sticks out
from under a green toque, his shoulders sag as if he has trouble
straightening them, and his face is shadowed by the weariness of
an old man and the grey evidence of a pending beard.

You up for biking? he says, his voice a kind of growl.

What?

I just thought.

Danny, it's Saturday. People sleep in, Saturdays. Sane people,
I mean. Still bleary-eyed herself, she sees Danny as a configura-
tion of chaos, his body one long torment. Come in, she says.
You're cold.

Danny follows her like a stray dog into the kitchen, where she
takes the pot with yesterday's coffee, pours a mug full, heats it in
the microwave and hands it to him. Danny curves both hands
around it, hunching his body over that small source of warmth.
Mia thinks of the derelicts on Main Street for whom the coming
of winter is a seasonal threat. She wonders whether it's sheer
gall that brings Danny to the Wittenberg bungalow, knowing
the vice principal is not at home. Danny's act of vandalism is
ancient history, her father's Camaro repaired and parked somewhere at a retreat centre.

Just let me brush my teeth, she says, relenting. She dresses, collects her helmet, gloves and warm jacket. The radio spits out news: Iraq. Kuwait. Oil.

Millicent brings two bowls of cereal with milk, offers one to Danny, who shakes his head. Mia eats hers standing.

Since the first snow melted, weeks ago, there has been no more. Streets will not be icy. But the morning air is crisp and if it weren't for the first rays of the sun showing above the houses in the east and the absence of wind, biking would be out of the question. They leave the house and Mia leads her bike from the garage. She hasn't used it since she switched to jogging in September.

Where are we going? She assumes they'll take a short ride down Kildonan Drive and maybe down side streets or lanes, but Danny heads toward Henderson Highway and turns north.

Lockport, he says.

You're kidding me, Danny. Lockport's twenty clicks.

By the time they reach the place where the paved shoulder becomes a bike path and the sparse Saturday traffic thins to a trickle, the sun is dragging along even with the tops of the trees. The sky is a timid blue. Along the highway silent yards display the shrivelled remains of summer: marigolds that blazed recently. Frozen pumpkins. Oak and elm tree skeletons. Mia is fully awake now. Exhilarated. Every muscle, every nerve alert. She feels the warm strength of her body, feels buoyant, weight-less, as if she could lift off and fly like those screaming gulls overhead. She craves speed. Thighs, knees work automatically, fluidly. Her torso is taut. She pulls ahead of Danny.

Brilliant idea, she calls back.

I told you.

And now the river begins to reveal itself between the leaf-less trees to their left. It flows north to the lake while vees of Canada geese head south, honking frantically. In summer Mia cycled the distance to Lockport regularly, rising early to avoid the heat, leaving behind the commercial stretch of the highway, entering a rural landscape with market gardens, small fields of grain, forage crops and churches. She observed new construction projects, large houses being built on lots squeezed between the river and the highway. There are four churches to pass. She knows them all, from the small orthodox chapel undergoing a slow renovation to the brown brick Catholic church with its two towers and neatly gravelled yard. Somewhere across the river is St. Andrews, the impressive stone church west of the river. Mia attends the Mennonite church on Edison Avenue, partly out of habit, partly out of loyalty to Bev, who was baptized last year and is a member. Mia has thought about baptism, an undertaking so significant it frightens her.

They don't make you sign anything, Bev has assured her.

But I'd really have to mean it, wouldn't I?

Of course.

A few early joggers are out. A woman walking her dog calls a cheery good morning and Mia calls good morning back. Occasionally she slows down to let Danny catch up. When he does, he's pumping hard. This is good for him, she thinks, resuming speed, leaving him behind once more. She'll make him work to catch up.

Eventually Danny no longer tries to catch up and Mia stops to wait for him. When he does, he's gasping for breath. They wheel their bikes off the highway onto a driveway with a small shelter where garden produce is sold in fall: corn and carrots and potatoes. She turns the CLOSED sign to OPEN and grins at Danny, who doesn't grin back. They sit side by side on a red bench, Danny still breathing hard as if his heart is beating overtime in his narrow chest. Mia doesn't tell him he's out of shape, but simply waits, glad that the sun is higher now, warmer. She looks at her watch. She had intended to visit GranMarie this morning. "Tea and history," her father calls these sessions.

When he can speak without gasping, Danny asks, How's Jeremy?

Mia doesn't believe Danny is concerned this morning about Jeremy's welfare. The tension has not left his face, he is having trouble getting his breath and this makes her uncomfortable. Danny wants something from her.

I'm asking about Jeremy, Danny says when she doesn't answer. Your new nephew. Remember? His voice rises for no reason, becomes harsh and by the time he gets to the question mark it has taken on a tinge of annoyance.

Jeremy mostly sleeps when I'm there, Mia says. Like an angel. But at night he howls and doesn't let Alice sleep. She doesn't say that Brian sleeps in the living room so he can rest and go to work next morning. That he's tired of walking a cranky baby. That he takes his cameras and tripod and heads out the door saying, I've got my job to think of. He hasn't taken one picture of Jeremy.

Yeah, well. He's landed in a shitty world, poor kid. What do you expect?

Danny, what's wrong? Mia asks, alarmed by his bitterness. Are you okay?

Why wouldn't I be? He turns away.

Mia wants to fill the silence with words, wants to return to the quiet beauty of the morning sun, the peace that settled while she was pedalling. But Danny is slumped next to her like a half-filled sack of potatoes.

Look at me, she says, impatiently. What she sees in Danny's eyes is not reassuring and when his cold hand reaches for her wrist, grabs it and holds it hard, she is afraid.

What? she says when he doesn't speak.

You gonna be my friend, Mia?

Danny, for God's sake, haven't I always been there for you?

You better be, he says through gritted teeth. His voice is hard and demanding, his eyes flint, she can't look away from that direct, aggressive gaze.

The two remain fixed on the bench, his hand tight around her wrist, their eyes locked. Mia doesn't know what to do or say. Then, as though Danny's words have chained her to him, her head nods an involuntary assent. His grip tightens. Then relaxes. He releases her hand.

Still far from Lockport, they remount their bikes and turn back. Mia's wrist is burning but the rest of her shivers and she pedals hard to warm up. She leaves Danny behind. His troubled face. His icy hand on her wrist. But before long she slows and lets him catch up and keep pace with her.

~

In early November Millicent stands at the window of her daughter's kitchen, staring out into the drab street where the wind is playing cat and mouse with dry leaves, wedging them up against fences and shrubs. Winter is coming, her least favourite season, and she shudders at the prospect before turning to the pot of tea waiting for her. Her mother, an English war bride, taught her the correct way of making tea and she has not forgotten the procedure: warm the teapot, measure the tea leaves, pour boiling water, let the tea steep, pour the milk before you pour the tea.

Here I am, Millicent thinks, pouring tea, a middle-aged woman in a middle-class suburb. How did I get here, and what have I accomplished? What did I think I was going to do with my life? Did I miss a turn in the road somewhere? No, she tells herself. I won't think that way. Not today. I'm here in my daughter's house to do something that needs doing and no one but me can do it. Alice will be grateful. My family will be grateful.

In the bedroom Alice lies sleeping, exhausted, while in the

boys' bedroom Jeremy will soon wake from his nap and set up a fuss. She will shush him so Alice can rest longer. Lucas has a play date with a boy from the Church of Abundant Joy whose mother has seen Alice struggling with her two children and has taken pity.

When the doctors first told Alice, Your son has Fragile X Syndrome, they merely confirmed what the family already suspected. Alice has not challenged the verdict. She has not broken down or raged against God or looked for pity. Everything will change, she says, even when no one shares her optimism. Jeremy will come through this. He will be well.

Millicent thinks, He will live among us, be part of the family. We will surround him with attention and love, give him what we can. She knows his condition will eventually hamper the coordination of his limbs, sabotage the development of his brain, and make his mouth want to remain open so that saliva runs down his chin. People will stare. Or turn away from him. Millicent is determined to love this grandchild the way she's learned to love Lucas, with a devotion that will override lethargy. That is the hope she has clung to since Jeremy's birth.

Her daughter is chasing solutions and experts, credentialed or not. Like a child chasing bubbles. Recently Alice heard of patterning, an exercise regimen that stimulates the reluctant brain by guiding the body through stages of physical development. To everyone's surprise, Brian is cooperating with this concrete alternative to prayer. Although it's much too soon, Jeremy too young to be patterned, Brian has brought home lengths of lumber, gathered his tools and is building the necessary equipment: an exercise table, a wooden tunnel through which Jeremy will be made to crawl, a device for suspending him upside down so oxygen and blood can rush to his head.

What's this? Joseph has asked. You're transforming the basement into a rehab hospital?

We'll recruit volunteers, Alice says. They'll help us guide Jeremy through the exercises. We'll make a schedule. The whole neighbourhood will help. They'll want to.

Millicent, skeptical, has voiced no objection.

A friend of Alice's has urgently recommended an herb with an unpronounceable name. You make a tea of it and give it to the child three times daily.

Millicent is afraid her daughter will be consumed by this flawed child. And Brian, whom Millicent has never cared for, will lose interest. And Lucas, whom she loves, will be neglected. Millicent, guilty of so much neglect it doesn't bear thinking about, will devote herself to Jeremy.

She turns to the plate of raw beef cubes on the kitchen counter and remembers a time when she loved cooking. She was not a bad cook. Now, riding the wave of energy triggered by Jeremy's birth, she will revive that skill. Alice's church people brought casseroles in great variety, a service that has softened Millicent's attitude toward them, but lately the casseroles have tapered off and several days a week she makes the supper and, if Alice asks, stays overnight. She has discovered which dishes Brian prefers, which ones he refuses to eat. Beef in any form is safe, and even Lucas likes stew. Alice eats anything, always in a hurry, often standing up. She's losing weight.

Sipping tea, Millicent reviews the supper menu: stew and beets and carrot sticks—Mia, not Joseph, has finally harvested the carrots. Coffee for Brian and Alice, tea for herself. That leaves dessert. Is there time to bake a pie? Lemon is Joseph's favourite and suddenly Joseph is in her mind. His broad shoulders, the confident bearing that first attracted her, his blue eyes, his thick, straw-coloured hair, firm hands, hands that once stirred her body to life. It's four o'clock and he'll be at his desk or somewhere in the school, her hardworking, conscientious husband. Whom she doesn't deserve. She has always known that in a vague sort of way. Known that she has not been a good wife. The heaviness that settled on her with the weight of concrete has been to blame. And she has been to blame for not winning the fight against this malaise, this noon-day demon. She knows that even now it is there watching. Waiting to catch her in a moment of weakness.

Mia will have to find something for supper tonight, for herself and Joseph. Mia seems so much older than her years, so much more mature than Alice ever was. And wiser than her mother. Mia too deserves better. Millicent sets down her tea cup and dials.

Mia, it's your mother.

Oh hi, Mom. You doing okay? How's Jeremy?

Sleeping. Sweet as a kitten. What's for supper over there?

Dad won't be home.

But you—you have to eat.

Kurt's coming by, we're going for pizza.

Kurt?

Our new neighbours? Just down the street?

Oh, yes, Millicent says. She has no idea who Kurt is. Has Mia mentioned him before and she hasn't listened?

He's at basketball practice. He'll come by when he's done.

When Millicent hangs up, she goes over the conversation. There is something more, surely, that she should have said to her daughter. Questions she should have asked. She ought to have probed her about this Kurt whom she has never seen. Or perhaps she has? He will drive or walk Mia home and they will be alone in the house, maybe for hours. She has not met the new family. She's known very few of the neighbours who have lived on Kildonan Drive over the many years since the Wittenbergs bought the bungalow.

She thinks of Danny, who doesn't come as often now. Last year he was always hanging around like an untrained puppy that trailed Mia home. From her bed, the refuge where she brought her heaviness, Millicent often heard them coming in and chattering. Millicent has always assumed that Mia will outgrow Danny, but what does she know? She is afraid she's had as little success at being a mother as at being a wife.

Why will Joseph be home late?

In the bedroom Alice stirs.

~

When her father called—Don't expect me for supper, I won't be home until late, you'll be okay, won't you?—a wave of loneliness swept over Mia, but when the phone rang again and it was Kurt—Want to go out for pizza? I'll come by after basketball practice—she was instantly buoyant.

And now she is restless, watching the clock, impatient for Kurt to arrive.

If Mia were inclined to be suspicious, she might see a pattern in her father's frequent "I won't be home for supper"s. Besides school duties and meetings at the divisional office, her father is on the Board of Stewards at church and sings in the choir. Lately he's missed Sunday morning service, she's noticed. Too busy.

Today he's given no explanation for skipping supper at home. And her mother didn't ask where exactly he said he'd be. Nor did her father ask about her mother. Does he usually? She's not sure.

Lodge likes your Dad, Angela wrote this morning, boldly, on a loose-leaf page. She added "Alot" before folding the page and passing it to Mia during English class.

Angela's head is so glutted with melodrama and romance there's no space left for anything even faintly philosophical, and if the poem in this morning's English class had been Elizabeth Browning's "How do I love thee?" there might have been no need to write surreptitious notes. But the poem was about war. Wilfred Owen describing the young men leaving for battle as *grimly grey* and their deployment like *wrongs hushed up*. Chilling words that reminded her of the threat of conflict in Iraq.

Mia would have ignored Angela's note, but she knows how quickly Angela senses the sparks of passion developing beneath a stairway or half concealed by the open door of a locker or shooting across a classroom. She's quick to report who is an item with who. And always on the button.

You're crazy, Angela, Mia said, on the way to the next class.

Oh, believe me, Angela shot back. And don't be so innocent. Think teachers don't get the hots for each other? Your dad's pretty cool, you know. He's a looker. And Lodge is pretty cute herself.

Oh shut up, Angela, Danny said. All you think about is sex.

Angela paid no attention and Mia wondered if Danny ever thought about sex. But what alarmed her was Bev's silence. She expected Bev to laugh at Angela. Or argue with her about Hedie Lodge and her father. But Bev said, That poem about war. Wasn't it depressing? Didn't it just make you want to do something, anything to prevent war?

Between biology and maths classes Mia saw her father and her English teacher talking together near the main office door as if they were good friends and had much to tell each other. Was there an intimacy she should have sensed? She wants to deny this possibility, wants to stop trying to recall missed clues. Nothing should spoil the anticipation of pizza with Kurt. She closes her eyes and conjures the blue and sparkling waters of the Aegean Sea. She is on her back, floating, weightless, the water rippling around her. Somewhere below her the sleek forms of fish glide like silver missiles through the darkness.

But although the Aegean Sea calls to her, she also imagines flying right over Greece, heading farther east to the world she is learning about from her grandmother. Is that world real or the dream of an old woman? She has pored in vain over maps searching for a place named Wassilyevka. What would it be like to walk along a street through the village her grandmother remembers from the country of her birth? To wander through the cemetery and read the names engraved in stone? Names her grandmother repeated on Saturday. Names of the dead.

Both Bev and Angela are signed up for Greece. Danny isn't, of course. Kurt? If she knew he was coming her earlier excitement would return. She'll ask him.

Back in September, for a brief while, Mia wanted to sing in the school choir, run for student council, join the drama club, try out for volleyball and travel to Greece. She wanted to fill her last year with activity as if she needed to create memories to take with her into life. But soon she found herself drawing back, as if to gain distance from life, to observe, to learn by watching how it all works. Sometimes Mia is afraid she's inherited her mother's sadness, an affliction capable of paralyzing you. Other times she believes she is being called out of the crowd, set apart for some reason. A sense of difference is surfacing, opening like a water lily on a still pond.

Last Sunday Pastor Heese spoke about being in the world but not of it. Mia can't imagine not being of the world if Kurt is in it.

Mia has given up on Kurt and is making Kraft dinner when he finally arrives.

Sorry, he says. The coach was really hard on us tonight. He looks pleased at this. Something smells good around here.

Over Kraft dinner and Cokes Kurt describes Jason, his friend back in Churchill, where Kurt's family lived until his father's transfer to Winnipeg.

Jason was the best, he says. A total athlete.

Was?

His snowmobile broke through the ice.

Mia flinches.

Jason was good at everything, he says. He was aboriginal. And I'm half aboriginal too. Kurt watches for Mia's reaction, but all she says is, Did you have a girlfriend? Up north?

Kurt tilts his head, mulling over the question. Yeah, he says slowly, but, well, we were more like just friends.

Mia senses that in thinking of this girl, this "*just* a friend," Kurt has momentarily forgotten basketball.

He tells her then how polar bears are invisible against an expanse of frozen snow, how their numbers are rapidly decreasing because the ice is melting. He describes the splendour of aurora borealis trailing its graceful swirl of ribbons—red, green, yellow—across the black sky on long winter nights.

You're a good listener, he says, interrupting himself. You sit so still. Like Jason.

Mia smiles, grateful for the compliment. She wants to know more of Kurt's life, every fascinating detail. She wants the whole story. Wants Kurt's voice to hold at bay all other stories: Danny's. Or Hedie Lodge's. Jeremy's. Even GranMarie's. But Kurt has come to the end of what he wants to say. She fills a bowl with chips, brings out more Cokes and they watch an old movie on TV: *Back to the Future.* She forgets to ask whether Kurt has signed on for Greece.

When he leaves it's late and her father still isn't home. Too exhilarated for sleep, Mia takes a book from her shelf, a play by Anton Chekhov. *Uncle Vanya.* She turns to the final scene, which she loves, reads it, then closes the book and sits down at her computer.

The Photograph
(Assignment #3)

It was mid-May and the morning mist lingered over the village of Wassilyevka. The air was heavy with the threat of rain. The yard surrounding the home of Abram and Hanna Franz was immaculate, the kitchen garden free of weeds in case anyone should choose to inspect it, and tables in the swept-out granary laden with fresh **Zwieback** and **Platz**.

Elena Sawatsky stood eyeing the colourful kaleidoscope on display in the flowerbeds. Her heart ached for Hanna as she bent to pick daisies to pin on the satin and lace that trimmed the freshly constructed rectangular wooden box resting on a bench in the front room, where curtains were drawn to shut out the sun. Elena had already pinned blue and yellow pansies to the white sleeves of the dress worn by the round-cheeked angel asleep in the box.

Any moment now the first guests would arrive.

The photographer walked into the yard and began fussing with his paraphernalia. He kept an eye out for the first drops of rain. Abram came of the house to greet him, while Hanna removed her apron and smoothed her straw-blonde hair. If she had looked into a mirror it would have reflected back to her a pair of blue eyes darkened by sorrow. She coaxed five-year-old Maria out of the house, away from the wooden box into which the girl had been staring intently, looking up from time to time to assure her mother that she had seen Käthi's eyelids flicker and open just a tiny slit. She was positively sure her sister was getting ready to wake up.

A neighbour hoisted the box in his strong arms, carried it out through the door and set it on a bench in front of a lilac hedge. He went back for two chairs.

Judith Bartsch emerged from the house with little Simon,

who clung to his oma's hand. "Go to your papa," she told him, pulling her hand away, nudging him forward. "Over there. Close to Käthi. Quick now, it's going to rain."

The boy ran toward his father, and the family arranged itself around the box, facing the ominous contraption with its black cloth hood. The parents sat on the two chairs and Abram lifted Simon to his knee. Maria stood quietly between her parents. She wanted to take her mother's hand, but it was balled into a tight fist. Four pairs of eyes stared at the camera and even Simon became **mäuschenstill** when the strange man's head disappeared inside the shrouded black box.

No one that day could have known that the picture of this family tableau would one day find its place in a brown velvet-covered album belonging to an old woman on a far continent, in a future no one at this funeral could imagine. The old woman would stare long at the pictures in the album and old sorrows would surface.

Hanna believed she had turned to stone. She was no longer truly alive and never again would be. How was it possible that a child, happy and sturdy, its round limbs in constant motion, the legs made for kicking, the arms for reaching out, that such a child could become so still within just a few days, still as the stones that lined the path to the street. The fever that came without warning had burned fiercely for twenty-four hours, consuming the twelve-month-old life entirely. Almost as easy as snuffing out a candle. And so quickly that the face of her little daughter lost none of its freshness. But no matter how unravished she appeared, Käthi was no longer capable of stirring.

Well-meaning villagers said solemnly, "God gives and God also takes away."

Elena Sawatsky said nothing as she pressed the hand of her heartbroken friend.

Käthi was carried in her box back into the dim house accompanied by her family and when the last villager had crowded in, the preacher read: **Alles Fleisch, es ist wie Gras** (All flesh is like grass) and also **Der Herr ist mein Hirte, mir wird nichts mangeln** (The Lord is my shepherd, I shall not want). Then everyone joined in to sing all eight stanzas of "Stimmt an das Lied vom Sterben" (Join in the song of dying).

Maria held Simon's hand as the family and their neighbours followed Käthi through the village toward the church, the air around them heavy with moisture. The box had been nailed shut: their little sister could no longer be seen. Behind the church, next to a white cross with the name "Susannah" on it, they stopped and formed a rough circle around a freshly dug grave that looked to Maria as if the earth had opened its mouth, ready to swallow the sky. Simon wanted to play in the mound of earth beside the grave but Maria said, No, and held him back. They watched as the box was lowered into the waiting hole. Their mother stared down as if she might follow the box into the darkness. Elena stood beside her while their father bent to pick up a lump of earth. He dropped it into the hole and it landed with a dull thump on the lid of the box.

"Come," Maria said to Simon. "Let's go home. It's going to rain."

The marriage of Hanna Bartsch and Abram Franz had been celebrated on the bride's eighteenth birthday. They had met at a wedding the previous year and, sitting across from each other, gazing into each other's eyes, sipping coffee, nibbling at **Zwieback**, they had fallen so permanently in love that a wedding was planned for the following summer.

For one year the couple lived with Hanna's widowed mother, then all three, with the couple's brand new baby girl, moved to The Promised Land, a property Judith both treasured and resented. Her sons, Hans and Peter, had tilled the rich soil and kept it productive, more productive than the old farm. But the brothers had become infected with strange dreams—dreams of travel and adventure. Of faraway places. One year, after completing the spring seeding, they left for settlements east of the Ural Mountains, where they found land, and as if a new country had swallowed them, they were seldom heard from.

Abram Franz, when he took Hanna for his wife, had promised his mother-in-law that he would care for The Promised Land, but he had insisted on living near that land, in the village of Wassilyevka.

Within the first year of her marriage to Abram, Hanna had given birth to Maria and the following year to Susannah, whom they had to leave behind the church, deep in the earth, three years ago. Simon, like Maria, did not have to be buried.

Today, it was Käthi.

Two more births lay ahead—Eduard and Jascha—and two more deaths, but today that future was mercifully veiled.

When Hanna had been about to give birth to Käthi, she had sent Simon and Maria to Oma Bartsch, telling them: "There will be such a surprise when you come home." She assumed they would miss their mother. But the children were happy with Oma, who entertained them by deftly eviscerating a chicken, stripping it of feathers and burning away the fuzz. She let them watch while she supervised the constantly nattering Russian maids, who were up to their elbows in flour, shaping round balls of dough, capping them with smaller balls into which they pressed a firm thumb, leaving an indentation that was still there when the pan of **Zwieback** was pulled hot from the oven. Sometimes they watched the collaborative production of a mountain of egg noodles for chicken soup. The dough was mixed, rolled out, cut into broad strips, the strips stacked. Then with a sharp knife needle-thin noodles were shaved from the end of the stack. Snick, snick, snick. When the maids tossed the noodles and scattered them on the table to dry, the air was filled with flour dust and the children laughed.

When Maria and Simon came home a week later they were greeted by a cry from the wooden cradle beside the large bed where their mother lay, covered right up to her shining face.

"Come, Maria, come, Simon. See what I have for you."

Like all children, the Franz siblings were subject to childhood diseases, fevers that lay in wait to attack even the healthiest child. If Abram did not immediately harness the horses and drive at high speed to a settlement where a doctor could be found, he would come home to a dying child.

Abram was never inclined to rush for a doctor. He was an optimist who persisted in believing, against growing evidence, that children were naturally resilient and would recover. One didn't jump whenever a child sneezed. Children were meant to live, weren't they? Death should be for the old.

Death came for Judith Bartsch when she was in her fifties. At little Eduard's funeral she had already been too ill to attend. When the doctor first determined that Judith

Bartsch had cancer, he shook his head. The neighbourhood midwife came with her wealth of home cures and
stayed to commiserate.

A bold Russian maid marched in to inform her mistress
that of course there was a cure, and it would quickly restore
her to full health. But there was no time to lose. "This is
what you must do," she said with such conviction she
might have been emulating her mistress. "You set up a tub
in the yard and fill it almost up with camel milk. Pour in
warm camel piss. And camel shit too. Add these important
herbs"—she rattled off a list—"and mix everything up good
with water and let the sun warm it nice over noon. Then
you sit in it and do this every day for two weeks. You will
be well and clean."

A servant was sent to an estate thirty verst removed
whose owners Judith Bartsch knew remotely, to fetch the
milk of camels as well as their urine and excrement. A tub
was set up in the orchard where it would be concealed
from the street. The Russian maid supervised everything.
Every afternoon Oma Bartsch sat in her bath, stoic and
erect as a thin tree, her naked shoulders showing white
above the tub's rim, her knees bent to fit into it. A junior
maid was assigned to stand in attendance, equipped with
willow branches to swat flies away, as if she were guarding
the tsarina herself. Girded with patience and the determination to drive the cancer from her body and live, Judith
Bartsch sat dutifully for hours in the liquid muck. Her grand-
daughter Maria watched, wide-eyed.

The remedy, no matter how faithfully prepared by the
maid and endured by the mistress, did not conquer the
cancer. Maria was ten when her grandmother was laid
into the ground beside Johann Bartsch. "To rest," Hanna

told her children. A black metal marker announced: Judith, Beloved Wife of Johann Bartsch.

Hanna, grieving the death of three children, and once more pregnant, was given also the grief of her mother's death.

The maid grieved too. She had believed with her whole orthodox heart that her mistress would recover.

Oma Bartsch had been gone less than two years when it was Jascha's turn. He had just passed his first birthday, a red-cheeked, chubby boy already walking, when his forehead became hot and his eyes listless. Hanna dared to hope, though she didn't dare to speak that hope aloud, not even to Abram, who took one look and hurried to harness the horses. She pleaded silently with God not to let fever take from her this lovely boy.

Before the women from the village arrived to wash the newly dead son, dress him in white trousers and shirt, she cradled his unresponsive, silent body in her arms. Elena brought a hastily embroidered white pillow for his head. Hanna announced her refusal to sit at the side of another pretty casket, where a photographer was once more mounting his camera on its tripod to capture her grief.

"But we must have a picture." Abram was helpless in the face of his wife's grief and puzzled what to do. If his wife refused to sit for the picture, he must refuse too. Well, then, just the children, he said and ordered Maria and Simon to stand beside the latest family sorrow. Instead of looking at the camera, they gazed down on the little boy and later Maria would remember how unworthy she had felt to be alive in her clean school uniform when four of her siblings had never had the chance to grow.

After that no more children were born to Abram and Hanna. And no more children died. Grief tunnelled its way deep into Hanna's soul and guilt joined the grief. Why had she not watched more closely over her children? What kind of mother would let child after child fall ill and not be able to nurse it back to health? The marriage of grief and guilt became too much for the woman whose constitution was delicate, her shoulders narrow. The doctor pronounced: consumption. There were days when she could do little more than lie on her bed and cough. Maria heard it and worry created a small knot inside her. Could her mother die the way Oma Bartsch died? The way her brothers and sisters had died?

Maria and Simon remained alive. Their siblings, they were told, had been taken to a better place, if you could believe that. And Oma too. When Maria was older and heard the preacher read in church, One will be taken and the other left, she hoped she would always be the one left, in the village of Wassilyevka, in the house with the apricot orchard and the white picket fence. With her parents and Simon.

~

Mia, rereading her latest assignment, is cautiously pleased and hopes Miss Lodge will be pleased too. Once launched into her story, GranMarie had seemed to inhabit that long gone time in a distant village without faltering or trailing off in confusion.

Dad, I've written another story, Mia says, trying to sound casual. Want to read it?

Love to, he says. But can it wait? I've got choir practice and after that … after that I've got a meeting. A … a … late meeting.

With Mr. Solinsky?

Mia thinks she sees her father nod. He doesn't look at her. He never misses choir, she knows that. But a meeting after choir? He is toying with his car keys.

Mom, my latest story. Can I read it to you? she holds up the pages.

What's it about?

"Death" would be the honest answer, but Mia doesn't want to encapsulate GranMarie's story within such a bleak word. It's not one she wants to blurt out to her mother. It's about my Mennonite ancestors, she says.

Well, I guessed that much. Is it a happy story?

Not exactly, no. Not happy.

Of course I want you to read it, her mother says. But not right now. I feel a headache coming.

~

A week later Joseph Wittenberg interrupt Mia's English class to remind students of a change in parking regulations along the street. He stands behind the desk, next to Hedie Lodge. Mia looks down at the poem the class was reading when her father walked in:

Two roads diverged in the wood, and I—
I took the one less travelled by,
And that has made all the difference.

When the vice principal leaves and the class resumes, Miss Lodge asks, Why do you think the poet says, *And that has made all the difference?*

Mia, hoping to erase from her mind and the minds of her classmates the way her father and Miss Lodge stood so close together, says, How it applies to us, is that the choices we make,

I don't mean whether I grab cornflakes or Cheerios in the morning, or if I put on blue socks or white, but important decisions, well, they nudge us in a certain direction, they start us on a path and we go ahead and maybe we're taken too fast into the future and it's not easy to go back and start over. To retrace our steps. We're sort of set in motion. Thing is, we don't always think about how our choices affect the future. Not until we get there. And then it makes sense or—maybe we realize it was all wrong. But it could be too late. I mean it might be ... What I'm trying to say ... Here Mia's rush of words flounders and fails. Anyway, choices are important, she ends, lamely.

Yeah, like who to ask out for a date, someone says.

Or who to have sex with.

It's like which university to go to.

Like you've got choices?

It's way, way more, Bev says. It's what we devote our lives to. What we choose to believe.

Comments bounce across the room, none of them earthmoving. Mia is embarrassed with her foolish outpouring. Robert Frost deserves better. After class Miss Lodge calls Mia to her desk: Can you drop by after school? I have your latest assignment. Jane Kerr overhears the summons and out in the hall she says, grinning, Well, well, we all know who the teachers favour, don't we?

Oh just shut up, Jane. Angela's comeback is swift and Mia is grateful.

Your dad and Lodge look good together, Angela tells Mia. And can't you just feel those sparks fly? *Sparks*, Mia.

Angela's remarks have trumped Mia's eagerness to know what Miss Lodge thinks of her story; she drags her feet when she returns to the classroom at the end of the school day. She has slung her backpack over one shoulder, her parka over the other as if to signal that she's in a hurry. When she enters the room, the teacher rises from her chair as if she recognizes the presence of someone who merits respect. She is wearing a brown jacket over a white blouse. The contrast suits her. Mia thinks they could wear each other's clothes, they are so similar in build. For several seconds—it seems much longer—teacher and student appraise each other and the appraisal goes beyond clothes, eye colour, hairstyle, gestures, demeanour, though all of these are included.

I've read your latest story, Miss Lodge says. She takes the manuscript from her desk and holds it in her hand.

And? Mia keeps her voice cool. Looks away.

Those children who died, the teacher says, is that a story you grew up with?

No. I just heard it recently.

That's not quite true. Mia has paged through that brown album often when visiting her grandmother and over the years those little figures nestled like dolls in their white beds have become permanent fixtures in her memory.

I found it very moving, Hedie Lodge says. The way you describe that little girl, as if she's asleep. You capture that so well.

Mia wonders if her teacher sees her at this moment as a student who has written a competent story or as Joseph Wittenberg's daughter whom she must impress.

I think she looks at them every day, Mia says.

Your grandmother?

Yes. She stares at pictures of the dead children.

And what does she say?

Not so very much. She thinks they're better off.

Why?

Because of what they didn't have to go through.

I hope your stories will eventually include you, the teacher says.

Mia thinks the story would then have to include her father. I won't get that far, she says. This project will end when they all emigrate. I won't even be born.

And neither will my father, she calculates silently.

Does your grandmother enjoy telling you her stories? Does she like being your source?

Sometimes. She's becoming just a bit … I mean … sort of … disoriented.

Older people sometimes have small strokes that are barely detectable, Hedie says. It might not happen a second time. Your grandmother might go on being quite—lucid.

Hedie Lodge sits down, gestures Mia toward a desk. The change of position or her teacher's sympathy or the reminder of GranMarie's frailty, or all three, serve to open a door. Mia begins describing how she found GranMarie confused and dull-eyed in front of a sink full of clean dishes. How this worries her. She is about to say something about her father being too busy to look in on his mother, but stops. She will not speak of her father to this woman who, no matter how kind, is, according to Angela, crazy about her father.

The door that opened, shuts.

Are you thinking of becoming a writer? Hedie Lodge asks after a silence during which neither teacher nor student shows any evidence of haste.

You've asked me that before, Mia says. She draws back. Draws into herself. She rises and turns to the chalkboard. In the space where students are allowed to write a "Thought for the Day" someone has written in a neat cursive: *Blessed are the peacemakers*. Mia smiles. Only Bev Plett could have chosen that wisdom. Bev, who is pure of heart. Mia turns to leave.

Your writing is good, Mia, her teacher says quickly, rising too, the assignment still in her hand. It's really good. I wanted to tell you that. Any time you want to discuss your writing, I'll ... I'm here to help.

The teacher's offer brings Mia back into the dialogue. Are you going to let us read a Chekhov play?

Miss Lodge looks as if Mia's question comes at her like a stray spitball. Chekhov?

We should, Mia says. *Uncle Vanya* would be good.

Well, I suppose it's a possibility. The teacher's tone suggests that she doubts her class is equal to Chekhov. With good reason. Mia can't imagine her classmates getting serious about social and economic upheaval in an era long gone, in a country they have no reason to care about.

Have you read *Uncle Vanya*? Hedie Lodge asks.

Mia is embarrassed and pretends not to hear, pretends to study the large poster of the Globe Theatre beside the door. Her teacher is probably wondering if her request for Chekhov is just showing off or an outright challenge. Mia tries to appear detached.

And so does Hedie Lodge, who says only that she has scheduled modern drama for after the Christmas break. She hands Mia the assignment which is marked A plus. Mia wants to yell, Yahoo, but she keeps her face serious, leaves the classroom and breaks into a dance, down the hallway, down the stairs and out into the street.

The snow crunches underfoot and more is falling as Mia turns down Kildonan Drive, running, her step light, convinced Angela's reactions are always over the top.

~

Joseph Wittenberg arrives late for choir practice and waits for an opportunity to slip unnoticed into his place. The sopranos are singing "Lo, How a Rose E'er Blooming," and from out of the past the German words float into Joseph's brain: "Es ist ein Ros' entsprungen." The song recalls the sum of all his childhood Christmases and nostalgia washes over him. He is surprised that Christmas is already on the rehearsal agenda. *Amid the cold of winter when half-spent was the night,* the sopranos sing on this icy winter evening. Bill Steiner interrupts the singing to tell them that a few voices are going flat and pulling the others with them. Listen, he says. Listen to each other. Joseph slips in through the side door of the choir loft and finds his place in the baritone section.

Bill gives him a thumbs-up welcome and someone calls, Hi, Joe. It's only at his church that he is still called Joe. He smiles self-consciously, nods to his neighbour, wonders who the new baritone to his left might be. Someone wants to know if he's got the school population under control and someone else hands him the music for Handel's "For Unto Us a Child Is Born." The song is familiar. Joseph has sung Handel's *Messiah* many times since he first joined the choir. Millicent endured the performance of the oratorio, declaring it an ordeal.

Joseph joins in on the long runs—a child is b-o-o-o-o-o-rn— and the choir is so alarmingly shaky everyone laughs. Bill Steiner has his work cut out. They manage somewhat better with the exuberant litany, *"And His name shall be called Wonderful, Counsellor, the mighty God, the everlasting Father, the Prince of Peace."*

Bill's face is animated, his conducting charged with energy, and the choir responds. The empty sanctuary fills with exultation, with the proclamation of hope fulfilled and joy overflowing. Beneath the glorious splendour of the music lies the simple fact that a boy is born.

In the Wittenberg family too a boy has been born and his name is Jeremy. Joseph has not given much thought to the name or why Alice chose it. It has never occurred to him until this moment that Jeremy, derived from Jeremiah, is the name of a prophet. Prophets were called to proclaim suffering. But they also spoke of hope. So far Joseph hasn't seen anything very hopeful about Jeremy.

The rehearsal ends with "Love Came Down at Christmas." The song is new, but by the time they have sung it through once Joseph has learned the uncomplicated baritone line. The melody still echoes in his head when, not much later, Hedie lets him in, lets him love her and their loving is passionate and also desperate because at Christmas Hedie will not be here. She is flying home to Toronto. Joseph doesn't say, I wish you would stay, and she doesn't ask, Why don't you come with me? Neither course is possible; a solution is nonexistent. But his need for Hedie, *that* exists. And hers for him.

~

It's noon and Mia strides through the front office, slips past the secretaries and knocks on her father's office door. She hears his "come in," enters, sees Hedie Lodge sitting across from him. The English teacher turns and smiles. Her father smiles too. Both are self-conscious and this irritates Mia. She asks for lunch money, though that is not the reason she came.

Remind your father I'll need a ride to Alice's right after school, her mother said this morning. I didn't get a chance. He left early.

Mia doesn't want to mention her mother in the presence of Hedie Lodge. Lunch money is neutral. Her father hands her several bills, no questions asked. Mia feels she has blundered into territory where she isn't welcome. Where the atmosphere is slightly off. She leaves without another word.

At the entrance to the lunchroom she is assaulted by the beat of heavy metal blasting from speakers attached high up on the wall, away from grasping young hands. The music attacks her with the force of hammer blows and almost drowns out the babel of voices rising from the long tables. Noise rides on every dust mote, filling the cavernous room she is about to enter to its four corners and all the way up to the high ceiling. Mia wants to turn back. More so when she spots Danny just inside the lunchroom entrance, undecided and forlorn. He didn't used to look so hopeless. What's he doing here? She's pretty sure he has an art class. Now she will have to rescue him, bring him with her to the table where Bev and Angela are saving a place for her. Bev will move over good-naturedly to squeeze him in; Angela will radiate displeasure. He's such a nothing, she said yesterday. Smarten up, Mia.

Danny's presence will reroute the conversation, it will not be what she has counted on. Not that she intends to unload over juice and sandwiches the fact that her father is having a tête-à-tête with Hedie Lodge, now, this very minute. That is a detail she wants to blot out. She has counted on Angela's chatter to distract her, and Bev's common sense to provide an oasis in the day. She wishes Kurt's schedule wasn't always so overloaded with basketball. She would like to stare at him over a ham and cheese sandwich.

Mia hangs back and hopes Danny will place one foot in front of the other and make his way to one of the tables. Hopes that someone will wave him over. But Danny turns around, as if forced by the noise and confusion to retreat. When he sees Mia his face does not light up with relief, as she expects. Come, she says, taking him by the black sleeve of his shirt. He pulls away sharply and turns once more to scan the sea of faces in the lunchroom, as if looking for someone, and then Mia sees that someone is waving to Danny. From a far table Jane Kerr beckons imperiously. Danny pulls away from Mia and strides toward that summons.

From another table Angela is waving with both arms. She is calling Mia but the amplified music drowns out her voice. Mia heads in the direction of those waving arms.

~

When Mia walks into Peter McBride's afternoon history class, Kurt is standing beside the teacher, who is pointing him to an empty desk near the windows. Students surround Kurt, offering enthusiastic high fives.

My timetable's changed, he tells Mia, who has detoured in his direction. Because of basketball practice, he adds.

Mia smiles all the way to her desk.

Near the end of the class Peter McBride allows a digression from his lesson on Western Civilization to the Middle East where conflict looms. His permission stirs up a hornet's nest of opinions.

They should just bomb Saddam all to hell.

Yeah, let 'em have it, those Arabs.

The US must have tons of weapons piled up somewhere. Why don't they just friggin' use them?

No—the UN should pin an embargo on Iraq. That's the only way. That'll crush them properly.

Yeah, whatever. Make them suffer.

War or embargo, Bev says, either way it's the innocent who are going to suffer most. Women and children. And the poor.

Mia is sure that Bev is remembering Sunday's sermon. Pastor Heese titled it "The way of peace" and said it had never really been tried by the nations. The nations are always calling on young people in large numbers to die waging war, he said. Why

141

wouldn't it be just as reasonable to die waging peace? The only person in this history class who might be willing to die waging peace would be Bev Plett, Mia thinks.

Yes, Kurt? The teacher acknowledges the new student's raised hand.

So how come we're all solving the problems in some foreign country? What about here?

Like what? a student asks.

Yeah, what?

Like there's conflict in our province. Our city. Ever been on Main Street at night? Ever seen those people with no place to go? Ever seen those Indians lined up at the mission? Yeah, I'm talking about us. My people. Kurt speaks with an even voice. No hostility. A bit sardonic.

The volley of opinions about the Middle East ends in embarrassment. The class is silenced. Those who know Kurt like him. Those who don't are surprised to learn he's aboriginal. No one wants to antagonize this tall, handsome athlete. Even Peter McBride seems unable to come to the rescue. It's Angela who speaks. She's been eying Kurt since she walked in. You're right, Kurt, she says. You're absolutely right. She doesn't know what she's saying, Mia thinks, and waits for Bev to say, Peace begins at home. She wouldn't be upset if Bev should decide to quote Pastor Heese.

Good point, Kurt, Peter McBride says finally. By the way, class, I should have introduced our new student. He's Kurt Brady. And as he's just demonstrated, he'll bring a new perspective to our discussions. Welcome, Kurt.

There is applause. The teacher, before returning his class to Western Civilization, turns to Bev: We'll come back to this war, he says. We want your perspective. She blushes.

When the buzzer sounds, Mia leaves the classroom with the rest, wondering if her father is a pacifist and if so, is it by conviction or because he has no need for force? Her mother is incapable of aggression. And where does she, Mia, stand?

Wait up.

If only the voice behind her and the footsteps crunching on snow were Kurt's. But they're Danny's and the words are urgent. She turns to see his forward-thrusting body, his nervously swinging arms.

Hey, Danny. What's the problem?

Just wanna walk with you. Why do you right away think there's a problem? His injured tone is fake. Mia is not fooled.

They head down the street toward the highway. Mia hopes Danny isn't planning to walk home with her today. Right now she isn't wild about his company. Doesn't want to invite him for supper. She thinks Kurt will call this evening. She hopes.

When they near the highway, Danny slows his steps and she slows hers. They come to a stop. They have hardly spoken.

Hey, Mia, I'm wondering can you like help me out? There is a hint of a quaver in Danny's voice and Mia's antennae flare, ready to snap up signals. You want to come for supper? she says. No idea what's on the menu.

I ... I need some cash. Seriously. I have to head downtown for some ... for new gym shoes. I forgot my money. I mean, my mom's short on cash right now, and ...

Mia does not look down at Danny's shoes. Shoes are not the issue. The issue is something else.

The Henderson Credit Union with its convenient bank machine is within sight and the glance Danny sends in its direction makes his intention blatantly obvious. The credit card Mia sometimes gets to use is at home, inside a glass dish on a kitchen shelf. Only for household buying, that's the rule. And she has no cash. She can't help Danny out. She is safe.

I'll walk home with you, Danny says, gaining control of his

voice, which is no longer diffident. Not something she can brush off. Does Danny plan to hide behind the hedge while she goes into the house to get the cash or the piece of plastic he seems to believe can save him?

You're going to be there for me, remember? he says, holding their conversation over her like a threat. Well, I haven't asked for anything, have I? And now when I do you're holding back? If this was the other way, Mia, I'd help you, and you damn well know it. I wouldn't let you down. Well, so now I need your help. Just a little bit of help.

No, she says, I can't. She turns and begins running.

Danny calls after her. Please, Mia, please! Please! His voice rises to an animal howl. She runs faster.

That evening Kurt does not call. Instead, it's Danny. He is counting time, he says. He is doomed. Friggin' doomed, Mia. He lowers his voice to a whisper, as if he finds it difficult to speak. Or as if he's afraid of being overheard.

Can't you just say no? Mia has only the vaguest notion of who it is Danny must say no to.

You haven't got a clue, he whispers again, hoarsely. You just friggin' don't know, do you, Mia, what's out there? How things work?

No, Mia doesn't know.

These guys, they don't take no for an answer. They don't give a shit.

I'll meet you at the credit union, she says, her voice a whisper to match his. She hangs up, finds the credit card on the shelf, and holding it clutched in her hand she's out the door and into the dark street, running.

~

Joseph is surprised that adultery can be so easily arranged. At first it's Wednesday night choir practice that provides the opportunity. And the alibi he hopes he'll never have to produce. And then the church's aging boiler needs replacing and the parking lot renewal slated for spring is under discussion. We'll meet every Monday for the next while, the chairman of the stewardship committee has warned. Keep those evenings free. And every Monday Joseph impresses the other members by arriving well before starting time. I'll have to leave a bit early, he tells the committee apologetically. School stuff. It piles up.

No rest for the wicked, eh, Joe? the chairman says.

Joseph's attempted smile is stiff. And brief. He chooses a place near the door. When it's nine o'clock he sends a sheepish excuse-me glance in the direction of the chair, slips out and before nine-thirty he is holding Hedie in his arms, once more surprised at his good fortune. His happiness. All challenges, all obligations fall away. All concerns for a building's heating systems, an institution's administrative opportunities, the gym renovations, a family's failures melt in the warmth of Hedie's apartment. And the comfort of her body. There is joy here, with this woman who wants him as much as he wants her.

Afterwards she asks, What do you want most of all?

You mean for Christmas? Joseph teases.

All right, for Christmas. What do you want most for Christmas?

I want this to last. Joseph buries his face in the lustre of Hedie's hair.

What does it mean to be Mennonite? Hedie asks. What's that all about?

The question is a rude intrusion. Peace, Joseph says. Mennonites always say they want peace.

And do you think that's realistic? Is it possible? Peter McBride says there's no hope for peace in the Middle East.

Joseph's response is to turn toward her and reach once more for the separate and precarious contentment he has found with Hedie Lodge.

~

The day begins innocuously, snow falling intermittently, harmlessly on the other side of the small window of the vice principal's office. Yellowish light falls on three framed paintings of a black Camaro hanging above Joseph's head. The world has settled into sombreness that can be lightened only by anticipation: Christmas and the winter break, a reprieve for teachers and students. Already it's the Advent season, daylight in short supply. The gloom beyond his window does not infect Joseph, but he thinks of Jeremy and this sobers him.

The doctor thinks Jeremy's biological family ought to be tested, Alice told him yesterday. Everyone.

Even your grandmother? Joseph asked, wryly.

Of course. And Aunt Sue and Uncle Phil. Have they never been tested?

Joseph can't say. He doesn't know. He is trying to imagine what his mother will say. Will she understand that she is implicated? What will she think, should it be discovered that her legacy to the latest generation is disease? A dismal inheritance of which he, Joseph, and Phil too, appear to be the carriers. And Mia. What does this mean for Mia?

The inevitable knock at the door. He glances quickly at the papers in front of him, the most recently tweaked plans for the gym. He has been dawdling. Has done very little this morning. His mind before Jeremy slipped in was filled with Hedie Lodge. Come in, he says.

It's Mia, her face as grave as this winter day.

So which furious teacher has sent me my favourite student this lovely morning? Joseph says, then stops, ashamed of his fabricated heartiness. It will not do. More than jocularity will be required to brighten his daughter's mien.

Dad, Mia says.

Well?

I'm always here about money, she says.

Joseph knows she's not here for lunch money. Sit down, Mia, he says, but she remains standing, the desk between them.

I have to talk to you, Dad. Before you get your bank statement.

Oh, I think my account is good for lunch money, he says, grabbing again at the straw of pretence. What is it his daughter will tell him?

What she tells him is clearly not the whole truth. It is a prepared story, about helping Danny out because his mother is laid off and this is all a secret, Joseph must promise not to speak about it, not let Danny know he knows. The details that pour out are incoherent, incomplete—the Haarsma family in need, Mia pressured, the credit card, the meeting with Danny at the credit union, her reluctant withdrawal of the alarming sum he demanded.

Joseph should be outraged but he feels only numbness as his daughter makes her confession. She is crying, and her sobs bring him to his feet. He walks around the desk and stands behind her, takes her by the shoulders, turns her round to face him, then pulls her close in a clumsy hug. He thinks of Hedie Lodge, the scent of her dark hair. The richness of her laughter.

Don't be afraid, Mia, he says.

Mia pulls away, wipes her eyes with her sleeve. She steadies her voice: Dad, I'll pay you back. And you can't tell anyone. Promise. Her words are no longer a plea. They are a reasonable demand and the look in her eyes tells him he cannot refuse her. Joseph wonders if she suspects his late nights more than

Millicent does. He makes no promise. I'm sorry about this, Mia, he says. Everything will be all right. It's not the end of the world. He can tell she doesn't believe him any more than he believes her story. But what right has he got to demand his daughter's honesty?

I'll pay you back, she says again as she backs away, dabbing at her face before she leaves.

Joseph returns to his work, which has suddenly become onerous. Even the thought of Hedie Lodge holds little comfort.

The Factory
(Assignment #4)

It was for love of Hanna that Abram Franz sold the farm in Wassilyevka and moved his family to the town of Barvenkovo. "Life will be easier for you there," he told his wife, who could not stop grieving the loss of her babies. "There will be no orchard, no large garden. You won't have to worry about hiring a swarm of maids to cook for the farm help. You will get stronger. You will be well."

But Hanna knew that it wasn't only his love for her that motivated Abram. Her husband had farmed with passion, guiding the plow that turned furrows in the rich soil of the steppes, seeding the fields in spring or fall, bringing home the harvest. His horses were not the best in the village, but they were good animals that made him proud and made farming a pleasure. Her husband had loved The Promised Land that, according to family lore, had cost Johann Bartsch his life. But now he was in the grip of another passion. An industrial revolution was spreading across the country toward southern Russia and the possibilities stirred Abram's imagination. He dreamt of machines that would transform the way grain was grown and harvested. Machines, the revolution promised, would speed up farm labour. Food would be more efficiently produced. He sold his land and began to build a small factory in Barvenkovo, a town only fifteen verst east of the village of Wassilyevka.

His neighbours shook their heads. We are people of the land, they said, quoting from the Psalms: **Live in the land and enjoy security .... Those who wait for the Lord shall inherit the land.** Didn't those words state clearly what the Lord required of them?

Hanna hoped her husband knew what he was doing. She had not inherited her mother's skill in taking charge, not over the hired help, not over her husband. Barvenkovo was not far from Wassilyevka and she would return often to see her friend Elena. It might heal her heart, if not her lungs, to put distance between herself and the graves of her children.

It was spring when the drab town of Barvenkovo with its muddy streets became home to the Franz family. Abram worked long hours, with energy and optimism building the factory where farm machinery would be produced. He named it Lutzch—a ray of light.

When Elena came to visit, Hanna said, "Yes, we are happy." But her friend knew better. How can a woman be happy when she has buried so many children? How can she consent to live fifteen verst away from their graves? Neither Hanna nor Elena could have dreamt how great a distance one can travel from the place that is home, away from the graves of loved ones. Hanna would never know that a descendant of hers, a teenager, would one day sit beside an old woman whose memory waxed and waned like the moon, though less reliably, and turn the pages of an old photo album with pictures of pretty children who lay motionless as if they had just been put down for a nap.

Hanna's health did not improve when they moved to Barvenkovo. She continued to lose colour and weight. She fretted over Maria, who was thin and sure to catch fever but never did. Simon, who had roamed as unrestricted as the geese and dogs in Wassilyevka, flew into a rage when he wasn't allowed in the factory. "You'll just be underfoot," Hanna told him when Abram left for a day's work. She never raised her voice and when she smiled it was a smile tinged with sorrow.

Machines, it turned out, excited Hanna's husband even more than land. He too would say he was happy, on fire with energy and dreams. He sent his best employees to Germany to learn how bigger and better machines could be built. The factory gave birth to the prototype of a tractor, a crude and clumsy contraption that sputtered and chugged to life like an ill-tempered monster. Abram invited a photographer to record this still-to-be-civilized creature. That photograph would one day be selected, along with photos of lifeless children, to cross the ocean.

To Hanna it seemed that her husband was becoming obsessed with the factory and its mechanical offspring. That he loved it like a wife and couldn't tear himself away from it.

In summer we'll travel to the Dnieper River, Joseph promised his children. It's where I learned to swim. There's an island in the river where they grow watermelon. You've never tasted anything so sweet.

But summer came and although Simon clamoured, "Dnieper River, Papa, Dnieper River. You promised," there was never enough time.

In fall, Maria found friends at school and was happy. And too young to be aware of rumours of a revolution, this one not industrial in nature, fanning out from Petrograd, spreading like a virus to all corners of the empire. Suspicion surfaced everywhere, even in Barvenkovo, where the hired workers of the new Lutzch factory became less diligent, spoke seditiously amongst themselves and eyed the factory owner with envy and hostility.

Winter was coming. In the safe circle of her small family Hanna knit woollen stockings for her children and baked **Pfeffernüsse** while snow fell softly on Barvenkovo, covering the grey town square, the rutted streets, the bleak yard of the factory. Everything was white. Forgiven, Hanna thought. She sang carols with her children, "Leise rieselt der Schnee." "Welchen Jubel, welche Freude." Let others prepare for what might be coming toward them from Petrograd; she would prepare to celebrate Christmas.

~

Mia counts the printed sheets of her story—three scant pages composed at home on her computer when she should have been in English class. She doesn't often skip school, and never English class, her favourite, but today she hadn't been able to face a teacher in whom her father may have more than professional interest.

Rereading the story, Mia is not satisfied with herself. Miss Lodge will think she's slacking off. And what excuse can she give? That GranMarie's arthritis has flared up, and who wants to badger an old, pain-ridden woman for stories? That Danny's in trouble and she's worried? Mia sets it all aside—the too-short story, pain of arthritis, drug money, even Jeremy—because tonight she's going to the school dance with Kurt.

He finally asked you? Angela says. About time.

Have fun, is Bev's comment. Bev is not going to the dance. She is going to a meeting of her church's Christmas hamper committee. She has agreed to organize the collection of toys and canned food.

When Mia and Kurt arrive there's a crowd at the entrance to the gym. Inside, a forlorn cluster of multi-coloured balloons bobs and sways while criss-crossed red and green streamers—a nod to Christmas—limply festoon the stage. The decorations are pathetic, as if the dance committee deems the old gym unworthy of real effort and expense. A strobe light sweeps brazenly across the crowd, cutting the darkness, leaching the red and green streamers of their brightness, blinding the upturned faces massed around the stage where the band is warming up, making up for its lack of skill by belting out a strong beat at which the crowd claps enthusiastically. Teenagers, frenzied or shy, mill about, waiting to dance.

When the band is ready, Kurt takes Mia's hand and leads her across the floor, navigating around or through clutches of students. They find an opening in the mass of bodies and turn to face each other. Mia wants to say something, tell Kurt that this is great, a good turnout, but that would be bland and anyway, conversation is impossible in this noise. They dance and past Kurt's shoulder Mia catches sight of Angela, her blonde hair an unmistakable spot of light in the crowd. She's wearing a deep green top. When she sees Mia she waves wildly and yells something across the sea of heads. Mia doesn't wave back.

Jane Kerr's gyrating body moves in, dark pants, leather jacket open to show a white skull imprinted on a black T-shirt. The hypnotic sweep of the strobe light catches glints of metal, a chalk-white face punctuated by darkly made-up eyes. In the glare she looks eerily bleached. Seen Danny? she mouths. Mia turns from her and places her hands on Kurt's shoulders as the last rhythmic beats of the song fade, its final chords swallowed by the crowd's roar of appreciation.

When the band takes a break there's a rush for the exits, a streaming toward the drink machines, the washrooms or out the back door, where smoking begins on the steps. The supervising teachers stalk the halls, alert for trouble. Mia sees her father, whose turn it is to be the administrator attending this dance. He's talking to Peter McBride, the history teacher. Instinctively Mia looks around for Hedie Lodge, then remembers that her English teacher told them, I'm not on duty until after Christmas. She smiled at them and told them to have a great time. Did she know that Joseph Wittenberg would be on duty? Did she try to negotiate a trade with Peter McBride?

Jane Kerr is heading in their direction again but Kurt pulls Mia toward the drink machine, where they wait in line with guys from the basketball team, the Saints, who talk only about tomorrow's tournament, and Mia has nothing to say. She won't be at the tournament. She'll be at Wild Oak Estates, sixth floor, like every Saturday morning, and if GranMarie's memory permits, she'll be transported to Barvenkovo. She looks around for Angela's new green blouse, but it's nowhere to be seen.

There's a commotion in front of the girls' washroom. Miss Avery has emerged clutching the arm of a tall girl—Jane—who struggles free, and Joseph appears, takes charge of Jane and marches her away. Mia grabs Kurt's hand and tugs him away from the basketball team, back into the gym, where the dance is about to resume. In the crush of bodies Mia hears a voice spit out: Dirty Indian! She recoils. Kurt face is tight. When they reach the middle of the gym she raises her arms to draw him close, presses her cheek to his and they dance that way until closing time.

Leaving the school, they hold hands as they walk together in the cool darkness toward Henderson Highway, the snow crisp under their feet, the sky star-spangled. Mia doesn't want the evening to end. She wants more. She has never been so happy.

She asks, Did you see Danny at the dance? Her question is interrupted by a screech of brakes, a crunch of tires on snow. Hey, Kurt, a voice calls through the darkness. Action's at the 'Villa. Hop in. Kurt hesitates briefly, then guides Mia toward the car and climbs in after her.

The hotel lounge is filled with students, laughing, smoking, drinking or learning to drink. Kurt orders Cokes. They sit with his basketball buddies, who are one hundred per cent convinced the Saints will win tomorrow's tournament. The dance has slipped from their radar. As if it hasn't happened. Mia listens to their conversation and tries not to stare at Kurt.

It's one o'clock when they leave with Kurt's friends. Kurt is dropped off first. He squeezes Mia's shoulder when he gets out and calls a general 'Bye, guys, see you tomorrow, into the car. Mia watches him run up the steps.

Where to, gorgeous? the driver asks, and she indicates the white bungalow.

No way, someone says. We got a cute chick in the car and we're letting her go? Let's hit the road. He's only teasing, but Mia cringes. When they stop and she gets out at her door, several voices call a casual Good night, see you tomorrow.

Her father is still up and lets her in. Kurt bring you home? he asks.

Mia nods and walks past him to her room. That night she dreams she is swimming with Kurt in the Aegean Sea. The water is green, the sky above them a blue meadow. They swim away from shore, their heads two objects bobbing on the gently rolling waves. Then she realizes with a jolt that it's not the Aegean Sea but the wide Dnieper River they are in and its current is too strong for her. She struggles against it but can't make headway. Kurt is far ahead. Wait! Wait for me! she tries to yell but her voice is a faint gasp. She is choking. She hears Kurt calling: There's watermelon up ahead. You've never tasted anything so sweet.

~

Alice is scheming to bring the whole Wittenberg family together at Christmas. She asks her father, When have we last been together, all of us? She isn't prompted by her father's long separation from his brother Phil, but by Jeremy. And Lucas. And Taylor too, of course. Alice believes Aunt Sue will arrive with a suitcase full of wisdom and pockets full of advice. She believes this even though their correspondence hasn't flowered. Aunt Sue takes weeks to answer letters, and when she does, the reply is brief and misspelled and says more about weather and kitchen renovations than about Fragile X and the children who have it. But once she's here in person, once Aunt Sue sees Jeremy, she'll snap into action and take Alice under her wing.

Alice can't clearly remember what Taylor looked like at the last visit. Skinny, she thinks. Colourless. Most certainly he'll be sturdier by now. She's been sending pictures—she's taken them, not Brian—of Jeremy, and Lucas too, lots of them, but there's never been one of Taylor coming her way.

Please say you'll come, Aunt Sue, Alice writes, no longer asking for Mia's assistance. Mia is going to a hockey game, not because she's crazy about the Winnipeg Jets, but because she is head over heels with Kurt, as she should be, in Alice's opinion.

I think it's time you and I talk face to face, Aunt Sue.
I want to show you our darling Jeremy. And I've simply
got to see Taylor, who must be quite tall now. He'll just
love my Jeremy, I know it, and so will you. And Lucas,

he's such a good boy. What a beautiful way to spend Christmas, imagine, all of us together, one big family. On Jesus' birthday!

Alice is about to add, I am so very hopeful for our boys, as I am sure you are, Aunt Sue, but lately Lucas has wanted either to fling his racing cars at his brother or just curl himself into a lifeless lump on the couch, and Jeremy has been nothing but listless. Alice's hope has been tested and become frayed.

The visitors will fly in from Toronto two days before Christmas and stay in the white Wittenberg bungalow. Alice takes this for granted. You and Uncle Phil will sleep in my old bedroom, she writes, as if this will be an incentive. And there will be a place for Taylor too.

~

Joseph is unexcited about a reunion with his brother, but he doesn't oppose it. It's been more than a year since he last saw Phil, who is five years younger and was never the playmate he longed for. Their mother, still trying to make sense of the country she had come to and consumed with putting bread on the table for her boys, had held Joseph responsible for every quarrel that escalated to the point of annoying her. Even mischief Phil manufactured on his own was blamed on Joseph. This rankled. Joseph liked things orderly; Phil attracted chaos. Joseph went willingly to school; Phil discovered that an afternoon could be passed pleasantly at the pool hall or on the riverbank biking or smoking with like-minded classmates. The brothers found no common ground they could occupy together. He wonders if that isn't still true.

The two-week break in the school year, longed for by students, teachers and administrators, looms bleakly for Joseph: Hedie is flying to Toronto and he will be left behind. With Millicent and Mia. And Alice's crew. And now his brother Phil. Of course he loves them all. Dearly.

Millicent has nothing to say about the proposed arrangements. She has begun cutting back on time spent helping Alice. Sometimes she is irritated with her daughter, who seems to assume that giving birth to Jeremy has entitled her to redraw the boundaries of the existing world and expand the territory over which she can wield power. Millicent wants to ask Joseph, Do you think Alice is using Jeremy to her advantage? Like when she was a teenager and knew how to get what she wanted? Deadlines were extended, curfews modified, deserved anger deflected. But Joseph is never around long enough to be asked.

Millicent is thoroughly sick of Fragile X. The endless weight of its details. The whole tiresome biology. As for the visitors from Toronto, I'll just leave that on Joseph's plate, she tells herself. He's the problem-solver. Joseph hasn't spoken to her about Christmas, which in recent years has come and gone without fuss or planning or real celebration. Joseph hasn't spoken to her about anything at all recently, as if their worlds don't overlap. He doesn't find me attractive, she thinks. I'm not a good wife.

I think it's a really stupid plan, Mia tells Alice. Do you realize you're doubling the occupants in the Wittenberg bungalow? How is Mom supposed to like that? You're just edging closer to the deep end, Alice, with Jeremy. You're eating and dreaming miracles and now you're dragging Phil and Sue into the mix. You think Aunt Sue will pull a solution out of her sleeve? What does Brian think?

He's on strike, Alice says. Everyone at the TV station is on strike. And I'm not changing my mind.

~

The guests arrive to a city decked out for Christmas, fir trees bristling with lights, neon angels brightening the short, dull afternoons, traffic clogging the snow-covered streets.

Aunt Sue admits she's had no time for shopping in Toronto.

No problem, Alice tells her, eagerly. We'll go tomorrow. Mom will take Jeremy, won't you, Mom? He's got a touch of fever.

Polo Park mall is a chaos of garish lights and makeshift booths cluttering the wide mall. Bargains everywhere. The voices of shoppers compete with amplified carols—"Jingle Bells" and "O Come All Ye Faithful." Undaunted, Alice and Sue embark on a foray through racks of children's clothes, tables of on-sale toys, kitchenware.

I love shopping in a mall I haven't been to. Sue, tired when she arrived from Toronto, is revived, a woman on a mission.

Alice is elated at the prospect of conversation that will surely follow the hectic rummaging. She buys nothing, insists on carrying her aunt's packages and is soon exhausted, trying to catch her breath in one slow cash register lineup after another. Can we stop for coffee? she begs. They push their way to the food court, bring their coffee to a crowded table. Sue lights a cigarette and they fumble with the parcels to make sure nothing is missing.

Aunt Sue, there's so much I have to ask you, Alice begins, but her voice is drowned in the general noise. Alice raises her voice. When Taylor was born, she says, how soon did you know?

Know what? Aunt Sue asks, looking away.

How soon did you know he had Fragile X?

Sue shifts in her chair. Not right away, I guess. But eventually you realize.

Tell me, Alice says, her voice a plea.

Tell you what? Sue looks around at the crowds. She looks annoyed. Uncomfortable.

We have this problem, Alice says. Our children have this ... this condition. You and I, we're the mothers of special boys. I don't know about you, but for me ... I feel like I'm on shaky ground sometimes. Actually most of the time. Do you feel like that? Are you afraid?

When her aunt doesn't reply, Alice says, Of course I believe God can make a miracle. I do. She looks at the woman across from her, waiting to hear that she too believes in miracles.

You know what I think? Sue says, mashing her cigarette, not looking into her coffee or at the crowds, but facing Alice, who shrinks back from the older woman's steely eyes. I think what's been dumped on us is cruel and unfair. Right from the start I raged and ranted against it. I screamed, I cried till I had no tears left. I took it out on Phil. And what good did that do? Be reasonable, I told myself. Don't let it all hang out. So for a while I pretended that everything was just hunky dory, I smiled at everyone. And nearly went crazy. By the time Taylor was four, I was a wreck. And that's when I looked in the mirror, so to speak, and decided I deserved better. I deserved a life. So I took a course in flower arranging and now that's what I do. And that's where I should be right now—it's Christmas rush and I'm needed, my supervisor at the florist shop where I work didn't want me to go. But here I am. She shrugs.

Flower arranging, Alice says. That's beautiful. Isn't it beautiful work?

Sue laughs ruefully. You have no idea how heartily sick I get of flowers. Daisies, mums, Alstroemiria, glads. Roses—you can get sick of roses. Did you know that?

Alice shakes her head, incredulous.

But it gets me out of the house, doesn't it? Away from you-know-what. And it's income. Not much income, but I can buy a few hours of child care and do some shopping. She gestures toward a dress boutique. Alice, she says, setting down her cup. You've got two of them. Get yourself a life. Get a job. She gestures toward the shops as if that's where Alice should be, selling goods, making change. Don't you want to accomplish something? she asks.

Yes, Alice says, I do. I am. Don't we accomplish something caring for our very special children?

Special? Sue spits the word out. I hate that expression. As if special equals good. Not in this case it doesn't. You can't change them. Once more she fixes Alice with her gaze, but a gentler one. You think I'm hard, don't you. You think I've become unfeeling.

No, no, no, you haven't …

Yes, I have. I protect myself. And now, if you don't mind, I'd rather not talk about it. Especially not here. She gestures at the crowd.

Alice reaches across the table with her hand, but the table is wide and her aunt needs both hands to light another cigarette. Alice withdraws her hand. We haven't really talked, she pleads. We haven't spoken their names. We haven't even said "Taylor." We haven't said "Lucas." And "Jeremy." Her voice is barely audible in the noise around them. Aunt Sue, who has tilted her face to direct the smoke away from the table, can't hear a word of it.

The two women finish their coffee in silence.

~

While the women are shopping, the brothers, with Mia, Lucas and Taylor, even Brian, who takes time off from the picket line, are at the community centre skating rink. Joseph watches Lucas skate, not with skill but with dogged stubbornness. He watches Mia tag him, ·Hey, buddy, then skate away, slowly, so he can stumble after her, catch up and tag her. Phil helps Taylor lace up his skates and leads him patiently by the hand, steadying him as they make a determined round of the rink, always staying close to the boards.

Although Joseph hasn't skated in years, he soon finds his glide and as he passes Phil and Taylor, he wonders what's kept his brother's heart from breaking. Or maybe it has broken, and he's learned how to keep the shards hidden. His brother has changed, has lost that streak of daring, that youthful bravado. He has become meek. Joseph is appalled at that meekness. Seeing Mia at the far end of the rink he gives chase, his limbs stretching, the speed exhilarating, his heart pounding. He catches up, grasps his daughter's hand and pulls her with him. He waves when he sees students from GSC and they wave back. A whole string of skaters grab hands and form a snake that surges forward crazily with exuberant speed and then, when the lead skater's blade digs in and holds, the whip swings in a wide arc and cracks. The end of the screaming whip escapes, by a whisper, a collision with the boards. A sharp whistle puts an end to that. Several skaters are ordered to leave the rink.

Joseph is glad he's not in charge here. He is not the one who must enforce rules. He is on vacation. Free. And desolate. Hedie is in Toronto.

His daughter's cheeks are ruddy from the cold air and the exertion. She laughs up at her father and he wants to throw his arms around her.

I think your daughter is going to be a writer, Hedie told him again last week. He didn't know what to say to that and anyway wanted only to make love. He had left choir practice early to come to the apartment overlooking the Assiniboine River. Their last time together before Christmas. No gifts, they'd agreed; they needed nothing but each other. At choir practice Bob Steiner had concentrated on "For Unto Us a Child Is Born," polishing every phrase until the whole piece shone.

Winded after a dozen swift rounds of the rink, dodging skaters, flying past clusters of kibitzers on blades, father and daughter leave the ice and head for the stands, where they sit down to watch the children. Joseph spots Lucas plodding doggedly beside his father. So far the boy has not fallen even once, but now he does and Brian is there to pick him up. Phil and Taylor complete another round of the rink.

Dad, Mia says, when they've been quiet long enough. Dad, do teachers on your staff ever, you know, fall for each other?

She can't be serious, Joseph thinks, yanked away from the pathetic efforts of Phil and Taylor. I don't know … I haven't a clue … well … I guess it happens, he blusters. I guess it could. It, it might. It probably does. He's floundering. He's defensive.

Ever happen to you, Dad? Mia is staring out across the rink.

Joseph musters a laugh to show he understands that she's joking and naturally expects a joking reply. But the laugh is a groan, and he can't offer an answer. He too stares out across the rink.

Dad? Mia's question is a soft whisper. And very clear.

A scream issues from the far end of the rink. Lucas in a burst of bravado has torn away from Brian, charged into a gaggle of skaters, and crashed down on the ice where his forehead is gashed by another boy's skate.

Joseph and Mia rush down from the stands. Lucas howls like a stuck pig, there's blood on his ski pants, his legs are kicking as Brian carries him off the ice and into the van, skates and all. Joseph follows them into the van. The party is over.

~

Although it's almost Christmas, there isn't a single candle lit in Marie Wittenberg's sixth-floor apartment. Her family, nervous about her increasing forgetfulness, has quietly removed all candles and matches. She hasn't noticed. She doesn't think of candles.

Phil comes to see her after the aborted skating party and brings Taylor. But not Sue. Sue is a daughter-in-law, like Millicent, and daughters-in-law have never warmed to Marie, who has never warmed to them. She is carefully polite, but considers them permanent strangers.

Say hello to GranMarie, Phil instructs his son. Give her a hug.

Taylor hangs back from the old white-haired woman, afraid to step close. When he finally gets up the nerve to approach, Marie takes him by the shoulders and holds him away from her for a close look. He has the Franz family's blue eyes, she says. The boy's brown hair is cut short and his ears stick out noticeably. His lips are parted as if he breathes through his mouth. He doesn't look quite like other children, though Marie rarely sees children nowadays, only the occasional one brought to Wild Oak Estates. Dragged in, the way Taylor was, most likely, to greet an ancient, unfamiliar grandparent. In her opinion, Taylor's features are perfectly acceptable. When she draws him in for a hug, his resistance weakens, though he doesn't hug her back.

Phil helps her make tea and she finds milk and a few biscuits for Taylor.

This is our boy, Phil says, the words an expression of love. And anguish.

He's a good boy, she says.

Phil tells her of Taylor's special-ed classes and that he has joined a bowling club this winter.

I knock 'em all down, Taylor proclaims, as if he's discovered he's safe here. I knock 'em everyone down.

Marie's apartment contains no toys, has little to offer a child. She doesn't think Taylor would like the photo albums, he's too restless. She watches him wander to the kitchen and come back with the seashell.

Careful, she says, alarmed. And regrets it. What would it matter if he dropped the shell and it broke?

Careful, Phil echoes and takes the shell from the boy, who looks as if he will cry but instead begins to open cupboards and closets, picking up objects: What's this for? Why you got no toys?

Let him, Marie tells Phil. It's all right.

Phil keeps careful watch, knows just how far to extend the reins, when to draw in.

When they leave, Phil wishes his mother a Merry Christmas. I'll come again on Boxing Day, he says. Joseph has told him their mother has decided she will refuse to leave her apartment this winter. Unless I have to, I mean if they carry me out or something. She won't come to any of the celebrations. I've done enough Christmases, she says.

Say good bye to GranMarie, Phil tells his son. Wish her a merry Christmas. This time the boy does not refuse his grandmother's hug, but grabs her roughly.

Easy, Taylor, Phil cautions.

Come again, Marie whispers into the boy's prominent ear. And before he can pull free from her she adds, Not everyone has to be the best at school. You are a good boy, Taylor.

When they leave she feels proud, not of her son or her grandson but because she has done something right. What she said about school, and telling Taylor he was a good boy. She should have followed that with, I love you, Taylor. What was so difficult about that?

It's school she thinks about when she's alone again, and what is there to do except remember? Her schooling was cut short when disaster descended on the town of Barvenkovo. On the country, really, but what did she know then about the ways of armies and nations?

There are places she remembers, sometimes with vivid clarity, sometimes dimly: Barvenkovo, from where her family fled. Yalta with its beaches and battleships. Wassilyevka, a place of refuge and grief.

Her mother, whom she adored, floats into view, a ghost, pale and ephemeral against the backdrop of dark clouds hanging over the horizon and everyone waiting for what they would bring. The word "emigration" surfaced in every adult conversation. Who could have seen what was coming?

Marie has learned to choose where to locate herself in that vast territory called "the past." This week she has inhabited a large railway station on Winnipeg's Main Street. The waiting room with its high dome is packed with immigrants newly arrived, their voices echoing in the vaulted space. The scene is a chaos of bags and boxes, children clinging to their parents, wide-eyed. Babies crying. Awkward teenagers looking for solidarity with other teenagers. Old women, slumped, exhausted, tired of noise and motion. Tired of travel.

Marie is an old woman now, a woman who moves too slowly and is too soon tired. And too much preoccupied with things of long ago.

Today she moves out of that station, the place of arrival in a prairie city that doesn't yet know that its future will include a stock market crash, joblessness and poverty. The immigrants, escaped from the country they love and long for, don't know what awaits them.

Marie's family, together with other immigrants, rented rooms in a two-storey frame house in the city's North End. They shared the kitchen and slept in every available corner. Simon no longer needed a place to sleep. But she must not think of Simon, whose absence cast a shadow on the arrival in Canada. Instead, she must remember how the immigrant children ran in the streets at evening and played happy games. Her father, who in Barvenkovo had always risen early, eager for another day in the factory, hopeful for the future, and in Wassilyevka returned to farming, had turned silent in Canada. As if the ocean voyage had robbed him of speech and all energy. As if it had broken him.

Evenings, when everyone else had settled into silence, the men could be heard talking. There was land available. Small acreages. On Edison Avenue.

Marie rises and takes from the shelf a thin album, not the brown velvet one, brings it to the light and turns to the first page, where a series of snapshots chronicles the transformation of the plot of land her father acquired on Edison Avenue. First, a stand of scrawny poplars, bare, it must be fall; then, the trees felled and lying helter-skelter as if a storm had swept through; then the trees moved aside to make a clearing; then the skeleton of a modest building; finally a small, unpainted house standing bravely on snow-covered ground.

In that house Marie's father would collapse one day like one of those poplar trees, felled by a massive stroke that would put an end to his need for land.

Her name, when they moved to Edison Avenue, was still Maria.

She looks for a picture she believes to be hidden behind a snapshot of the long, muddy stretch of road that was Edison Avenue. She removes the snapshot and finds underneath it the black-and-white likeness of a young man with pale, earnest eyes, a broad forehead and curly hair she remembers as reddish and greying slightly at the temples. There's the hint of a smile on his pleasant, boyish face. She stares at it, unsmiling, slips the picture back into its hiding place and closes her eyes.

Small houses sprang up on Edison Avenue, each with a shed or two attached. A garden was carved out of gumbo, potatoes and carrots and peas planted. Also geraniums, petunias, camomile. Every day the small homes spilled their life into the street. Fathers left early to trek along Edison Avenue on the way to the streetcar that carried them to jobs in the city. Children poured out, collected in groups and streamed toward the school on Henderson Highway, streamed home for lunch several hours later, then back to school for the afternoon and home again after four. The women, after clearing away the breakfast dishes, worked in the yard—kitchen garden, chickens, a cow they must milk and lead to pasture in the unclaimed land behind their houses. Sometimes the cows were stubborn, and if the woman was small or elderly or pregnant, the task became difficult.

In time there were marriages. Young women became pregnant. Those not married served as domestics in the large homes of prosperous Anglo Saxons in River Heights.

Maria, seventeen, stayed home to help her stepmother in the household while her father left for work, her stepbrothers for school. When they came home, she coaxed them to speak English to her, but they were impatient to play in the street. There was never an end to cooking and cleaning, sewing and gardening. Maria knew she should relieve her stepmother of responsibility for the cow.

On Sundays, the Edison settlers gathered in one of the homes for worship. Their voices joined in harmony, in songs of praise to God, who had brought them out of communism's red clutch just as he had brought the people of Israel safely through the Red Sea and out of bondage in Egypt. Jakob Neufeld, ordained in Russia, was their leader. His deep voice intoned the scriptures: *Bless the Lord, O my soul: and all that is within me, bless his holy name.*

Before long the newcomers built a small wooden church and the young people formed a choir. The young women working as maids in the houses of the wealthy came to choir practice when they could, sharing stories about the new world they were discovering. The English world. Maria envied them. She wanted to step into that world too, learn its customs and its practices. Most of all she coveted their English words and phrases. Others are moving forward, she thought. I am standing still.

On the river side of the highway, in a large two-storey house, lived Agnes McKay, the great-granddaughter of one of the Selkirk settlers who had farmed here a century ago. She lived alone, aging, ripening like fruit in late summer. When the German-speaking immigrants arrived with their large families, their foreign language and their rumoured abhorrence of war, and settled along Edison Avenue, she observed them from a distance. With curiosity. And apprehension. Would they be clean? Would they be troublesome? Would they breed and multiply, populating this northeast extension of the city until they outnumbered her kind of people?

Were they a threat, she wondered, or was there, within this new population, a solution to her dilemma?

Look, she said holding out her hands, her sweater sleeves pulled up to display wrists that were inflamed and swollen. Rheumatoid arthritis, she told Elena Franz. Hurts like bloody hell.

Elena stared at the bare, deformed wrists, the twisted hand that disappeared into a sweater pocket, fumbling for a pack of cigarettes. She couldn't understand the English woman, who was really Scottish, but because she spoke English would always be referred to by the newcomers as "de Lady." Mrs. McKay's words might be gibberish to Elena, but no one could fail to understand that such angry swelling of the joints must cause unbearable pain. A woman with such hands, Mennonite or English, Lady or not, must find it hard to peel potatoes or knead dough.

It was Maria who unscrambled the implications of Mrs. McKay's visit and latched on to the thread of hope it offered. There was, after all, an escape for her. A way to learn how to live in this country. How to speak its language.

Isn't it our Christian duty to help this English lady? she admonished her parents. Two days a week—that's all Mrs. McKay asks for. Don't we have to help our neighbour even if that neighbour lives on the other side of Henderson Highway? And can't speak German? And maybe never goes to church? And smokes?

Maria argued her case vehemently, confident that the weight of Holy Scripture was firmly on her side. That they'd be hypocrites if they didn't help Mrs. McKay when she needed help. Please, please, she begged. I'll bring home every cent. You can buy a butter churn. A washing machine.

From the start Agnes McKay called her new girl Marie and the name held.

That summer the kitchen and garden Marie laboured in with most devotion were not her stepmother's but Agnes McKay's. There were, thank God, no chickens. And no cow.

In Agnes McKay's kitchen, Marie learned to bake a flaky lemon pie and raisin scones and prepare tea the right way. In her employer's garden she planted, weeded and harvested peas and beans and radishes.

Years ago a crabapple tree had been planted behind the house. It was huge now, offering shade under its spreading branches and promising a harvest of tart apples in fall. Those apples, Agnes McKay told Marie, will make you an excellent pie. She sat on a wooden bench away from the tree's shade, bared her aching wrists to the sun's warmth and smoked one cigarette after another as she watched its leaves unfold in spring, then the white blossoms, then the green apples that in fall would turn red.

My ashes will be scattered under that tree one day, she told Marie, gesturing with her arm, flicking ash from her cigarette. Or maybe on the Red River. I guess that's when this godawful pain will finally stop. Cremation, she said. They burn you down to ash and toss you around and that's the end.

She spoke so matter-of-factly that Marie was shocked. She had never heard of cremation. Her mother and siblings lay buried in black earth in a far country. Simon had been wrapped in a blanket and lowered like a parcel into the black water of the Atlantic Ocean.

Death was the end? On Sunday Brother Neufeld had read the story of Lazarus, who was raised from the dead by Jesus who said, *I am the resurrection and the life.* The congregation believed that only communists lacked decent beliefs and her employer was no communist.

Oh yes, she told Marie one day. The Reds. We've got them. Right here in our own city. She shuddered.

Mrs. McKay, childless, had been widowed a decade earlier. Her nephew, Ronald, who lived in River Heights, would drive his aging aunt to appointments—bank, doctor, lawyer—and shopping at Eaton's. If the outing was exclusively for shopping, Marie might be invited along. She trailed Mrs. McKay up and down escalators, carrying her bundles, marvelling at the abundance of goods on display: thick towels in pretty pastel shades, elegant white linens, gadgets for slicing and grating, all sizes of mixing bowls, spatulas, spoons for stirring. And the exquisite bone china her mistress admired. Royal Doulton. Which pattern do you like? Agnes would ask, but Marie was speechless before such opulence. The shelves at home held barely enough plates and bowls for the family, mostly bought at the Goodwill store.

Gloria likes plain white, Agnes said, but I like patterns. After lengthy indecision, she would select a plate or bowl in a delicate pattern called "Angelique" and bring it home and place it in the already crowded china cabinet.

Who is Gloria? Marie wondered.

Ronald, who had returned to his office on Portage Avenue, appeared again promptly when the shopping was done to drive them home. Sometimes he appeared at his aunt's house just at the end of Marie's work day and insisted on driving her home. This embarrassed Marie. She made sure he didn't attempt to navigate Edison Avenue when it was waterlogged during or after rain.

Where did you go to school? he asked. Why did your people leave Russia? Were you driven out? What was your life like? He kept his eyes fixed on the young woman beside him who looked down and stammered and tried bravely to answer, to pretend each question was nothing more than an opportunity to practise the new language. When he provided a word she needed, Marie blushed. This English man was older than she was—mid-thirties, she guessed, or even forty. He was handsome in an amiable sort of way. His hair was reddish and thinning, his eyes blue, not the blue of the eyes in her family, but diluted. It was not from Ronald but from Agnes McKay that she learned he was married. Gloria.

Sometimes Ronald suggested they go for a drive before he brought her home. If Marie hesitated he would say: This is where you live now. You have to practise speaking English. You need lessons to learn a new language, it doesn't just happen. He spoke gently. And urgently.

He drove down Portage Avenue, pointing out the ornate

moulding on the Birks building, the Hudson's Bay store. He slowly navigated Broadway past the Manitoba Legislature. Made of Tyndall stone quarried in our own province, he told her proudly, watching for her reaction. She repeated to herself the unknown words—legislature, quarried, Tyndall stone. They drove through Assiniboine Park, where they caught glimpses of elk and deer and Ronald listed tigers and bears which they didn't see but which Marie imagined living in barred cages. They crossed the bridge to St. Boniface. This is where the French settled, Ronald said, on the east side of the Red River. Marie wanted to ask why, but he was already gesturing toward the stately cathedral. Once he stopped at a restaurant and ordered tea and nesselrode pie and Marie thought she had never tasted anything quite so delicious. She didn't dare ask what "nesselrode" meant, but she repeated this word also, in her head.

They covered a good deal of the city, but Ronald never headed toward River Heights, where he lived along that other river, the Assiniboine, in a house Marie imagined to be large and handsome with tall trees lining a wide driveway and roses at the front door in summer.

Explanations were necessary every time Marie came home late. And how easily they came to mind. Mrs. McKay needed her to finish washing the walls in the living room, my goodness, they couldn't have been done in years. Or Mrs. McKay dropped a jar of canned beets and with her arthritis flaring up this week she couldn't be expected to clean up the mess herself. Or there was unexpected company and tea had to be made and cookies served to three ladies.

When the muddy length of Edison Avenue froze over and snow covered roofs and gardens, Agnes McKay announced that at Christmas she would visit her sister in Regina. For three weeks Marie would not need to come on Tuesdays and Thursdays. She would have a holiday.

But Ronald McKay, driving Marie home, unfolded an alternate plan and during the entire Christmas season Marie's family saw her trudge off to work as usual, a key to Agnes McKay's house in her pocket.

Throughout the fall, Brother Neufeld's Sunday texts, it seemed to Marie, had been aimed at keeping the immigrant youth pure and faithful as they mingled with the English, at school or at work, especially the young women who worked as maids. "Your body is God's temple," he said and turned to face the choir, the sopranos and altos in the front row blushing in their Sunday dresses.

But the moral force of Brother Neufeld's sermons was pitted against an alliance of other persuasive forces that assault an awakening young woman, immigrant or not: the body's burning desire; dreams of perfect happiness; opportunities that open up so naturally. So miraculously.

Marie, denied further schooling in her new country, was learning instead the miracle of a woman's power over a man. And his over her. It was a heady education. Three Tuesdays and three Thursdays given over entirely to pleasure. Each morning she pretended to clean the spotless McKay house, dusting, mopping, looking around as if she were the mistress here in this home she shared with Ronald.

She prepared lunch: an egg salad sandwich, or Scotch broth from her employer's recipe book and laid the table, then waited impatiently for Ronald to come home to her. During the holiday season Ronald was less tied to his office, or perhaps he simply left orders for his secretary or neglected the office entirely in order to sit at the table with this fresh-faced young immigrant whom he never tired of instructing. Our premier here in Manitoba is John Bracken. Right now we have a Liberal government.

Marie watched his hands, the way they handled the cutlery or spooned soup or buttered bread.

They had the run of the entire house—kitchen, living room, dining room, bedrooms. It was not in Agnes McKay's bed but in a guest room that Ronald's most intimate instruction happened. There he taught Marie the landscape of a man's body, the pleasure of exploring it as he explored hers. How quickly what had seemed forbidden territory became familiar ground, and Marie believed she now knew everything there was to know.

Once they went shopping at Eaton's, where Ronald stopped at the perfume counter and they sniffed samples of exotic toilet water and cologne.

Which do you like? he asked.

With Ronald so close beside her every scent was sweet and dizzying. Marie couldn't choose. It was Ronald who selected "Pure Desire" in a cut glass bottle with a rose-shaped stopper. At another counter he found a snowflake-spangled Christmas card, on which he wrote: With all my love, Ronald.

He took her arm and led her out into the afternoon dusk so she could see Portage Avenue lit up. They walked toward the display in the corner window, where a toy train travelled repeatedly through fabricated tunnels while miniature mice danced around an enormous Christmas tree that glittered with rainbow-coloured lights as snow fell and dolls reached out their artificial arms and opened their mouths to say, Ma-Ma. Marie stared entranced at this children's winter wonderland.

On the third and last Thursday Ronald was late. While she waited, Marie went to the bookshelf where, right from the beginning of her employment, she had pulled down books and, drawing her finger beneath a line of words, made her way slowly down one page, then another, shaping the words with her mouth, noiselessly, and sometimes aloud, if Agnes was not nearby.

The first book she managed more or less to read through was *Mansfield Park* written by Jane Austen.

You can borrow it, her employer said. Take it home.

At home there were no books and little time to read, but Marie found the time and grasped something of Fanny Price's loneliness and longing for a home.

On the last day alone with Ronald she couldn't sustain the pretence that Agnes McKay's house was *her* home. She scanned the shelves, pulling out the books by Jane Austen. She was agitated, listening for Ronald at the door, the possibility of disappointment growing like a tumour inside her.

He came finally. He'd been delayed, helping his wife rearrange the heavy furniture in the dining room. Marie pictured a dark oak table like Agnes McKay's and matching chairs. She didn't ask if his wife suspected anything. Ronald had never mentioned her before. Had never spoken her name: Gloria.

This time with you, Ronald said, it's my best Christmas gift. It's everything I want.

But he was distracted during love, his body palpably present, but his thoughts elsewhere. Had they returned to his office? To his wife? Marie tried not to be terrified as she sensed a withdrawing, a separation, a parting, as if from a country you must leave forever.

Afterwards Marie declined Ronald's offer of a ride and insisted on walking home alone.

The houses, strung like beads along Edison Avenue, were already lit with coal-oil lamps, and most windows framed Christmas scenes with candle-lit trees. Like Christmas cards, she thought. She imagined warmth inside each house. And joy.

The previous Sunday the immigrants had marked *Heil'ge drei Könige* and Jacob Neufeld read the story of the magi, *We have seen his star*. The church had been hushed except for crying babies. They all sang "Freue dich, Welt" (Joy to the World) one more time.

Tonight the sky was overcast and starless. Marie was cold. Her breath formed small white puffs that hung in the chill air. She felt no joy, only the dull weight of foreboding.

~

The Church of Abundant Joy does not observe Christmas, Alice tells Aunt Sue. In our theology one day is like every other. So I thought we'd all go to the Christmas Eve service in the Mennonite church. Where Dad sings in the choir. Where Mom and Dad were married. Where Mia and I grew up. I'll stay home with Jeremy, Millicent says, and the offer is so convenient, Alice is relieved when no one objects. She knows her mother would prefer to stay home and avoid the noise and the people. The constant presence of her husband's relatives has worn her out, every room in their bungalow occupied every minute. She has headaches. Joseph, unable to help the headaches, hovers around her as if he senses that she expects something of him. Is it easier for him if the sea of faces in the sanctuary, lifted to the choir, will not include Millicent's?

Although the Wittenbergs arrive early they must search for a place in the parking lot. Once, the people of this congregation walked to church, but most have long since moved from Edison Avenue, a street their immigrant parents once considered a community. Now they have built bigger and better houses on newer streets.

A middle-aged couple welcomes the Wittenbergs with smiles and handshakes. Someone helps Taylor remove his parka and someone else unwinds Lucas's bright blue scarf.

Look out, Lucas mutters, clamping a hand on his bandaged head. You gotta look out.

The foyer is cluttered with damp boots and jackets. Teenagers with red Santa hats are handing out programs and candles. A strapping youth bends down to offer one to Lucas. Hey, who beat you up? he asks.

Lucas, baffled, grabs the candle.

The youth hesitates when he spots Taylor, held fast by his father, his mouth moist, but gives him a candle too. Be careful with it, buddy, he says.

Hey, Joe, a booming voice sings out and the chair of the stewardship committee slaps Joseph's shoulder: Merry Christmas!

Hey, you too, Joseph says and introduces Phil before making his way to where the choir is assembling.

Alice, who would feel at home in any church, shepherds the Wittenberg flock into the sanctuary. A string ensemble is playing a Bach chorale, "Jesu, meine Freude," and the Sunday school children are streaming in through a side door to take their places. Mia spots Bev, who is shepherding the smallest.

Alice is about to lead the family too far forward but her sister stops her halfway and, squeezing past several pairs of knees, they settle into the pew, Mia between Brian and Alice, who holds Lucas. Sue is last and sits near the aisle.

The evening unfolds as such evenings do. A teenage girl is confronted by an angel with large, drooping wings, who hands her a baby and says, Don't be afraid, Mary. It's real, Alice whispers in Lucas's ear. It's a real baby. The boy's eyes are huge. Yeah, he says. Like Jeremy, Mom, like Jeremy. Because he speaks too loudly, Mia wants to say, Shhh. Alice folds her arms and begins rocking them as if they hold a baby. Lucas watches her, then folds his arms too.

The smallest children toddle forward to sing "Away in a

Manger," their voices high and wobbly and pure. Bev crouches watchfully behind them.

Mary places Jesus in a manger crafted of rough poplar saplings and a teenage boy comes forward to stand awkwardly beside her. When the choir sings "Love Came Down at Christmas," Alice whispers, Yes, yes, love, as tears stream down her face. Mia can hear her father's voice carrying the baritone line and she is proud of him.

A choir of youthful angels, haloed and tinselled, skips in on stockinged feet to sing "Glory to God in the Highest" and then a ragtag passel of shepherds stumbles in from the foyer at the back and forms a wavering procession that makes its way along the centre aisle to the manger. They have been trussed up in tea towels and bathrobes and armed with makeshift crooks that stab the air dangerously. The shepherds are followed by smaller children camouflaged as sheep. When one of them goes, Baa, Baa, an annoyed shepherd turns and says, SHUT UP and threatens the lamb with a staff.

Taylor and Lucas are awestruck and mercifully silent.

The choir rises to sing: *For unto us a child is born, unto us a son is given, and His name shall be called Wonderful, Counsellor, the mighty God, the everlasting Father, the Prince of Peace.*

Three men step forward from the choir. Each one is given a silver crown, a cape of shiny brocade and a gift wrapped in gold fabric. When Lucas sees that his grandfather is the one in the blue cape he blurts, Opa, Opa, and the congregation laughs with the young visitor. Then as the star above the holy family is lit up everyone joins in the refrain, *Star of wonder, star of night, star with royal beauty bright.*

After this the figures in the story become motionless, forming a tableau at the front of the church where the light catches the tinsel and sequins and sets the scene aglitter. Behind them hangs an empty wooden cross, the only permanent decoration in the church. Tonight its familiar stark lines are upstaged by the amateur splash and splendour of the nativity story.

It's still there, Alice whispers, nudging Mia. The cross. It's there.

The church lights are dimmed and the teenagers who earlier handed out programs light the candles nearest the aisle and whisper, Pass it on. Rows of tiny flames appear and soon the sanctuary is filled with flickering lights that bravely dispel the darkness.

Dangerous, Mia warns.

But so beautiful, Alice whispers, her voice choked. The boys are speechless. Phil and Brian keep close and nervous watch over their sons' tiny fires.

When all candles are lit the congregation stands to sing "Silent Night, Holy Night," and even Aunt Sue is singing. When the song ends everyone streams toward the back. Sheep and shepherds become children once again, angels cast off their wings and all the candles are blown out.

The Wittenberg family follows the flow from the sanctuary to the crowded foyer, they find their coats and boots, their car in the parking lot and return to the white bungalow on Kildonan Drive.

~

And then it's Christmas day. The Wittenbergs' festive dinner is prepared by Millicent and Mia with sporadic assistance from Joseph and advice from Alice, who said over the telephone, You can skip the sweet potatoes, kids don't eat them, Brian won't for sure. Remember that steamed pudding you used to make, Mom? We could have that. I'll bring dinner rolls and juice.

Instead of steamed pudding there's chocolate cake. Millicent spent an entire, exhausting afternoon making it from the recipe in the magazine she had opened on the day of Jeremy's birth. It rose nicely and came out of the pan easily but even the frosting can't make it look like the cake in the picture.

Aunt Sue has not volunteered to help but when it's time to prepare the salad she squeezes in beside Millicent and begins slicing cucumbers and tomatoes while Mia mashes the potatoes. Joseph has found a chef's apron and is carving the turkey.

Lucas is damp with excitement, anxiously demanding, When the presents come, when? Where Santa anyway? Mom? I need presents. His small face is a twist of worry.

Jeremy is handed from one arm to another, and accepts each transfer with dull complacence. His eyes wander around the room, unable to focus on anything for long. The excitement may keep him awake at night, but for now he is exhausted and some-one lulls him to sleep.

Taylor is on the floor drawing a picture on a large sheet of paper provided by Mia. A huge blue face looks out from what might be the second-storey window of a crudely outlined house. It's God, he declares loudly and when no one responds he repeats with increased volume, It's God. God lives up. Very high.

And has a blue face? Brian jokes, and seeing the boy's bafflement adds, gently, Why don't you draw a bunch of angels?

No, Taylor isn't going to draw angels. Angels are too conscrated.

Complicated, Mia corrects and offers lavish praise for his messy crayoning. When she posts the picture of God on the fridge door, Taylor beams.

When everything is ready, Joseph produces a seating plan he worked out this morning.

Always the efficient VP, Dad, Alice jokes. She takes Brian by the hand and leads him to his designated place.

Lucas and Taylor find themselves seated on either side of

Joseph, who pulls from his pocket two hockey toques and says, You have to wear them. You're the Winnipeg Jets. The two boys break into giggles. They have not, so far, discovered how to play together.

Mia senses the merriment around the table and is glad for it. Her father, as if he's a mechanical toy come magically to life, makes a point of drawing out everyone, teasing the children, calling out to Millicent, You're a super cook. And to Mia, You're a first-rate assistant. He keeps a deliberate smile on his face, but Mia can see that the effort is wearing him down. Embarrassed by his determination, she wonders if he is counting the days until he will see Hedie Lodge again. She looks away and sees that her mother is also watching him.

Phil pours wine and they drink to the season and to each other.

Everyone digs in.

Then Alice rises:

I want to say something. Last night in church when those sweet little kids sang "Away in a Manger" and the baby wasn't a plastic doll, but a real baby, warm and soft, it was just such a miracle and that's when I wanted so much for Jeremy to be in that manger with the angels around him, singing a lullaby. Singing him to sleep. And last night I dreamt he was walking, oh I know he's not old enough, but in the dream, you know? He was surrounded by lambs, white and soft. And his face shone like a star.

She stops and looks around as if she has forgotten where this speech is headed. No one says anything. An uncomfortable silence has fallen over the plundered table. Over the whole family. Brian is folding and refolding his napkin. Joseph clears his throat and stares off into the distance.

Christmas is all about love, Alice says, regaining her voice and momentum. And hope too. We all have such great hope, don't we? For our children? For Taylor and Lucas? For Jeremy? Her eyes move around the table, from face to face, pleading with her family to summon hope. Her words are unsteady. She sits down and lowers her eyes.

Mia wishes Brian would put his arm around her sister, but his eyes are downcast too, and it's Aunt Sue who gets up to give Alice a hug.

Mia thinks the manger scene last night was charming, yes, but also amateurish. The teenagers who played Joseph and Mary had been so obviously nervous, so obviously stifling their giggles. Maybe they were infatuated with each other. She expected the real child to begin wailing, and it did, near the end. But there was a moment when the teenaged Joseph stood perfectly still and looked down on the child like a real father, and Mary leaned over the manger, and a woolly sheep nudged its woolly neighbour, and Mia had felt a shiver of holiness. And peace.

The awkwardness around the table is broken by Millicent, who says, It's time for presents. There's commotion as the family rises from the table and everyone groups around the Christmas tree. Santa appears in their midst and Taylor and Lucas are beside themselves. A fabricated ho-ho voice pronounces the two boys elves and Santa produces elf hats to replace the toques. Mia becomes assistant to the elves, reading out names so they can deliver the gifts.

Like the wise men, Taylor shouts. Like Uncle Joseph.

Like Opa, Lucas mumbles and looks around. Where Opa?

Alice has insisted that Brian bring his video camera and it whirrs as Taylor clumsily tears the paper from hockey gloves, a badminton racket, a baseball bat. He stares at each gift, dumbstruck. A thread of drool slides from the side of his mouth, dribbles down to his shirt and soaks into the wrapping paper.

Look, Mom, a ... a ... Lucas can't find the word, his face below the white bandage reddening with anxious excitement.

His words become a jumble. Brian's camera, panning the room, captures the boy's stunned amazement and moves on to other faces, Alice's radiant now with joy; Phil's guarded, anxious; Millicent's etched in weariness; Joseph's Santa face. And so on round the circle.

GranMarie should be here, Mia tells Alice. We should have brought her.

Absolutely, Alice says. Absolutely. She'd just love to watch the boys. Why isn't she here?

Mia has asked for gifts of money to help with the trip to Greece, and she opens each envelope gratefully. But the gifts will not underwrite her travel to Greece—she will direct the money to her father's bank account. No, Mia, no, he'll say. I want you to go to Greece. But Greece has been overshadowed.

Brian comes from the kitchen with beers. Aunt Sue pours more wine.

When the children's excitement has abated, and before crankiness can replace it, a temporary calm settles on the Wittenbergs. Why don't we sing? someone says and everyone looks to Joseph, but it's Alice who suggests "Deck the Halls," and when the last *Fa la la la la* has been sung someone calls out "O Little Town of Bethlehem" and after that "Good King Wenceslas," for which the men and women—even Sue—sing alternate verses, and then it's "Rudolph, the Red-Nosed Reindeer" and the boys laugh and try to join in and merriment floats teasingly through the house.

~

The next day the Wittenberg clan is gathered once again and the surprise is GranMarie, wrapped in a green and blue paisley shawl and seated in the best chair in the toy-littered living room.

All the adults stand around the shrunken matriarch, looking down on her as if she is an exotic creature from a foreign country. Joseph has settled her into the chair and now stands beside her, a dutiful attendant.

Blame Alice, she says. Squeezed me into the van with Lucas and … and—she searches for the name of the baby. I didn't want to come. I told you. Her face breaks into a smile.

Alice hugs the old woman. You did so want to come, Gran-Marie. I could see it. And we need you here. She rushes off in the direction of the baby's whimper.

Joseph echoes his daughter dutifully. Yes, Mother. We need you.

What for? she says sharply, the smile gone.

While Joseph gropes for an answer to the sharpness, Mia chimes in, Because you're the one with the stories, GranMarie. Our stories.

Well, I hope you're not expecting me to tell you stories.

No, no, Joseph says. It's Christmas. Just enjoy yourself.

In all this confusion? The old woman looks round warily.

Mia shepherds Lucas and Taylor to the front hall, where they struggle with boots and scarves and toques. When I bring them back they'll be lambs, Mia promises and leaves with the boys, letting in a gust of icy air.

Phil pulls a chair close to his mother. She smiles at him politely, as if he's a guest she must entertain. Well, she says, here we are, and leans closer to him. You remind me of someone I knew.

Do I look like my father?

Your father? Now that's a funny question. She draws back, as if to study Phil from a distance. Her hands become restless, her fingers move nervously along the fabric of her black skirt.

GranMarie hasn't had her nap, Millicent says. Want to lie down, GranMarie?

The old woman looks up, offended.

Brian finds his camera and draws up a chair. Have you got a picture of your husband? he asks, and when she looks confused he directs the question at the brothers. You guys have a picture of your dad?

Joseph and Phil look at each other as if neither can remember and Phil says, I don't even know if we called him Dad or Daddy.

I think we called him Papa, Joseph says. We spoke German then.

Millicent goes to join Sue in the kitchen, leaving Marie Wittenberg with her sons. And Brian. The old woman lets her eyes rest on each in turn, as if she wishes to memorize the details that distinguish one from the other. Her fingers stop moving and when she speaks her voice is clear: I remember a time when our father would have prayed when the family was gathered together like this.

Prayed? Phil looks up as if he is closing in on details he has been looking for.

Marie sits upright, her eyes are alert, the blue of them intense. When she doesn't speak Joseph repeats Phil's question: Our father prayed with us?

I'm not talking about your father, she says. I'm thinking about mine.

So ... so your father was the one who ... prayed? Joseph says.

All three men look uncomfortable. Talking about fathers is unfamiliar enough; talking about prayer even more so.

Well, Marie says, it could have been my mother. Someone prayed, that's all I remember.

What did they pray for? Joseph asks.

Well, everybody wanted to get out, of course.

Out?

Out of the country. Marie sounds impatient, as if her family should know this and not have to ask.

Tell us about our father, Phil breaks in, his voice urgent. I want to know about him. What was he like? Where did you meet him? When did you fall in love?

His mother's head swivels to face her younger son, her eyes alarmed, as if speaking about love will require more effort than she has available. She stares accusingly at Phil .

Love, Joseph thinks—when has he last spoken that word? Only in the comfort of that apartment overlooking the Assiniboine River. But he has promised himself not to think of Hedie or their winter trysts, not while the family is together in this house where he is the host and should say something to rescue his mother , whose eyes are beginning to close. She is dozing off, leaving the three men in uneasy silence.

Phil clears his throat. Do you think she—he nods toward his mother—is she the one we can thank for this Wittenberg thing our boys are cursed with?

Joseph waits for his son-in-law to speak, but Brian picks up his camera and aims it like a gun at the sleeping woman.

For God's sake, Joseph says.

Brian shrugs. Lowers the camera.

Joseph says it might have been their father and Phil asks why their mother never talks about him.

Whatever happened to your father? Brian asks. Where is he?.

Joseph shrugs. Alice thinks everybody should be tested, he says.

Including her? Brian indicates the sleeping woman. Either of you two up to suggesting it to her?

Their mother rouses and Phil repeats his unanswered question: Mother, where did you meet our dad? When did you fall in love?

Marie Wittenberg's fingers begin once more to worry the fabric of her skirt. She looks at a spot above the heads of the men. Love is patient and kind, she says. Her words, rising from a neglected corner of memory, float like released butterflies into the room. Her face softens and she raises a hand in a feeble gesture of dismissal just as Sue returns to the room and Mia comes in with Lucas and Taylor, all three pink and glowing.

The telephone rings and Joseph goes into the den to take the call, shutting the door behind him.

~

Joseph, I'm afraid it's bad news. Ab Solinsky's voice is grave. It's about Hedie, he says.

He doesn't say Hedie Lodge or Miss Lodge. Just Hedie. Joseph's throat tightens and speech is impossible. He can only listen.

A traffic accident, Ab says. I'm afraid it's pretty bad, yes. It happened the day after she got home. There was snow and the streets were icy. Her spine's injured. Broken, actually.

Will she live? Enormous physical effort is required for Joseph to force out those words loudly enough for the principal to hear.

Oh, I'm sure she'll live. She's so healthy in every way and that's got to be in her favour.

But you don't really know, Ab, Joseph says, his words a groan. You don't know.

We'll just have to wait and see. Ab's voice has become gentle as if he's comforting a child. Are you all right there, Joseph?

I'm fine.

Be sure to call me, Joseph. If I can help.

Yes.

We'll be in touch.

Yes.

A final pause and the principal hangs up.

In the houseful of people, there is no one Joseph can go to and speak the words that come automatically to mind: I have to go. I have to be there. With Hedie Lodge. There is no one he can say this to. Who would make sense of it? Numb, he stumbles out of the den and back into the living room. There's an awkward hush, as if no one has spoken in his absence and all time has been suspended, awaiting his return. His mother looks up. And so does Phil.

What the hell, Brian says. You see a ghost?

Millicent has returned to the room. Who was it? she asks. Who called?

Joseph's knees weaken and he finds a chair, lowers himself into it. His body is a burden unconnected with him, his tongue paralyzed. When he can finally speak his voice is hoarse and raspy. The principal, he says. It was Ab Solinsky.

Good God, Joseph, Brian says, they surely didn't fire you? At Christmas?

Joseph tries to pull himself together. He mustn't fall apart. Not at Christmas, with his brother Phil here, and Brian taking pictures of everyone and their mother present who is old but not easily fooled. And Millicent. Elsewhere in the house Jeremy has awakened from his nap and Alice comes into the room carrying the baby. She hands him to Brian, who is still trying to figure out how to hold this special boy. He gestures as if to swing him high, then hesitates, convinced that everything about Jeremy is fragile. Lucas, still in his wet boots, makes a beeline for his brother. Someone yells at him and Brian holds Jeremy out of his brother's eager reach.

Marie Wittenberg sits upright in her chair. Who's going to pray? she says.

Millicent walks slowly toward Joseph and sits down beside him. She places her hand over his. What's wrong, Joseph?

From across the room, still in her parka, Mia watches her parents.

Storm

Joseph and Mia leave for the airport with the Toronto visitors and Millicent is alone in the house, alone with the aftermath of Christmas. Before he left, Joseph asked if he should stop at Safeway, did she need something. He looked at her but she turned away.

At the last minute, Sue had hugged Millicent and then called Taylor to say goodbye. The boy had mumbled a few agitated words and Millicent said, Enjoy your flight, Taylor, words too formal for a young boy.

Millicent scans the detritus of celebration surrounding her. I will clean up, she tells herself, put things away, find places for all the presents. The white sweater is from Mia. Everyone, it seems, has given Joseph a shirt, the boxes are everywhere. She hasn't finished unwrapping the new breakfast dishes Joseph surprised her with and now she doubts that she ever will. And there are those gifts he received at school, bottled mostly, from the secretaries, the staff, the school board. From Ab Solinsky.

This morning, to calm Taylor's nervousness about the flight, Mia sat him beside her on a sofa. I'll read you a story, she said and held a children's picture book so Taylor could see. The story was about a mother and her boy and the words *love you forever* kept repeating. Taylor, who should have been too old for such a book, was mesmerized.

Love is too complicated. Instead of dwelling on it Millicent sets her mind to creating order out of chaos. But the melancholy kept at bay during the Christmas bustle, and jolted aside by Ab Solinsky's phone call, is creeping back into the crannies of her body and she cannot shake free of it. Joseph has been with another woman. With Hedie Lodge, Mia's English teacher. He has betrayed her, but all she can think of is the shock in his eyes after that phone call. Shock and confusion that he tried to conceal so the family could go on celebrating Christmas and life could continue. Millicent believes a good wife could have prevented the calamity that has invaded her family. Prevented the look of dismay on her husband's face. She has failed Joseph and is to blame and this failure has now come to haunt her. She must not sit here, helpless. She goes to the closet, finds a garbage bag, hauls out the vacuum cleaner, rubber gloves, a bottle of detergent, then, exhausted, stares at them helplessly.

She will begin with the gifts. But that too is daunting. A good wife should not be daunted. She wills herself to go down to the basement, where Phil and Sue and Taylor slept over Christmas. They have stripped the beds, leaving piles of linen on the floor. Millicent walks past them to the corner bar where she selects one of the gift bottles and carries it up to the kitchen and looks for a corkscrew. Before she opens the bottle, she makes two more laborious trips down to the bar, carries bottles up and conceals them in her half of the bedroom closet. There—she has accomplished something. She almost smiles. She is taking initiative. She is going to be a good wife. She steps to the window, looks up at the featureless sky, and suddenly she is overtaken by a fury so urgent she has to grab a chair for support. She is angry—at the world, at her empty life. Maybe at God and definitely at Joseph.

In the street, snow is falling and a wind has picked up.

~

The wind turns to storm and the falling snow becomes a blizzard. Huge drifts make streets impassable, driveways snow-clogged, the neighbourhood a white desert. Mia feels as if she's stranded in a shoulder-deep bank of snow with no way out. To settle her restlessness, she picks up *Nicholas and Alexandra,* a biography Miss Lodge loaned her the last week of school. This will give you a background for your grandmother's stories, the teacher said. Mia knows the story of the Romanovs ends horribly. She wants a happy story, something to keep grief at bay.

With the city shutting down, even Kurt's basketball practices scheduled for the holiday week will be cancelled, but it wouldn't be impossible for an athletic teenager to walk to the white bungalow several doors down. He will come and they will talk about Hedie Lodge and even though he is not in her English class, he will be as shocked as she is. He will share her sorrow.

When Kurt doesn't come, Mia calls him and he tells her about the snowmobile his father bought, a Christmas gift for the whole family. I reported to the emergency centre, he says, excited with his new toy and its possibilities. I'll be picking up nurses who can't get to work. And bringing back the stranded ones, the ones who've done two shifts.

I hope those nurses are all good-looking, Mia blurts out.

Kurt laughs. I better get going, he says, and before he hangs up adds, I've got a job at McDonald's. Starting January.

Disappointed, Mia turns reluctantly to *Nicholas and Alexandra* and reads her way toward the Russian Revolution, surfacing from time to time, dazed, to hear the wind still howling across the city.

It's too cold for jogging, but she pulls on her warmest boots and parka and heads out to face the razor-sharp wind, the snow needling her face. She pushes into the storm and is charged with a surge of energy. Just as she nears Kurt's house, a snowmobile comes roaring and grinding through an enormous drift that blocks the driveway. As the driver revs the engine, the churned-up snow strikes her with the force of a hurricane.

Kurt! she calls into the blinding whiteness. Kurt! Wait! Wait for me!

The snowmobile charges through the drift and turns ahead of Mia to plow its way along Kildonan Drive. She tries to go faster, tries to run and catch up with Kurt. It's impossible. She keeps calling, but a blast of wind snatches her words away. And her breath. Knee deep in snow, alarmed by the storm, and disappointed that Kurt didn't see her, she stumbles and falls forward.

There is no one in the street. Mia, still fuelled by disappointment, begins pushing with her arms, flailing against the snow. She tries kicking with her feet but every movement is difficult, her body cumbersome and her energy draining away. Warm from her struggle, she relaxes and lies still. This snow bed is surprisingly soft and comfortable. No wonder people fall asleep in snow. She closes her eyes. When drowsiness threatens to overtake her, she knows she should fight it. People who fall asleep this way may never wake up. But it's so much easier not to fight. Is this what it's like for her mother in her battle with depression? Mia pictures her mother as she lay in bed this morning. Pictures Alice. Lucas. Jeremy. Her father's grief-etched face.

Cold is creeping more insistently into her body and wind-blown snow swirls viciously across her face. Soon all warmth is gone. With huge effort, Mia forces herself to move. Her arms, her legs. Everything is slow, slow as molasses, but she keeps on struggling, inch by inch. She embraces the challenge and is rewarded by a flow of adrenalin. She knows she isn't stuck for good.

When Mia arrives at Wild Oak Estates she is too spent to run up the stairs.

Were they chasing you? GranMarie asks. She makes tea and Mia is warmed.

GranMarie, do you have a story for me?

What kind of story?

A happy story. Do you have one?

Happy, the old woman muses. I could tell you something that happened one spring. GranMarie goes to her rocking chair and settles into her Scheherazade role. It happened at Easter, she says.

The Fugitives
(Assignment #5)

No one in Barvenkovo had ever actually seen Tsar Nicholas, though photographs of him and his tsarina, Alexandra, were given a place of honour in many homes, the handsome couple seated facing the camera, surrounded by their charming daughters in summery dresses and, in a crisp sailor suit, the young tsarovitch who lived in constant danger of bleeding to death. Everyone knew that the tsarina, in fear for her son's life, clung to every word of counsel that came from the mouth of Rasputin, a devilish holy man.

"He is simply evil," Hanna Franz pronounced, in front of the young Maria. "Godless." Hanna considered the scandalous stories linking Rasputin and the tsarina malicious inventions concocted by enemies of the royal family. And she had prayed that the tsarina would be granted strength to resist the advice of a madman. And to reject his company. Abram and Hanna believed monarchs and emperors, though imperfect, were ordained by God to rule and the people they ruled had an obligation of loyalty towards them.

When the first rumours of the overthrow of the tsar reached Barvenkovo, a confusion of excitement and gloom settled on the town. "Where is respect for authority?" Abram wanted to know. Hanna was shocked at the lack of compassion for a mother whose son was the victim of the bleeding sickness. When the imperial family was murdered, Abram wanted to keep the news from his wife. "Don't tell your mother," he warned Maria. But such news cannot be concealed. A neighbour blurted the story to Hanna, who would not stop crying.

The deposed and murdered tsar and his family were not uppermost in the minds of Abram and Hanna on the night they left their home and climbed with their two children into their droshky after nightfall. Hanna and the children huddled together while Abram urged the horses on and they moved as swiftly and stealthily as darkness and deeply rutted streets and the clip-clop of horses' hoofs allowed. The direction he had struck led away from their solid brick house with its sturdy furniture—the oak table, the handmade wooden sleeping benches with feather bedding folded into them, chests of drawers filled with hemstitched shirts and linens. It led away from the Lutzch factory toward the outskirts of the town.

The opposing Red and White armies were poised to converge on Barvenkovo and the town was no longer safe for owners of property or employers of peasants and the landless. Insurrection was in the air. A sympathetic worker at the factory had taken Abram aside and whispered in his ear. "For you, it is very dangerous." Shocked by the scarcely veiled hatred in the faces of some of his workers, Abram had acted decisively.

"Quick," he ordered tersely. "Warm coats for everyone. Blankets."

Maria was ordered to pack cheese and roasted **Zwieback**. Simon was sent to find his mother's woollen shawl. Hanna boiled water for **Prips**, which she poured into bottles. Abram harnessed the horses. Everything was stowed hastily in the droshky and they set out like fugitives into the night. It was April, Easter week, and although the days were warm, the nights remained damp and cool.

Their vehicle took them past the small shop where the best candy in Barvenkovo was sold, past the broad roof of the town's market and past an abandoned warehouse. Abram stiffened when just ahead of them a shape stepped out of the darkness at the side of the street, raised a lantern and called out: "Halt! Halt!" The shape was accompanied by several others, some of them armed, their weapons glinting in the lantern's light. The Franz family was ordered out, their wagon and horses commandeered for purposes more urgent than the needs of fear-driven fugitives. Wounded soldiers were waiting to be taken to the train station. A driver was needed too, Abram was told, and he knew it was useless to object.

He folded Hanna's shawl more tightly around her shoulders and ordered the children to carry the bundles. He pointed to the warehouse they had just passed. "It will be open," he whispered to Hanna, then repeated for Maria when he saw how his wife's face paled and her thin shoulders trembled. "If there's a cellar, go down. I will find you." He gave Maria his lantern, relieved when the waiting men made no objection. Then he climbed back into the droshky, took the reins and drove away with men he had no reason to trust.

Yes, the warehouse was open. Maria shone the lantern around until they found a trapdoor to a cellar. Hanna went first and her children followed, feeling their way down the broken ladder into blackness so deep it threatened to overwhelm their weak light. Hanna felt she was leading her children in a descent into hell. They groped in the subterranean darkness, testing the ground under their feet, bumping against obstacles. The obstacles were wooden crates, a few of them sturdy enough to sit on. The mother kept her children close, one on either side, so they could lean against her and she could place an arm around them, or they around her. They shared the blanket Maria had grabbed and braced themselves to endure the slow passage of the hours until the breaking of a new day that would bring hope of rescue.

Dull thuds of distant gunfire somewhere over Barvenkovo punctuated the sombre hours and occasionally the trio could hear the tramp of feet passing by in the street, and voices, agitated, shrill. "Shhh," Hanna cautioned and they held their breath until their lungs were ready to explode. Hanna struggled to control her rasping cough.

No one must hear. No one must know there were fugitives hiding in the empty building. But a cough has a life of its own and though she tried to smother it in her shawl, she wasn't always successful.

Simon shrieked into the darkness, "A rat, Mama! There's a rat! I saw two eyes."

"Sssh." Hanna placed her hand over her son's eyes. "Sssh. No rat, Simon. You're just imagining things." But she knew he was not. She had heard scuttling in the dark and had seen the light of the lantern reflected in two pinpoint eyes. "Sleep, Simon," she said. As if anyone could in such a place.

Maria wanted to scream too, but instead she sat tense on her box, pressed so close against her mother she could feel the heaving of each smothered cough. Only this morning, when the world still held together, Maria and her friend Nettie had slipped out of the orchard and hurried along the street, keeping close to the picket fences, avoiding adults who would tell them to run home, quick, it's not safe in the street. They saw Petya wandering sadly down the lane like a lost, unwanted dog. At least he wasn't surrounded by the village rowdies who always found a way to torment the hapless boy. Nettie had brought a few pennies to spend at the small shop and the girls shared a handful of red candy. The storekeeper's cat had brushed against their legs and they bent to stroke its black fur, then, giggling, flew home, passing a yard where two boys were grooming their riding horse. One of the boys had waved a brush and shouted some kind of warning, but the girls only giggled harder and ran faster. Maria had come home just as her father arrived with the news that they must leave.

And now she was in this black hole, without her father, her brother scared half to death and her mother unable to stop coughing. Her own bed, the family house, the street running past it, had become a faint and distant dream. Would they ever see their house again? She wondered where the tsarina and her daughters had hidden when they were driven out of the palace and whether their mother had coughed like hers. She thought of Petya. Was he asleep in his bed, safe because his father owned no factory and no land?

Hanna knew it was morning when shafts of light fell through cracks between the floorboards and narrow ribbons of light created a striped pattern on the dirt floor.

"What's that!" Simon yelled, waking. He had dozed, off and on. Now he noticed thin, pale fingers poking through gunnysacks filled with something bumpy.

"Potatoes," Hanna said. "They want to grow because now it's spring." At least we won't have to starve, she thought, if help is slow in coming. If it comes at all. Maria would say no to a raw potato. Not for me. Simon would refuse too. Hanna, knowing more, fearing more than her children, wondered if it would come to that—hunger so urgent they would tear open the sacks and pull out these abandoned potatoes and eat them raw after brushing the loose dirt from their skins.

The gunfire of the previous night had stopped and the noise from the street seemed like the ordinary bustle of a day beginning. Maria thought she heard birdsong as she pulled out the **Zwieback** the Russian maid had toasted to a crisp yesterday before she left Barvenkovo and fled to the village of her parents. Maria handed one to Simon while Hanna unwrapped a bottle of cold **Prips**. Simon wanted to dip his bread into it, but there were no cups, they had to take turns drinking from the bottle.

All day they waited, listening for footsteps that might signal Abram's return. And their rescue. Or the opposite:

discovery by bandits or soldiers. Hanna rationed the bread and cheese, alert to any sound from the door. No one came. With better light, she saw that there were enough crates to arrange as makeshift beds for her children. She set them to work, preparing for another night. Maria lured Simon into games. To scare away the rats she sang: Ein **Blümlein steht im Walde**. She wondered if that forest was as dark as this hideout had been last night. Hanna walked around in the damp cellar, hoping to restore warmth to her feet and fingers.

At night the gunfire resumed, the rats came to life in the dank darkness, Hanna shivered under her shawl and Maria dreamt that a monster with eyes like stars was dragging her from her bed. Simon slept through it all.

The lantern light died, its fuel spent.

On their third morning underground, Hanna rose chilled to the bone. They were out of food. Her coughing, aggravated by the damp cold, had become constant. Her chest was raw. She stiffened when she heard the door to the warehouse creak open. "Ssh," she cautioned and pulled her children close, pressing their faces against her skirt. The trap door opened and a square of light appeared on the cellar floor. A dark figure was descending the wooden ladder. Panic rose in her throat and she was afraid she would not have enough strength to control it. Were they discovered, or rescued? She had almost despaired of rescue, hadn't dared to believe it when last night she had noticed the gunfire had not resumed.

The descending figure was Abram. It was really Abram, gaunt and unshaven, stumbling down the ladder, everything about him grey. In the underground gloom he seemed much older than when he'd left them, but he greeted them with a show of good cheer and the children left off clinging to Hanna and came forward timidly. "Papa," they said. "Papa."

Abram helped Hanna climb up the shaky ladder. The children followed and all four emerged into the blinding glare of the morning sun.

"The horses, Papa?" Simon asked. "Where are the horses?"

Abram shook his head. "Wait," he said, taking Simon's hand. He let Hanna and Maria get a head start; a group of four would be too conspicuous. Their long trek through the streets of Barvenkovo must be as unremarkable as possible. Hanna, whenever she was sure she couldn't take one more step, summoned another breath, another small burst of energy. Every time she saw someone approaching or heard footsteps or merely thought she did, she longed for the earth to open up and swallow them, all four. Maria gripped her mother's hand, pulling her along the last stretch toward home.

The door to their brick house was swinging crazily on its hinges, and when they entered they found themselves in a peculiar haze. The bedding had been slashed, releasing clouds of goose down. The down sailed slowly, dreamily around the room, drifting, floating until it occupied all available space. Maria thought she was walking into a dream, a dream that must be harmless because how much harm can feathers do? But the mud-streaked floor carried the prints of enormous boots, drawers had been yanked right out and lay overturned in the mud, their contents of hemstitched pillowcases and linen towels flung every which way. Someone's knife had gouged the oak table's gleaming surface. When she saw the gash, Hanna broke down and wept.

"But we are alive," Abram said. "And they have gone."

Maria wanted to ask the question that had troubled her at night in the cellar when she couldn't sleep: Who exactly were "they"? But her mother was sobbing in her father's arms and Simon was running like a dervish from room to room, feathers swirling around his blond head.

~

Rereading her story, Mia thinks Hedie Lodge would probably tell her she's included too much information about the tsar's family. It slows the story, she would say. But it was Hedie Lodge who gave her the book about the Romanovs in the first place.

Hedie Lodge will not return to George Sutton Collegiate, Angela says. She made her mother call the school and that's as much as the secretary would say. In the Wittenberg house the teacher's name is not spoken: it is a burning coal no one wants to touch.

On the Saturday when GranMarie had finished her story and a cup of tea, she told Mia that on Easter mornings the priest in the orthodox church in Barvenkovo would greet his congregation boldly with the words: *Christos voskrese!* (Christ is risen!) and the congregation would shout back: *Voistinu voskrese!* (He is risen indeed!)

Even the year you hid in the cellar, GranMarie?

No, no. That year ... that year ... Suddenly, GranMarie was no longer sure what happened that year.

Well, I guess if they had any sense they'd be at home, hiding, wouldn't they? Mia said.

Praying, GranMarie said and closing her eyes chanted: *Gospodi pomiluj, Gospodi pomiluj, Gospodi pomiluj.* It means God have mercy, she explained when she stopped and opened her eyes. She repeated the Russian words for Mia and they recited them together, over and over, like a mantra. Mia liked the feel of the words on her tongue. She wanted them in her story, but that would be showing off.

Mia does not regret the hours of work spent on this story, which the new teacher may not accept. The task has kept her mind off the Wittenberg sorrows, and the story has taken such hold of her that she wants to continue telling it.

Mia begins a letter: Dear Miss Lodge, but the words that should follow do not come. How is that possible? Hasn't she just written something much longer and more complicated than a letter? She gives up and next day during a lull in the storm ventures out to buy a get-well card at the drug store. "Thinking of You," the card says. Mia signs her name. But where will she send the card? She addresses the envelope to Hedie Lodge at George Sutton Collegiate, omitting her return address. The secretaries will forward it. She is about to seal the envelope, when she pulls out the card and writes her address below her signature. Then she adds: You are taking the less-travelled road and that will make a difference. She seals the envelope and holds it in her hand, thinking of what she has written. The words are arrogant. Cruel. She tears the envelope and its contents into small pieces. Tomorrow she will buy a new card. This time she will not add stupid sentiments.

~

On the first day of classes after the holiday, Hedie Lodge's classroom is in a state of disarray. Mia feels the tension when she walks in. Her classmates are not, as might be expected, exchanging holiday news in shrill, competing voices, complaining that the blizzard spoiled their vacation, why couldn't it wait until January so school would have to be cancelled. The conversation this morning is muted and it isn't about who picked up extra hours at Wendy's or who skied at Banff; who travelled with their parents to a Caribbean beach or spent the holidays with grandparents in rural Manitoba; which lucky student's parents came across with which new videos, clothes, hard cash; who was utterly and completely bored over Christmas.

Desks stand awry while their ought-to-be occupants move quietly around, stand together in pairs, in ragged groups, or alone at the windows staring out at the January snowscape, static now that the wind has died down. Hedie Lodge has not returned and her absence is to blame for the disorder. Mia hears her name move from tongue to tongue.

She could of died. The words are scarcely above a whisper.

Nearly did.

A rock fell off a cliff.

A rock? No way. An avalanche hit the car.

In Toronto? Get serious.

I heard the streets were icy. You know—Ontario? They ice up worse than here in Winnipeg. She lost control.

Her boyfriend was driving.

No, her brother.

No way. *She* was driving.

Is she crippled?

Yeah.

No way.

Who have they got to replace her?

Who knows.

I bet we'll get like some dumb sub.

This news is not entirely negative: with a substitute teacher no one can be expected to work. The voices gradually gain pitch and volume, interrupt and clash, and chaos replaces the hush.

Mia is tense, afraid Angela will say something linking the absent teacher with her father. It must be so tempting. But

Angela has had a busy social life—by telephone during the worst of the weather—and is sleep deprived. None of the comments are hers. She stands dazed at the window and has not spoken.

Neither has Danny Haarsma, who arrived late, slid into his place, put his head face down on his arms and there he is still.

The substitute, late because he's not familiar with the northeast part of the city, arrives at last, accompanied by the vice principal. The two men carry a stack of books each, paperback texts, slender new volumes. At the appearance of the VP all conversation stops, students return to their desks, straighten the rows and turn as if with one pair of eyes to study the man who is to replace their disabled teacher, Miss Lodge, who has now become understanding and wise and they will be completely justified in maintaining loyalty to her, and therefore withholding it from the stranger who is moving toward her desk: a small man with black wavy hair and a dusky face. And glasses through which he peers with pale eyes. He looks pleasant enough. He smiles.

Mia, had she turned to scrutinize the substitute, would have detected a trace of weakness in that smile, but she is looking at her father, who is businesslike and makes no attempt to smile. His jaw is firm, his hair showing the first touches of grey, and the gaze of his blue eyes, intensified by the blue of his shirt—a Christmas gift—sweeps the class like a search light. Angela is right—her father is handsome. And despite his calm exterior, shaken by the accident that has befallen Hedie Lodge. She doesn't need Angela the romance expert to tell her that.

Can I have your attention, ladies and gentlemen, he says. I'd like to introduce Mr. Yakimchuk. He'll be your English teacher for the next while. I know you'll make him feel right at home. This last is spoken with deliberation and authority. And more than a hint of warning.

Yak-Yak-Yak. Mia hears mumblings and a snicker behind her. She bristles. Some idiot dares to snicker in her father's presence. It's contemptible. Rude. She has not spoken much with her father since Christmas and he has said little to her. What happened to Hedie Lodge is wedged between them, keeping them apart in their grief. But she wants her classmates to respect her father.

You will each receive a copy of a brand new text, recently ordered, Joseph Wittenberg says. Paid for by taxpayers, AKA your parents. Take good care of them.

Parents? Take care of our parents? someone whispers.

Mia strains to read the title. Can that be a Chekhov play?

They're all yours, the vice principal says and nods crisply to Mr. Yakimchuk before he leaves, closing the classroom door behind him.

How old do you think he is? Angela has come awake. Her note travels lightning-quick from three rows over and lands on Mia's desk. She crumples it.

Hedie Lodge's English students, even in their final year of high school, cannot resist making mileage out of the vulnerability that automatically disadvantages a substitute. While copies of *Uncle Vanya* make their way along the rows, one dropping on each desk, a small tempest of the kind that springs from nothing is already brewing.

Uncle Vanya!

Uncle Vanya?

What kind of garbage is that?

Garbage like we had last term—Arthur Miller.

That was *Death of a Salesman*.

That was in grade eleven, stupid.

I hated *Death of a Salesman*.

I hate plays, period.

Excuse me! A hand waves wildly, the corresponding voice unwilling to wait. Excuse me, Mr.Y ak, Yakim—the student turns to a neighbour—maybe we should just say Mr. Y?

As opposed to Mr. Who?

Sir, is this a good book? someone asks. I mean what's the value to me, the student, of reading a drama written by some dead foreigner? I'm not planning to become an actor. Or a playwright. Or even a stagehand. So why should I read a play? Plays generally stink, in my humble opinion. The cocky orator looks around for approval. A response comes quickly:

That's because you're a total idiot and you're missing a bloody brain.

The hubbub stops. Everyone is shocked to hear Mia Wittenberg speak up. Loudly. Slowly. Clearly. Mia is surprised too. But mainly furious. At her classmates for being stupid donkeys. And at this teacher for not standing up to them at once the way he should. The bantering so far is good-natured but it will quickly become malicious. And now, having spoken, she will be seen as siding with the administration. She doesn't care.

Miss Lodge is injured, she says, her voice unsteady. Seriously injured. Her life will never be the same. Ours won't be the same. Can't we just for one minute be serious?

Silence follows Mia's outburst. Even Bev Plett has nothing to add. Cowards, Mia thinks and wonders if this man will let her continue with her family story. Will she have to renegotiate? She will not join a group project. She will be bold. And demanding. She wonders if group projects will be part of this man's method. If he is the kind who lectures, he's dead.

The eyes of the class have been focused on Mia, but now one by one they turn away to search each other out, or to survey the room, gauging the lay of the land. Mr. Yakimchuk uses the temporary lull to send around a sheet of paper with a list of textbook numbers.

Sign your name beside the number that matches the one in your copy of *Uncle Vanya*, he says.

And that's exactly what some students do while others,

already recovered from Mia's scolding, sign at the wrong place or with the wrong name, creating confusion that the man with the unfortunate name will have to sort out. A false calm settles on the class while the sabotage is carried out.

A few students will dutifully read all of Anton Chekhov's play; a very few will like it. Others will read Coles study notes at least. Few will grasp the significance of the social upheaval central to the play. Or its despair.

Mia is surprised that this text was actually ordered. What was Hedie Lodge thinking? And what was she, Mia, thinking on that autumn day when she suggested the Chekhov play and her suggestion became a challenge for Miss Lodge? They are both to blame. And the hapless man standing before the class is saddled with the fallout.

Someone thrusts an arm into the air, the hand at the end of it flapping like a frantic bird. Excuse me, Mr. ... . Mr. Y, —whatever—shouldn't we be remembering the poor? I mean the kids. I mean here. Right here in Winnipeg. The poverty capital of Canada. It was in today's *Free Press*.

We should raise money, someone chimes in earnestly.

And collect clothes.

Yeah, scarves and socks.

Blankets. It's going way down to minus 35 tonight.

There's no more need to raise hands, the topic itself is permission to speak, to disrupt the class. It offers a focus and Mr. Yakimchuk doesn't need to be there at all.

Toys for Kids, we'll call it. (This is popular.)

I've got tons of GI Joes at home.

My old Barbie dolls. I'll bring them.

Barbie dolls! She's got bloody Barbie dolls!

Books for kids.

We need a committee.

Should we run this by the student council?

No. This is our baby. A class project.

Miss Lodge would like it, don't you think?

We'll call it the Ms. Lodge Save the Children Project.

A wave of energy fuelled by genuine concern, pure emotion, student opportunism and sheer mischief rolls over the class. Mr. Yakimchuk clears his throat as if he means to speak, but a student with a strident voice tinged with self-righteousness cuts in. What's with the narrow vision? Haven't you guys heard? The UN is getting ready to bomb Iraq. It's going to be all-out war, trust me. In the Middle East. And here we are so damn smug, so totally local. Disaster is brewing. Just watch our not-so-friendly giant next door roar into action.

And now Bev speaks. It doesn't have to happen, she says, her voice urgent. There doesn't have to be war. We should all … we should … She hesitates and at this moment the buzzer sounds, putting an end to all consideration of war or poverty or literature. Saddam Hussein and Anton Chekhov are both forgotten along with the city's poor. And so is Mr. Yakimchuk, who takes off his glasses and wipes them clean, as if to better watch as his students rush out the door.

Mia gives the new teacher a curious glance as she leaves. She's thinking that if Bev had completed her sentence she would have said, We should all pray.

The new school term has begun and there's Danny loitering near the lockers, waiting for her.

~

In the staff room Peter McBride joins a cluster of teachers huddled over coffee at a window table, retelling, arguing, speculating, guessing. Here too Hedie Lodge is headline news. Here too, information and gossip intermingle. She will not return to GSC, that much is certain.

It's a pity, someone says. She was popular.

A damn good teacher.

She will be permanently disabled. This is less certain.

Joseph Wittenberg flew to Toronto when it happened. To be at her side.

Absolutely not. Peter McBride is emphatic. And angry at this bit of hearsay introduced so glibly into the discussion. His outburst drives the idea underground, where it will lurk, waiting for an opportunity to surface again.

The teacher who chairs the social committee holds up the card she's bought for Hedie. The words WE'RE ALL ROOTING FOR YOU form a blue arc above a pastel spray of field flowers, yellow, mauve and white. I'll wire flowers too, she says, and if someone doesn't pay me, I'll be on your case. She hands the card around to be signed.

Joan Gustav opens the card and reads aloud: "With best wishes for a speedy and complete recovery." Tacky, she mutters. Cliché. She signs her name to the embarrassing card and passes it on.

This is hard on Joseph, someone says. Coming like this, on top of his grandson's disability.

What disability? Apparently not everyone has heard that Fragile X has surfaced in Joseph Wittenberg's family. Those who have are sympathetic. The biology teachers are more than ready to jump in with explanations. There is hubbub. There are questions. It's not an auspicious start to the new term.

This will really unnerve him, someone says.

Nothing unnerves our man, trust me. He'll handle it. Peter McBride wants Joseph left alone.

Tom Gibbs dashes in for a cup of coffee and reminisces, with anyone who will listen, about Hedie Lodge's car. How last

November he supervised his students as they replaced the fuel pump while expressing unanimous contempt for the small, low-powered model.

Joan glances uneasily toward the door as if expecting the VP himself to appear. Not likely. It's the first class of the new term and only those with a morning spare have the luxury of coffee and gossip. The administration will have plunged right in, dealing with a dribble of new students, exam follow-ups, and the replacement for Hedie Lodge.

Peter McBride pushes his empty mug to the centre of the table and gets up to leave. He turns to his colleagues. Whatever's gone on between them, let it rest already. Give the guy a break. He's got to move on. How about we all move on with him? How hard can that be?

It's not that simple, Claudette Avery mutters. She has just signed her name on the card for Hedie. At one time Claudette may have believed, perhaps hoped, that Hedie Lodge would provoke an occasion for Joseph Wittenberg to stumble and she, Claudette, would gain ground and overtake him on his way to the top. But Hedie will not return.

Tom Gibbs swallows the last of his coffee and dashes back to the automotive shop where he'll inflict on his aspiring mechanics a review quiz that will reveal how much or how little they can recall about transmissions, spark plugs and electric circuitry.

Claudette pours another cup of coffee and wonders if Joseph's heart is broken and how badly. All fall she expected Mia to come to the guidance office. Not for emotional support or stroking or consolation. Mia Wittenberg doesn't look as if she would ask for any of that. But even a good student like Mia needs information about scholarships and university programs. Mia, however , has not come. What is she waiting for?

~

The windless icy air mass that has descended on the city evidently means to stay. Night after night the thermometer falls to minus 30 and the sky is clear and black and seeded with stars. In the warm Gulf region, the UN has deployed its military forces ready to begin the bombardment of Iraq. Newspaper headlines scream predictions of imminent bloodshed and doom. Will it be this week? Will it be tomorrow? Television brings images of Iraq and Kuwait and Saudi Arabia into the city's living rooms. The world is waiting.

In the Mennonite church on Edison Avenue the pastor has announced a mid-week prayer meeting. It's what we do, he tells his congregation. We pray.

We have to be there, Bev tells Mia over the phone. I'll meet you at the church. Mia has not been to the church since Christmas Eve. She knows Bev will not invite Angela, who would claim she had homework and anyway is not Mennonite.

It's freezing cold, Mia says. She is reluctant to leave the warm house, but her friend's conviction is formidable. Yes, she says. I'll come with you.

Only if your dad drives you. Millicent has emerged from her bedroom in time to see Mia grabbing her jacket and has untypically intervened. Mia knows her mother is not concerned only about the temperature but also about Edison Avenue, which is not the safe thoroughfare it once was. It has become a bus route and the apartment blocks that have replaced the bungalows that long ago replaced the humble homes of the first Mennonite settlers are shoddy rental walk-ups. The population is transient and police cruisers are a frequent presence.

The prayer vigil is not on Joseph's agenda. He has not heard about it. But when Mia says, Please, Dad, he knows he cannot let this opportunity pass. This opening his daughter offers. And anyway he can think of no excuse, no urgent school business. Like Mia, he has not been at the church since Christmas Eve.

Not at choir practice, not at stewardship meetings. He finds his boots and winter parka.

The sanctuary is cold when they arrive, something wrong with the furnace. A small cluster of people huddles together in the four front pews. Bev is waiting for them. She leads the trio, late, toward the first pew, but Mia tugs at her parka sleeve. No. They slide into the fifth pew, Mia between Bev and her father. She can see her breath, white and frosty. On a low table, a cluster of lit candles.

Pastor Heese does not climb the steps to his usual place behind the pulpit, but rises from the front pew and turns to face the small evening flock. His voice and mien are earnest. He begins reading:

> How beautiful upon the mountains
> Are the feet of the messenger
> Who announces peace,
> Who brings good news, who announces salvation,
> Who says to Zion, "Your God reigns."

The phrase "good news" takes root in Mia's brain and her lips move automatically to repeat the words. Good news, good news. And then she whispers a single word: Jeremy. She wants to speak it out loud. Wants to say a prayer, but she can't get past his name: Jeremy. And then she thinks of Hedie Lodge, disabled. Please God, she wants to pray. Heal her. Let her walk again. She thinks of her mother, who could use healing too. And her father? But all such petitions would be too enormous to put into words.

When Mia thinks of Danny Haarsma she turns her hands palm up and curved like two empty cups on her blue-jeaned knees.

The pastor continues reading:

Blessed are the peacemakers
For they shall be called the children of God.

Bev is sniffling beside her and Mia isn't sure whether it's from the cold or is she crying. The pastor calls forward a teenager who reads the prayer of Saint Francis of Assisi: *Lord, make me an instrument of your peace ...*

He stumbles in his reading. When he comes to the line, *not so much seek to be consoled as to console,* he reads "controlled" and "control," causing Bev's sniffling to become a nervous giggle. She jabs Mia with her elbow and both girls struggle to suppress their laughter.

Then everyone sings:

Dear Lord, redeemer of our lives,
Forgive our foolish ways.
Reclothe us in our rightful mind:
In purer lives thy service find,
In deeper reverence, praise.

Drop thy still dews of quietness,
Till all our strivings cease;
Take from our souls the strain and stress
And let our ordered lives confess
The beauty of Thy peace.

Mia listens for her father's voice but he is silent.

Let's bow our heads to pray, the pastor says. Let's all pray quietly and I'll pray in conclusion. When all heads are bowed, there is silence, a long stretch of it, and Mia imagines the people in Iraq praying too. The men bent to the ground in the mosques the way she's seen on TV. The mothers at home, terrified for their children. And whose side is God on, really? Her father's lips aren't moving. Bev is quietly crying.

When the pastor breaks the silence it's with a simple prayer for peace around the world and in the hearts of everyone here assembled.

The benediction follows:

Live in peace
And the God of peace
Will be with you.

When it's over no one moves, as if they must stay together, or as if the cold outside deters them. Joseph is first to rise. He leaves quickly and the girls follow him into the frigid winter night and the sudden darkness of the parking lot.

Look, Mia says. She has tilted her head back to look at the sky, the vast black canvas spangled with a zillion glittering stars and the cold, bright planets. There is no moon.

There's Orion, she says, pointing. And the Milky Way.

Bev spots the Big Dipper.

Joseph comes to stand beside Mia. He puts his arm around her and looks up too. Mia shivers but doesn't shrink from him.

We can get a better look, he says. Come on. They drive east, out of the city. When they have escaped the last street lights, Joseph turns onto a side road and parks. They get out. Above them aurora borealis is a spiralling of light and colour, a celestial stage show that draws their gaze upward to its extravagant splendour and holds it there.

It's awesome, Bev says, her voice quavering with cold and emotion. It's just so beautiful. So amazing. So way above everything. More powerful than war, don't you think, Mr. Wittenberg? Thanks for bringing us.

Mia thinks if Bev will just be quiet they will hear the music of the spheres. They will hear angels singing.

They return to the city, drop off Bev and when they come home, Millicent surprises them with hot chocolate. She looks depleted, as if the effort of making it has exhausted her.

You should have seen the sky, Mom, Mia says. You should have been with us. She bends to fill her mother's cup and catches a whiff of alcohol on her breath.

Before the end of the week UN forces commence a bombardment of Iraq. Mia is getting ready for school when the radio announcer's voice announces the war to the world. She wishes she could stay home, considers skipping her first class, history, where Mr. McBride will allow the class to discuss this breaking news, unleashing a stream of opinions, unexamined ideas and ignorant suggestions. She isn't sure she's up to it. She thinks of how she shivered at the prayer vigil. She remembers the glorious night sky.

In the hallway, she finds Bev bending to pick up a poster someone has torn down and scrunched into a ball. Last week Bev joined like-minded students in posting "No bombs on Iraq" signs wherever they were allowed. She is crying and Mia knows her friend too is thinking of that evening at the church.

All Mia can think of to say is: We can't win every time, Bev. She holds out her hand for the crumpled poster.

Bev finds a tissue, blows her nose and wipes away her tears. We weren't wrong, Mia, she says pointing to the crumpled poster. We weren't wrong.

~

It's Friday afternoon, GSC's long halls emptied of students and staff, Joseph Wittenberg in his office, writing with his fountain pen on a white sheet of paper. He is composing a letter and so far he has written the greeting and one sentence:

Dear Pastor Heese.

In view of my inability to fulfill my church duties, I hereby give notice that I wish to resign from the stewardship commission and must also withdraw from the choir.

He adds a sentence: I owe the church an explanation. But what should he say next? What should the owed explanation include? He puts down the pen, closes his eyes and composes a possible list.

My duties as vice principal at George Sutton Collegiate keep me occupied more each year and I find myself overextended. (But isn't everyone at the tail end of the twentieth century overextended?) My wife is not strong and I must take that into consideration when budgeting my time. (When has he ever taken Millicent into consideration in measuring out his days?) My daughter has given birth to a child who will not thrive and my entire family is emotionally and psychologically drained. (But what is he actually planning to do to help Alice? And who in this world is not saddled with grief and disappointment?) I have committed adultery and am not fit to serve any longer in the church.

Joseph has no intention of telling the pastor any of this. The church is not as much in need of an explanation as he is of confession. He needs the confidentiality of a confessor. The privacy of a confessional. Absolution. A Mennonite church insists on the priesthood of the individual believer; it also insists on democratic discussion. Of everything. At one time adultery would have required a full airing in the presence of the members. He doesn't know if that has changed.

And what does God require? Joseph wonders. Does God, observing me, think, Well, I've given him free will, haven't I? As if free will is not also a burden. And anyway, is God really there? There, but aloof and distant? There and stubbornly silent? Where was God when Hedie Lodge, who is needed here at GSC, was driving down a Toronto street on a winter day?

An interruption would be welcome, but the phone doesn't ring and no one knocks. Joseph looks at his watch. His mother will be waiting. He stares at the unfinished letter.

It's the choir, Joseph thinks regretfully, that he will miss most. Those harmonies accompanied by the majestic swell of the organ: *Holy God, we praise your name ...*

Do integrity and honour require him to withdraw his membership from the church he has been part of since he was a teenager? From which he has come unmoored?

Just how did that unmooring happen? When did it begin?

Joseph was thirteen when his mother bought a house in North Kildonan, on Edison Avenue, the street where she had lived when her family first arrived in Canada. Neither he nor his younger brother Phil wanted to leave their city home, but they weren't consulted. Their mother simply gave notice to the landlord and began packing. A small white house with green trim became their home. From here the boys walked to school every day, and on summer evenings let the kitchen door bang shut behind them as they ran out to play baseball in the field that opened up where Edison Avenue ended. In winter they joined other boys to haul water to an empty lot to make a hockey rink. Joseph possessed a strong body that moved with easy fluidity. He was good at sports. He forgot about the city.

Edison and the parallel streets were a far cry from the self-contained colonies and villages the Mennonites had come from, Joseph knew that much. In this corner of the city they attempted to fashion from their chunk of land a community of like-minded people, people with a shared history, a shared language. And a shared faith. Sundays, Joseph walked with his mother and brother the short distance to the church that would soon be expanded. During the week there was boys' club, German school, then youth gatherings, and later he joined the choir, the baritone section. His rich voice persuaded the choir conductor to assign the baritone solos to this young chorister. He was popular. He loved singing in the choir. Still does.

But Joseph has let his mind meander too long in the past. The visit with his mother will be short. He crumples up the letter and begins again, writing the greeting and first sentence of the original letter on clean paper, signs his name, addresses an envelope and affixes a stamp. Outside it's colder than he expected and he's not properly dressed even for the short walk to the parking lot. On the way to Wild Oak Estates he stops at a mailbox, takes the letter from his pocket. It's halfway through the slot when he pulls it back. He is not satisfied with the letter. And not satisfied with himself. He jams the letter into his pocket. The cold stings his ears. He should have worn a toque under his parka hood. Don't you know any better? his mother used to say when he came home frostbitten. And suddenly he can't bear to face her. He turns around, and with the wind at his back returns to his car and drives home.

~

Marie Wittenberg blames the weather for the increased pain in her joints. Examining her swollen wrists and distorted fingers,

she remembers Agnes McKay's thick red hands and a sympathy
stirs in her heart, as if now, so many years later and Agnes long
gone, they have become sisters in pain.

For Marie there has been little reprieve this winter. The pills
have lost their potency, pain has raged in her joints, and often
she rises only when the low sun's rays filter through the venetians, imposing strips of light over the floral wallpaper. Some
days, when she has become mobile, she plays old tapes—a male
quartet singing, *On that resurrection morning when the dead in
Christ shall wake, we shall rise, Oh yes we'll rise.* The voices are
animated and she imagines the men dancing.

Today she's chosen a tape of German songs, as if only the
language of her childhood can offer comfort.

Wehrlos und verlassen sehnt sich
oft mein Herz nach stiller Ruh ...
(so defenceless and abandoned
my heart longs for quiet rest ...)

The song echoes the longing that wells up so frequently this
winter. It is a longing for another country. But is it a country
left behind or one still to be arrived at? While morning is the
time when pain attacks her body most fiercely, it's also when
her mind is at its sharpest. Today the words Fragile X Syndrome
float to the surface of her consciousness. Such big words for a
child's illness. There was a time when parents didn't ask so many
questions, like where did the disease come from? What caused
it? They simply believed it was sent by God, to remind them of
a divine presence. And of the fragility of life. She imagines life
and death as two figures moving toward each other, pausing,
stepping aside to avoid the other and at some point colliding.
Another loved one carried to the cemetery behind the church
and placed in the earth. Another grief for a mother to carry.

Another emptiness. And always the return to feeding the family, tending the garden, harvesting grain.

Harsh fevers took her siblings from this world before they could grow; before revolution could threaten them; before houses and land had to be abandoned; before an ocean had to be crossed; before they landed on an alien continent.

On Edison Avenue.

The faces of those dead children are blurring, their memory growing faint, and she hasn't taken down the brown velvet album in weeks. But the face of her mother always demands her attention. Marie can see it clearly without opening the album. Her mother did not live to cross the ocean. She never walked along Edison Avenue or planted a garden beside a small wooden house, or led a cow to pasture like the other women, or watched her children become adults. If it had been her mother instead of Elena there on Edison Avenue, everything would have turned out differently. Everything would still be different.

"Maria, I think from now on you will be the one to lead the cow to pasture," her father said on a rainy late-summer day on Edison Avenue. "You can see, can't you, it's getting too much for Elena."

It was true. Her stepmother had gained weight and moved awkwardly from stove to table, from chair to pantry. Maria had considered taking on responsibility for the cow, but hadn't known how to make the offer; she didn't speak easily to her stepmother. Concern for Elena was not the motivation. She was propelled by fear. The unmistakable signs of life taking shape inside her own thin body could not be denied though the evidence could still be hidden under a loose dress or a full apron. Her morning queasiness had so far gone unnoticed. But not for long. A solution was needed. Desperately. Her father would never know how his words brought hope to his daughter. How they came as the answer to a prayer that had for weeks trembled unspoken in her frightened heart.

Early on, Ronald McKay had presented a solution to the problem of her pregnancy. He had made inquiries, obtained the name and address of a woman who had ways and means. He offered to take her there and of course he would pay. The risk, he assured her, was not great. Didn't she want to be relieved of this worry? He himself was very anxious to be relieved of it. It frightened him. He showed more than a little surprise when Marie didn't grasp at the offered solution.

Agnes McKay, first to suspect Marie's predicament, let fall the information that girls sometimes went away for a time and when they returned, took up their lives again and all was well.

Marie shook her head. For her, all would not easily be well. Where would she go without her family knowing of it?

When summer gave way to fall Mrs. McKay informed Marie that she intended to sell her house and move into an apartment downtown. It will be inconvenient for you to come there, she said. I'll find another girl.

What about your ashes? Marie blurted, thinking of the apple tree.

Agnes McKay shrugged, as if she had given up on the ashes, then said, I'll tell Ronald to have them scattered on the river, and Marie wondered which river.

Any books you want? Agnes McKay asked. You can take them.

Marie chose the Jane Austen novels.

Joseph believes he is her firstborn. It's better he should. Better he should never learn of the foetus that might have become a child—boy or girl—except for her father's convenient sugges-tion that she should relieve her stepmother of a cumbersome chore.

She is grateful that her father never learned of that aborted child, but she wishes he had seen Joseph. And Philip too, of course. He'd be proud of his grandsons, especially the older one. But Abram Franz died that winter of a stroke and within a year Elena remarried—a widower with means to care for her and her three sons. He took her to live on the West Coast.

Marie also left Edison Avenue. She moved into a rented room in the city's West End and found a job at Eaton's, in the lingerie section. She made no effort to contact her stepmother, who never wrote to her. It was only when she returned to Edison Avenue with her two young sons that she learned of Elena's death, some years earlier. She wished then that she had known and had found a way to go to the funeral. She would have seen her two stepbrothers and her half-brother. But she could not afford to indulge in regrets, and although curiosity about her brothers surfaced from time to time, it was overshadowed by the cares and duties of the day.

On Edison Avenue she learned too that she wasn't the only woman on the street to be relieved of an unwanted pregnancy by a cow straining so hard at the rope that the woman at the other end of it could not hold on to the life inside her. Even if she wanted to.

When is Mia coming? Marie wonders. Today? Tomorrow? And how many more stories does she need? The responsibility of storytelling is becoming burdensome. She wants an end to it. Thank God, it won't be necessary for all stories to be told. Didn't Mia say the assignment will be finished when the school year ends? Well, then, there's no need to worry. They won't get as far as Edison Avenue.

Joseph never speaks to her of Edison Avenue. On his sporadic visits she's noticed that his hair is showing grey around the temples and his shoulders have begun to sag. More than once she's found herself wanting to scold him: Don't slump as if you're carrying the world on your shoulders. Like your grandfather lugging a sack of feed for the chickens on Edison Avenue. Sit up. Give your lungs space. It was advice her mother once gave her, but you don't tell a grown man what to do even if he happens to be your son. Even if he emerged miraculously from your body, a body that's become slack and wrinkled as a worn sock.

And you don't scold him for visiting seldom and leaving as quickly as the sparrows that perch for two, three seconds on a branch of the elm outside the window and then, poof—are gone.

~

February rolls in, cold and bright, the groundhog in retreat. Millicent, rising late, ties a dressing gown around her nightdress and forces herself to pour a cup of the coffee Joseph made before he left for school. She sips it at the kitchen table where sunlight brightens the checkered cloth and the faded floral wallpaper. Not so long ago, fuelled by anger, she'd believed she could strip the walls and paint them bright colours—a peachy coral or warm yellow. And once, after Jeremy's birth, she'd believed it was within her power to stave off calamity. Not Fragile X itself, but its toll on her family. But anger and energy have dissipated; she can't even stave off the torpor that creeps in and settles its weight on her spirit. She has given up resisting it.

Right now she is waiting for Mia to leave before she retrieves a bottle from its hiding place in her closet. She'll pour from it a generous dose of relief. Joseph seems to have forgotten the bottles in the downstairs bar. She hopes he has properly thanked the givers of gifts that will make it possible for her to endure the leaden hours of this short winter day.

But one day the supply will run out, and then what?

When Mia finally leaves, Millicent brings the bottle to the kitchen, sits down again and pours a glass. She lifts the glass for the first sip. Then another, longer drink.

This morning the decades of Millicent's life appear before her like a bleak landscape leached of vitality. The road ahead looks just as dismal, just as endless. Her own worthlessness is to blame for all of it. She refills the glass and lifts it to her lips.

~

DANIEL HAARSMA, REPORT TO THE OFFICE IMMEDIATELY.

The firm and resonant voice of Joseph Wittenberg, only slightly distorted by static, issues from the intercom, interrupting the English class. Mr. Yakimchuk, whose status has been upgraded from substitute to term position, has just given each student a copy of *The Glass Menagerie* and reminded them to locate and return the unfortunate *Uncle Vanya* texts. He has declared *Uncle Vanya* inappropriate and completely irrelevant. The cheer that greeted this wisdom is the most welcome sound he has heard so far in this classroom.

For once Mia agrees with him, though she resents his implied criticism of the class and their former teacher. She wishes she had never mentioned Chekhov to Hedie Lodge. She turns to look at Danny, seated at the back of her row. He's not moving.

Daniel, I assume you heard that. I assume you're not altogether stone deaf, though your hearing is peculiarly selective. Over the past weeks Mr. Yakimchuk has discovered sarcasm. It has become his weapon of choice. Last week the vice principal had to speak to the English class about mutual respect between students and teachers. He reminded them that each student represents the school both in the classroom and beyond the school boundaries.

Neither sarcasm nor her father's intervention can save Mr. Yakimchuk. He will not survive. Mia finds no joy in that.

Danny's limbs unfold slowly, unwilling to eject him from his desk and propel him forward. His face is hard as sheet metal. And pale. He moves clumsily along the aisle, arms dangling, and when he's next to Mia, she reaches out to let her fingers brush his sleeve. He ignores the gesture, continues toward the door, opens it, turns to look back, not at Mia, but carefully around the room as if to register each face. His last cold glance is aimed at Mr. Yakimchuk. Then he is gone.

So, what's up with Danny boy? Angela's predictable note finds a circuitous route to Mia's desk. Is he going strange? Is he stoned? For once Mia knows more than Angela, and wishes she didn't.

Mr. Yakimchuk begins reading the introduction to the new play straight from the book, interrupting himself to explain that the Wingfield family is poor and Tom Wingfield is a frustrated young man, a bird with clipped wings. The teacher drones on. Heads nod.

Mia sets her mind on Tom's poverty. What does she know about poverty? When she was in fifth grade her father set up a bank account for her and it grew like the ten talents in the Gospels. This year it would have financed her trip to Greece if she hadn't withdrawn it before Christmas to repay her father. Her Christmas gift money replenished the account, but yesterday she withdrew the entire sum.

You don't know these guys, Danny said, his voice, his thin body, his restless hands an agitation that scared Mia. They don't give up, he said. They're fuckin' armed. And they'll get you every time. You wouldn't believe how they operate.

Mia's stomach curdles. She doesn't want to believe that Danny is trapped in a web of drugs and dealers right here at the school, but she suspects his locker was searched during the recent visit to the school by three uniformed officers. Her father refuses to speak of it. Did someone at Kmart catch Danny shoplifting? She knows only what he chooses to tell her.

That's the absolute last, she told Danny yesterday, handing him the money. That's all I've got. She does not intend to use the family's credit card again, though she could. It still has its place on the shelf in the kitchen, and her father has not reprimanded her for anything since Christmas. Mia wants Danny to leave her alone. She wants the space he's occupied to be filled with good things. Like Jeremy. School. Her mother. Kurt? Kurt is preoccupied: it's basketball season. But still, he might call tonight and suggest a movie. Or, if they can afford it after pooling resources, a Jets hockey game. Mia is not excited about hockey, but she will sit through anything to be near Kurt.

Mr. Yakimchuk has reluctantly agreed to let her continue with her individual project. She must visit GranMarie and record the next story. Her grandmother's small apartment has became a welcome oasis in this long winter.

When Mia comes home after school, there's a letter from Hedie Lodge. She stuffs it into her jeans pocket. She's eager to read it but not in this dreary house. Her mother's door, as usual these days, is closed. She turns on the TV, finds *The Young and the Restless* and quickly flicks them off. Curiosity overpowers reluctance; she pulls out the letter.

Dear Mia:

This winter I've been given a gift—the gift of time, lots of it. Time for thinking, remembering, reviewing, rationalizing, blaming. This isn't fun and I don't intend to bore you with it. Most of all I'm grateful to be alive. It could so easily have been otherwise. I'm not sure I'll recover completely, ever. But I believe (at least at this moment I believe) that to live with a disability is better than not to live at all.

I am paralyzed. Waist down. But I can write and you are someone who will appreciate how important that is. This morning after rehab the sun slid out from under the clouds. I can't tell you how I miss the brilliant prairie sun.

Do you know what I think of most often? Our English classes. I seem to have forgotten anything unpleasant that happened there. Sometimes our discussions of literature managed to be lively, don't you think? All of you are so vivid in my memory. There was such energy, enthusiasm, silliness. In retrospect it was all good, though I wasn't always able to steer the ideas in the right direction. Was I terribly serious? Too stern?

I know you signed up for the trip to Greece and must be looking forward to it. And you'll be applying for university. Are you considering writing as part of your future? I know, I know I've asked you this before.

I'm writing this letter slowly with my more-or-less undamaged right hand, on a day when I have more hope than fear.

I just wanted to tell you how much I enjoyed each one of your stories. I hope you are continuing this project. Your family stories are wonderful and you must tell them. And I would love to read them.

And Mia, I hope your own story unfolds as it should: beautifully.

I've made mistakes, Mia, and I think you saw that all along. I'm afraid to think how I have hurt your family. Sometimes what seems like an opportunity, an invitation to happiness, turns out to be something else altogether.

I'm still trying to figure out this place where life has brought me.

I hope everyone in your family is happier than I can ever be.

Your friend,
Hedie Lodge

Mia reads the letter three or four times, folds it, shoves it back into the envelope and places it between the pages of *Uncle Vanya*, which she has not yet returned to Mr. Yakimchuk. She heads for the door, grabs her running shoes. She pauses, mid-lacing. There are other uses for the letter. She returns to her room, takes it out of the envelope, unfolds and smoothes it. She clears a space on her desk and places the letter in the centre of that space, the envelope beside it, and once more leaves her room, this time with the door ajar. In the hallway, the idea achieves full clarity. She goes back to switch on the desk light.

Her mother, despite her lassitude, is not chained to her bed. There is evidence that she sometimes enters Mia's room: pants picked up from the floor and hung over a chair, scattered books stacked neatly, the blinds opened to let light in, the violet watered. If she sees light in an unoccupied room, her mother will automatically switch it off because in the Wittenberg household economy is ingrained.

Mia also knows about the bottles. Where her mother hides them. And that her father has insisted on getting her doctor to refill the prescription for antidepressants.

She leaves the house and begins running. Sidewalks have been cleared of snow. She slows down at Kurt's house, just in case, but there's no sign of him. In fall she hoped Kurt would be the one she could depend on. For companionship. Someone besides Angela and Bev. A reprieve from Danny. But the coach has his eye on Kurt too, and sets rigorous schedules. Angela has found someone with broad shoulders, a thatch of dark hair and an inviting smile. Bev is on the committee that's planning graduation.

Mia tries not to think about Danny. Instead, she lets the details of Hedie Lodge's letter roam freely in her brain as she runs. The question about her writing. The praise for her stories. Her mother has never shown such interest in her writing. What does her mother think about in the course of a day? At night, with her husband bunked in Alice's old room? What could jolt her out of this depression? Does she still worry about Jeremy? Or her younger daughter? Does it ever occur to her that a daughter could worry about her mother?

Is it possible that Mia does not simply want to open her mother's eyes, jolt her out of lethargy, but actually wants to hurt her? Troubled, Mia keeps going, reaches the park, runs down every snowy path. Dusk arrives too quickly; gloom occupies the park. Headed for home, she thinks her mother may not have noticed the desk light. It's not too late. She runs faster, arms pumping, shoulders in motion, her body thrusting itself forward as if against an impediment.

When she's even with Kurt's house she stops, facing the front steps. She imagines the door opening, Kurt running down the steps to join her. They will jog back to the park, find a field of snow and lie down side by side to make snow angels. They'll struggle their way through snow down to the river bank and look up. There'll be a moon. They'll see the North Star and under that star Kurt will kiss her for the first time. Fuelled by this fantasy, she runs up the steps, rings the door bell. Twice. When there's no answer she bangs on the door, then, when the front light goes on, she flees down the steps and, arriving at the

Wittenberg driveway, is surprised to see her father's car. She's even more surprised to find both parents at the kitchen table. Her mother's hair, dull and loosely tangled, skims her dusky rose bathrobe, fallen open to reveal her nightgown. Her father is wearing the leather slippers Alice bought him for Christmas.

No meeting, Dad? Mia tries to be casual.

Cancelled. He offers nothing more.

Mia is aware that her mother is watching her. She hangs up her jacket and walks to her room. When she turns on the desk light she sees the envelope, letter neatly folded inside it and placed beside the copy of *Uncle Vanya*.

Her father calls from the kitchen, Mia, come join us, I'm making tea. His voice is steady.

The three sit together at the table without speaking, as if gripped in a sombre pact to maintain family solidarity. Mia feels a rush of loyalty toward both her parents. Joseph fills the tea cups.

Did anyone call? she asks.

No. No one.

~

The next day at school Peter McBride announces a meeting for all participants in the trip to Greece, including teachers and parents who will come as chaperones. In fall, Mia hoped her father would be one of those. Then she became afraid Hedie Lodge would come too. That fear is long gone, replaced by others.

I won't be at the meeting, Mia tells Bev and Angela. I'm not going.

Not coming to Greece! Mia, what's with you?

You're just kidding, aren't you? Mia?

Angela is genuinely alarmed; Bev incredulous.

I'm thinking of getting a job, Mia says. And I'll work on my English assignment. And spend time with my grandmother. None of these excuses satisfy her friends; Mia knows, but she moves to her next class with a sense of relief.

~

Lucas has been up a half dozen times, thirsty, hungry or simply checking: You here, Mom? You here?

I wouldn't leave you, sweetie, Alice says and tucks him in once more. Good night Lucas. She kisses him.

Where Daddy? Lucas says. Want Daddy.

I want him too, Alice thinks, her hand on the boy's hot forehead. Go to sleep, she says.

Jeremy was feverish again today and restless, Lucas demanding: Need blue truck. Mom. What you did with blue truck?

Her mother has stopped helping with meals and Alice scrambles to do the shopping, then the cooking. She is too exhausted to eat.

Brian said he'd be home by ten. It's already nearing midnight. Toasted raisin bread with cheese? Brian likes that. Should she put on the coffee or will Brian want a beer? Before she can decide, she hears his key in the door and then he's standing in the dim hall removing his jacket. She walks toward him, raises her arms like a robot, lets them circle his neck. Her slight body slumps against his and he is forced to hold her or she'll slide down to his feet. They stand like that for long moments during which Alice holds back her tears; Brian doesn't like her to cry, it leaves him helpless. He feels helpless too often. But now in the closeness and the silence he tightens his hold on his wife's fragility, her ribs, her small chin digging into him. The sobs she is withholding pulse against his chest. He lifts her, carries her to their bedroom, lowers her onto it, lies down beside her and finally she can let go the worries that have become a canker inside her. The sobbing is a sustained keening that threatens to spill into the room where the boys are sleeping. Alice forces herself to stop and when Brian moves toward her, she holds him close and will not let him go.

~

Millicent holds in her hand the vial with medication.: Three times a day with meals. She has not yet taken any of it, but now she will.

Joseph's bottles—she can't help thinking of them as his property which she has stolen—have mysteriously disappeared. Was she too greedy? Or has Mia had a hand in this? If a new supply has to be found, plans will need to be made. She has no strength for plans.

There is a simpler remedy. A remedy that frightens her.

Hedie Lodge has written to Mia. Has praised Mia's writing. The letter has verified Millicent's failure as a mother. The failure has been spelled out clearly and for that she is grateful. Although addressed to Mia, the letter is clearly also meant for her. It is a warning. And a cue. Nothing remains now but simple action. Hers.

The letter also concerns Joseph, Millicent knows that. Even if his name is not mentioned, he is surely meant. She thought, that evening, of showing the letter to him. But she lacked courage. Today she will be brave.

Millicent's affliction has settled like a pall on her innocent family, much like the pall that rests on Taylor and Lucas and now Jeremy. She can no longer bear any of it. Was there ever a grandmother as ineffectual as she is? The alpine evidence has piled up and hesitation is out of the question. She cannot make things better, but she can at least remove from her husband, from her children and grandchildren—and from Hedie Lodge too, though that's too late—a burdensome presence.

I'll escape the darkness, Millicent thinks. Darkness that is not a tunnel with a light at the end. I could claw my way toward even the tiniest pinpoint of light, but there is only the darkness.

She turns the vial in her hand. She opens it.

Yalta
(Assignment #6)

The port city of Yalta was recovering from a bloodbath when the Franz family arrived, Hanna coughing and exhausted, Simon saucer-eyed, Maria carrying her mother's three-legged stool. Abram Franz took Hanna's arm gently and led his family into the city.

Civil war had raged in Crimea, opposing armies pitted savagely against each other. Officers, so the hushed rumours claimed, were hacked to pieces, their limbs and torsos thrown into the Black Sea. The city's population was terrorized and devastated.

Shops in Yalta were still eerily empty and the people, recently emerged from hiding, looked warily over their shoulders as they queued for bread. A hush hung in the streets. The sanatoriums, hastily restored and painted white, shimmered like beacons from the tree-covered hills.

We've never been this far from home, Maria thought with a shiver. Barvenkovo seemed a world away. Before they left, her father had said he wasn't sure they would ever again call Barvenkovo home. The civil war had replaced the prosperity promised by the town's flourishing, smoke-belching industry with a day-to-day uneasiness and fear for the future. The new authorities had purchased the Lutzch factory but that was a charade. Abram had received just enough roubles to buy a pair of shoes for Hanna.

"Mama is wearing Lutzch on her feet," Simon had shouted as he ran laughing out of the house.

Abram had warned his family that the journey from Barvenkovo to Yalta would not be a pleasure trip, though he refrained from saying outright that they would be travelling from one devastation to another. Hanna had questioned whether the journey should be undertaken at all.

"Yes, it's a risk," Abram admitted. "But we have to try. In Yalta you will get your strength back. You won't be so tired. Your cheeks will have colour and you won't be always coughing." As if, once his wife arrived at the Black Sea, she would become the vivacious, sturdy woman he had married.

"And anyway," he might have added, "what have we left to lose?"

Simon could not be convinced that the trip would be anything but a thrilling adventure; why was everyone so frightened? He had watched impatiently as his father fashioned the three-legged wooden stool. "Who's that for?" he asked. "Me?"

"We don't want Mama sitting on the floor of a baggage car, do we?" Abram replied. He hoped to obtain space for his family through the good graces of a sympathetic officer who would have commandeered a train for his troops. And sure enough, a persuadable officer found room for them and their luggage and the stool in a corner of a baggage car. But no one could guarantee a safe arrival. All rail connections and schedules were in perpetual chaos and at any station, even between stations, they might be ordered out.

Before they arrived in Crimea they were transferred to a ship that took them across a stretch of the Black Sea, its waters still seeded with unsprung mines capable of ending any journey. When they finally arrived in Yalta and felt its firm streets under their feet Hanna declared it a miracle.

The Franz family settled in for a second miracle—Hanna would be healed.

"You came all this way? With this sick woman? And young children?" The doctors stared at Abram, shocked. As if he had committed an atrocity or was stupidly blind to the new realities that now ruled this ransacked place.

Hanna was admitted to a recently reopened sanatorium halfway up a hillside and assigned to a freshly painted room with windows facing the sea. Light poured in, dazzling the white walls, blinding Hanna as she lay on the clean bed. The doctor announced that her left lung would have to be collapsed. He ordered rest. The windows were to be kept open to let the healing Black Sea breezes waft in. And her diet must be supplemented. Eggs were recommended. With sugar, if sugar could be obtained.

Abram found a room to rent and proceeded to establish a routine for his children. Simon was not easily confined to one room and had to be entertained. Every day after breakfast Abram took one of the eggs they had brought from Barvenkovo, broke it into a cup, added a half teaspoonful of sugar and beat it with a fork until it foamed. He covered the cup with a clean handkerchief and, holding it with care, climbed up the path to the sanatorium. Maria and Simon tagged along behind. The path led past empty shops, past an old hotel waiting to be rebuilt, and up the steep incline to the white sanatoriums gleaming through a screen of leafy chestnut branches. Brother and sister followed their father into the clinical atmosphere and antiseptic smell of the room where their mother lay pale as a ghost, in a white gown on a white bed hemmed in by white walls.

Maria began to think of her mother as a saint. She'd been taught to speak her prayers directly to God and had little knowledge of saints, though once or twice her teacher had taken the class to the orthodox church in Barvenkovo and the priest had introduced the young Protestant visitors to worship, instructing them when to kneel, when to bow. The children were entranced by the colour and bustle in the church, the incense that sent wisps of smoke and smell swirling around them, the mournful harmonies of choral music; the altars where people knelt, the linen-covered table where the prayers of the people, scribbled on bits of paper, were read by a priest. Candles sputtered everywhere, and the busy back-and-forth was nothing like the simple service in the plain Mennonite church they were accustomed to. Maria had stared at the icon wall from where the austere faces of saints, haloed with gold leaf, glittered in the faint light, and a multitude of piercing eyes followed her.

The eyes of Maria's mother shone too, in a way that sometimes frightened her, as if, before directing their attention to her children, those eyes had been gazing on visions in another place. Not this white room. Not the city of Yalta with its beech and chestnut trees and green surrounding hills, not the Black Sea where they would soon swim, not even the house in Barvenkovo which they could no longer call home, but a place much farther away. A better place, Maria thought. A beautiful place.

Hanna rarely smiled, and when she did, her daughter thought of sunrise.

Maria would not have wanted to be anywhere else but here in Yalta with her mother. A fragile, temporary peace hung over the city nestled in hills and lapped by the Black Sea. Here her father, whose factory had kept him always away from his family, was free of work. He filled his days visiting his wife, entertaining Simon, making meals with Maria, who helped tidy the rented room and took her turn in the bread queue. Maria felt secure in the circle of her small family and didn't miss her friends. She and Simon had been promised that they, children of the steppes, would swim in the Black Sea and Simon was beside himself. "The sea, the sea!" he demanded. "When am I going to swim in the sea?"

And there was Livadia—the summer palace of the tsar's family. The place where the royal children had come to spend leisurely summers. The tsarovitch in his sailor suit, the princesses in flowery dresses. All gone now. "Led like lambs to the slaughter," Hanna had lamented. She was shocked to hear that Livadia was now open to the public, open to ordinary people who had hated the tsar and wished his family no good. For her part, Maria was thrilled at the prospect of walking where the princesses had walked. But she knew better than to clamour like Simon.

When Abram had called Maria aside one day in Barvenkovo and told her the tsar and his family were reported dead, murdered, Maria had felt as if her world was being squeezed by a monstrous hand. "Don't tell your mother," he'd said. But her mother had known and she had cried.

Here in Yalta Maria tried to imagine the youngest princess, Anastasia, in a white dress, playing with her brother Alix in the gardens at Livadia. Impossible that they could be dead.

Mid-summer, when the scarcity in the markets showed

no signs of easing and they were running out of the flour, sugar and eggs they had brought, Abram spoke of returning to Barvenkovo for fresh supplies. "I'll go alone," he said. "I won't be long."

"Don't leave us," Hanna begged. "You won't be safe."

Only when Abram promised to avoid Barvenkovo and go instead to Wassilyevka, where he would visit her friend Elena Sawatsky, did she consent to let him go. Elena's husband had taken ill with typhus in spring and Hanna wanted news. When Elena had come to Barvenkovo to wish her friend a safe journey she had whispered, "I'm pregnant."

"What a time to bring a child into the world," Hanna had said to her husband and Maria heard her add, "I'd give my right arm to bring another child into the world."

"Look after Simon," Abram told Maria and made the landlady promise to look in on the children. He didn't need to remind Maria to avoid the sea. And to visit her mother every day. "Don't be afraid, Maria," he said.

When her father left, the landlady said to Maria, "You are the mother now." Maria didn't need to have the seriousness of her responsibility pointed out. She felt sure that some danger she couldn't see threatened them and she must protect Simon and even her mother. against it. Simon was not always cooperative, but when Maria noticed her mother's face gaining a touch of colour she thought she could bear anything. She kept her mind on her father's return with food and news of home.

"He'll come back and we'll all go down to the sea," she assured Simon as they trudged uphill to the sanatorium, Maria carrying the cup with the last beaten egg. And we'll go to Livadia, she thought, although she had dreamt one night that the palace was haunted by shadows of the children who once played there, the faint voices of Anastasia and Alix wailing through the empty, elegant rooms.

Whenever Maria stood in line for bread, she dragged Simon with her. "Don't grab me," he complained. "You're always grabbing me." But Maria remained relentless. On one humidly hot day, in a discouragingly long line, her hand let go of her brother's and she slumped onto the sun-baked ground. Simon screamed. Someone bent over Maria, a glass of water appeared, her head was raised.

"Don't tell Mama," Maria warned her brother when she had regained enough strength to walk slowly back to the rooming house where the alarmed landlady put her to bed.

Even Simon was beginning to understand that their mother needed to be protected.

Late one night Abram returned. Another miracle, Hanna would insist next day. The children wasted no time investigating the bags of roasted **Zwieback** their father let them open while he held on to the carefully packed eggs. Simon grabbed the bread, squealing like a hungry pig, as if Maria had not fed him during their father's absence. Maria poured lukewarm **Prips** and he dipped the bread in his cup, letting it become soggy, then sucked it noisily. Next morning she broke the dry, capped buns into bowls of milk for their breakfast. On Simon's she sprinkled sugar.

They brought some to Hanna, who immediately dipped one in her still-warm tea. The children watched, standing near her bed. It was a reunion Maria would always remember as serene and beautiful, all four of them together in a place that was brilliant and white and safe.

"How did you find Elena?" Hanna asked.

Abram had had time to prepare for this question. "What can I tell you about your Elena?" he mused, evasively. "She has her boy to look after. I could see how he's growing."

Hanna did not enquire about Elena's pregnancy in the presence of her children. She dipped the **Zwieback** a second time, lifted it to her mouth, then paused and looked up at her husband. "I have a feeling I'm eating funeral food," she said and let the bread fall from her hand. "Tell me, Abram," she demanded.

Yes, he admitted, the **Zwieback** had been baked for the funeral of Elena's husband. Abram had missed the funeral by only one day. The leftover baking had still been fresh and soft and he had been hungry after the journey from Yalta. Elena had roasted the rest and insisted he take some back with him. For Hanna. For the children.

Hanna wept, her hoarse sobs racking her lungs, her thin chest heaving.

"Elena said I should bring you home," Abram said, taking his wife's hand. "She said she would find room for us all. She wants to take care of you. Help you get well." He did not say that Elena, left alone with a farm and a young boy and a pregnancy, also needed help.

Hanna's sobs eventually stopped, and her convalescence continued. Slowly. By October she was allowed to walk with her family on the wide promenade along the Black Sea from where the battleships were not visible. Her husband's arm supported her; the two children skipped ahead. In a newly reopened shop Abram bought a beige shell, pink inside.

"It will be our souvenir from Yalta," he said, giving it to Hanna, who put it to her ear.

"Yes, I hear it," she said. "The sea."

"Give it to me," Simon shouted. "I want to hear the Black Sea."

His mother handed him the shell. "It's not the Black Sea,"

she said. "It's a much larger ocean and the waves are beating against the shore of another country."

"What country?"

"Far away. Listen."

In November Hanna declared herself so homesick she no longer wanted to stay in Yalta. "I must go back," she said, and Simon cried, "Me too. Let's go home."

"Where will we sleep?" Maria asked. Her father had explained that their house in Barvenkovo was now occupied by strangers and the town unsafe for them. It might be simpler, Maria thought, if they all stayed in Yalta. They had gone swimming in the Black Sea only once and still hadn't visited the tsar's summer palace.

"We will stay with Elena," Hanna said. "She is alone now. We must help her in the fields." "We," as if she had miraculously acquired strength for field labour, which in any case would already be completed.

Abram had no other plan to offer. He would have preferred to return to the clang and clatter of the Lutzch factory in Barvenkovo, to the noisy production of plows and harrows, the heat of the foundry where huge flywheels were fashioned and laid on the ground behind the buildings to cool. He had learned to love the industry, with its stench of oil and grimy black smoke. But his body had retained the familiar rhythm of field work, his hand holding the reins, guiding the plow, the sun burning his face. He would not be unhappy to return to Wassilyevka as long as Hanna was well.

The doctors reluctantly discharged Hanna. "But she must go regularly for treatment," they warned, writing down the addresses of doctors in Kharkov. "And she must rest."

On the last morning Maria boiled the remaining eggs while her father tied their baggage with cords for the journey home, but not to Barvenkovo. They had not visited Livadia even once. The hours for public tours had been curtailed, and on the few occasions when they tried, the palace had not been open. They had walked to the beach several times to swim, but never for a whole day as Simon demanded.

"Your mother is waiting for us," Joseph always said and Simon ran enraged into the water, stubbing his toes on the rocks that cluttered the beach and the sea bottom. His father rushed to retrieve him. At the sanatorium the boy refused to smile for his mother. "I want to stay here," he cried.

"We'll come again," Joseph promised. "Your mother will be well and we'll be tourists and see everything we want to see. You can stay all day at the beach." But he spoke without conviction, as if he doubted his own words.

Maria knew no one her age in Wassilyevka, the village her parents once called home and where Elena lived. She couldn't imagine living in a farming village in a house that didn't belong to them. We are returning, she thought, but we are not going home.

~

The Wittenbergs are ushered into a bright room dominated by potted plants, a ficus in one corner, a large fig tree in another, hanging spider plants above a lamp. All of the greenery looks real; all of it is fake. The counsellor seats them at a table and moves the vase with silk roses to one side so she can see everyone. Mia sits nearest the door and holds her English assignment on her lap where her parents and the counsellor can't see it. The assignment is due today. She would like to reread it one more time when all this is over, but she'll have to hurry, and the meeting will have to be quite short if she is to be on time for English class.

Maybe rereading isn't such a good idea. Flaws will be revealed, weaknesses, omissions, and she'll just want to keep on adding, deleting, editing and Mr. Yakimchuk will not extend the deadline, even if she should tell him of her mother's crisis, which of course she would not dream of mentioning.

Don't forget, he never fails to tell her, you are riding along on privilege. And privilege can always be revoked.

His threats annoy Mia, who is glad that she has enough raw material for the next several stories because now she must stay with her mother on Saturdays and evenings when her father is at a divisional meeting for administrators, or summoned by the principal for some emergency at the school.

The current emergency has long lurked in the Wittenberg bungalow but now it is brazenly occupying it completely. Millicent has come closer than she's ever come to being swallowed by the darkness that all her life has lain in wait for her. Yes, all my life, she tells the counsellor who has convened this meeting. I didn't just wander in the wilderness, she says. I settled in it.

Can that be true? In spite of all the accumulated evidence of her mother's struggle, Mia is appalled.

Joseph sits beside Millicent, fidgeting nervously as if he can't believe the Wittenberg family needs the services of a counsellor. Mia heard him assure the doctor that he will personally make certain his wife takes her medication as prescribed, but these counselling sessions, the doctor insisted, were not negotiable.

Mia watches her parents from across the table. She wishes her sister could be here with her unfailing optimism. Of course I'll be there, Alice said when she was told about the appointment, and wrote the date on her calendar. But this morning she called to say Jeremy had come down with a fever.

It was Alice who had pounded at the door three days earlier and called, Mother! Mother, are you there? And when she
opened the door and saw what she saw, called an ambulance. I
felt like I was sent by God, she said later. Sent to stop the worst
from happening. She'd had Jeremy with her, but thank God, not
Lucas. He would have gone berserk, she said. God just took care
of everything. Jeremy slept through it all like a sweetheart.

But today Jeremy is sick and Alice is not here.

The counsellor rallies the trio in front of her. We need the
total picture, she says and directs them to visualize their household on Kildonan Drive, the three people who occupy it (Papa
Bear, Mama Bear, Baby Bear, Mia thinks as she stares at the fake
fig tree), their coming and going, the goals they can reasonably
set for themselves. The future, immediate and long-term.

We will talk about how you, Millicent Wittenberg, fit into all
of this, the counsellor says. In your own view and in the view
of your husband, Joseph, and your daughter, Mia. We will work
our way through. We will put the pieces of the picture together.
The counsellor makes eye contact with each person as she
names them. She has an enormous head of platinum hair and
yellow metal jewellery to brighten her navy jacket.

Who does she think she is? Mia is not impressed as she considers the woman's long, bejewelled fingers holding the sheets of
papers she'll distribute to her clients at the end of the meeting.
Mia turns to watch her mother.

Maybe the worst is over, Millicent is saying as she raises her
face to the counsellor. Millicent's face is thin and white but her
eyes have life in them.

Mia is not going to take for granted that the worst is over.

I'm taking the medicine, Millicent says, her voice soft but
steady.

And it'll be up to me to make sure she takes the right dose,
Mia thinks, wondering if her father is thinking the same thing,

and who will actually guard the supply and oversee the measuring out?

The counsellor rises to print in large letters on a flip chart: THE WITTENBERGS. And under that, three headings: MILLICENT, JOSEPH, MIA. She intends to make a list under each name, she explains. Of each person's strengths. Of what they can contribute. Of their wished-for outcome.

Next she's going to promise us our hearts' desires, Mia thinks and shifts in her chair. She wonders if this woman sees the Wittenbergs as an item on her agenda. Another file in her bulging case load.

A situation such as this—the counsellor gestures toward Millicent—can be viewed as an insurmountable problem, but it can also be viewed as an opportunity. She pauses. An opportunity for change. Change for the better.

A poster under the clock features a smiling young woman with a perfect complexion and teeth; the caption under the woman says: Love the skin you're in. Love, Mia notes, is a word no one in this room has spoken. As if love has nothing to do with the pieces the counsellor wants them to put together. And with the total picture.

Would everyone like some water? the counsellor asks and reaches for the pitcher at her elbow.

Joseph sighs as if he is being offered milk and a cookie.

Mia looks at her father. We are both absent from school, she thinks. We are AWOL. She glances at the story she holds in her hand, the story of Hanna Franz, her grandmother, released from the sanatorium, going home. Well, not really home.

Why don't we just all go home? Mia wants to say to her parents and the counsellor.

An ear-splitting wail, coming as if from nowhere, fills the room and all three Wittenbergs jump up, hands clapped to their ears. The counsellor remains seated, annoyed at the interruption.

I should have warned you, she apologizes. I knew we were in for a routine check of the alarm system.

Joseph takes the alarm as a signal for their release, they need stay no longer. Mia is relieved—she will deliver the essay on time. She is also glad the others can't see into her critical mind. The counsellor has no choice but to book another appointment for her clients. We'll continue right where we left off, she says with all the good cheer she can muster while the Wittenbergs troop out one after the other.

~

Several weeks later Millicent surprises her family with a roast beef dinner complete with Yorkshire pudding and mashed potatoes. Not much is said around the table, but Mia senses a small current of new energy. Her father's face is hopeful as he takes second helpings of everything and declares the meal delicious. Her mother doesn't eat much but passes the dishes and receives Joseph's praise with a faint smile. The medication is working.

No dessert, Millicent announces, and adds, with amused defiance, You didn't think I could do this, did you?

Of course you can do it, Mia says, uncertainly. And I know you'll do it again.

The dinner's marvellous, Joseph says. It's wonderful.

~

When it becomes safe to say that Millicent has rallied, Mia becomes restless and gets a job at McDonald's. Also a driver's licence. You might have to take late shifts, her father says. You'll need the car. Streets are icy on the day of Mia's test, but she passes it easily.

Sometimes her shift coincides with Kurt's, who has worked at McDonald's since Christmas. They are both at the counter the day Danny Haarsma appears in the lineup and Kurt takes his order for a hamburger. Want a drink with that? he asks.

Danny, counting his change, hadn't noticed Kurt at the counter, but hearing the familiar voice he looks up. Uh, no, he says, shuffling the coins. Wait a sec. Yeah. A Coke. He puts money on the counter, takes his Coke and hamburger and is about to leave when he sees Mia. His eyes focus. When do you get off work? he asks.

Mia stutters something incoherent before turning to the next customer.

She gets off when I do, Kurt says. His words are brusque, his tone a warning. Danny walks away.

Kurt and Mia leave together when the shift is over. At first they walk, then break spontaneously into a jog. You're not going to change him, Mia, Kurt says. Better just keep him out of your life. Mia suspects that Kurt knows more about Danny than she does. That he's heard things she has not. She would like to ask him but her voice would be unsteady. Not because of Danny, but because Kurt, who is running so close beside her, has her well-being in mind. He wants to protect her.

~

In mid March the days are long enough for the sun to melt the surface of the snow. Spring is in the air. The Gulf War is over, though oil wells continue to burn in Kuwait, mothers in Iraq mourn their dead, and the destruction has scarred cities and countrysides. The world has lost no time in turning its attention elsewhere.

One morning Millicent sees two crows swoop down and settle like black paper cut-outs on a white drift shrinking in the garden. That evening she announces her intention to volunteer at the thrift store in the city's North End. Joseph and Mia exchange nervous glances. They don't know what to make of it. Both are relieved that the family counselling sessions will soon be over and that Millicent is taking the medicine apparently even when she's home alone. She is recovering, but this unusual initiative is baffling. They can't believe she will actually spend a six-hour shift in a dingy space smelling of dust and old clothes.

I'll drive you, Joseph says.

No, I can take the bus. Millicent's tone is firm; Joseph is silenced.

Becoming a do-gooder, Mom? Mia asks. That's so totally Mennonite. How come the thrift store?

Someone from the church called, Millicent says. From *your* church. She looks at Joseph. They need volunteers.

Joseph appears to be ready to object to this impossible plan, but isn't sure he has that right.

Well, good for you, Mom, Mia says. She can't imagine her mother pulling on boots and a warm coat every Thursday, waiting at the bus stop and mingling with thrift store customers who might as well be from another planet.

Jesus always sided with the poor, didn't he? Alice says. And we should too. She hugs her mother. You'll be their angel, Mom, I know it. She doesn't say Millicent should be helping her with Jeremy and Lucas as she used to—a plan that has occurred to Mia.

On Millicent's first day at the thrift store March has become a lion. Well before opening time, shivering customers are waiting for the door to open. She sees them stamping their feet in the snow and peering impatiently through the frosted glass.

Millicent is assigned to the front counter, where she's partnered with Elaine, a short stout woman who says, You pack. That's easy enough. I'll handle the till.

When the store manager flips the sign from CLOSED to OPEN the people pour in, bringing with them clouds of frigid air. Millicent watches the chilly flow of shoppers divide into tributaries, one stream flowing toward the clothes racks: women's sweaters, teen clothing, boots and shoes, pants, mittens and men's underwear. All women's blouses are fifty cents today, a homemade sign announces. Another stream heads for kitchenwares and another continues down the main aisle toward the sofas and fridges crowding the back of the store.

Millicent is mesmerized by the restless swirl of people in motion. A whole new world she didn't know existed in her city is opening up before her like a movie. A red-faced woman with a gaudy East European kerchief in green and gold floral design knotted firmly under her chin is holding the door for a raven-haired man struggling to manoeuvre his wheelchair in off the street. More icy air blows in. Three boys, all more or less the same size, come with their mother, tear away from her and run toward the toys.

Come back here, the mother yells. Right now.

Millicent thinks of Alice and feels a twinge of guilt.

The raven-haired man rolls his wheelchair to a rack of vinyl records.

Retired? Elaine asks, appraising the new volunteer.

No, I-I'm—I mainly work at home. She is surprised to be considered retirement age. She looks down at her clothes, black turtleneck sweater and nearly new jeans. She touches her hair with her hands.

I come every Thursday, Elaine says. Been coming now for six years.

Millicent has no reply. She mulls over the fact that she and Elaine will meet every week on Thursdays and wonders if she will find a place in this Mennonite effort to help clothe the poor and furnish their rooms with used furniture.

The woman with the floral kerchief is first at the checkout counter. Her face, less red now, is lined and sagging. She heaves an armful of goods onto the counter and Millicent reads out the prices for Elaine, then shoves the items into plastic bags she helped smooth out before the store opened. A dozen women's blouses, six pairs of pants, men's and women's, a pair of men's long underwear, three quilted jackets, several pairs of socks, polyester neckties, a good wool coat, a mountain of children's clothes and some well-used bedsheets. The total amounts to thirty-four dollars and fifty-seven cents.

I buy for Ukraine, the woman says, gesturing with her arm toward the bags Millicent has filled. All this I buy. You give me please discount.

I can't, Elaine says, shaking her head and holding out her hand for the money.

I buy here so much, the woman objects, her voice rising to a high-pitched whine. Every day I buy. Please, a discount. She holds out a twenty.

Sorry. Elaine's voice is gentle.

The woman digs into her pocket for another ten, looks directly at Elaine, who takes the money, and when the woman doesn't offer the rest, simply shrugs.

Everything's already so cheap, Elaine says after the woman leaves, still muttering that in Ukraine they suffer, they are poor, you don't know how poor, they have nothing, they are there so close to death, as she walks stiffly out into the cold street.

I was close to death too, Millicent thinks.

In the afternoon, there's a lull, the flow of people almost at a standstill.

So how come you decided to volunteer? Elaine asks.

I … I … needed to do something … you know … something to get me out of the house. My family thinks I've gone crazy.

Elaine eyes her appraisingly.

You guys got any kids' boots? A tall aboriginal woman, two girls in tow, stops at the checkout.

Elaine looks at Millicent. Nods.

Over here. Millicent leads the trio to the rack of footwear. She looks down at the children's feet and points out several pairs that might fit, but the woman ignores her. Which? she asks her children, who sort through the selection like mittened animals.

I remember shopping for boots when my children were this small, Millicent says timidly.

The woman holds up two pairs of boots for her girls, who sit on the floor and kick off their old footwear.

Girls, Millicent says. I have two daughters. Like you.

Girls are good, the woman says, glancing up at Millicent. Mine don't give me no trouble. So far. Touch wood. She taps a wooden shelf.

Boots in hand, the children and their mother follow Millicent back to the checkout, where she puts the boots in a bag while Elaine rings them up. Her eyes follow the family out the door into the cold. Where will they go with their boots? Where do they live? What will that tall woman serve her children for lunch? The older girl must be school aged. Why isn't she at school today?

That evening at supper, while Mia serves chilli she made after school, Millicent can't stop talking about the thrift store. She describes the girls trying on used boots, the man in the wheelchair, the woman who came shopping for Ukraine.

Ukraine, Mia says. That's where GranMarie comes from.

Yes, our roots are in Ukraine, Joseph offers, wanting in on the conversation.

My roots are in England, Millicent says, annoyed with herself for not making the connection between the Wittenberg family and Ukraine. Then she goes on: Whenever the backdoor buzzer rings, it's somebody dropping off donations. Next time I'll take something with me, something we don't need. We don't ever use that blue stoneware breakfast set.

Joseph looks up. That breakfast set was his Christmas present for Millicent.

You're really going to lug all that stoneware on the bus? Mia is skeptical. Both she and her father are astonished at the way Millicent has led the conversation over supper. Millicent is surprised too.

The next day, Millicent begins cleaning the kitchen cupboards. Mia finds vases grouped on the counter beside the blue stoneware, a coffee grinder and an old toaster. The table is covered with stacks of tea towels and tablecloths and napkins, clusters of serving spoons, carving knives, extension cords, salt and pepper shakers, a pretty crystal bowl she can't remember ever seeing and a dozen wineglasses.

Looks like we're getting ready to move, Joseph says, when he arrives home. Where to?

We have so much, Millicent says. It's not fair.

Mia thinks of Danny, who lives with his mother in a shabby house on Edison Avenue. The bus stop in front of their house is always strewn with litter. Poverty doesn't exist only in the inner city, she tells her mother. It's here in the suburbs too.

In the following weeks, the Wittenberg kitchen is slowly emptied of all things unnecessary. And of some things that aren't. Joseph will look in vain for his favourite mug, Mia for the pot in which she likes to cook pasta. Two African violets disappear from the windowsill. Millicent packs them in a carton padded with old newspapers and waits for a mild Thursday.

You didn't ask me, Joseph teases. I'm the one who watered the violets. He is cautiously delighted at Millicent's sudden display of industry. It's a miracle. He hopes it will last.

My mother's reinventing herself, Mia tells Bev. One of these days—bingo—she'll emerge like that proverbial butterfly from that proverbial drab cocoon.

Privately, Mia watches her mother for signs of happiness. Some days she seems nearer to it than any other Wittenberg.

~

Mia, still nervous about driving her father's Camaro, turns into Alice's driveway hoping she won't find her sister euphorically upbeat or the baby sick and squalling. As soon as Alice lets her in, Lucas sidles up muttering, Anniemie, Anniemie. He pokes at the bag she's carrying. She holds it beyond his reach with one hand and with the other pins the curious boy firmly to her side. Her sister, Mia sees, is exhausted.

I've got something for a good boy, Mia says, releasing Lucas.

He tries to stand stock still, but both hands flutter like the wings of a butterfly and his body quivers with wanting what's in that bag. His eyes shift from it to Mia's face. What? He whispers, hoarsely.

Well, let's see. Mia pulls a bulky, wrapped package from the bag and hands it to him. His clumsy fingers tear at the paper and pull out two stuffed animals, a brown bear and a black cat with four white paws. Lucas grunts with pleasure. I liberated them from one of Mom's thrift store piles, Mia tells Alice.

I remember these, Alice says. Aren't they just so cute? You're a lucky duck, Lucas. Say thank you to Auntie Mia. She hurries off in the direction of Jeremy's whimper.

Lucas move his animals around with clumsy hands. Mia remembers how his birth catapulted her father over the moon and pulled her mother briefly out of sadness. Even at the first signs that not all was well there was no alarm. Lucas was adorable, he'd get over it. Today his helplessness exasperates Mia. He lets go his animals, as if unable to think what else a bear and a cat might do.

Give them pretend food, Mia prompts, impatiently. Popcorn and cookies. Make them talk.

Lucas grasps the bear with one hand, the cat with the other. His face becomes taut with the effort of making animal sounds that never amount to anything but small, pathetic woofs. Mia grabs the animals and before Lucas knows what's happening a cat and a bear lunge at him with exaggerated meows and hisses and a threatening roar. He lets out a desperate wail and Alice comes running, Jeremy in her arm. Embarrassed, Mia sets the toy animals on the floor beside Lucas. Her sister laughs awkwardly and offers her the baby. Mia cradles him close to her chest. How fragile he is. His small hand reaches for a silver button on her jacket and bumps up against her throat instead.

Alice asks, So is Mom still giving away everything plus the kitchen sink these days?

She's starting on the furniture, Mia says. Remember the gold velvet cushions I used to spread on the floor to build a yellow brick road? They're gone. And so are those small nesting tables you always arranged for your tea parties. Should I have kept them for you?

Those old things? No way. Who needs more clutter? Alice retrieves Jeremy, who has resumed squalling, and rocks him, walking back and forth, back and forth in the kitchen with detours to the hall and living room. Isn't it a miracle, Mia, how Mom is concerned for the poor? God has given her this precious gift of compassion. It's wonderful.

Mia bites her tongue. Yeah, she says. Mom's fast becoming Winnipeg's Mother Teresa. Just watch her leave us and head out for heathen lands.

Oh Mia! Alice chides, and placing Jeremy on the table, lets herself down on a chair. Mia sits opposite her. Alice, she says earnestly, leaning toward her sister, how do you do it? She expects Alice to say, as she's said so many times, One day at a time. It's entirely possible. I'm not alone.

Instead Alice crosses her arms on the table and lowers her head onto them as if she is putting herself to rest the way she puts Jeremy to rest in his crib. Mia reaches across Jeremy and places a hand on her sister's head, on the tousled, lustrous hair that everyone admired because it complemented her dark eyes and fresh face. So pretty, they said. No one ever told Mia with her straight brown hair and serious grey-blue eyes that she was pretty. Today she's noticed lines around Alice's eyes. Her sister is aging. Mia places her other hand on Jeremy and for a while the only sound is Lucas muttering to his bear and his cat. Then Alice raises her head and reaches to clasp Mia's hands in hers. You're blessing me, she says. Your hand is blessing me.

Mia, embarrassed, says, Just showing my pastoral skills.

There is silence, then Mia asks again, But how do you manage? She gestures toward Jeremy. Toward Lucas.

Not very well, some days. But I have to carry on, don't I? Who else is going to do it? I'm the mother. And, here's what

I've discovered. There's always that tiny bit of energy left. New strength, new something. There must be a special source of it and it's labelled "for mothers only."

And you're telling me that supply never runs out? It's new every morning like manna in the wilderness? You're not going to admit you're exhausted?

Alice pulls her hands from Mia's and lets them fall in her lap. You've no idea how exhausted, she says. She rises stiffly, lifts Jeremy from the table and with her free hand takes a bag of cookies from the fridge and calls Lucas, Snack time, sweetie.

He's got Dad's straw-coloured hair, Mia says, taking the bear from Lucas so he can hold the cookie.

And Jeremy's dark like me and Mom, Alice says. We've got no control over what we inherit from which parents, do we?

You're thinking about Fragile X, Mia says quickly. As if her sister doesn't constantly think about Fragile X.

Isn't it time you got tested? Alice says. You might be a carrier, you know. And pretty soon you'll be thinking of getting married, so it's important, don't you think?

Just like Alice to get straight to the point. To zero in on marriage. And then, babies. Babies that may or may not thrive. Mia squirms as she feels Alice studying her slender, firm body as if to discover its childbearing potential. Does Alice ever wonder if GranMarie might be the source of her sons' affliction? Does she really believe Jeremy can be healed? Does she think her sister should even consider having children?

Lucas abandons his animals on the floor and, munching his cookie, leaves the room a dozen times and returns a dozen times bringing Mia his Lego blocks, his motorized trucks and cars, his games. His blond hair is damp, his cheeks flushed.

Slow down, Lucas, Mia says, glad of the interruption that makes it unnecessary to answer her sister's question. She gives the boy another cookie and he runs away.

Tell me about the trip to Greece, Alice says.

Mia is relieved that Alice isn't pushing the test for Fragile X, something she knows she should take seriously.

You must be all excited, Alice says. Is Kurt going?

Yes, everyone's excited. No, I don't think Kurt's going. And I won't be either.

And then, as if her sister's plate isn't already heaped with more trouble than she can digest, Mia tells her about Danny, how he's caught in the grip of substances he can't resist. And can't pay for. How he's been caught shoplifting at Kmart and how she has given him money, used the family's credit card, emptied her own savings account and nothing is ever enough.

He says if I don't help him out he'll have to rob his mother. He's scared. Terrified. I saw his mother on the street last week. I was shocked. She's so terribly gaunt. And old. Her hair's gone grey. It was blonde and pretty when we were kids. Danny's destroying her. And himself. Mia looks away from Alice as she confesses the things she has been unable to speak about to anyone.

It's Alice's opportunity now to offer the blessing she desires to offer, but there is nothing she can do except kneel beside her sister and press her face down on her blue-jeaned knees. Oh Mia, she croons. Mia.

~

Joseph Wittenberg stands side by side with Ab Solinsky in the school's cavernous gym where workmen are sanding, sawing, painting. It's a productive bustle and the satisfying aroma of building products tickles their nostrils. But the project is behind schedule and the principal is growing impatient. Joseph knows he must reassure him, tell him there's plenty of time, the gym will be completed well before June. This year's graduates,

Joseph's daughter among them, will be the first to march forward through a sea of faces—parents, friends, teachers—to receive their diplomas in a smartly renovated facility. Joseph, who has stood with his principal through the long months of this project, should now say, There it is, Ab. All but the finishing touches. You've done it. Congratulations.

Well, perhaps congratulations are premature, but a measure of enthusiasm is expected. Today Joseph feels no enthusiasm. Everything seems wearisome. The gym project, the graduation exercises, details for which—cap and gown rentals, flowers, photographers, a suitably eminent commencement speaker, programs, the printing of the diplomas—are constantly on his mind. He has been trying all day not to think about *Homes and Gardens*, the glossy magazine that arrived with yesterday's mail. The cover showed a brilliant burst of red and yellow tulips. He should have planted new bulbs in fall. Fresh varieties are available. That purple frilly kind. The first shoots could soon be poking up from the hard ground of his garden.

Hearing no affirmation from the man beside him, Ab gazes across the empty space and says, I think we'll make it. And if we do—and all this is confidential, of course, Joseph—I'm thinking I might retire this year. He looks at Joseph, expecting astonishment, discreetly tempered, of course. And gratitude. But Joseph continues staring into the gym.

You'll be first to know when I decide, but I just want to tell you, I think you're ready for the position. You deserve it.

I don't deserve anything, Joseph thinks. Ab's announcement is not a surprise. He's been expecting it for several years, with hope and eagerness, even impatience. But over the winter everything has changed.

I don't know, Ab, he says. I don't know.

You're not letting this go by? Ab is shocked. You're not jumping ship? Are you leaving GSC?

No, no. Where would I go?

Ab waits for more.

I've been thinking, Joseph begins. It's not a bad idea to step back, you know, reenergize. I've never taken a leave of absence.

You mean now? Ab is incredulous. What about your career? This could be your big break. It's your time, Joseph. Ab sounds offended.

And Joseph is surprised too. He has spoken words he hadn't intended to speak, words whose meaning and implication he hasn't thought through: Leave of absence. This possibility has lain dormant. Unspoken. The last thing he wants to do is disappoint his principal. He's disappointed too many people already. Mia. Millicent. He doesn't want to think how he has disappointed Hedie Lodge. In the weeks following her accident she was always in his thoughts. She was there in his dreams, vibrant and unhurt. When he woke up, he was eager to call her. Not right then but soon. He would hear her voice. He would tell her he was planning to fly to Toronto during school break. And he'd assure her she would recover, there must be new medical breakthroughs.

Thanks for the heads-up, Ab, he says. I'll think about it over spring break. And don't get me wrong. I'd love the job. Only …

Only what, Joseph? Ab is impatient. His scrutiny has reached the far end of the gym where the basketball hoops will be placed. Can't you just see it? he says. The bleachers packed, our Saints in action, the crowds cheering their wins. He turns to Joseph: You have to be here next season to see it.

Joseph laughs, but there is no mirth in his laughter. Saints, he says. Whoever came up with that name in the first place?

What's wrong with the name?

Nothing. I'm just saying—saints, holy sorts. I'm thinking how the teams are at each other like animals. Everyone out to win—the kids, the crowds, the coaches. Got to get to the finals.

SARAH KLASSEN

Got to win the trophy. Remember the final match last year? Remember that wild brawl? Saints is a weird name for a team that's supposed to fight to win.

Oh, now you're talking Mennonite, Ab says. You're thinking pacifism. Conscientious objection. You and your people with your one-track focus on not fighting a war. Ab's sudden hostility is palpable. Joseph wonders if Ab is thinking of his father, killed in World War II.

Being Mennonite isn't just not taking up arms, Joseph says. It's ... it's about doing what's right ... what you know is right.

Passing up a promotion—is that right?

It's about feeding the hungry, Joseph says, ignoring Ab's question. It's about sheltering the homeless. And creating a community of people who care for each other. It's not so completely passive as you seem to think. Joseph is about to add volunteering in a thrift store, but he has said too much already and Ab Solinsky has stopped listening. His attention has returned to the gym, where next year the Saints will shine in all their glory.

This gym is state-of-the-art, Joseph says, placing his arm on the principal's shoulder. It will be the envy of all the other high schools. What you've accomplished, Ab, is extraordinary.

~

Spring break, and although Mia has her driver's licence, she's jogging to work. When she passes Kurt's house she slows down hopefully before resuming her tempo. Their shifts have not coincided so far during this week of school vacation and she feels lonely. Bev and Angela will be turning golden brown under the Mediterranean sun, swimming in the clear waters of the Aegean Sea, meeting gorgeous Greek boys and buying kitschy souvenirs. What will we get for Mia? they'll ask each other. Poor thing, Bev will say, she's missing all the fun, and Angela will

262

say, Well, it's her fault, isn't it? and Bev will mount a courageous defence. Then Mia will slip from their radar.

I don't get it, Angela said before they left. You're telling me you can't afford the trip? Your dad won't come up with the cash? I can't believe it.

Both she and Bev wanted an explanation, but Mia didn't tell them how her father had tried to insist that he'd pay, but she had stubbornly refused him. And how gratified she felt when her decision caused him misery.

Now Mia is lonely.

You're always doing homework, Angela complained over winter. Who in their right mind would slave away like you do on an essay for Yak-Yak? If you don't look out you'll turn into a zombie. You'll just disappear from the landscape.

I don't write for Mr. Yakimchuk, Mia argued. I write because the stories are gifts. From GranMarie. They're my history and that's important. She didn't say that she loved writing the stories because Angela would not believe her and even Bev might not understand.

But Angela is right, Mia thinks now. All winter I've sat hunched over my computer while a whole other world, a world of carefree pleasure and laughter and friends, is passing me by. If I'm lonely, it's my own fault. It occurs to her then that writing, by its very nature, must always be a lonely employment. But isn't it lonely just to be a human being?

In my final school year, she thinks, I've composed and polished a handful of not bad stories, letting them absorb me, letting them fill my time, stories that only Mr. Yakimchuk will ever read—and maybe not even he. I've enabled Danny's drug habit. I've found my first job. I've more or less kept the friendship of Bev and Angela. And I'll graduate, but there will be no scholarships. I've neglected math and biology (except for details about

Fragile X) and Mr. Yakimchuk will see to it that my English mark is modest.

And as for Kurt, Mia hasn't been able to figure him out.

Near the end of the school break there is another letter from Hedie Lodge

Dear Mia:

Thanks for sending me your story about Yalta. Your new teacher is right to let you continue with your family history. He'd be unwise not to. You've worked hard on this, I can tell, and it's good.

Spring is here and the forsythia in bloom. But I'd give anything to be at GSC where our English class will be getting ready for graduation. (I've written "our" as if I'm part of it, though I know I'm not. Not any more.)

This is a time of life when you should be carefree, Mia. You shouldn't be burdened with worry about your mother and your sister. I wish I could do something to help, but I'm not much help to anyone these days.

I'm worried that you're letting Danny pressure you. Don't let his addiction control you. You're not responsible for him. Can't you speak to the guidance people? Claudette Avery is pretty level-headed, I always thought. And what about your father? You shouldn't be left alone with this.

I shouldn't have ordered *Uncle Vanya* for our (there I go again!) class to read. What was I thinking? You were the only one in that crazy, silly, wonderful class able to appreciate it. I wanted to please you. Maybe win you over. That was unwise.

Still, I wish I could sprout wings and fly back to

Winnipeg for your graduation. But my flying days are over. Yours are beginning and maybe one day you'll see Yalta.

Recently I read (lots of time for reading these days!) that when the tsar and his family were shot, the bullets ricocheted off the bodies of Anastasia and her sisters because they had sewed diamonds into their clothes. The soldiers had to use bayonets. I don't know why I'm telling you this. It's too terrible.

I have slightly more movement in my right arm now. The doctor says not to hope for much more.

Your friend,
Hedie Lodge.

Mia folds the letter and places it between the pages of *Hamlet*, careful that no edge will show.

That evening Kurt calls. His dad has bought him an old truck, an early graduation gift, and if she isn't working, he wonders, would she like to test it with him? The truck is a rusted, rattling, noisy vehicle and the drive to Lockport the most exhilarating trip Mia has experienced. When they get back, Kurt suggests a movie. All through *Indiana Jones and the Last Crusade* Mia marvels that the world is so full of joy.

Later, too excited to sleep, she works half the night composing her next story for Mr. Yakimchuk.

Wassilyevka
(Assignment #7)

Three weeks after the Franz family settled into the house

of the widow Elena Sawatsky in Wassilyevka, bandits arrived in the village bringing their guns, knives, curses and a list of demands: grain, the best horses, food, a place to sleep.

"You are the owner?" they asked, blundering into the room where Elena lay, awaiting the birth of her second child. Mud dropped from their boots and their knives glinted.

"Give them what they ask," Elena whispered to Abram, fearful for her unborn child, and Abram escorted the intruders to the barn, trembling, because the children had been sent to hide in the straw. "You too, Maria," Hanna had insisted. Rumours of rape were rampant.

In the granary the bandits helped themselves to oats and rye, and from the barn took the best horses and did not find the straw-covered children, who hardly dared to breathe. Then they returned to the house and wolfed down the cabbage soup and bread set out for them and afterwards slept for an hour on Elena's best white linens as if they were pure of heart and their consciences untroubled. When the visitors departed at evening, carrying their deadly mission to another unsuspecting village, no blood had been shed and no one raped. The children were called in from their straw nests and the household sent up a prayer of gratitude that they were all still alive.

Four days later Elena's second child, a boy, came screaming and bloodied into the world.

"Poor little mouse," Hanna whispered. "No father. And he's pushed out by a woman who has to stare at sharp blades that easily could kill her. Such a beginning. The boy will not have a good life."

And then they discovered that the bandits had left behind them the seeds of death—typhus. The dreaded plague selected Abram and Simon. Father and son tossed and sweated in their beds, delirious with fever, hallucinating. Simon cried out in his delirium, "The sea, the sea. Take me to the sea."

Hanna, who had been ordered by the Yalta doctors to rest, rose early each day, stayed up as late as necessary to tend to the sick, wash bedclothes, moisten parched lips while Elena nursed her baby and directed the kitchen help as best she could from her bed. Neither Elena nor Hanna fell ill of typhus.

Maria too was spared. "Let me do that," she begged when she saw her mother lifting a pot of boiling water from the stove to make hot compresses or wash soiled linens.

"No," her mother would say. "This is too heavy for a young back. You must be careful. My back is strong. It's my lungs that are sick. You, Maria, have narrow shoulders. Like me. Straighten them. Always. You're still growing."

The growing had begun in Yalta. Maria had stretched and was still stretching and ruefully aware that her body was becoming awkward and spindly.

"The doctor said you should rest," Maria pleaded, but her mother only shrugged as steam from the heavy pot swelled and swirled like a cloud, enveloping them both. Through the cloud Maria saw her mother as insubstantial. Ephemeral.

Obviously now was not the time to see a doctor in Kharkov, as Hanna had been ordered to do by the Yalta physicians. There would be time for that when her husband and son were fully recovered. Anyway, no one was foolish enough to travel anywhere these days. Train schedules were erratic, cancellations frequent. Madmen and murderers were rumoured to be lurking in the streets. The people of Wassilyevka huddled in their homes, waiting for whatever else was heading their way to arrive. Behind closed doors they schemed escape. From this village. From this country. There was talk of passports and visas. The price of train tickets for a large family. To Moscow. And out of Moscow. And the fare, by boat to—where? Nothing was certain.

Except death, Maria thought.

Simon recovered first, then Abram. When she was convinced that they had survived the typhus, Hanna allowed herself a full night's sleep, then a daily **Mittagsschlaf**, and soon she remained all day in bed. Maria, untouched by typhus, thought of herself as an unsightly, ineradicable weed towering above pretty flowers and useful vegetables. Not even a deadly plague bothered with the ugly weed.

Hanna Franz died on a warm day in spring, apricot and plum trees in blossom, the air fragrant with promise. Birds of all kinds sat on their eggs. Storks had returned to Wassi-lyevka, to the same nests where every year they fussed over their always-hungry fledglings. The bandits had moved on to distant villages, and an uneasy peace hung over the village. Hanna died quietly, her family gathered at her bedside.

Elena's seemingly safe and solid house, Maria thought, was a house of death. Elena's husband had died here and bandits had infected it, forcing her father and brother to fight for their lives. Her mother had been brought from Yalta into this house of death. She couldn't understand why some were chosen to die and some spared.

On the day of Hanna's burial, birdsong filled the air and the friendly sun sent its warmth down on the mourners as they made their way to the cemetery behind the village church where on Sundays they sang in harmony and the preacher admonished them. One Sunday they were counselled to "remain in the land" and on the next to "flee corruption."

Perhaps the villagers sensed that a time was coming when four-part harmonies would no longer fill the church. Instead the sanctuary would become a storage house for grain in good years, and when the harvest failed, it would be empty and neglected, succumbing to ruin. And rats. The congregation would be gone, not home to the noon meal after the Sunday sermon, but scattered in all directions like seeds carried by a rude wind.

Today the scene was not so much sombre as peaceful. Hanna was now at rest; she had reached a place of peace, the preacher said after reading **Blessed are those who die in the Lord**. The grieving congregation sang, **Es erglänzt uns von ferne ein Land** (We glimpse a distant shining land). For some of the villagers, the distant land they dreamed of was Canada, a shining promised land. A refuge from the wilderness of their present lives.

Maria did not cry. Could not. She had prayed daily for her mother, believing with her whole heart that God wanted her to recover, like her father. Like Simon. Hanna's death left her incredulous at first. Then numb.

Her father took his grief out of the house and into the barns and fields of Elena's farm, where there was work to be done. Simon clamoured to ride a certain horse he had taken a liking to. Elena looked after her children and organized her household. Maria was left to drift aimlessly around the yard, feed the chickens or wander toward the garden, where she sometimes pulled weeds or hoed the hard ground. Anything to keep her away from Elena's domain, the kitchen, as if that had become unsafe ground.

Over time a hard shell formed, encapsulating Maria's grief. She carried it around the yard, along the village street and to bed at night. It crept into her dreams, all of them filled with the shape of her mother's thin body, sometimes upright in the train coming home from Yalta, sometimes stirring a pot, her head and shoulders enveloped in steam. But most often lying down: in bed, in a coffin, or in the earth. She didn't know then that grief was a tenacious companion and would travel with her to a strange country where there was no guarantee of a good future.

Meanwhile, life in the village continued. The harvest was poor that year. There were few pigs to slaughter in November, a rainy, dull month. At any time the bandits might return. The cowed villagers withdrew snail-like into their houses.

In Elena's house the bereft, thrown together by circumstances and harbouring their individual griefs, cautiously considered the space they shared and how to live within it. Tensions became discernible, though Maria could not define them. Or perhaps didn't want to. A sense of foreboding took root, a companion to her grief. It wouldn't be shaken off. Winter was in the air, but on rare sunny days she wandered through the barren fields and orchards. The entire landscape seemed to be shutting down.

At mealtimes, made bearable by the liveliness of Simon and Elena's older son, Maria watched her father, who often stared into his plate and forgot to eat. Evenings, she heard him speak to Elena in low tones before he returned to the room where he slept with his children.

"When are we moving into our own house?" she asked, studying his grave face.

"Where can we go?" he said. "And who will look after us?"

"I can cook." Maria was hurt that he doubted her ability

and chilled to hear her father speak so helplessly. So hopelessly. "Don't you think I can keep a house clean?"

She did not find friends in Wassilyevka. She wasn't really looking for them. After the summer in Yalta, she had come to think of her family as all she needed, and even with her mother gone she believed they could be self-sufficient, if only her father would agree. In fall, school did not become a part of her day as it did for Simon. Wassilyevka offered only primary school, which she had long ago completed. And Elena's house had no books.

Maria knew that the losses suffered by Elena and by her father and the general unrest in the village were the reasons its leaders tolerated the unorthodox household arrangement. But very soon it would be considered improper. She didn't speak of this to her father, but she counted on community morals to nudge him toward action, the action of finding a home of their own. The muted kitchen conversations left her uneasy as she lay in her bed, listening.

One evening when at last the voices fell silent and she settled herself for sleep, her father came to the bedroom. "Maria," he said, his voice gentle. "Come into the kitchen."

She got up and came, shivering in her nightdress, her heart heavy with dread. Elena sat at the table and watched her enter, motioned her to a chair. Maria shook her head and stayed near the door, as if she might need to escape. She wrapped her arms around herself.

Her father also remained standing. "Maria," he said, "we have decided to marry, Elena and I."

The words held no surprise for Maria, who had known all along that one day they would be spoken.

"We hope you can agree to this," Abram said.

A tightening in Maria's chest. The widow's eyes were on her. Her father's had turned away and were directed somewhere beyond this room. The sadness in his face reminded Maria of a picture she had seen of Jesus carrying his cross to Golgotha. Her tongue refused to move.

There was silence then, after which her father spoke again: "Maria?"

Still she couldn't speak. How was it that fate had crept spider-like into the kitchen and spun a web around them? A web so tenacious no one could escape.

Elena spoke finally. "If she can't say yes, we can't marry."

Possibly the widow did not intend to speak harshly. It wasn't until Maria was much older and in a different country that she would acknowledge that perhaps the widow too was terrified by the web she was trapped in. Elena rose from her chair as if intending to leave the kitchen.

Maria let her arms fall to her side. Her body, so recently warm from bed, shivered. Elena glanced back at her, giving her one more chance. Maria looked at her father. What he expected of her was unthinkable and cruel. How could he do this? How could he place into her unwilling hands the power to prevent the marriage she desperately wanted to prevent? He and Elena were forcing on her the responsibility of determining the future of this entire, miserable household. Time stood still for her as she felt, and tried to resist, the weight of this obligation. She could not say yes. Could not. But her head, as if it must, began to nod, not quite imperceptibly.

The widow sat down again, looked at Abram and nodded.

And now Simon was stirring, as if the enormity of his sister's decision had roused him from his dreams. He stumbled into the kitchen, warm with sleep, and Abram opened his arms to him. "Simon," he said, and Maria wished he would say nothing more but simply carry the boy back to his bed and let him sleep.

"Simon, now you will have a mother. Aunt Elena will be your mother."

Simon looked up, his expression changed from drowsiness to shock. "No!" he shouted. "No! I want my own Mama!" The words bellowed out from the boy like the outraged roar of a wounded animal. "I want Mama! Only Mama!" His hands became fists pounding his father's chest.

Abram held· him tight and carried him out of the room, leaving Maria alone with the widow.

~

Mia runs all the way to school and goes directly to the library, where she takes from the shelf a book about the Russian Revolution. GranMarie's voice had become almost inaudible when she told how that evening in Wassilyevka she had determined the future by nodding her head. And then she claimed she could remember nothing about the Revolution. Why should she have to dig up sorrows she'd rather forget?

No, no, she said vehemently last week. I don't want my birthday celebrated. I've had too many. I should be long gone. God has forgotten me. He's taking the others and leaves me here.

God had just taken a neighbour from down the hall and GranMarie had said, heartsick, How nice. That's wonderful. But wasn't it my turn?

Mia drove her mother and a birthday cake to Wild Oak Estates, where GranMarie accepted a small slice with her tea and sighed and said, I told you not to. Then she paused, dessert fork mid-air, and looked around. Where's Joseph?

He couldn't come, Millicent said. He was busy. No need to

mention that he was in the garden, digging. You know Joseph, she added.

I do? GranMarie looked up, baffled. But after another forkful of cake she spoke calmly about her pills and her arthritis and asked what she should do with her ragged spider plant that was no longer thriving.

Time is running out for GranMarie, Mia thinks, emerging from between rows of library books. She sees an approaching figure and tries but fails to avoid a collision. *The Russian Revolution* flies from her hand and lands on the floor.

Dammit, Danny says, startled by the impact. His arms have automatically reached out to keep her from falling. Dammit. Sorry. He speaks too loudly and his eyes dart wildly, not stopping anywhere for long.

What are you doing here, for God's sake? Mia steps back from him.

Yesterday Danny was summoned over the intercom to the vice principal's office. For the last time. He must not be seen on the grounds of George Sutton Collegiate. Mia thinks her father will have been kind when he expelled him, if not for Danny's sake, then for hers.

What're you up to these days? Danny asks, his voice strangely pitched, his face turned toward her though his eyes refuse to meet hers.

Mia bends to retrieve the book, then takes Danny by the arm as she used to do when they were children and he needed rescuing. From his own ineptness. From a teacher's harsh remark. From bullies.

He shakes her off.

Come, she says. She has no wish to talk to Danny but she must get him out of the building before an administrator sees him. She guides him along an inconspicuous route out of the library. She knows this meeting isn't accidental; it will complicate things.

Around the corner they meet Angela, whose eyes spring wide as she gives Danny's presence an indiscreet thumbs down. Mia ignores her, hurries Danny out of the building, down the side steps. She stops near a caragana shrub that borders a paved walk. Danny becomes wary, glances nervously over his shoulder, as if he's picked up the scent of danger and must determine the nearest escape route. He brings his mouth close to Mia's ear: Help me. Just ... this ... once.

Mia shrinks from him. Now she's the one looking around for escape.

C'mon, Mia. I'll never ask again. Never. I swear. I ... swear ... to ... God. His hand reaches for her wrist, clutches it.

Mia yanks away from him. She wants to cover her ears, but she's holding *The Russian Revolution* in her left hand and the right is moving toward her sweater pocket where her fingers curl around two twenties.

Could you run up to Safeway, her mother had said at noon, handing her a list. Now, with Danny's need closing in like a steel net, her fingers separate the two bills, pulling one from the pocket.

Danny takes it, turns it over. What the hell, Mia, this all you got for me? This is it?

His words, a confusion of outrage and disbelief and near terror, unnerve Mia. She pulls out the other bill. He snatches it from her hand and runs.

Danny! she calls after him. Danny! She sees him dash into the parking lot, where he dodges cars and trucks and then is gone. When her eyes can no longer follow him she is terrified. And then she sees Kurt coming toward her. The guy's got nerve, he says, showing up here totally stoned. I hear he's out. For doing drugs.

Yes, Kurt, I know. Mia feels hollow and guilty. *The Russian Revolution* is unbearably heavy in her hand.

I thought you were smarter than that. Kurt's annoyance jolts Mia out of shock into fury.

What has smart got to do with it? she spits out, not caring who might hear. You don't know anything, Kurt. You don't understand. She lifts the heavy volume and heaves it, but he is already walking away.

~

It's Tuesday, not Thursday, but Millicent has agreed to help out at the thrift store because one of the regular volunteers is on vacation. Tuesdays are slack, the woman at the till says. Her name is Nettie and she's small, elderly, speaks with a flat Mennonite accent and moves with the agility of someone much younger. Her eyes are alert to any movement at the door, at the clothing racks, beside the shelves of dishes, at the entrance to the fitting room.

Look at her, she says, nudging Millicent. An aboriginal woman comes through the door. She wears a smart leather jacket, her skin is flawless and her bearing confident. Morning, ladies, the newcomer says. When she sees Millicent at the counter she pauses. Good morning, Mrs. Wittenberg, then continues toward the book section.

Millicent turns a quizzical eye toward Nettie, who says, She comes regularly, and always buys books.

How did she know my name?

Nettie shrugs. She is folding newspapers. We'll need them for packing glassware, she says. That's if we sell any today. See that box of cups and saucers? If you want, you can find room for them on the china shelf. I'll manage here.

Millicent heads off to shelve the dishes. When she passes the book section the aboriginal woman looks up from the book in her hand. I don't think you recognize me, she says. I'm your neighbour. Teresa Brady. She offers her hand and Millicent takes it, baffled.

I'm Kurt's mother.

Oh ... Oh yes, yes. Of course. Kurt. I'm Mia's mom.

I know.

How ... how do you like your new home, Millicent says, before remembering that Kurt and his family moved into the neighbourhood last summer and may no longer consider themselves new.

Fine. The neighbours are friendly. We like it. Kurt likes school.

When Millicent has nothing to say, Teresa adds, Nobody calls Kurt "Indian" at school except once in a while and I've only been called "squaw" once and that was by an Indian kid who should know better. You'd think he'd respect me as an elder. She laughs heartily and Millicent thinks there is no fear in this woman.

You look much too young to be an elder, she says. And too young to have a teenage son, she thinks.

I teach at Urban Circle down the street, Teresa says. I drop in here on Tuesdays mostly to find something to read. What do you read?

Mia's reading a play these days, Millicent says, dodging the question. She says it's written by a Russian. I can't remember the title. She moves on with her box of dishes, embarrassed that she can't name a single book she is reading. Embarrassed that she knows so little about anyone anywhere. Dismayed, she wonders if she forgot to take her medication this morning.

And then Nettie is calling: Millicent, I need you up front.

Millicent sets down the heavy box and hurries back to the checkout, where a gaunt man, his head shaking uncontrollably, his jacket buttonless, has piled a crumpled armful of shirts and four blue bowls on the counter. She is saved. By Nettie's call for help. By this derelict from the street. She is needed to fold those crumpled shirts, wrap newspapers around the bowls and shove the "experienced goods," as Nettie calls them, into plastic bags.

Millicent reaches for newspaper, picks up one of the blue bowls and recognizes it. It's from the breakfast set she brought here weeks ago. She holds the bowl with both hands. It has a delicately embossed border that she notices for the first time. What possessed her to give the dishes away? They were a gift and if she could she would take them home with her today.

She picks up the newspaper again and sees a picture of a woman dancing. I used to dance, she says to Nettie. I was pretty darn good.

Nettie stares at Millicent, who packs the bowls as if they are delicate porcelain.

Teresa Brady drops an armful of books on the counter. Look what I found! The book she is holding up is *Sense and Sensibility*. It's by Jane Austen, she says. An early copy. Do you like Jane Austen? She is looking at her neighbour.

Mia does, Millicent says, defensively. And my mother-in-law's got a whole shelf of Jane Austen's books. Millicent has no idea whether Marie Wittenberg reads anything these days. She drops the books into a plastic bag. Come again, she says, managing a smile.

Teresa Brady doesn't ask, Are you okay, Mrs Wittenberg? But Millicent can see the question on her neighbour's face.

When Teresa is gone, Millicent excuses herself, runs upstairs to find her coat. She wants to leave. Instead, she searches the pockets and yes, her pills are there. She will not go home. She will pull herself together. And before she leaves the store, she will go to the book section and find a novel, not by Jane Austen. She will buy it. Take it home. Read it. All of it.

It's almost closing time and Nettie says, Just watch, now we'll get a string of customers. Always happens. And sure enough, a half dozen latecomers push through the door and begin rummaging through clothes or LPs or appliances. A tired-looking woman with limp, greying hair is first to bring her purchases to the counter, a pair of jeans and several pairs of socks. Millicent bags them.

These for your son? Nettie asks.

The woman nods and takes the parcel from Millicent.

Good bye, Mrs. Haarsma, Nettie says.

When the woman leaves Nettie tells Millicent, Mrs. Haarsma's lost her job, poor thing, and her son's a problem. Drugs.

Danny? Millicent whispers, but the line of late customers is restless and she must call out the prices on the used goods for Nettie to ring up.

Rain

April brings rain, rain, rain, and everyone believes the Red River will overflow its banks. But then the sun emerges, the rain stops, the earth sucks up the moisture and by mid-month the afternoon temperatures shoot up to the high twenties. Along Kildonan Drive tulips are blooming and maple branches thicken with buds.

Joseph—shorts, T-shirt, tools and gloves—is in his garden, digging. Bags of garden soil, peat moss and sheep manure are piled on the driveway. He will spread everything evenly across the flower beds and kitchen garden. Replenished, the garden will thrive. He has made a list of perennials he will add this year: deep blue delphiniums along the back fence, astilbe, two or three pink cone flowers, hydrangea and dahlias. If only he had planted a dozen new tulip bulbs in fall.

It's Saturday. He refuses to let Ab Solinsky and gym renovations intrude. Or the looming textbook inventory or commencement exercises with their myriad details. One detail is taken care of: Bruce Cameron, the MLA, has agreed to be the commencement speaker and Ab Solinsky is pleased. Good, he said. The *Free Press* will pick that up.

Joseph plans to work here in the sun all day, stopping only for a quick trip to The Plant Place to select geraniums for the planter, not white but scarlet, and German ivy and white trailing lobelia. It's too early for other bedding plants. Too early for vegetables.

No gardener in spring knows what summer will bring, Joseph muses. Or what the harvest will be like in fall. As he continues to dig he whistles because today he is full of hope.

~

It's Friday and Marie Wittenberg should be preparing for Joseph's visit. She should pick up the crumpled tissues she dropped, return the brown velvet album to the shelf, fill the kettle—but something in the room, or in her life, has shifted, as if a page has been turned or someone has dimmed the light.

A pale glow falls on two shadowy figures seated side by side in the compartment of a moving train. Mother and daughter. And now she can see the father sitting opposite, and beside him, a boy, his face pressed to the window, counting empty storks nests. Or horses. Or cows in a meadow. "That's number thirty," he'll say, shouting above the clackety-clack of the train. It's November, but although the landscape appears grey and bleak, the mother says, "Look, Maria; look, Simon, how the trees bend in the wind! And the lovely sky." She says this not once, but repeatedly. She has colour in her cheeks, her eyes are bright and hopeful. The father places a hand on his wife's knee and smiles at her. Maria thinks she has never seen anything as hopeful as her mother's eyes. And never anything as sad as her father's smile.

Marie knows how the story ends. Death was stalking them. How their happiness could not hold, and suddenly she finds herself in frightful silence, shivering with cold and despair in the doorway of Elena's kitchen. The widow seated on a wooden chair. The lamp's pale flame fluttering on the table where next morning, after a sleepless night, they will all sit down to breakfast and then rise to go about the day's tasks, each one bearing a portion of sorrow mixed with fear that will follow them all the way to the house on Edison Avenue. Her father committed a terrible sin for which she forgave him because she loved him. But she has not forgotten. She longs for the mother who was happy on the train. Marie herself will soon embark on her last journey. It's high time she boarded the next train. Or boat. And if there is a promised land waiting somewhere, that will be a bonus.

Marie Wittenberg begins humming with an unsteady voice the song sung at her mother's funeral: *Es erglänzt uns von ferne ein Land.* And then Joseph arrives and she hasn't prepared the tea.

I'll do it, Mother, he says.

She sits at the kitchen table and watches Joseph glance at the unwashed cups and plates, the uneaten fish sandwich. A pot of soup heating on the stove. He turns it off. Marie notices the cluster of pills on the table.

I never loved your father, Marie says, raising her hoarse voice.

Joseph stops pouring tea and waits for his mother to continue. When she doesn't, he places the steaming cup in front of her. She doesn't reach for it, keeps her hands folded on her lap. I never loved him, she repeats.

Joseph doesn't look shocked to hear that his parents' marriage may have been flawed. What I remember about my father, he says, is how he would arrive at our Langside house, out of the blue it always seemed, and then, just as suddenly, he'd leave. When he stopped coming I hardly noticed. I never really knew him.

There is a very long pause before his mother says, It was wrong, very wrong of me.

What?

To marry your father.

Then why did you?

What could I do? I wasn't fit for this country. What could I do except clean other women's houses? Might as well be cleaning my own. I couldn't depend on my father—he was gone. And did I want to depend on my stepbrothers? God forbid.

She still hasn't touched her tea.

Did you ever love someone? Joseph asks. He stops, as if surprised he's blurted the word "love" to his mother.

Another long pause, during which the old woman shifts her gaze away from the window, picks up one of the pills, then stares at Joseph, whose eyes are blue as her father's. Her husband had grey eyes. He was not cruel. He didn't drink. He was simply inconsequential.

She married Edward Wittenberg when she was living in a basement room in the city and worked at Eaton's. Edward was also alone. They moved into a house on Langside Street and there he gave her two sons in whom he showed little interest. There is no picture of him on the oak dresser.

Joseph is watching her. Did you ever love someone? he asks again.

There was someone. Yes. Marie's voice is steady.

Joseph waits for her to go on but now she's toying with her cup. Finally she says, I miss my mother. Her voice is plaintive as a child's. She takes the cup with both hands, raises it to her lips and lowers it again.

Mother, did you forget your pills? Joseph asks. We're thinking,

Millicent and me, that you might enjoy Meals on Wheels. His mother turns a startled face toward him. Mia agrees that it's a good idea, he says, to bolster his case. When Marie continues to stare, baffled, he adds, All right, not necessarily every day, Mother.

No. Oh no. Marie speaks with an emphasis that lets Joseph know what she thinks of his good idea.

I met him on Kildonan Drive, she says, not far from where you're living. He came into my life like a surprise, a good surprise. Here was someone who actually saw me, who knew I was there. All of a sudden I was important to another person. Her voice trails off and Joseph assumes she's lost her train of thought. But then she rallies: Well, I thought I was important to him. Her words have a bitter edge now. She leans back in her chair and closes her eyes.

I should go, Joseph says, uncertainly. You look exhausted.

You always rush off. His mother's accusation is knife-sharp; her eyes are open. Am I so boring?

Baffled, Joseph says, Why don't you tell me? Tell me about the man you loved.

And what will you tell me? Marie snaps back. You never tell me anything.

All right, Mother. You tell me about the man you loved and I'll tell you about the woman I loved. He looks up to see if she accepts the challenge, a challenge that thrills and scares him.

The man I loved was my father, Marie says, tracing the rim of her cup with a thin, unsteady finger. She smiles, oddly.

Joseph is confused. And irritated.

Marie takes her first sip of tea. All right. Let me tell you about this man I loved. His name was Ronald.

Joseph listens as she unfolds her story.

The sun is low in the sky when Joseph leaves his mother's apartment, walks down the five flights and finds himself in the mellow light of a spring evening. The scent of Russian olive trees in blossom fills his lungs. From Henderson Highway the siren of an emergency vehicle shrieks above the steady noise of after-supper traffic, the roar of revved motorbikes, the screech of brakes. The apartments across the street are disappearing behind the newly green elm trees. He looks around as if he is seeing and hearing and smelling for the first time. He is not sure whether he is completely drained or completely saturated. He gets into his Camaro and drives home accompanied by his mother's story about the man named Ronald.

If he should test his mother tomorrow morning, the way students are tested, on what he's told her about Hedie Lodge, would she remember anything?

I'm going to bed, I'm tired, she said when he finished his confession.

Emigration
(Assignment #8)

The Franz family left home before daybreak and, as the distance between them and Wassilyevka increased, Abram and Elena looked steadfastly ahead.

"The Lord keep you," the villagers had said, and some had begun singing, **God be with you till we meet again,** but Abram said, "Sshhh. Better not. Better keep quiet." The neighbour who had agreed to drive the family and their belongings to the train station in Barvenkovo urged his horses forward. Had the travellers looked back they would have seen the village become smaller and smaller until it faded in the pre-dawn gloom.

Abram and Elena did not allow themselves to look back. When the threat of looting and violence had subsided, the farm that was Elena's had recovered and for several years prospered. Hope returned, and a near normal life, for which they were thankful. But soon the gusty winds of change, temporarily abated, picked up and blew once more, sweeping across the steppes with a new regime's decrees and demands and bold proclamations of equality and freedom. Uncertainty and apprehension returned to the village and once again longing for a better country stirred in the hearts of its inhabitants.

Abram and Elena fixed their fearful gaze on the future into which they were headed with their blended family. "His, hers and theirs," the neighbours joked, and it was a familiar, friendly joke because such blending was common among their people. In this case, "his" were Maria and Simon; "hers," two lively, growing boys, and "theirs" another boy born one year after the wedding of Abram Franz and Elena Sawatsky.

The two oldest children did not hesitate to look back. Simon was leaving behind four sleek black horses, animals he loved to ride or help hitch to a plow. They had been sold to a neighbour. Maria, long since finished with childhood, knew she would never return to Wassilyevka. But she would never forget its white picket fences, tidy yards and fragrant orchards. Nor would she forget the terror when bandits came. Or the grief when her mother died. She believed that whatever was to come could be no worse than what had been.

"We are not fleeing," Abram insisted. But he had told Elena he hoped to travel as unobtrusively as possible past the two Russian villages that lay between Wassilyevka and Barvenkovo where they would board the train for Moscow. That meant leaving before dawn, before the Russian villages woke up.

"You are making a terrible mistake, Abram," a neighbour had warned repeatedly. "You are selling your wife's farm and setting out on a dangerous journey to a strange country. On a different continent. Your stepsons will grow up and they'll blame you for selling their inheritance. Their birthright. Can you guarantee them land in Canada?"

Hearing his own fears spoken aloud had unnerved Abram. He had become ill and remained in bed for a week. The journey to Yalta—it seemed long ago—had been dictated by his love and fear for Hanna. He had not hesitated. The sale of the Lutzch factory in Barvenkovo was not a matter of choice: the state had decided. But here in the village private sales were still possible and he must choose: sell or stay. Elena was desperate to get her young sons out of the country where they would grow up to future service in the Red Amy. Sell, sell, she begged. She summoned the doctor from Barvenkovo, who said he could find nothing wrong with her husband. "This sickness is of another, deeper kind," he said and took his leave.

When a buyer had appeared with money enough to pay for the farm, Elena had argued, pleaded and cajoled until Abram finally said yes and the sale was made.

Abram had taken Maria with him one last time to the mound of earth behind the village church. Neither one had spoken. Maria knelt to place on Hanna's grave the pink roses she had cut from Elena's garden. She positioned them beneath the bronze cross that marked the site while Abram watched, his eyes dry, his heart heavy.

"We'll come back some day," he'd said when his daughter

straightened up from the grave, then added a cautious "God willing." Neither father nor daughter believed this would happen. They knew of no one who had crossed the ocean and then returned.

Within the year the skeptical neighbour would write to Abram Franz: "What is it like in Canada? Is there a place for me in that country? Can you help me?" Abram wrote back to offer help but the neighbour was not heard from again.

All that was still in the future. A future toward which the plodding horses were transporting the parents with their five children, their possessions belted and roped into a collection of baskets and boxes. So much baggage, although they had taken only what was essential and a few non-essentials they couldn't possibly part with. Maria had snatched up the Yalta shell. Elena had baked bread for the journey. One loaf contained in its cooled centre the wad of tsarist roubles Abram insisted on taking with them to the promised land.

When they arrived in Moscow he found temporary lodging for his family while he made the rounds of government offices, where he answered questions posed by officials who were unwaveringly suspicious, always slow and always counting on bribes.

"Why are you leaving?" they asked. "Where do you think you are going? You are foolish to leave a country that is taking a brave step forward into a glorious future."

Abram could not envision a glorious future, not here, and not in the country to which he was leading his family like a timid Moses whose faith and confidence were frayed.

While they waited for their documents, Abram took Maria and Simon to see the embalmed body of Lenin lying in state in Red Square. Maria thought he looked pale and grotesque. Simon said he was ugly. "Like a dead pig."

When they finally boarded the train that took them away from Moscow, away from a country they loved, it seemed to Maria that her family scarcely breathed the entire distance to the border, where a huge gate stood, its dark ironwork stark as a gallows. The ominous red star at the top glared down accusingly on all deserters. The Franz family couldn't see it from their car, but they knew they had reached that fabled symbol when silence swept like a wave toward them from the front of the train as it slowed, approaching the dreaded gate. When it stopped, Abram glanced at Elena, who held the cloth sack that concealed the guilty loaf. Several officials with coldly curious eyes boarded the train for a final scrutiny of visas. Occasionally they lingered with a passenger to ask questions. When an officer approached the Franz family, Abram and Elena, and Maria too, forced themselves not to avert their eyes. The children's innocent curiosity, they hoped, could do no harm. The agent scanned the family with sharp eyes, then demanded their visas, but asked no questions, and moved on.

When the last official stepped down from the train, it remained motionless for an excruciating eternity, and Maria thought she would explode. Then, slowly, deliberately, like an elephant whose time has come to lumber on, the train began to move. When the gate was scarcely behind them the train stopped again and the passengers were ordered to gather their belongings, step down and walk a distance to another train on a track with a different gauge. The silent column of emigrants moved silently and quickly.

When this train finally moved, an explosion of shouts, sobs and laughter erupted in the emigrant cars. Abram snatched the sack from Elena's hands, tore the loaf from it, broke it open, pulled out the roubles and laughed triumphantly.

The roubles were useless. Perhaps Abram Franz knew this, but he knew also the importance of celebrating a miracle. They had come through the Red Sea, praise God, and emerged safely on its far shore. Not everyone who had tried had been so fortunate.

For the moment, the past left behind and the future not yet in clear focus, there was hope for the Franz family, and they allowed themselves a shiver of excitement. They did not know that after they had admired the splendid old city of Riga, lived for weeks in cramped immigrant quarters in Southampton, finally boarded the SS **Metagama** and found themselves on the grey expanse of the Atlantic Ocean, sorrow would once more find them.

In Wassilyevka Simon had grown into a sturdy farm boy. He was not sick on the sea journey like his parents and Maria. He played games with his younger brothers and made up fabulous stories about the place they were sailing toward. There would be horses, he promised. One for each of them. Jet-black steeds if that was what they wanted. Indian ponies if they preferred. When pain began to stab him in the stomach, he didn't complain. When it grew worse, he continued telling stories. When something inside him was about to burst, he stayed in bed. Abram was still weak and shaky, Elena forcing herself to attend to her boys. It was Maria who found the ship's doctor.

It was too late.

The Franz family, surrounded by other seasick emigrants, gathered on deck to hear the captain intone: "Ashes to ashes, dust to dust." One of the emigrants translated the words into German. Odd words, Maria thought, considering that it was the watery depth of the vast Atlantic Ocean her brother was lowered into, the shrouded body breaking its rough skin and vanishing without a trace.

~

What do you think, GranMarie?

Mia has been reading aloud from the typed sheets of the final instalment of her assignment. She has stopped before the end, leaving out the part about Simon. Her grandmother has nodded off from time to time and now looks around, distracted, and says nothing.

Did you hear what I was reading? Mia asks. Is this how you remember it? She taps the pages. Grandmother and grand-daughter sit side by side in the usually sun-filled room that today is dull. Rain is forecast. What happened to the roubles? Mia has asked this question before, but received no answer. In her story she has declared them valueless.

How should I know? the old woman mumbles. How am I supposed to remember all that? You, you're young. You tell me if it's true.

Mia gathers up the pages of the story. It is incomplete. The arrival in the promised land is missing. And there is nothing about Edison Avenue, where her great-grandfather and his wife settled their family. Mia wants the whole story, but GranMarie is tired of telling it.

Did you ever want to go back to where you were born? Where your mother is buried? Mia presses close to GranMarie, who pulls herself together and leans toward her granddaughter: Impossible, she says, her voice a whisper. They'd be after us in a minute.

Who, GranMarie?

Well, the bandits, of course. GranMarie pulls back, annoyed at the girl's slowness to understand. And the Red Army. The whole godless business.

Mia rises, fetches the Yalta shell from its place and, uncurling

GranMarie's hand, places the shell in her palm. At first her grandmother looks startled, then frightened. Her eyes fill with tears. I had a brother, she says. Can you tell me where he is?

Mia sits down again and takes the old woman's hands in hers. The clock is ticking and she should deliver this last assignment to Mr. Yakimchuk before the deadline. She strokes the ancient papery skin.

The apricot orchard, GranMarie says, rousing herself with effort. We had an apricot orchard. After dark when no one was about I liked to walk there. The moonlight fell on me. Like milk. She closes her eyes and holds her face up to catch that moonlight.

Outside the wind has increased.

Listen, Mia says. The wind.

Oh but the trees are used to it, GranMarie says. It makes them strong.

~

Mia is late with her assignment and Mr. Yakimchuk shakes his head. You surely didn't think I'd make an exception for the vice principal's daughter? he says. Some things aren't possible even for the privileged. His smile is strained, his words tinged with sarcasm, the only resource he has left. It's been rumoured that the teacher who came to replace Hedie Lodge has applied for a permanent position at GSC. A counter-rumour claims that he's been terminated.

Chilled by her teacher's hostility, Mia doesn't argue. In spite of her mistrust of him she feels sorry for this man with the obviously Slavic name. His students have done their ruthless best to create a hell for him. She would like to hear *his* story. When did his family emigrate to Canada? She's pretty sure they must have come from the western part of Ukraine, maybe near Lviv. Principal Solinsky, she's learned from her father, was born near the Carpathian Mountains. The eastern part where GranMarie lived was populated mostly by Russians, she's discovered through her research. Her grandmother has always referred to that country as Russia, although on the school's atlas it's Ukraine.

Mr. Yakimchuk has never commented on the setting for her stories, as if it holds no interest for him. Has he bothered to read her assignments before hastily scrawling his blood-red judgement in the margin? "C" or "quite good"?

You should complain, Bev has said. You're not getting a fair mark. But Mia shakes her head.

Once—Mr. Yakimchuk must have been in a magnanimous state of mind—he put "A minus."

Now he gestures impatiently. He wants Mia to leave.

I hope we'll get to finish *Hamlet*, she says.

We wasted all that time on *Uncle Vanya*. He speaks accusingly, as if he knows Mia is to blame.

Story in hand, Mia turns and leaves her teacher's sarcasm and his lack of curiosity about Ukraine. Mr. Yakimchuk is right: everyone's time was wasted with the Chekhov play. They might as well have been twiddling their thumbs.

Leaving, Mia worries about Danny, who last night called although he'd promised he wouldn't. His voice was hollow and he didn't insist when she gave a flat No to his urgent Please, Mia, please. You've gotta help me. You've gotta.

It had been surprisingly easy to say no to the friend she'd last seen vanishing into a parking lot. She had felt nothing, as if whatever once tied her to Danny had rotted away and he no longer mattered. But today indifference is impossible. Danny still exists. And so do those with power to threaten and terrify him.

Mia wonders how Danny's mother lives with all of this.

~

Danny hears his mother's steps as she enters his room to see if he has opened his eyes. Danny, you'll be late for school, she says. You're going, aren't you? Promise me you'll go.

He moves his head on the pillow. His mother does not know that he is no longer a student of GSC. He has kept the news from reaching her.

I've got three today, she says, and he knows she means inter- views. They're across town. But I'll be home for supper. Will you come for supper? Her voice is wistful. Pleading. And empty of hope, as if today she can expect nothing to go her way.

When he hears the door bang shut, he burrows deeper under the covers. But sleep eludes him and his brain spins and spirals like clockwork out of control. His body is a turmoil of need. It wants, wants, wants. The world has shrunk down to this one craving that so far he has been able to satisfy. With help from Mia. Jane Kerr. Inattentive staff at Kmart. He's never taken from his mother.

She will be gone until supper. Armed with this knowledge and propelled by his body's need, he stumbles out of bed. The air is cool on his bare chest. His mother has left a window open and he can hear birds chittering.

In the kitchen he dials Mia's number.

You have reached the Wittenberg residence. Please leave a message.

When he hears the beep, Danny brings his lips close to the mouthpiece: Why aren't you there for me? Bitch.

And now there is no other way.

Danny can't remember when he last stepped inside his moth- er's bedroom. The double bed in which his mother once slept with his father takes up most of the room. A floral blue and grey spread has been thrown hastily over the bed, his mother's night- gown is a white splash on the floor. One dresser drawer is open. On top of the dresser, several photos. He steps closer to see. A framed picture of his father is all but obscured by a large box of tissues. He picks up the photo and takes it to the window, where he peers into the face of the man on whose strong shoulders he was carried. Because his father was very tall, or the ceiling very low, he had believed he was perched on top of the world, a prince carried by a devoted and trustworthy monarch.

But that could not have happened here in this house on Edison Avenue with its crumbling foundation and a roof that needs new shingles. That was another house. In Holland. Where one day his father put him into a wagon and pulled him along the street until they left the houses behind them and, continuing along a country road, came to a pond where ducks and swans floated on the water. Danny was delighted when his father put him in a boat and they rowed across the pond and the ducks swam away but one swan stayed. He had asked if they could take it home and his father said what would they do with such a great bird.

But it's so pretty, Danny said. Or thinks he may have said. We shouldn't just leave it behind.

His father said they'd be leaving behind more than just a beautiful bird.

This incident with his father and the swan has stayed with him, embedded in his memory from which all the rest of Holland has vanished. He can't remember flying across the Atlantic. Nothing? His mother used to ask. Well, I sure can. You screamed and screamed the whole way and wouldn't sleep and the other passengers kept glaring at me. I wanted to disappear.

So they came to Canada, to Edison Avenue, and one day his father was gone. Danny can muster no anger against his father. No emotion whatsoever. He returns the picture to its place and now he notices another photo: his last year's school picture. He holds it close and sees himself a year ago. He is looking straight at the camera, not smiling, his eyes slightly wary, as if he's not at ease. The bright light shining on his neatly trimmed hair gives it radiance. His black shirt stands out against a background of blue and mauve swirls.

Danny puts the photo down and looks around for this year's picture but of course it's not here because in September, when the grade twelve students posed in blue gowns and caps on loan for the day—a foretaste of graduation—he was absent. And then he missed the retakes the following week. Mia and Bev had teased him: Hey, Danny, no picture, no graduation.

Danny turns to the open drawer. Pulls it all the way out, dumps its contents on his mother's bed and runs his fingers through her underwear and stockings. Nothing. In the next drawer he finds sweaters, maroon wool, pastel acrylic and worn white cotton, but though he rummages through them he finds nothing. His agitation increases and his hands shake almost uncontrollably as he tries the next drawer and the next. And then, in the shallow top drawer crammed with envelopes and old postcards and pictures of relatives in Holland, his unsteady fingers find what they are looking for. He takes the bills—a modest roll—and leaves the plundered room.

He doesn't need to call Mia and hear her say, No, Danny. No more. Not ever.

Bitch.

Jane Kerr will not let him down. She will be there for him because his urgent need to have will mesh with her willingness to supply. And today he has enough. For what he owes and what he needs. Jane will come, a fairy godmother bearing gifts, and his hands will stop shaking, and his knees will regain strength. His mind will focus. Everything will be good. There will be ecstasy and everything will change. He'll get a job. He'll pay his mother back. Of course. Soon.

It's possible that right this minute his mother will be starting her first interview. She'll get a job.

Danny wills his clumsy finger to dial.

~

Leaving McDonald's, Mia tries to set her mind on the matter of the graduation gown but all she can think of is Danny's message, which kept ringing in her head as she took orders for fries and hamburgers and now, walking slowly home, she still can't root out his words. No one has ever called her a bitch.

You have to have a gown, Angela keeps telling her with genuine concern. You're running out of time. Both Bev and Angela have long ago shopped for gowns and accessories with their mothers, who offered encouragement and credit cards and advice. Bev has asked a boy from the Mennonite church to be her date and Angela vacillates between a muscled six-foot football player and a Patrick Swayze–look-alike from Mr Gibbs's automotive class. The latter drives his father's red Corvette.

Mia can't imagine her mother shopping for a gown and shoes and jewellery. Her mother is still intent on reducing the Wittenberg household, a slendering on which she thrives. She isn't interested in acquiring things.

Your mother is out of the woods now, Mia's father says, adding, Well, almost.

By the time she reaches Kildonan Drive, thoughts of Gran-Marie have replaced Danny's message. Her grandmother is losing the desire to eat or move and after telling her last story, she'd said, Are you finished with me now? I'm tired.

I've learned something this year, Mia thinks ruefully. I've learned how to add flesh and blood to the bare bones of a plot. And I've got GranMarie to thank, not Mr. Yakimchuk. What should stop her from bringing her grandmother's story to a conclusion? Even though the school year is ending. Even though

Mr. Yakimchuk has refused her last assignment. She will not ask GranMarie for more, but will bring the Franz family to their destination in her own way. Mia keeps walking and ends up at her sister's door.

Of course I'll go shopping with you, Alice says when Mia mentions the graduation gown. We'll go tomorrow. I'll take Lucas next door and I'll bring Jeremy. He'll be no trouble. We'll have a blast, the three of us.

Mia arrives on her sister's driveway next morning, but Alice fails to appear until Mia goes to the door. A distracted sister lets her in.

Oh, I'm sorry, Mia! I completely forgot to call. I had to take Jeremy to the emergency last night. He had trouble breathing. It was so awful, I was so scared, Mia, you can't even imagine. He's home now. He's okay. But I have to stay with him. I'm sorry.

Mia hears Jeremy's raspy breathing from the bedroom. She bends down to enfold Lucas who has flung himself at her and says, Jeremy was very very very sick. His voice is a burble, his whole body quivering and damp with excitement. He draws a big, slow breath and lets it huff out noisily in imitation of his brother's difficult breathing. Your brother will be all right, Mia promises.

Could of died. Mom? Anniemia? Could of?

Alice has returned with the baby. Don't worry, sweetie, she says, reaching out to stroke the boy's hair. He'd have gone straight to heaven. The angels would take good care of him. that's what angels do.

Lucas stops trembling and Mia feels his small form grow tense as if his unique brain is straining to make sense of what his mother is telling him. She restrains a smile at Alice's home-spun theology of heaven. She remembers how Taylor drew God at Christmas, insisting that God was somewhere high up. As

SARAH KLASSEN

far as Mia is concerned God's whereabouts are a mystery and
the nearest thing to heaven would be sitting beside Kurt in the
movie theatre, his arm around her. His hand warm on her thigh.

Lucas surfaces out of his incomprehension. Jeremy was very
very very sick, he repeats, watching his aunt.

Your brother will be okay, Mia says, still holding him tight.
Look, he's sleeping now. He just closed his blue eyes. He's going
to grow up big and strong. Just like you.

Mia thinks that if Lucas were a different boy he might ask,
Do babies in heaven grow up? Do they get to be big boys? But
Lucas is Lucas and Mia wonders how her sister, rocking Jeremy
and oblivious to everything else, would answer such questions.
Come, Lucas, she says and takes him by the hand. You and me
are going to the park.

But your gown, Alice says.

The gown can wait. Let's go, Lucas. I'll swing you real high.

Yeah, yeah, yeah, Lucas mumbles. To heaven.

~

Millicent watches Mia shove book after book into her backpack, pausing now and then to run the palm of her hand across
a jacket as if she's caressing something live. Millicent remembers how her daughter used to ask for change to pay for overdue
books and often she'd bring the change back and say, The librar-
ian forgave me. As she should, Millicent always thought. Mia
never lost or defaced a book.

Mia, that's a pretty hefty backpack, Millicent says, concern
in her voice. You won't be running to school today. She pauses,
smiles and adds, School year's nearly over. Are you glad?

Mia's response is a small twist of surprise that becomes a
half-smile. Glad? she says. Yes. I guess so.

Better get going, Millicent says gently, or you'll be late. She wants to hug her daughter but instead picks up the morning paper, moves to the dining room window, glances at the headlines. After Mia leaves she will tackle today's agenda: sorting clothes. She has already emptied a drawer of sweaters and socks onto her bedroom floor, pulled pants and blouses and skirts from her half of the closet. She'll wash them this afternoon, and tomorrow pack everything that's going to the thrift store on Thursday. She has left Joseph's side of the closet unculled.

The sky is cloud-covered, it's going to rain, and light falls stingily on the front page of the *Winnipeg Free Press*. Mia comes to stand beside her mother. Look, she says. Look at Dad's peonies, and together they admire the new plants in Joseph's perennial bed.

This summer I might help with the gardening, Millicent is saying just as the black Camaro coming along Kildonan Drive turns in at the driveway.

Must have forgotten something, Mia says.

Can't be his lunch, Millicent muses. I haven't packed lunches for him since before you were born. And not for you in years. She is amazed at this. Amazed at how time has flown. Millicent goes to the door to meet Joseph and Mia follows. The man who enters is not the bearer of good news. Millicent thinks he has aged. He is on his way to being old.

What, Dad? What? Mia asks, frightened.

Joseph steps inside and shuts the door. It's Danny. Joseph glances at Millicent, hesitates, as if he can say nothing more because he must shield her from this grief.

As if my work at the thrift store means nothing, Millicent thinks. As if I haven't been taking my medication regularly. As if I haven't survived a man's unfaithfulness. She puts down the *Free Press* and steps closer to her husband, compelling him to address them both.

His mother found him, Joseph says. He overdosed.

Mia raises a hand to her mouth and stares at her father.

Millicent braces herself against this new disaster that will sweep them all into its vortex. She reaches with clumsy, unpractised arms to enfold Joseph and Mia, who has pressed her face against her father's shoulder. Millicent holds on to both of them. Tightly.

~

Two students carrying flutes walk up to the stage and begin playing a melody that floats sombrely through the cavernous space of George Sutton Collegiate's newly renovated but still unnamed gym. Bach, Mia thinks. She is sitting beside Bev, four rows from the front. The word "bitch" rings in her head. Insistently.

Already the refurbished gym has been the venue for a school dance, the last one of the year. The student council and their supporters festooned it with streamers and banners, blew air into bunches of balloons, rented strobe lights, hired the best live band they could afford and sold tickets. Teachers scheduled for supervision reported a civilized affair: fewer than a dozen smokers caught in the washrooms. Three or four unregistered guests ordered to leave. No fights. No drugs (detected). No weapons. The troublemakers who cruised in late declared the event boring, the entire student council wimps and the supervising teachers spineless scum. Then they left. Students danced until one o'clock.

In a few weeks, desks will be hauled from classrooms into the gym and lined up in long rows for the final exams. Final torture, some students call it and some teachers agree. Maths students will be seated alternately with history students, like a checkerboard, to minimize cheating, and teachers will invigilate, some casually, some like hawks. Ab Solinsky will appear midway through an exam and stand at the entrance, arms folded, surveying with satisfaction the quiet sea of teenage heads bent over problems and questions, their foreheads wrinkled with indecision or smooth with confidence. He'll raise his eyes to the far reaches of the restructured space he is so proud of. And would like named for himself. Mia's father will stride in from time to time to chat with on-duty teachers and check on the paper supply. If the exam days are hot, the gym will be the coolest place in the whole building.

And at the end of June friends and families of the graduation class will crowd into the gym and sit facing the stage lined with pots of hothouse chrysanthemums. The graduates in blue caps and gowns will file in to receive their diplomas and accept a handshake and congratulations from Ab Solinsky, who is retiring.

Mia is surprised to see the gym fill up so quickly. With Danny drifting to the periphery of school life this year, then asked to leave, she doubts he had many friends left. No one should be so bereft. She pushes away the suspicion that the students streaming in may be lured by crass curiosity, and that only death can provide Danny with a measure of significance. A small share of the school's attention. She thinks the silence may not be so much respect as a consequence of her classmates' uneasiness with the Grim Reaper.

The two flautists are playing "O Danny Boy." Bev is dabbing her eyes with Kleenex. The song is an odd choice for a student of Dutch descent, but Mia can't think of what she would replace it with.

When Mr. Yakimchuk asked his English class who would prepare a tribute to their classmate, everyone looked at Mia, but she shook her head, I can't, and the ensuing back and forth led nowhere until finally Angela volunteered. Okay then, she said. I'll do it. For Danny, I'll do it. No one thought she was a good choice. Mr. Yakimchuk looked nervous, as if he was sure she would say something embarrassing, something that would reflect badly on him. He waited for someone else to step forward, but no one did.

You have to help me, Angela told Mia when she realized what she'd agreed to.

Mia, marvelling at how quickly Danny's death had altered Angela's opinion of him, tried to suppress her misgivings.

The assembly rises as Danny's mother is led in, a slender, greying woman in a beige dress, her back slightly bent. She is not crying but keeps her head down and clings to the man leading her in. A small entourage follows, then the administrators, and finally Angela Leclaire trailing them, pretty in her frilly white blouse.

When Mrs. Haarsma is seated and the formal party has reached the stage, the school's vocal group steps forward and Mia sees her father leave his place beside the principal to join the baritone section. They sing a jazzy version of "Amazing Grace," the harmony provided mainly by her father. Mia closes her eyes to listen. *I once was lost but now am found.* Danny, she thinks, was lost but never found. Never properly searched for. She avoids looking at Angela on the stage.

Principal Ab Solinsky steps forward to face the gathered silence. He speaks of George Sutton's loss, a young life cut short, a future unrealized, a tragedy that touches them all. As his words drone on, Mia senses the beginning of a vast restlessness behind her. This assembly will not erupt as student assemblies sometimes do. Death will keep any heckling at bay, there will be no catcalls, no outbursts of rude laughter. But a spell has been broken. The masses are bored, even the students who minutes ago were audibly sniffling.

As the principal's rhetoric swells and dissipates in the empty space above the mourners, a scene takes shape in Mia's head: The quiet room, where Danny, lifeless, lies for hours before he is found. The blinds are drawn, light of the dawning day cannot get in. Bits of paraphernalia lie scattered around the body: Empty vials? Needles? Mia's imagination falters. The noise of traffic on Edison Avenue intrudes on the death scene. Danny's mother opens the door to his room and calls out to her son, Wake up, time to get up. When she discovers him crumpled on the floor she bends to touch the cold, blanched face. She shakes his inert body, trying to rouse him from sleep. But he doesn't move. She cannot wake him. She steps to the window to let in the sunlight that will warm her son. Bring him back to life.

But the sun sheds light only on what has been lost. For the rest of her life the mother will try to rid herself of what the sun revealed. Danny, Danny, she cries, her wail circling the room.

Mia reins in her imagination, and hears Danny's last message: "Bitch." She can't erase that telephone message or blot out the flat and non-negotiable "no" she gave Danny when she spoke to him for the last time, not knowing it was the last time. With great effort she closes the door on that scene, only to have it replaced with GranMarie's wispy, white hair and thin face. She pictures her grandmother stretched out, perfectly still on her apartment bed, eyes closed. And then Jeremy comes to mind, unbidden, a small boy's body, asleep like the children in Gran-Marie's album, white daisies pinned to his sleeve.

An old woman at the thin end of her life. A child with Fragile X and scant hope for thriving. And Danny. Who should be taken and who left? The idea startles her—who is to say? Who decides? God? If so, what was God thinking, choosing Danny for this tragic exit in the spring of the year when he should be graduating?

Angela has stepped to the podium and is well into the tribute Mia helped her prepare. The familiar words flow from her friend's brightly lipsticked mouth: .

It's not just your accomplishments that identify you, Angela is reading, *not the awards you win or the marks you get in school. That's not who you really are. There's also that part of you that wants things so badly it hurts, the part of you that reaches for things that are always out of reach. The part that's vulnerable. And scared. The part of you that wants a life. That needs friendship. At least one friend to count on.*

At this point Mia had wanted to conclude the tribute. They were seated in the library, near to closing time. Better to end it while we're ahead, she told Angela, fearing what else might come into her friend's head to say. But Angela had stormed at her. What? Cut it short like his life is cut short? Just like that? You'd leave it all half-finished? God, Mia, first you refuse to speak at his memorial and now you think we're wasting time on him? Wasting words? So Mia backed off, letting Angela ramble ahead on her own, which is what she is doing now, naming things Danny loved, making them up because, really, what did Angela know about him? What did anyone know?

For the ending Angela has insisted on quoting from *Hamlet,* the drama they'd been reading in class with Mr. Yakimchuk. A tragedy to end the school year. Mia steels herself, expecting to cringe at the bizarre comparison—Danny and Prince Hamlet— but finds herself smiling. She puts an arm around Bev, who is sobbing beside her as Angela reads, her voice steady, pure and completely sincere:

Good night, sweet prince;
And flights of angels sing thee to thy rest!

The gym empties quickly. Danny's mother climbs into a car
that takes her away with her sorrow and her drab clothes that
contrast sharply with the students' cheerful shorts and T-shirts.

Classes are over for the year. It's time to hang out at McDonald's or the NorVilla, gather in groups on the lawn in front of the
school, smoking, laughing. Or roar away in cars or hang out in
the park or plan the next party. Or even study. The sky is overcast, the air warm and muggy. It's going to rain.

Mia says good bye to Bev and heads home, not jogging but
walking. Kurt overtakes her, falls into step and when they get to
his house he doesn't turn in but continues with her to the Wittenberg bungalow.

You were his best friend, he says.

Mia turns to study Kurt's face, as if she must discover what he
really thinks of Danny.

I used to think he was like a ... you know ... like some project for you, Kurt says. You took it so seriously.

Mia studies the smooth, strong line of Kurt's jaw, the curve
of his mouth.

I was wrong, he says. You were really his friend.

Mia lowers her eyes. She wants to tell him about Danny's last
phone call. Wants to say, Can't you see? I failed him. But she is
quiet. She wants Kurt to touch her, hold her. She wants to feel
his body pressed hard into hers. His mouth on her mouth. She
wants to be saved from grief.

Kurt picks a leaf from the cotoneaster hedge and crushes it
between his fingers. The first drops of rain are falling.

Want to come in? she asks.

He hesitates, then shakes his head. I better study. He begins
to leave, but turns back, opens his arms and pulls Mia in for

friendly, light embrace, then quickly releases her, just as the rain becomes a steady drizzle. See you, he says as he turns to run. A few steps and he turns around once more, sees Mia watching him.

You'll be going to grad, he says. As if that is in doubt.

Mia holds her breath and waits for him to ask her to be his date, but Kurt says, Danny should be there, graduating with us.

Yes. Mia shrugs.

Well, see you then, Kurt says, turns and runs into the rain.

Mia is too distracted to study. Her mother is in the bedroom, still sorting clothes. Her father is at school, chairing the committee of staff and students set up to select a name for the new gym.

When he comes home, Joseph announces that the name of the new gym will be the Ab Solinsky Sports Hall. And that he, Joseph, has requested a leave of absence for the coming year.

~

The rain that began the day of Danny's memorial service continues falling. All the new leaves are dripping moisture and the ground is soaked. Millicent takes a large bag of clothing and an umbrella with her to the bus stop, refusing Joseph's offer of a ride to the thrift store. Before she settles down with a textbook to cram for exams, Mia runs in the rain and comes home drenched. Joseph's garden glistens, black and wet.

~

In her bedroom at Wild Oak Estates, Marie Wittenberg is getting out of bed when her foot catches on the mat. She stumbles and falls face down. The force of the impact fractures a thigh bone. Pain blazes through her body and won't let her move. She loses consciousness. If the sun were not shrouded in overcast, it would find her there and shine its warmth on her thinly clad body, on her bare ankles sticking out from her flimsy nightdress. It would illuminate her ashen face.

Hour after hour she lies, emerging at times from the grey murk of unconsciousness only to sink back into it. Sometimes she tries to move her arms and legs as if she must propel her body forward toward solid ground because she is drowning in the Black Sea. She struggles to reach shore, a spread of warm sand where she might gain a foothold. But the Black Sea beaches are stony, she will stub her toes and cry out and fall. She has already fallen. Rain clatters against the window.

Rescue comes toward evening. Mia has telephoned repeatedly and getting no answer, grabs the key to her grandmother's apartment, laces up her running shoes and races through the rain along the familiar route, afraid of what she will find. She lets herself in, heart pounding, trying to brace for the worst, and when she sees the small mound that is her grandmother gets down on all fours beside her, water streaming from her shoulders. GranMarie, she says. GranMarie, I'm here. It's okay. I'll help you. But when she touches the bent leg, her grandmother opens her eyes and screams and a neighbour comes running.

The ambulance arrives and GranMarie, sedated, is brought to a hospital bed, where she sleeps as if she will never waken. Surgery is scheduled for the next day, a doctor informs the family.

You can't be serious, Joseph says. Surgery for this old woman?

Cruel, Mia thinks.

But the doctor is adamant: the bone must be pinned. There is no other way.

Mia abandons the particulars of genes and chromosomes and DNA—the bits and pieces out of which the looming biology exam will be made—and arrives at the hospital at midday after her grandmother's surgery. She finds the old woman motionless on blue hospital sheets, as if she is done with the whole business of life. Her eyes are shut. Unwilling to disturb her, Mia leaves.

When she returns the next day, GranMarie is agitated, moaning and struggling to raise her leg above the guard rail of the mechanized bed. Her thin arms flail like erratic sails of a broken windmill. When Mia places a restraining hand on GranMarie's leg, the leg pushes back with amazing strength, pushes against the bedrail, determined to get out of this cage. *Jesus, Jesus*, Gran-Marie moans. *Gospodi pomiluj. Gospodi pomiluj.*

The nurses are baffled. What language is this woman speaking?

Mia watches the old eyes fill with tears that spill over onto her sunken cheeks and roll onto the pillow and it seems that a life is escaping with that thin watery trickle, as if the body can no longer contain the strong spirit it has housed for nine decades.

On the third day, Mia can see that GranMarie is past delirium, no longer hallucinating. She lies docile on the hospital bed, her arms straight at her side, above the covers. Joseph comes to stand at her bedside, helpless and awkward. He can't stay long. Then Alice is there, kneeling, lips moving in prayer. When she rises she hugs Mia and says, I have to go. The boys are at the neighbours. Alone with her grandmother, Mia touches a hand and it twitches back as if such contact is painful. GranMarie's eyes open, then fall shut like the heavy lids of a china doll. Mia pulls a chair close to the bed.

A while later her grandmother opens her eyes and asks, Is this real? Or are we dreaming? Then she sleeps and when she next wakes she peers at Mia as if to determine who this person might be, sitting silently at her bedside. Is that you, Mama? she asks, surprised and uncertain, but also eager. Is it really you? She attempts to raise a hand.

Shh, Mia says. Shh. She guides the hand back to the side of the body.

Her grandmother's breathing is sometimes shallow, sometimes hard and rasping. Mia tries to match her own breathing to GranMarie's and finds the intervals between breaths eerily long. The gaunt body doesn't shift and the old woman finds speech difficult. Are we there yet? she gasps. Mia wonders if her presence is an intrusion, an interruption of a strenuous task her grandmother is in the midst of and must at all cost complete.

And suddenly Marie Wittenberg's blue eyes become bright as nails. She looks directly at the girl, opens her mouth and says, with obvious effort: I ... love ... you ... Mia.

Mia looks at her watch: it is exactly three-thirty. She keeps her eyes fixed on the almost imperceptible rise and fall of the sheet that covers the still-breathing form. So this is what dying looks like. She wonders if her grandmother is in pain. Should she leave and allow her to finish in privacy this arduous and slow work?

Once again the lids open, and the lips move. Mia, a faint voice says, I'm going away.

Where to, GranMarie?

Well, home, of course.

Shortly afterwards the nurse comes and reaches under the covers with her hand. The feet are cold, she tells Mia, who nods as if she understands. She leans forward in her chair, unwilling now to miss this departure.

She watches and waits. Death is in no hurry. And then, into Mia's brain, emptied of biology and Danny's death and everything else, stream the words she will speak in tribute to her grandmother. The stream becomes a flood, there is so much to say, so much life to acknowledge. Mia knows she will be the one to speak even if Alice is the older grandchild. She will end her tribute with the lines from Anton Chekhov. She has memorized the words and now she lets her lips move to form them:

We shall rest! We shall hear the angels, we shall see the whole sky all diamonds, we shall see how all earthly evil, all our suffering, are drowned in the mercy that will fill the whole world.

The rain continues falling. On stunted oaks in the park, on pavement, on Joseph's garden. It seeps into the earth and all underground life is soaked through. Water pools in low spots on lawns and roadways. The air is saturated.

On the hospital bed the old woman has stopped breathing.

~

Marie Wittenberg's entire family attends her funeral. Phil and Sue fly in from Toronto with Taylor. Alice comes with Brian and the two boys. If Jeremy becomes too restless Brian will carry him to the cry room at the back.

I be very good, Lucas tells Mia. Very, very.

Pastor Heese has insisted the funeral must take place in the Mennonite church on Edison Avenue where Marie Wittenberg is a member, though her name has long ago been transferred to the "inactive" list. She is one of ours, he says. She belongs. He begins the service by reading:

No eye has seen,
no ear has heard.
no mind has conceived
what God has prepared for those
who love him—

A small number of church people have braved the continuing rain, parked their umbrellas in the foyer and now they rise to sing: *When we all get to heaven.* Joseph walks forward to read a short obituary. Mia is appalled. How is it possible to whittle her grandmother's rich life down to such bare bones? Her father didn't ask her for help, probably scribbled down what he knew at his desk in his office, his mind on year-end duties, the commencement program still to be finalized. Does he even guess how much his daughter knows about Marie Wittenberg?

And then it's Mia's turn. She will not fill in the spaces of GranMarie's life left blank by her father, though she could. Nor, after all, will she recite the lines from *Uncle Vanya* because then she might cry and what would be the good of that? She'd cried when she walked home from the hospital for the last time, rain falling steadily, the dying woman's words echoing in her head: I … love … you … Mia.

She addresses her grandmother:

GranMarie, I can't remember whether you ever gave me a doll or a book or jewellery. I don't think you did. But over this past year when we sat for hours together in your apartment, you told me stories about a country I have never seen and people I have never met. Stories of fear and love and loss. Stories of travel. You gave me the names of ancestors: Johann Bartsch, Judith Bartsch, Abram Franz, Hanna. And names of places: Wassilyevka, Barvenkovo, Yalta. You gave me the best gift you had to give. I will treasure your stories and one day I will tell them to my children.

Joseph and Millicent are seated in the front row, facing a small table at the foot of the pulpit. The table is covered with a white cloth on which a vase crammed with red roses sits beside a photo of a young Marie Wittenberg and an urn containing her ashes. Ab Solinsky and Peter McBride have come to show support for Joseph. They sit near the back, poised to leave early.

Marie Wittenberg's death has come at an inconvenient time in the school schedule.

Good bye, GranMarie, Mia says. I love you too. She steps down and sits beside her parents.

While the small gathering makes its way through a final song—"There's a Land that is Fairer than Day"—people begin to leave. There will be no parade of mourners following Gran-Marie's body to a cemetery; her ashes will be taken to the white bungalow on Kildonan Drive. Someone pulls roses from the arrangement on the table and distributes them among the family members. Mia presses her lips to the soft petals.

When the Wittenbergs leave the church, the rain has stopped. By evening the sun is out and at nightfall its descent sets fire to the western sky, turning what's left of the clouds scarlet, then mauve and pink. Mia, alone in the rain-drenched back yard, watches, entranced. The view from GranMarie's sixth-floor window would be spectacular.

~

The day after the funeral Mia muddles her way through the biology exam. There has been little time to study for it. Fragments of information float through her brain and she reaches for them in desperation. If the questions were about Fragile X she would know what to write. But they are not.

Complete disaster, she tells Bev and Angela.

Bev tries to console her: No way, Mia. You probably aced it.

You're just being modest, Angela complains. Anyway, it's over. What about your grad gown? Get going, Mia. Get with the program already.

That evening Kurt calls to ask if she'll be his date at the grad banquet and dance. That is, if you're still free, he says. Are you?

Yes! Yes! Yes, she is free! It's all she can do to sound casual. She is so totally ready to exchange the ashes of mourning for the oil of joy. She wants to shout, Hallelujah! Maybe she didn't totally screw up bio.

~

Charged with purpose, Mia drives to the Polo Park shopping mall on Saturday and picks out a yellow dress. It complements your tan, the clerk says. And your lovely brown hair. No one has ever used the word "lovely" to describe any part of Mia. Does this woman really mean it? You'll be stunning. Trust me. The clerks smiles, hands Mia the bag with the yellow dress.

Driving home, Mia wonders if Kurt thinks her hair is lovely. Why did he wait so long to ask her? Could it be possible that other girls turned him down before he called her? Or did the grad party fail to register on his radar until the last minute because this rite of passage just isn't very important to him? She has run with Kurt, sat in the same history class, worked beside him at McDonald's, but he is still a stranger.

~

Joseph and Mia are emptying the apartment where Marie Wittenberg spent her last years. Joseph is dismayed at the quantity of his mother's possessions. He would like to make short shrift of the task, but Mia is in no hurry. For his daughter this is a labour of love. He watches her open a drawer with yellowed handkerchiefs, old postcards and letters. She finds a faded sepia photo of a clumsy contraption with large wheels. Look, she says.

Joseph takes it from her, puzzled. What's this ancient beast?

It was made in the Lutzch factory, she says. GranMarie told me. It's like a tractor, for farm work.

Joseph dimly remembers hearing about the factory. It never interested him. Now he realizes that Mia knows more about it than he does.

In a corner of the drawer, Mia find an envelope and in it a card. She unfolds it and reads, "With all my love, Ronald." Ronald?

That's one story I know, Joseph says. He reaches for the note.

A love story? Mia holds the piece of paper away from him.

Yes.

Is it about Yalta?

No. Edison Avenue. Joseph waits for Mia to ask for more, because suddenly he is ready to tell her the story, but Mia is rereading the note and then turns deliberately to the drawer. Joseph feels rebuffed. All winter he has felt his daughter's aloofness and here in this apartment, it creates a palpable distance between them. Frustrated, he picks up the beige shell from Yalta. He studies it, turning it this way and that. On the night of their mutual confessions his mother had said, Your grandfather bought that shell for your grandmother the summer we lived in Yalta. The year after the tsar and his family were murdered. Isn't it beautiful? To please her he had said, Yes, and she said, Well, you can have it. But you'll have to wait till I'm gone. It won't be long.

Seeing him examine the shell, Mia says, When I was small, GranMarie held the shell to my ear and told me to listen and I would hear the sea. She wanted me to have it. When you're grown up, she'd say.

Joseph does not contradict her claim.

In another corner of the drawer Mia finds a wad of crumpled bills. She gasps and smoothes them out and with obvious excitement tells her father how they were wrapped in dough, baked and brought to Canada. Didn't GranMarie tell you that story?

Joseph hears the question as an accusation. He shakes his head, ashamed, and says, If she did, I wasn't listening. Joseph marvels how his mother's stories have skipped a generation and settled with Mia. Except one. He takes the roubles from her and examines the scrunched face of the tsar. Look, he says, the date, it's 1900. Mia, you get the shell. I'll keep these roubles.

Mom should be here, Mia says, taking the shell. She's the expert at sorting. She knows how to get rid of things.

His hands full of useless roubles, Joseph is glad Millicent isn't here. He wants to speak to Mia. Remember that skating party at Christmas? he says. The question you asked me?

For a moment Mia doesn't know what he's talking about, and when she remembers she says, brusquely, Sorry, Dad. Was that too close for comfort? Okay, I shouldn't have asked. It was none of my business. She rummages in a drawer as if this common task of emptying the room is all that matters.

You had every right to ask, Joseph says. Yes, I loved Hedie Lodge. I made love to her and betrayed your mother. And you. And my church. I was unfaithful to all of you. And I keep thinking if you can forgive me then maybe your mother can too.

Mia has never heard her father speak so contritely. And she has never before been given the burden of such a confession. It is too much. It is unfair. She turns the shell over and over in her hand.

Joseph does not press Mia. He folds the roubles and shoves them into his pocket. He makes no objection when Mia claims a perfume bottle she finds shoved into a corner behind a stack of plates as if someone had intended to hide it.

~

The next day Joseph is sitting in the principal's office waiting for Ab Solinsky to put down the receiver on a telephone conversation that's going on too long. Joseph looks about him at the space that would be his to occupy next year if he had chosen differently. Several framed certificates hang on the wall. A shelf holds Ab's golf trophies. The central piece of furniture is a massive oak desk—does it belong to the office or is it Ab's personal property? Joseph is not caught up in regret. Instead he runs through the details he must attend to in order for the school year to end well.

If anyone had warned him that his daughter would graduate without being singled out for some honour or recognition he would not have believed it. Every year of her school life Mia has received prizes—for good attendance, good writing, good attitude. She's been praised for her contribution to student life. Her grades have been excellent. But at this afternoon's awards ceremony, where Kurt walked away with the title of "best athlete," Mia did not receive a single scholarship or school award. She has not been chosen valedictorian. In her final year her involvement in student life has been as unremarkable as her final report card: B in biology, the other sciences a modest pass, in English only a C. What unsettles Joseph most is that Mia has not said anything about her plans for the next year. Does she have plans?

Damn! Ab slams down the receiver. Bruce Cameron is bailing out on us.

How come? Joseph asks, shifting quickly into problem-solving mode. Commencement is only days away.

He left yesterday with the premier's trade mission to Hong Kong. That was his office informing us. As if George Sutton Collegiate doesn't count.

He's doing what any MLA would do, Joseph says.

It's a big letdown for the school. It's a slap in the face. Ab is furious.

I'm on it, Joseph says, rising briskly, keeping his voice upbeat. We'll get someone else. But as he leaves the principal's office, strides down the hall and out to the parking lot, his churning brain fails to throw out even one potential replacement speaker.

At home he finds Mia and Bev stir-frying vegetables in the kitchen. Millicent is there too, paging through the latest issue of *Canadian Living*. They're featuring soups, she says.

We've just lost our commencement speaker, Joseph announces. His wife and the girls sense the urgency in his voice and turn to him. Any bright ideas? he asks.

Good riddance to the MLA, Mia says. He would have given us the usual upward and onward speech. Go get 'em. Reach for the top. Anything would be better. She tends to the stir-fry.

Ask Pastor Heese, Bev says. He'll do it.

Mia looks up, astonished, and Joseph finds himself wanting to laugh. There's still time, he says, evading Bev's suggestion.

~

Commencement day has come and Joseph watches from the stage as the students file into the Ab Solinsky Sports Hall, Mia near the end of the long, snaking line, far from Bev and Angela. And Kurt. Somewhere in that crowd of friends and relatives Millicent and Alice are watching the procession. And Hedie Lodge should be here, too.

Also present, right here on the podium, is Reverend Edward Heese, pastor of the Mennonite church. He wears a beige jacket, yellow shirt, his tie is indifferently knotted. He looks as relaxed and comfortable as if he is in his own church and knows every one of the assembled guests personally. I'll see what I can do, he said when Joseph called. All I can promise you is I'll be short. And he chuckled.

The program had already been printed with Bruce Cameron's name and the title of his address: "The Key to Success." Ab Solinsky had liked the title. He'll tell our graduates to shape up and conquer the world, he told Joseph. He'll be excellent. It's what they need.

And it's what Mia would consider cliché, Joseph refrained from saying.

Great title, Edward Heese said when Joseph apologized for the short notice and showed him the printed program. I think I'll just borrow it, if that's okay. And Joseph wondered uneasily if he planned to simply quote his favourite Bible texts.

When the graduates are seated, a hush falls over the assembly, as if the gravity of this milestone has cast a spell over them. Then the speeches begin and the graduates listen attentively. No one whispers or fidgets. The valedictorian reviews highlights of the graduating year—the great school dances planned by a great student council; the fantastic trip to Greece; the smashing successes of the GSC Saints. This state-of-the-art new gym. And of course lasting friendships.

When it's time to introduce the commencement speaker, Joseph's uneasiness returns. He identifies Edward Heese as a man from the community, a pastor of a local church—he doesn't say which—and someone who has the interests of youth at heart. Heese walks forward carrying nothing in his hand. No notes, no Bible.

True to his promise, the speech is short. He addresses the students as friends, reminds them that they hold the hopes and the future of the community. Don't let the world sell you short, he says. The shining red apple of success will be held up to you like a prize. You will be urged to reach for wealth and power and popularity. You will be pressured to believe that you deserve the best and life is short. But does the world know what you're really capable of? Does it know the passion and brightness of youth? Does it understand the real desires of your heart? Your hunger and what will satisfy it?

For his Sunday sermons, the pastor uses his hands and here too he raises them as he begins reciting: *If I speak in the tongues of mortals and of angels, but do not have love, I am a noisy gong or a clanging cymbal ... . Love is patient; love is kind; love is not envious or boastful or arrogant or rude. It does not insist on its own way; it is not irritable or resentful; it does not rejoice in wrongdoing, but rejoices in the truth.*

Joseph is nervous. He doesn't dare turn to see if Ab Solinsky is displeased, but looks out into the audience where Millicent is seated, small and serene, listening to an ancient definition of love.

Love bears all things, Edward Heese continues, *it believes all things, hopes all things, endures all things.* This is your key to success, not the kind that simply accumulates achievements and celebrity, but the kind that lets you become the human beings you were meant to be.

Joseph's throat is dry by the time the pastor says: *And now, faith, hope, and love abide, these three; and the greatest of these is love.*

The students, impatient for their diplomas, offer modest applause and Ab Solinsky steps importantly to the podium. Relieved that Pastor Heese has kept it short, Joseph takes his place at a table stacked with scrolled diplomas, calls the students forward alphabetically, hands the appropriate scroll to the principal and watches him do the honours.

By the time Mia's name is called, the tension that has held the crowd is slackening, the audience becoming restless. Joseph watches his daughter walk forward. The mortarboard cap covers a good part of her broad forehead. Her hair streams out from under the cap and falls on her blue robe. She is composed and walks up the long aisle with grace. Joseph feels shaky as he hands her scroll to the principal. Mia ascends the steps to the stage and approaches the podium. Ab Solinsky shakes her hand, presents her with the diploma and speaks his congratulation as he has done with every other student. When he lets go Mia's hand, Joseph leaves his place at the table, almost emptied now of scrolls, steps forward and puts his arms around Mia's blue-gowned shoulders. He draws her into an embrace and kisses her on one cheek, then the other. The entire assembly explodes in exuberant applause, wild cheers, foot-stomping that doesn't stop. A dam has burst and all the pent-up excitement, restrained during the formalities, breaks through in an unstoppable surge. The clapping and whistles and cries of Go Mia, Go, Girl, do not die down until she has completed the long walk back to her place.

~

The dining room at the Fort Garry Hotel is a sea of pastel green linen and white daisies, gleaming silver and sparkling glasses. Kurt—in his rented tuxedo—takes Mia—in her yellow dress—by the hand and they find the table they will share with Kurt's basketball friends and their dates. Angela and Bev with their escorts are at the next table. Beside them is Jane Kerr, her head resting on the green linen, her face grey. Her escort's chair is empty but he comes in suddenly with several hotel staff armed with damp cloths to wipe away the evidence of Jane's misfortune. Bev looks as if she might cry. Angela is hiding a smirk.

Kurt attacks the salad with a healthy appetite but Mia isn't hungry. She excuses herself and heads for the washroom, a large, immaculately tiled space, shining and clinical. She has it all to herself. She sees her reflection in a full-length mirror, the yellow dress against a dazzling background of white cubicle doors.

She steps closer and stares at the slender girl with blue-grey eyes and straight brown hair. (You're not getting it done? Angela said, alarmed. Not even for the dinner and dance?) The girl in the mirror moves her hands up along her thighs and hips, along her slender waist, they cradle her breasts and then trace the lines of her throat and up to her tanned cheeks. She practises a smile. Bev has told her she should smile more. It makes you beautiful, she said last week and Mia laughed.

Here I am, Mia thinks, at the grad party, in the women's washroom of one of the city's finest hotels, admiring myself in the mirror. How ridiculous is that? The girl in the mirror is laughing, that's how ridiculous. The laughter is spontaneous and it softens the young face and Mia can see that it is beautiful. And thank God she hasn't thrown up and her face isn't pressed to the hotel linen. All is not lost.

When she returns to her table, everyone is well into the entree—roast chicken and mashed potatoes.

You okay, Mia? Kurt asks.

Mia nods. She sees that Kurt is nervous and doesn't quite know what to do with the quantity of cutlery, what to say, how to move and act at a formal dinner. He has no more experience with dating than she has. She listens to the banter around the table, smiling. In spite of the awkwardness, excitement hums around the table. This is a big day. A rite of passage.

When they get up to dance, Kurt and Mia are both tentative, their movements cautious at first, every touch light. They let the music draw them in and Mia lifts her face so Kurt can press his cheek to hers. Then they are close, their bodies in synch with the music and with the warmth and rhythm of their blood.

Afterwards there is a party at the home of one of Kurt's basketball friends, and here the music is louder, the beat more demanding, more intense. Everyone is drinking and laughing and moving to the pulse of the music, drawn into the vortex of its bold rhythm. The giddy heat of sex fills the rooms. Couples find secluded corners. Shoes are kicked off, clothes rumpled, the rest of the world is forgotten. The past school year, the pomp and speeches of the graduation ceremony, the diplomas received, the unfamiliar formality of tonight's dinner—all have become history. The future is of no concern. Only the moment matters.

Time for the riverboat! The student making the announcement has cupped his hands around his mouth and bellows: All aboard! This party's on the move!

To the river! someone answers and there's a tumult of motion and noise.

Mia finds Kurt with other escorts at the kitchen counter scarfing pretzels and guzzling beer as if they haven't eaten all day.

The river cruise, she says. Do we have to go?

Kurt downs the last of his beer. Don't you want to?

Mia shrugs, and Kurt, looking around at his departing friends, does not try to change her mind. He takes her hand and they slip out the door and into Kurt's truck. Before long they are driving north on Henderson Highway and then along Kildonan Drive. He's taking me straight home, Mia thinks, relieved. And disappointed. But Kurt slows at Bur Oak Park, and stops the truck. He walks around to Mia's side, opens the door and offers her his hand. They enter the park together, and walking slowly, follow the paths familiar to them both. Mia finds nothing to say and Kurt too is silent.

They have walked for a long while when the sound of a horn cuts through their silence: the *Paddlewheel Princess*, a brilliantly lit island of pleasure, is rounding the river bend. Dance music and laughter emanate from all decks, filling the night with the carefree happiness of youth.

Mia stops to listen and Kurt stops with her. Every year, from spring to fall, she's watched paddlewheelers ferrying tourists back and forth along the Red River, but she's never once taken the excursion.

Kurt, she asks, have you ever been on the *Paddlewheel*?

No. This would have been my first time.

And I've kept you from it, Mia says and thinks, I've spoiled it for both of us.

It's okay, Kurt says. He leads her off the path and stops, takes off his jacket and spreads it on the damp grass. They settle on it, leaning into each other. Kurt puts his arm around Mia and she rests her head on his shoulder. The boat with its celebrating graduates has passed out of sight, and when the sounds of merriment grow faint and die, Mia feels unutterably sad .

And suddenly the girl reflected in the washroom mirror flashes into Mia's mind. Behind that girl stands a shadowy figure, a Kurt-look-alike in a dark jacket. His face, just above the girl's shoulder, is tanned, his dark eyes searching for hers, his hands moving up along her thighs. Although he is smiling and the girl is smiling too, they are strangers.

And now, Mia thinks, these strangers are going to have sex. For the first time. On dew-damp grass. Above them, framed by leafy oak branches, hangs the lopsided orange face of the waxing moon. The girl is still in her graduation dress. Her yellow graduation dress.

Heat

The Canada Day fireworks have scarcely fizzled out when a heat wave rolls like artillery into the city, leaching it of vitality. Lawns turn brown, leaves on trees and bushes lose colour and become dust-clogged. Flowers open their petals only to let them droop. The population accepts defeat as abjectly as the vegetation. The noise of street repair projects—constant, grating, monotonous—undergirds the torpor claiming young and old. Air-conditioned offices and rooms offer reprieve and on weekends those who can flee to the beaches. Everyone waits for rain.

The Wittenberg household is waiting for air conditioning to be installed. Three weeks at the very earliest, the salesperson warned. Joseph has promised Mia a graduation gift—a used car. She'll need it for university. But Mia has not registered for university, and in this heat he can't muster the effort to shop for a car. Every morning he waters his garden and by evening

331

the ground is cracked and hard. The carrot greens are spindly and the perennials drooping. But the weeds are flourishing and the geraniums blooming blood red. Defeated, Joseph returns to the house, takes a beer from the fridge and goes down to the basement, slightly cooler than the rest of the house. He finds a comfortable chair and reaches for the large brown envelope on the coffee table. It contains his mother's stories. Or rather Mia's version of them. Written for Hedie Lodge. Of whom he must not think. He begins reading.

No cooking, Joseph has told Millicent, but she rises early, boils potatoes and eggs before the worst heat and for supper there is potato salad.

~

On Thursday Millicent takes the bus as usual to the thrift store, where Elaine sets up a fan to move the hot and humid air around. Business is not brisk. The customers are as limp and lifeless as everything else.

My husband has a leave of absence, Millicent tells Elaine.

Does that mean you'll be travelling to all kinds of exciting places?

We have no plans, Millicent says. Travel is not something she has craved, but today a trip to somewhere cool is not unappealing.

Maybe a trip south in winter? Elaine suggests. A Caribbean cruise.

A cruise would drive my husband crazy, Millicent says. On our family camping trips when our girls were little Joseph loved setting up the tent or splitting wood and building a fire. My husband was happy cooking hot dogs and hamburgers over a barbeque. He always had to be doing something. And all the while he'd be singing. After supper he'd take the girls on hikes and they'd come back with stones and flowers and whatnot. When they were older, he loaded bikes for everyone.

Millicent stops, embarrassed. She has used words like "our girls" and "my husband was happy," she's mentioned his singing. She has been describing an outdated version of Joseph, a version so long past it has no reality. She can honestly remember only one family camping trip.

For Millicent, long out of touch with women friends, Thursdays with Elaine have become a highlight, a time of camaraderie that's close to friendship. Now she has bored Elaine with her memories.

What about your daughter? Elaine says. The one who graduated. What's she got in mind to do?

In early spring Millicent told Elaine that Mia was graduating, though she's never spoken about Alice and her family. Mia has no plans, Millicent says, and then, afraid Elaine will think no one in the Wittenberg family ever makes plans, she adds: Not yet.

Because there are few customers, Millicent begins smoothing out crumpled plastic bags. It's true, she thinks, we are a family without plans. Looking for something more to do, Millicent tidies the bookshelves. She hasn't seen Teresa Brady for a while. Danny's mother hasn't been back since Danny's death.

The last customers leave, reluctant to face the heat, and Elaine locks the door and opens the till to count the day's sales. Millicent helps her, then steps out into the hot street and makes her way to the bus stop.

~

For Mia the bridge leading from school into summer is McDonald's. At least there's air conditioning. At least it's a job. But she is restless, and underneath her restlessness there is sorrow, the kind of sorrow triggered by knowing that nothing is permanent and the beauty she sees everywhere in spite of the heat cannot last. The pale blue of the sky in the early morning. Robins startling up from brown grass when she runs to work. The petunias and marigolds planted in pots along Henderson Highway and regularly watered by city crews in spite of the water shortage. The cheeky blackbird chorus. And the long and breathless evenings. Sometimes Mia shivers at the wonder of a single amazing moment. But how quickly joy gives way to frustration and longing.

Working side by side with Kurt at McDonald's has become awkward for both of them, and whoever leaves the building first after a shift does not look back for the other. Outside of work Mia does not see Kurt. They don't expect anything of each other, not since that early morning after the grad dance when they'd lain together on damp grass under the bur oaks, the familiar park wrapped in cool summer darkness. Not complete darkness—there was a partial moon and light was already breaking in the northeastern sky. Their hands fumbled with each other's clothes, their hot breath mingled and their damp skin touched. Their pulsing blood and impatient bodies urged them on, propelled them toward this necessary rite of passage. Everyone does it at grad, Angela had instructed Mia and Bev, as if explaining an initiation into life that must be accomplished before whatever is to come next can reveal itself.

When Mia pulled back and said, Do we have to? Kurt said, We want to, don't we? Don't you want to, Mia? His breath was quick and urgent.

When Mia didn't answer, Kurt groaned and rolled away from her. They straightened their clothes, got up and walked back to the truck, not touching. When Kurt dropped her off at the Wittenberg bungalow the eastern sky was a blaze of light. She ran up the steps without looking back. Her dress was creased and damp, the yellow fabric grass-stained. She was not sure whether she had made, or escaped, a fateful error.

When Kurt says he's quitting McDonald's because he's been accepted on the varsity basketball team and must attend basketball camp at the University of Manitoba, Mia is relieved. And desolate. The summer is passing, each day minutes shorter than the previous one. She wants to hold on to time, no matter how hot the summer is.

One day she sees Kurt drive by in his truck when she's crossing Henderson Highway. The black-haired girl beside him turns her large, dark eyes toward Mia. Mia waves and the girl smiles at her. This is what stories are made of, Mia thinks dully. But it's not a story she'd want to write, not unless she can determine the conclusion. The denouement she intends to compose for her grandmother's unfinished narrative has been put on hold, made impossible by the oppressive heat.

On Mia's Sunday off, Bev comes by and they walk together to the Mennonite church. There's no air conditioning and attendance is sparse with so many families at the lake, the teenagers working at summer camps, and members on vacation from worshipping God. Pastor Heese reads the story of Moses at the burning bush and announces that he's titled his sermon "Surprised by God." Mia's mind wanders from the sermon.

I wish God would surprise me, she tells Bev when the service is over. I don't know about you, but at my house we're all totally limp. And I have no plans, she might have added, but Bev has been accepted for a nursing program in fall and Mia doesn't want to dull her friend's happiness. Or evoke her pity.

From a rack of pamphlets in the foyer Mia picks up a brochure advertising a Mennonite Heritage Cruise. On the front there's a picture of a large cruise ship, the *Dnieper Princess*. Mia opens the brochure, glances through it, folds it and puts it in her pocket.

When she arrives home she finds Alice and her crew in the basement, where it's warmer every day. Our place is worse, Alice says. It's an oven, and Lucas echoes, An oven, Oma, an oven, Anniemie. Brian is having a beer with Joseph. Millicent has made cheese sandwiches and lemonade. She sets a bowl of apples on the table. Jeremy is fretful. Poor little man, Alice says. The heat's hitting you hard, isn't it, sweetie? Lucas, when he's eaten half a sandwich, lies prone on the couch. He refuses an apple.

And that's when Mia unfolds the brochure. Look, she says and holds it up. Look, Lucas. Want to go sailing on this ship?

Brian reaches languidly for the brochure, flips through it. Yeah, sure, he says. Who's volunteering to foot the bill for this fancy excursion? He holds the brochure away from Lucas, who has climbed down from the couch and onto his dad's lap.

Let's go, Daddy, Lucas begs,. Daddy, the boat. Let's go, Daddy.

Joseph takes the pamphlet from Brian. Wouldn't that be something, he says with zero enthusiasm. Yalta, he says, holding up a picture. The Black Sea. From the table beside him he picks up the brown envelope with Mia's stories. I've been reading, he says. About Yalta. About the Black Sea. So maybe I don't need to actually go there. He looks up and finds Mia looking right at him as if she's sending him a challenge. He looks away.

We should go, Mia says. We should all go.

The others look up, surprised. Emboldened, Mia says, We should do the cruise as a memorial to GranMarie. It's possible. Okay, I don't earn enough at McDonald's to get me there. But Bev's grandfather took his entire clan on a Caribbean cruise two winters ago. The Wittenberg family is smaller. It can be done.

Again she turns toward her father, her gaze an outright challenge. Dad's got his leave of absence, she says, and you, Mom, you should take a leave too from the thrift store. And I'll quit at McDonald's. Mia is on a roll. A feeling of power rushes through her.

You want *me* to come too? Millicent is astonished. I'm not even Mennonite.

Of course you have to come.

Alice says nothing. She is holding Jeremy, and her forehead wrinkles as she reads the brochure.

And suddenly Mia realizes that her plan, however brazenly she presents it, is flawed. She has not taken into account the complications of Fragile X. The feeling of power drains away. She sits down beside her sister. Maybe you can come too, she says. But she knows there is no way. Not even if Joseph pays.

It's okay, it's okay, Alice says, brightening. Brian is going to find us a rental cottage at Winnipeg Beach. We're going swimming, aren't we, Lucas?

The boat, Lucas pleads. The big boat, Mom. With Anniemie. He has climbed down from Brian's lap and is bumbling his way to his mother.

Mia intercepts him, swooping the boy up into her lap. She looks ruefully at her sister, who would have to stay behind with Brian. And with Fragile X.

Don't worry, Mia, Alice says. You guys should go. It's a great idea. We'll stay here. We'll be the fans rooting for you all the way. I can't wait to hear all about it. We'll be here for you to come home to. Me and my guys.

Mia wonders how often "my guys" would include Brian, whose job requires frequent trips away and whose absences might be a convenient camouflage for what is a kind of abandonment.

Well, if it weren't for my garden, Joseph begins, confident in his excuse.

Your garden's been neglected before, Mia counters, rallying once more. Anyway, the tour's in August. The beans will be finished and the carrots still in the ground. Sensing victory, she takes the brochure and holds it up like a flag. This cruise can be my grad gift, Mia says. Forget the car. Her boldness begins to galvanize the family.

Joseph, who has never desired to see the country of his ancestors, thinks that the heritage cruise is a whim, not a carefully thought-out plan. But it is his daughter's whim, and he owes her something. Something greater than a belated graduation gift. Mia has not only challenged him: she's offered an opportunity for some kind of atonement.

Okay, he says, surprising everyone, even Mia. We're going.

There's no time to lose. There are few places left on the cruise. Passports and visas must be obtained.

Look, Alice says, arriving on another hot evening with Lucas and Jeremy. I come bearing gifts. She pulls three notebooks from her bag, one blue, one yellow and one red. Assignments, she says. You have to write everything down. Every day. She fans out the notebooks and holds them up like prizes. Take your pick.

Lucas begs, Me, me, Mom! Me!

Joseph picks first. Red is for communism, he jokes as he reaches for the red one, cautiously as if it might explode.

Mia's our writer, Millicent objects. Why can't she do the writing for all of us? She picks the blue one.

Mia takes the one that's left. It's yellow like my grad dress, she jokes.

Alice looks as if she hasn't slept. Send postcards, she says. Lucas will be so thrilled, won't you, my munchkin?

Yah, Lucas mumbles. I eat 'em. Mom, I eat 'em all.

Jeremy begins to wail.

Looking at Alice, Joseph feels guilty. I feel like we're abandoning you, he says, apologetically.

Dad, don't be like that, Alice laughs. We'll be fine. And you'll bring presents. For the boys. Lucas will love that. And God will look after us. Like always.

Then how do you explain the Fragile X? Joseph doesn't ask.

He has been studying maps of the Soviet Union with the enthusiasm of a student tackling an odious assignment and Millicent, resigned, begins reading Mia's stories. It's your father's history, she reminds her daughter. Not mine.

Mia wonders if the cruise was a good idea.

~

By the time the Wittenbergs are ready to leave, the heat has let up and there are signs of energy returning. Mia receives a letter from Hedie Lodge and saves it to read on the flight across the Atlantic.

Dear Mia:

So the Wittenberg family is on the move. Whose idea was that? I know—yours. I'm glad for you. Did I ever tell you that Anton Chekhov lived in Yalta and wrote his plays there? His house has become a museum. Maybe you'll get to see it.

As for me, I'm an armchair traveller. Make that a wheelchair. Every non-traveller needs the stories of those able to leave home. Can I count on reports from a very good writer?

I've moved into a new "home." I should say "have been moved," since motion continues to be problematic. "Assisted living" they call it and I'll need plenty of assistance. This place allows me as much independence as I'll ever have. Everything's built for "wheelchair accessibility"—how I hate the jargon.

Sometimes I feel so completely caged in, I want to reach out and grab the steel bars and tear them away.

You are free, Mia. Fly. Fly while you can.

The other residents here are just as "independent" as I am. Most evenings Rob from next door comes over to play Scrabble. And cheer me up. He's lived here for three years. He's a survivor, he says, and makes me believe that I'll survive too. And that friendship is still possible even for someone as "mobility-challenged" as we are.

Travel well.

Your (not unhappy) friend, Hedie Lodge

P.S. Say hello to your parents. Only if you think it's a good idea.

Mia does not pass the greeting on to her parents.

~

The *Dnieper Princess* leaves Odessa on a warm and cloudless August morning with its full load of tourists. The passengers, still jet-lagged, have breakfasted in the pleasant dining room and are clustered in pairs or groups of threes and fours on the deck, watching as Odessa recedes and becomes a distant ghost-city. Some have already turned away from what they have left and are straining, like travellers at the end of a long journey, to be first to glimpse land.

The Wittenbergs stand apart, as if they are self-sufficient and there's nothing they need from people who are still strangers. The other tour members believe they are shy or aloof, and no one approaches them where they stand at the railing. All three are looking up, watching the gulls carve a symphony of spirals in the sky. When they spot food, the grey birds plummet, then, breakfast clutched in their beaks, they rise triumphantly, screaming up to the blue canopy of sky stretched above the dark waters of the Black Sea.

On this cruise the Wittenbergs will be more constantly in each other's company than at home in their white bungalow. Joseph is thinking of his office at George Sutton Collegiate, now occupied by Claudette Avery, who moved in as soon as the students, clutching their report cards, were gone. She will be the first woman vice principal at the collegiate. What pictures will she hang on the back wall, the space no visitor entering the office can avoid? When Joseph cleared out his office, he brought home the three framed paintings of his black Camaro and told Mia to pick one for herself. They belong together, she said, looking long at each. Danny worked hard at them. And so Joseph gave her all three, but so far no place has been found for them in the Wittenberg bungalow.

Someone Joseph has never met has been appointed acting principal for one year—the position is being held open for his return. If he wants it. But will the burning desire that once possessed him ever again surface? Or has ambition become a burden he no longer wants to carry?

Millicent carries a wary look as she eyes the strangers with whom she is travelling on this cruise ship with its cramped cabins, narrow stairs and confusing gangways. She is determined she'll learn to navigate the maze. She will not panic. Not even if she should lose sight of Joseph and Mia in the crowd. This morning the warmth and light of the sun enfold her and she is determined to be happy. She imagines sitting on a bench in Bur Oak Park watching Lucas clamber up the play structure, and Jeremy rustling through leaves on his chubby feet and calling, Oma, Oma, look at me! The scene is a pretty dream and Alice does not appear in it. What might her daughter be doing right this minute? They have crossed many time zones but Millicent has not learned to say as others do: At home it's midnight now, or: They'll be just getting up, or: Everyone's at work, no use calling home at this hour.

The burden Millicent feels for her daughter could weigh her down, but she has come this far and she will rise to any challenge of the journey she has begun.

The wind sweeps Mia's hair straight up as she turns her face to the sun. She is thinking of Danny, surprised that the memory of him has lost its sting, as if the long flight across the Atlantic has not only swallowed distance but also stretched time, and the grief over his spring suicide has receded the way the highway recedes in the rear-view mirror when you travel across the prairie. She can remember only a few times her family did that, Joseph at the wheel, Millicent beside him, she and Alice in the back, noses pressed to the windows as fields of grain, green or gold, rushed past.

She thinks of Kurt, enrolled in new courses, preparing to be a rising star on the university basketball team. Strange that at one time she expected he would pick her up in his truck or they would wait together for the university bus and meet for lunch, maybe not every day, but often. Kurt will not be thinking of her. Still, she wishes he could see her now, on the deck of the *Dnieper Princess*, tanned, looking out across the Black Sea or up at the hungry gulls. A longing wells up inside her, but it is not only— perhaps not at all—a longing for Kurt, who may be preoccupied with his dark-haired girl friend. The desire that surges so pow- erfully inside her is an indefinable blend of joy and sorrow.

She aims her camera at the gulls.

Mia believes that if GranMarie could have returned to this country and visited only one place it would have been Yalta, which now lies ahead of them on the Crimean Peninsula. But GranMarie never returned to the place where she spent six months when she was younger than Mia is now. Where she began a growth spurt that left her tall and gangly. Where her mother breathed the healing air and was restored sufficiently for her family to believe she would live. From where they set out by boat and train and arrived in Wassilyevka and came to a house that was never home.

Did GranMarie ever feel at home anywhere? Mia wonders. Does anyone?

She turns to her father, who is staring up at the sky. How handsome he is, with his blue eyes, the tan acquired over sum- mer, his firm shoulders, reticent smile. The sun has bleached his hair and now the grey hardly shows. Mia wonders if he's ever spoken to Millicent the way he spoke to her the day they emp- tied out the rooms GranMarie no longer needed. Did he tell her he was sorry? Must a mea culpa always be spoken or is it some- times best left unspoken?

Although Millicent prefers to stay close to Joseph and Mia, this morning she is first to leave the deck. She is walking cau- tiously along the corridor back to their cabin when a friendly, grey-haired woman intercepts her and asks, Where are you from? She is plump, older than Millicent.

Millicent is about to say Canada but stops herself. The woman, she realizes, is referring to earlier origins. Should she say England?

I mean what village were your people from? the woman says.

We ... we're going ... we're interested in Barvenkovo.

Oh.

Millicent knows that Barvenkovo is not on the general itinerary, not a place many Mennonites come from. And not a village, but a town, Mia has explained. We're also going to Was-seel ... , Millicent can't pronounce the name. What about you? she asks.

Come, I'll tell you. The woman introduces herself as Susan Loeppky, takes Millicent's arm, steers her toward a chair in the lounge and unravels a tale of how her grandfather was murdered in a village near the Dnieper River, the armed marauders spilling his blood on the floor of his own house, and then raping his wife and two daughters in the same room after forcing them to serve the bandits a meal of *Borscht* and *Zwieback*. When the terrorists finally left, the three women stepped through blood in their flight from the horror. They escaped to a nearby village, leaving the body of their husband and father behind in their need to find safety. They lived in the land like animals in constant fear of predators, depending on the mercy of strangers, fleeing from village to village, colony to colony. After years of war they crossed Poland, traces of blood still branded in memory if not staining their shoes, then entered Germany and finally crossed the ocean to Canada.

Millicent's brain reels. She wants Susan Loeppky to stop talking. She wants an end to this terrible story.

Quite a story, isn't it? Susan says, almost as if she is pleased with herself for being the dispenser of it.

Excuse me. Millicent rises, pale and unsteady. Can you tell

me how to get to the cabins? She is sure she will throw up. When they reach her cabin she waves Susan Loeppky away and closes the door after her. She feels queasy. Ignoring the nausea, she rummages through her luggage until she finds the blue notebook Alice gave her. And a pen. She sits down at the tiny table and, gripping the pen to steady her trembling hand, writes:

> These people I am travelling with are not my people. Their story is not my story. They frighten me. I should have stayed home with Alice and Lucas and Jeremy. What was I thinking? How will I ever make it?

She stops writing, turns the pen round and round in her hand, then sets it in motion once more, pressing hard on the page:

> I will not be afraid. Marie Wittenberg was never afraid and I won't be either. I'm here where I should be, with my husband and my daughter.

She puts down the pen, closes the notebook, slips between the sheets on her bunk bed and lets the Black Sea rock her.

~

That evening the passengers on the *Dnieper Princess* are seated in rows for a special lecture. A young historian—Adam Sudermann looks scarcely twenty—steps to the podium and announces his topic: "The Golden Age of Mennonites in Russia." It could also, he explains, be called "Before the Fall." He tells his audience—a full attendance, every eye on the speaker—that he plans to describe for them the decades bracketing the turn of the century, the golden era before revolution, civil war, terrorism, famine and typhus put an end to Mennonite prosperity on the steppes.

During this time—sometimes he refers to it as "the great flourishing"—the Mennonites, as if they had finally emerged from slumber, or stepped out of the revolving cycle of village life, opened their eyes, looked around and took small steps in the direction of that larger world from which tradition and conviction had kept them apart. A world against which the authoritative word—of their Book and of their elders—had warned them. Alarmed by this larger world, some packed up and emigrated to another continent, becoming the forerunners of a larger exodus to follow.

But others found the Russian world burgeoning with possibilities and were inspired to try new ways of living in the world. Institutions sprang up in the colonies: post-elementary and teacher training schools; hospitals and havens for the mentally ill; a school for the deaf and dumb; courses for deaconesses; agencies to oversee the welfare of orphans and widows. Families sent their sons—rarely their daughters—to St. Petersburgh or Germany to study engineering, photography or theology. They sent their overflow populations to places far from the mother colonies, places where land was still available for new settlements. The affluent purchased estates outside the colonies, hired local peasants and their own landless people to labour for them. Others became industrialists, built factories where farm machinery and furniture were manufactured. They lived in cities. Isolation was no longer satisfying—or possible or desirable. Their leaders dreamed dreams and had visions. By the 1920s the Mennonites had become a commonwealth that included the original colonies, daughter colonies, remote settlements and estates and urban Mennonites. Their farms and villages continued to thrive. They were the envy of their neighbours and drew the admiration of their government. They sent representatives to the Duma. They never forgot that they had been invited to this land by Catherine the Great, and that Tsar Nicholas II had visited the Mennonite colonies. Twice.

The young speaker's voice is clear and resonant with authority. He warms to his subject and draws his listeners into the spell of his eloquent portrayal of a bygone era. He is a graduate student and knows that he has staked out for his academic studies a time and place dear to the hearts of these travellers.

Mia is stunned. She has come believing she knows a good deal of what there is to know about the land of her ancestors. More even than her father. Hasn't she written stories about it? For Hedie Lodge. For Mr. Yakimchuk, who left GSC in June, relieved of his position. Haven't the stories become her own? Aren't they true? Haven't her father and mother read them in preparation for this family pilgrimage? The speaker's flow of words confronts her with a vast tapestry in which GranMarie's tales are faint and fragile threads.

I know nothing, she thinks, ashamed.

Joseph is embarrassed too. He looks around to gauge the reaction of his fellow travellers. He sees heads nodding agreement. He senses a subdued excitement. Are the others learning something new tonight? Or is the information this ardent student of history articulates so confidently familiar to them?

Millicent has become dizzy with the details. The unrest in her stomach has not subsided. The chairs are pushed too close together, she can feel Joseph's right arm touching hers. And Mia's left shoulder. This is a comfort, but will she be able to escape if nausea overcomes her? Surely it is enough if her husband and her daughter absorb this outpouring of history. She can't be expected to master it too.

The lecturer pauses to drink from the glass of water someone has brought to the podium. He turns a page in his notes and continues:

When you step onto the soil your forefathers owned, where they lived and raised their families, and pursued success and sometimes found failure instead, you will look for evidence of this former glory. And you may find traces—the remains of ornate stone fences in run-down villages, houses with unique architectural details like arched windows, once-stately windmills with broken sails. But if you are hoping to see more of the original grandeur you will be disappointed. You will find poverty and decay, and nothing will be the way your parents or grandparents described it.

Adam Sudermann ups the ante and begins speaking with the kind of fiery oratory Mia imagines once took hold of the prophets Elijah and Jeremiah. He asks, How did our ancestors view their place in history? On what did they build their identity? Were they still the exiles driven from Prussia to find haven and opportunity at the invitation of Empress Catherine, whom history calls "the Great"? What were they thinking when they moved from being the quiet in the land, humble farmers suspect for their insistence on pacifism, and stepped into positions on the larger stage of this vast country that was to become the Soviet Union? We know some were urbanized, the speaker says. We know they were not all equally successful or powerful or wealthy. Their landless populations grew. The disparity between the Mennonites and their Ukrainian and Russian neighbours also grew. Did they remember the poor among them—their own dispossessed, the peasants who worked for them? Did they continue to set their faith and trust in God? Did the democracy they maintained in village politics include everyone, not just men with property?

They taught their children that taking up arms was against

the will of God. Yet in the aftermath of revolution and in the chaos of civil war they abandoned their Anabaptist principles, armed themselves and confronted violently those who threatened them. They did not turn the other cheek. They shot and killed those who wanted to kill them. *Selbstschutz*, they called it. Self-defence.

Ripples of emotion speed through the audience like an electric charge. All three Wittenbergs feel it. When the young man stops speaking and gathers his notes, a forest of hands rises, slanting in his direction.

And what would you have done? someone shouts from the back row, not waiting to be recognized. Wouldn't you have done everything you could to protect your mother? Your sister? Girlfriend? Would you just stand there, watching? Spineless?

Someone interrupts with, That was just a few hotheads.

A very few, another voice adds, You have to put all this into context, for God's sakes. Not blow it up like it was a big deal.

We lost everything. *Everything.* This comes as a wail from an old woman who has boasted that she is going to see the village where she was born. That her family has donated medical equipment for the hospital her father started in that village. That she paid for the extra baggage and held her breath until it cleared customs. We are doing this because it's right, she's always explaining. Because we escaped.

Another voice chimes in: Well, we weren't exactly saints, were we? When our people came from Prussia to these steppes they occupied land without any thought to who'd lived there before them.

You're digging up ancient history, an accusing voice objects.

Isn't that why we're here? Mia thinks. She knows nothing of the *Selbstschutz*. Has never heard the word "Anabaptist." Gran-Marie never spoke it.

When Susan Loeppky rises to speak, Millicent rises too and,

squeezing past a row of knees, makes her way to the exit. I don't need to hear everything, she tells herself. I've had enough of the story. But at the exit she stops and turns to listen.

Susan Loeppky's voice trembles. My grandfather was murdered, she says. My grandmother and aunts raped. Her voice breaks. They lost everything, she sobs. Their lives were ruined. Completely ruined.

Millicent finds a chair in the back and sits down again.

My ancestors were the first from their village to move to the city and build a factory, someone says calmly. We have good reason to be proud of our heritage.

My parents were driven from property they'd struggled and struggled to ...

Our family had no land. Not one bloody *desjatin* ...

We're here in a country that robbed us ...

There is no end to the voices.

A man in a grey sweater rises and waits for an opening in the outrage. The *Selbstschutz*, he says, was our dark hour. It's part of our history and we have to accept it. And we have to remember not to blame the people who occupy the villages our forefathers built and work the land our people owned. They don't even know who we are. And maybe don't care. Just think of it—for over a century our people lived and worked and worshipped here and what's left of their work? *This place knows them no more.* He pauses and then says, But nothing stays the same. Even in the vast Soviet Union things can change. Things are already changing.

Nothing can change this godless regime, a voice calls out angrily. Not even God.

Adam Sudermann interrupts the angry voice to thank the man in the grey sweater. It's late, he says. Let's call it a day.

Millicent slips out ahead of the rest.

Mia watches the young lecturer who has unleashed this

Pandora's box of opinions and passions as he gathers his papers. Does he enjoy provoking people? Has he exaggerated? Was he showing off the way Peter McBride did when he dramatized the Winnipeg Strike for his teenaged history students?

Adam Sudermann must be the second-youngest person on the cruise, Mia thinks. And I'm the youngest.

~

When Joseph returns to the cabin after the lecture he finds Millicent in her bunk, asleep or pretending to be. She has left the light on. He finds his red notebook and opens it to the first page.

No one ever told me the Mennonites took up arms in self-defence. Here I am, first-generation Canadian, and what do I know about my people's history? My family story? Nothing, if Mia hadn't made me read her essays. Tonight was like a high school history class, the way the discussion almost got out of hand. Only a good teacher, or the right topic, gets that kind of reaction. Everybody wanted in. I felt like I was the only student with my homework not done. I actually found myself looking up to see if there was an intercom on the wall above the speaker's head. I expected a voice blaring into the room, telling me to come immediately to the office and account for my ignorance. To explain why I'm so ignorant of my heritage.

Non-violence. I had to think of that January evening when I drove Mia and Bev to the church to pray for peace. It was terribly cold and afterwards we drove out of the city for a good look at the sky. It was breathtaking, I have to say. The stars so bright. So startling. That fantastic display the northern lights put on for us. It wasn't all that hard to believe what Bev said, that there's actually something larger than what we see. Larger than all of the world's wars and violence.

So here's the homework question: Am I a pacifist?

Joseph stops writing, amazed at how much has appeared on the blank pages. And even now his pen keeps moving, doodling as he has done so often at staff meetings. Meaningless marks that fill the page. Fill time. Triangles, curlicues, loops and flourishes with spaces to be shaded in.

Behind him Millicent stirs in her bunk. He mustn't wake her. He puts down his pen and is about to close the notebook when his eye catches the last marks the pen has made: Hedie Hedie Hedie Hedie. The name slides off the page. Careful to make no noise, he tears the page out of the notebook, shreds the paper into tiny bits and drops them into the wastebasket. Then he takes the notebook and on a new page writes: Millicent. He switches off the light, climbs into the top bunk and closes his eyes. His wife's even breathing and the rocking of the *Dnieper Princess* lull him to sleep.

~

Just like I imagined, Mia thinks on the day after the lecture. The tourists have arrived in Yalta and are being escorted on a before-dinner walk. Beech and chestnut trees shade the streets, and the hills that rise protectively around the city are lush and green. Most of the tourists are middle-aged or older and content to stroll along the narrow path that winds through trees and up a hillside. The climb is gradual and no one is in a hurry. Millicent walks with Susan Loeppky; Joseph and Mia are at the rear of the column. A mother with two small girls in quaint frilly-skirted dresses and huge frothy bows atop their heads come down the hill toward them. The nervous mother takes her girls by their hands and averts her eyes from these strangers.

Millicent stops. Hello, she says to the woman. You have two lovely daughters.

The woman keeps her eyes downcast. The girls snatch shy glances. One of them smiles at Millicent.

A volley of boys shoots up from behind the column of tourists. Pen? they ask. Pen? Or maybe they mean pin. Gum? Dollar? Their importunity is rude, but Mia gives one of them a maple leaf pin and the lucky boy is instantly surrounded by his friends who chatter and argue in Russian, then turn as one and swarm like pesky gnats around Mia, holding out their hands and repeating, Canada, Canada, an instant mantra that evolves into insolence. One boy grabs Mia's arm, another comes so close his elbow jabs her stomach. She is surrounded and jostled by a gang of hostile, demanding boys whose words she can't understand, whose voices threaten her. She clutches her camera to her chest and raises a balled fist.

Stop! Joseph puts his arm around his daughter and draws her away from them. No, he says, raising a flat-palmed hand to keep the boys at bay. No more, he says, and they fall away, regrouping for their next assault.

The tourists reach the first sanatorium, a white painted building with a screened veranda set in a sheltering grove of trees. Everything is astonishingly close to what Mia has imagined, and she knows that beyond the white exterior there are white hallways and white rooms with white beds.

A young girl arrives, holding with great care a cup with a beaten egg in it. She walks quickly up the path to the sanatorium, steps through the door and goes directly to the room where her mother lies, patient and still. She kneels beside the bed. The mother smiles.

Mia thinks she wouldn't be surprised if that girl should appear at the door. She'll come running down the veranda steps, her brother tagging along behind. Mia takes a picture of the building.

It's not a girl but a thin man who strides down the steps and comes toward the tourists as if intending to order them away. When he reaches the path he stops and watches the foreigners until they have almost passed before calling out, Where from you are?

Winnipeg, Joseph calls back.

The man's eyes light up. Winnipeg Jets! he cries. Canada! Hockey!

Joseph smiles and walks back to shake hands while the other tourists, strung out along the path, stop and look back. In broken English the man tells Joseph he is from Novosibirsk, an engineer, and his collective has sent him here for a rest cure. He speaks loudly, dramatically, with too much feeling, like an amateur actor. This sanatorium, he tells them, is for those with ailments of the heart.

Mia wants to ask about sanatoriums that specialize in diseases of the lungs. The man is younger than her father, his hair thinning, his dark eyes too intense. What has his life been like? She pictures him living in a cold, white desolation similar to Canada's Arctic, his life cheerless, pared down to essentials. In the long hours of darkness he sits in a dim and chilly room reading, a single candle throwing a small circle of yellow light on the page.

Everything now is different, the man says, as if he is correcting Mia's version. Very good now.

Mia pictures him listening to a radio. News. Music. A hockey game.

A red-headed woman appears on the veranda calling, Ruslan! Ruslan!, her voice high-pitched and agitated. She runs down the steps, speaking rapidly in Russian, grabs her man's hand and pulls him to safety. Her eyes are hostile, or perhaps fearful, as if these strangers are not to be trusted, predators against whom she must protect her frail husband. She moves with the wariness of a cornered animal seeking escape. Her husband, once safe on the screened veranda, looks back at the group on the path. Wistfully, Mia thinks. She waves to him.

A voice beside her says, They still haven't got over their fear.

Mia looks up to see Adam Sudermann, last night's lecturer. He says, studying her, So you're from Winnipeg?

The prairie, she says. In winter it's pretty much like Siberia.

Adam falls into step beside her.

~

In the morning, their tour guide, Ludmila, announces the day's options. One of the buses will take them to Yalta's spectacular botanical gardens. Another will offer a tour of the city, which is both ancient and beautiful. A third possibility is the Livadia Palace. Anyone interested in the Chekhov house? They should take the city tour and ask the driver to let them off at the house and afterwards they can take the public bus back to the hotel. It is very easy.

Today I'm a gardener, Joseph says. How about you, Millie? She takes his arm.

Because of the Chekhov house Mia chooses the city tour.

Without us? Millicent asks, alarmed.

Let her go, Joseph says. It's you and me today, Millie.

Mia is not surprised when Adam, the young lecturer, boards the bus and sits down across from her. It isn't by chance, she knows that much, and knows too that when she gets off at the Chekhov house, he will follow her.

The sky is overcast, the air heavy and humid. Adam and Mia follow five or six others from their group who get off the bus and stroll through a garden full of hollyhocks and dahlias and cosmos toward the house, where a stout woman with coppery hair takes them in charge.

Here is Anton Chekhov's leather coat, she tells them, pointing. Our Chekhov, he was six feet tall. Here is the piano on which played Rachmaninoff. In this room sang Fyodor Chaliapin. Yes. And the furniture—here the guide becomes eloquent, her voice rising in tone until it becomes a kind of singing—it is our beloved Chekhov's same furniture, the bed where he slept, the table where he ate every day his food. Here, look—she points to yellowed sheets of paper kept under glass—the theatre bills of the wonderful, wonderful performances of his excellent dramas. The guide becomes almost ecstatic as she extols the accomplishments of the author.

She leads the foreigners into the next room. Look. Look here. His desk. Her voice is hushed now. And reverent. He wrote here *The Cherry Orchard*. He was a prophet, our Chekhov. The future, he saw it very clear. He could see, our prophet, the glorious revolution, and he could see maybe even the Great Patriotic War.

Glorious? Great? Mia is bewildered. What about GranMarie's tales of loss and fear and disorder, tales she has taken at face value? She looks up and Adam is smiling at her.

All history is a construct, he says. It's filtered through time and experience. And the historian's preconceptions and prejudices.

Mia doesn't reply, not sure whether Adam is trying to impress her.

As the guide continues, Adam whispers in Mia's ear, I wonder if Chekhov saw the carnage coming. I mean the whole bloody horror of it.

Did you ever read *Uncle Vanya*? Mia whispers back.

I haven't read anything by Chekhov.

When Mia and Adam leave the house, the other tourists have already gone. It is drizzling, the air warm, and by the time they find the nearest bus stop, the sky has opened and they are instantly drenched. Rain and mist obscure the hills surrounding Yalta and the two foreigners are enclosed in a moist curtain. The world is opaque. Mysterious.

Let's not take the bus, Mia says. Let's walk back. It can't be that far. She turns, wet and shining, to face Adam, who raises his hands to wipe the rain from her face. They are both laughing.

~

Joseph and Millicent have strayed from the group touring the botanical gardens and find themselves in a field of roses. Although the peak season for roses is past, the garden still offers the full spectrum of rose life: green buds, young roses tightly furled, roses partly opened, full blooms, faded roses with the last petals still clinging. And naked seed hips. They wander silently from row to row, from colour to colour, stage to stage. They see the amazing variety, the delicate shades of yellow, the pink-tinged whites, the bold reds, the bred-in hues of blue and mauve. This is a research museum and here are the astonishing results of human dreams and endeavour.

You've never tried roses, Millicent says. The moist air diffuses her soft words.

Roses aren't easy. I've never thought I could get them to grow. Our winters are so harsh.

All of life is harsh. Millicent's words are barely audible. She stops walking, surprised at what she has said. She looks up at Joseph, who has stopped too and is looking down at her.

Can you believe it? he says. All this is possible. He gestures with one arm, a wide sweep that takes in the entire charming gardens. What he wrote that evening in his red notebook—is that possible too? Joseph raises the other arm as if he wants to bless or embrace the entire world, but instead his arms move to enclose Millicent, only Millicent. Her head is crushed against his chest and her cry is the muffled cry of a small animal.

Millie, he says, Millie. Around them rain has begun falling, softly but relentlessly.

From out of the mist Susan Loeppky appears, her umbrella raised. Hurry! The bus is leaving. It's going to pour and you'll get soaked.

~

That evening Mia writes in her yellow journal:

> Today I walked in the rain with Adam. I have never
> felt so carefree.

These are the first words in the notebook. She has not written one word about the *Dnieper Princess*. Nothing at all about Yalta. Not one phrase about the Chekhov museum. She turns off the light, closes her eyes and pulls the sheets up to her breasts.

~

The Heritage Cruise has docked for several days at the city of Zaporizhe and buses are waiting to take the tourists to various ancestral villages and towns scattered on the steppes, places they have only heard of, never seen, except for several very old travellers who were born in this country and claim they have carried around with them all their lives memories of houses and land, barns and orchards, the cherished landscape of their childhood. The rest are armed with stories they've been told, maps they have copied from atlases, homemade family trees and sepia photos of buildings they will try to match with the ruined houses, churches and schools they expect to find.

The Wittenberg family—Vittenberg, Ludmila calls them—sit together at the breakfast table as they have done at every meal since the cruise set out. Mia has learned to look for a plate piled high with watermelon slices, red and sweet, just as GranMarie used to say. But this morning it's coffee and eggs and bread. Mia has never spent so much time eating with both parents. Here we are, she thinks. The Wittenberg family after our winter of discontent.

But though she is relieved that it is possible to be together like this, she is restless. What would it be like to sit at breakfast with Adam, who is walking between tables toward them carrying a brown folder in his hand—information about Barvenkovo and Wassilyevka that Joseph has requested. Only the Wittenbergs are interested in those places and Ludmila has hired a car for them. Adam, Mia guesses, stayed up late, searching through his papers for information.

All set? Adam asks, looking at each one, but mostly at Mia, who pretends to be preoccupied with bread and eggs. I checked with Ludmila, he says. She's confirmed your driver. He speaks English so he'll double as your interpreter. You won't be back till late.

You okay with everything, Millie? Joseph asks.

Millicent sighs. This morning she said yes to this day trip, which will be long and will require much walking in the oppressive heat blanketing the steppes. But now she puts down her cup and turns to Joseph: I don't know, she says. A quiet day in the cabin will do me a world of good. I think I'll just stay back and let you two do the walking. She gets up and leaves the table.

Mia looks at her father, who is watching Millicent leave. Mia is about to rise and follow her mother, but both she and Joseph remain seated. There will be extra space in the car, Adam must be thinking as he seeks Mia's eyes for a sign of invitation.

Why don't you join us, Adam? Joseph says.

I'll bring this, Adam gestures with his folder envelope. He hurries off to get ready.

When Mia and Joseph return to the cabin, they find Millicent lacing up her walking shoes. She has applied sunscreen and collected her wide-brimmed sunhat, dark glasses and a light sweater. Also headache pills. Her face is set. I've changed my mind, she says.

Let's go then, Joseph says, as if no dilemma exists.

Striding along the gangway that leads from the ship, they see Ludmila waving to them from beside a black Lada parked beside a row of buses. Adam stands beside her, the folder in his hand. Smiling. When he sees Millicent, his smile freezes, then fades. Ludmila waves once more, then hurries off to usher the other tourists into the right buses.

Joseph shrugs when he faces Adam and gestures toward Millicent. Mia, for whom the excursion has lost some of its lustre, avoids Adam's gaze until she is seated in the car next to an open window and he hands her the folder. She looks up then and their eyes meet in an exchange of disappointments.

Joseph rolls down his window. A uniformed steward is running from the ship toward the buses where Ludmila is giving directions. The movement of tourists seems to slow down, come almost to a stop, a hush, an intake of breath that is held and held until suddenly everything is in motion again, but the motion is more intense, everyone swarming, converging around Ludmila and the steward. Ludmila looks flustered. Perhaps even alarmed.

Have a safe trip, Adam says, stepping back from the Lada. His eyes follow the car as it takes the Wittenbergs away.

Before long the black Lada has left Zaporizhe behind and they are motoring at high speed along a highway winding north and east. It's still early and the hope that rises on a good morning in human hearts has infused the foreign passengers. They have every reason to be carefree. All responsibility for this day has been placed on their driver's shoulders. Vitaly has been told that the Wittenbergs want to see with their own eyes the land where their ancestors were born, laboured, grew old and were buried.

Vitaly has assured them that he knows the way. And knows too that time is short. They have only one day for this part of their pilgrimage and must be back before night, or at least before morning, when the *Dnieper Princess* will continue her passage down the river toward Dniepropetrovsk.

Vitaly wears a white shirt, his face is cleanly shaven and his hair damp, as if he's just stepped from the shower. He apparently speaks English—so far the only evidence is a brief good morning. When they pulled out of the parking area at the dock he had stared straight ahead and when they left the city, he stepped on the gas and the car surged forward.

Johann Bartsch, who a century ago travelled across the same steppes in search of land—the Wittenbergs have been unable to trace on a map the precise route he took—would be amazed at the velocity with which his descendants fly across the earth's surface in a vehicle able to negotiate swiftly and more-or-less safely the curves in the road. Bartsch's historic journey, much slower, over rougher roads, brought about his death.

An hour from Zaporizhe, the sun already high, a force to be reckoned with, the Lada's air conditioning fails and Joseph opens his window, letting in a blast of air that gusts rudely to the back of the car, startling Mia and Millicent. Conversation is difficult.

Millicent is worried the noise and force of the wind will bring to full bloom the headache waiting to emerge and hold her in its grip. She settles into her corner and fishes a bottle of pills from her bag. Joseph rolls his window back up but then Vitaly rolls his down. The wind whistles and wails. Millicent smiles at her daughter from behind her sunglasses. The smile says, I am not afraid. You do not have to worry about me.

Millicent has been battling nausea off and on since she stepped, still jet-lagged, on board the *Dnieper Princess* several days ago, but she is determined that nothing will erode the pleasure of this day for her husband and daughter. What Millicent looks forward to most is an entire day away from the loquacious Susan Loeppky, who waylaid her on the first day. She wants a serene day with Joseph and Mia. But will she be able to keep up with them or will the heat deplete her entirely? The shrill whistling of the relentless wind is unbearable. She sits up tall and refuses to imagine the cabin with its bunk bed and cool sheets.

The wind sweeps Mia's straight brown hair across her face. Its noise prevents her from hearing what Joseph is shouting at Vitaly, whose neck is pale, not tanned like her father's. His shoulders are narrow, her father's broad and sturdy. She has not had a good look at the driver's face. He seems vulnerable as he hunches over the wheel. Mia would like to know where he lives and what he does when he's not driving foreign tourists to the villages of their forefathers.

Most of all Mia wishes Adam Sudermann were here beside her, his shoulder, arm, thigh touching hers as the Lada jostles them over bumps in the road. She hardly knows Adam but over the last few days his presence has added a new excitement to the tour. She has placed on the seat between herself and her mother the brown folder he handed her when they left Zaporizhe. And also her yellow journal, in which she intends to write everything that will happen today. She pushes a strand of hair out of her face, fishes from her shorts pocket a cut-glass perfume bottle with a delicate, rose-shaped stopper and holds it up for Millicent to see. They smile and there is mischief in their eyes as if they are two schoolgirls sharing a secret.

The bottle contains a small portion of the ashes of Marie Wittenberg. It was Alice's idea. Why don't you take GranMarie with you, Mia? she said, gesturing toward the pewter urn on the dining room buffet. Scatter her somewhere. Somewhere GranMarie lived when she was young. Somewhere she liked to walk, maybe. Alice didn't have a clear idea of where that might be, but scattering ashes appealed to her. It had appealed to Mia too, but she knew that taking all of the ashes would not do—too heavy, too cumbersome. And there might be laws about crossing borders with someone's ashes. Certainly bringing a body into the Soviet Union would be a problem. Didn't the ashes represent the body?

She had torn a corner off the front page of the *Winnipeg Free Press*—the headline: "Heat Relents, City Revives," made a funnel that fit into the perfume bottle's narrow mouth and spooned in as much of GranMarie's ashes as it would hold, closed the bottle with the stopper, taped it securely to prevent spilling and packed it with her underwear. Then she returned the urn to the buffet, where a blue Moorcraft vase and a pair of elegant silver candlesticks had stood before her mother had wrapped them up one Thursday and taken them to the thrift store.

Mia did not tell her parents about the ashes until they stood that first day on the deck of the *Dnieper Princess*.

You did what? her mother gasped.

Her father threw back his head and laughed.

Mia wishes her grandmother could be here, not reduced to ashes but in the flesh, though anyone as scant of flesh as she had become would be blown away as easily as ashes by this fierce wind. And one more person in the back seat of the Lada, no matter how thin, would be a tight squeeze.

Mia turns to watch the countryside rushing by. Acres of sunflowers ready for harvest. Neglected villages. Fields of yellow stubble remarkably like the Canadian prairie.

Joseph, in front, has the best view. He too watches the unscrolling of a landscape that was home to his forefathers, to whom he has given little thought until recently. Vitaly has found his tongue and occasionally points out a good crop or a farmhouse. When they pass a village with thatched houses he says, Very old. Very poor.

Stop, Mia says. Storks.

Vitaly slows, stops and puts the Lada in reverse. Storks have built a massive nest on top of a roadside tree and five or six grown birds are standing upright in it.

They will fly in two weeks home, Vitaly says. South.

Aren't storks supposed to mean good luck? Joseph asks.

Vitaly grins. I hope, he says, and waits while Mia aims her camera at a stork flapping its clumsy wings until it's airborne. Then he drives on.

They pass wooden roadside tables where farm women sit with their produce: pails of beans and carrots, potatoes and turnips, apples piled up in pyramids. Their faces are empty of expression. Umbrellas meant to shield them from the sun are closed in deference to the wind.

Want some apples? Joseph shouts to the back seat. He instructs Vitaly to stop at the next vegetable stand and orders everyone out. Coffee break, he jokes, and Mia walks toward a pile of apples.

Four women guard the produce, their faces uniformly stolid. They have been talking to a man leaning out the window of a car parked on the road's narrow shoulder, but now they turn to the tourists. The man gets out of the car and approaches Vitaly. His face is grave and Mia wants to warn her father to stay clear of him. There is an intense, rapid-fire exchange of words between the two Russians, during which the stranger brings his face close to Vitaly's. Their driver does not back away, as if what he is hearing has him in its grip. Both men shake their heads repeatedly, slowly and with an air of shock and foreboding. They are not discussing the price of apples. The Wittenbergs can do nothing but watch and wait.

When Vitaly finally turns to them, he has lost his ability to speak English coherently. He blurts out phrases and fragments. Very big news, he says. Very serious. And rattles off a string of Russian names that mean nothing to the Wittenbergs. He says "putsch" several times, a word they are not familiar with. When he says, Our Gorbachev, the Wittenbergs repeat the familiar name, Gorbachev, relieved to have something to latch on to. Then Vitaly tells them that in Moscow tanks are rolling down the main street. Apparently the world is coming to an end. The president is dangerously ill. He is hiding. He is in prison. Nobody and nothing is sure. He might be on vacation in his dacha in Yalta, where the Wittenbergs have visited so recently.

Is it all bad news? Joseph asks.

Vitaly shrugs and speaks of shooting and soldiers. There is fear in his voice and Mia remembers GranMarie's fear of what she called "that whole godless business," and wonders if she should be afraid too. The milling of the tourists around Ludmila this morning suddenly makes sense. Their driver, shaken, repeats the word terrible, terrible, and mumbles something about the future. At the produce tables the women listen intently, as if they understand Vitaly's every English word.

I wish we had Ludmila with us, Millicent says.

We do not know, Vitaly says. Is it all bad or a little bit good? Is everything fly apart? We do not know. Nobody can tell.

Not knowing what to say, Joseph asks, Can we go on? To Barvenkovo? Is it safe?

Called back to this world, this steppe where the wind is still blowing, the sun beating down and nothing seems changed, Vitaly leads the Wittenbergs to the Lada. Of course, he says. We go. And soon they have left apples and carrots and the women ~arding them far behind. Vitaly, too overwhelmed to speak, concentrates on overtaking every vehicle ahead of him. Joseph hopes his daughter and especially his wife will not notice how narrow is the margin of safety each time Vitaly succeeds.

When they arrive in Barvenkovo it is almost noon, the streets sun-baked, the sky exhausted. The Wittenbergs step out of the hot car onto the hot pavement of the drab town and look around helplessly. Lost. They turn to Vitaly, who seems equally lost, but rallies, stopping a sombre-faced man passing by. The Wittenbergs assume he is asking directions, but the Russian dialogue becomes too animated for something so mundane. The two men, strangers, must be trying to grasp the enormity of what is happening to their country, to them and their families, to the whole Soviet system.

When the intensity of the dialogue abates, Vitaly motions his passengers back into the car. It's like being invited into an oven, Mia thinks. Like Hansel and Gretel. No one asks where they are going and when Vitaly stops at a walled complex with a metal plate at the entrance engraved with Ukrainian words, they do not at first realize that they have arrived at the factory Abram Franz named Lutzch: a ray of light. Vitaly points to the name on the sign and his grim face breaks into a wry grin. Krasnoya Lutzch, he reads. Red Ray of Light. Our glorious leaders, they have given to the name of your grandfather's factory a colour. He laughs and the laugh is bitter. The Wittenbergs smile nervously.

When Vitaly rings the buzzer, a woman appears and

reluctantly agrees to let them in. They find themselves in a courtyard overgrown with weeds and surrounded by crumbling brick buildings and decrepit remnants of rusted machinery.

Looks like the ray of light has pretty much gone out, Joseph mutters. For the first time he tries to picture his grandfather ordering labourers to their tasks, overseeing the process of making and assembling parts of machines. He has never tried to imagine what the factory mentioned in Mia's stories looked like. If he had, it would have been nothing as disconsolate as these ramshackle buildings and this dreary yard.

He asks, What do they make here?

Vitaly consults the woman, who shrugs. Apparently not much is made here. Shopping carts, small tools, the woman says. But only when they can get the material.

Here and there labourers enter or leave one of the tile-roofed buildings with shattered windows. Someone is trying to start a truck but the motor refuses to spring to life. The Wittenbergs leave Vitaly with the Russian woman and wander off, stumbling over stones and bits of rusted iron. Patches of Queen Anne's lace grow between huge wooden spools once wound with cords or cables. The delicate white flowers overlie the abandoned trappings of a failing industry with their fragile grace. Mia aims her camera to capture both the beauty and the decay. Millicent steps into the shade of a chestnut tree. I'll wait for you here, she says.

When Vitaly catches up with them he points to a building in the northeast corner of the complex. That one, he says, is maybe original. All the rest—he waves dismissively, as if all the rest is not worth considering. They walk toward the shabby brick building. Thick dust covers the cracked panes; some windows have no glass and gape, empty. Above a door the year has been carved into the brick: 1913. The Wittenbergs take in the date and add it to the name at the entrance as evidence.

Vitaly looks at his watch. The Wittenbergs, reluctant to leave the factory compound, follow him to the car. Mia fingers the perfume bottle in her pocket, pulls it out. Both parents shake their heads, Not here, although Joseph had suggested opening it in Barvenkovo. The Lada leaves the factory and stops at the railroad station, a low building with a ladder leaning lethargically against the wall beside the entrance through which they see no one coming or going. From this station Abram Franz and his second wife left their homeland with their children, the oldest, Maria, a teenager.

On the drive to Wassilyevka Mia holds the perfume bottle in her hand. I should have emptied it in Yalta, she says. Somewhere near that gravel path to the sanatoriums. But it's too late now.

When the sign "Wassilyevka" appears on the side of the road, Vitaly points and says, There. It is your village.

The village has one street, the houses neither new nor very old, simply unremarkable. None of them could have been built before World War II . There is no sign of life in the village, the heat having driven the inhabitants indoors. Gaggles of geese graze along the roadside. Somewhere in this village Hanna Franz and her children lie buried, but there is no sign of a cemetery or a church.

Joseph turns and sees Mia holding the bottle up to the light. Just say when you want to stop, he says. They continue along the street to where the village gives way to fields of yellow sunflowers on either side of the road.

Here, Mia says. Let's stop here.

Looks just like Manitoba, all those sunflowers, Joseph says. Getting out, Millicent?

Millicent climbs slowly out of the Lada and follows Joseph and Mia down through the ditch toward the sunflower field. There is no fence and Mia wades in, unseals the bottle. She removes the stopper, tips the tiny bottle and lets the ashes spill through the narrow opening and fall to earth in the shade of sunflower stalks. All three stand still. Mia would like to take the hands of her parents, form a ring. She imagines them dancing like pagans around GranMarie's ashes. If Alice were here she might say, We are standing on holy ground. She would sing. Mia wishes for ceremony, for words to be spoken, words of consecration or blessing.

The wind has abated, the sunflowers sway gently. Mia would like to wander among them, linger, maybe cross the field. She bends down, wanting to scrape up enough soil to fill the empty bottle, but the ground is hard and she gives up. She looks for flecks of the pale ash she dropped but can find none. The sun is lower now, not quite so hot.

Their driver is impatient and they leave the yellow field with GranMarie's ashes scattered where they will never be found. Vitaly turns the car around on the narrow road and soon they have passed again through Wassilyevka with its blank houses and grazing geese and are on their way to the highway that leads back to Zaporizhe.

Traffic on the highway has increased and Vitaly is in a hurry. He accelerates and they see ahead of them on the road a semitrailer loaded with long, enormous pipes. The Wittenbergs watch nervously as the distance between the Lada and the semi shrinks, Vitaly closing in and slowing only when he is almost on top of it—or so it seems. Then he veers left, finds himself in the path of an oncoming vehicle and is obliged to retreat into his lane. As soon as the vehicle whizzes by, Vitaly edges the Lada out again. Another oncoming vehicle. Another retreat, SWOOSH, and almost immediately the Lada noses out again, is about to pass the semi and once more pulls back. The back and forth, out and in, become a jolting rhythm that unnerves the passengers. Joseph tries to remain calm but the intensity and persistence of the man behind the wheel leave him worried. We're not in that big a hurry, he shouts, but apparently the driver doesn't hear him.

Then, as if he can read Joseph's mind, Vitaly allows the distance between the two vehicles to increase and the Lada proceeds at a more reasonable speed. The passengers relax.

When they approach a village Vitaly slows down even more. A family is seated in front of their home watching a tethered goat grazing on what looks like bare ground. A goat, it is good, Vitaly says, approvingly. The children wave and the Wittenbergs wave back. A magpie takes flight from its post on a picket fence from which most of the white paint has peeled. They pass an orchard of apple trees and yards ablaze with zinnias and hollyhocks.

They maybe don't even know, Vitaly says, his voice a mix of awe and despair. Nobody tells them yet. He shakes his head dolefully at the disaster he understands only in part. The disaster the Wittenbergs have momentarily forgotten.

And then with a lurch the Lada surges forward and quickly devours the distance separating it from the loaded semi. Bent over the wheel, Vitaly is completely absorbed, a hunter closing in on his prey. The Wittenbergs sit taut, appalled that their driver is determined to crash into the truck. They brace instinctively, Joseph shouts, No! Stop! You bloody fool! Millicent's scream is muffled by her hand clamped to her mouth. Mia's hands grasp the backrest in front of her and she presses her face into her arms. At the last minute Vitaly swerves into the other lane, accelerates, and had his three passengers looked up, they would have seen an obstacle of enormous dimensions hurtling toward them at breakneck speed and then suddenly reduced to slow motion as if the march of time had decelerated. There's a deafening crash of metal, a scream of brakes, a roar as if this morning's wind is funnelled directly into their ears, their heads fill with the unbearable thundering that builds and builds viciously and will surely blow their skulls wide open.

A final detonation and everything comes to a halt. The

roaring gives way to silence, immense and ghostly. Thick darkness covers the world. Time, as if completely spent, stands still.

~

Alice gets out of her car, unbuckles the two boys. Lucas stumbles ahead up the driveway and bangs impatiently at the locked door. Oma! Opa! he calls, as if he doesn't know they are far away somewhere on a big boat. As if they will appear and let him in because he is calling loudly. Alice lifts Jeremy from his car seat and can't resist kissing his cheek, warm and pink from sleep. She picks up the brown envelope from the front seat and takes out the keys to her parents' bungalow. She agreed to check the house every three days, but she's only come once so far and it's a relief that everything looks normal. She unlocks the door and Lucas catapults along the front hall straight to the kitchen. Oma! he calls out.

Alice walks through to the back door and unlocks it. Opa and Oma are still on the boat, remember? They're coming home. Soon.

Wanna be on the boat, too, the boy says. Mom? He tags on a plaintive Please.

You can go outside and play, his mother says, after checking that the backyard gate is shut. Don't trample Opa's garden.

Alice walks into her sister's room and places the brown envelope on the desk, relieved that Lucas did not get his sticky hands on Mia's pages and illustrate them with random crayon smudges. Alice cried when she read about the deaths of babies and was filled with thankfulness for her two boys, both alive. She cried too about her grandmother, just a girl, giving her heartbroken assent to her father's remarriage.

Marriage, Alice has learned, is not an easy road proceeding

in one direction. It's a bumpy business of new beginnings. Beginnings she must initiate. Let's just forget last night, she told Brian this morning when he left the house. She can still see how he turned back, actually turned back to look at her where she stood, Jeremy on her hip. She thought there was compassion in his eyes. Or was it an appeal for her compassion? For a moment she thought he might come back and hug her.

Last night was total disaster: Lucas knocked over the tall lamp in the living room and whimpered, I didn't do it, Mom. Brian, seated before his dried-out, tasteless supper said, I should have stopped at Burger King.

Alice was holding Jeremy in one arm. She raised the other and with her fist beat against Brian, pummelling his head, his chest, his shoulders as if she couldn't stop.

Alice wants to forget all that and this morning she hoped Brian could forget too, but he left for work without saying he would. The venetians in her parents' bedroom are closed and when she opens them the light streams in, revealing a thick layer of dust on the furniture. She settles Jeremy on the wide bed, her parents' marriage bed, and lowers herself beside him.

Alice has never given her parents' marriage much thought, has never allowed the evidence of flaws to register. She and Mia have never discussed it. Whether it's good or failing is not a question she's asked of any marriage, except lately of her own. And she's decided that, no, hers is not all that good, and sometimes she's tired of it. Brian is never at home, and when he is, he's one more person to attend to.

But sometimes a measure of peace makes itself felt in her family: Brian is home for three consecutive suppers; Lucas falls but gets up, unhurt and not screaming his brains out and driving Brian to distraction; Jeremy sleeps through a whole night and wakes with what is surely a smile. And last week Brian surprised her with a cake for her birthday. And a present: A bottle of perfume, gift wrapped. That day, gladness and hope rose like a helium balloon.

But why does the ground under her feet so easily begin to wobble?

Alice gets up to water the two tropical plants her mother hasn't taken to the thrift store because her father objected. Then she gathers Jeremy, walks to the back door. Let's go, Lucas. Mom's got to make supper. Daddy will be home soon.

No, Lucas says. Want Opa. He is standing in his grandfather's garden. After a dry start to summer there has been occasional rain and the garden is beginning to thrive.

Alice comes out and stands beside Lucas. Let's try a carrot, she says. Still holding Jeremy, she bends and, tugging at the greens, pulls out a carrot the thickness of her thumb. Lucas is delighted.

Brian has arrived home before them and he opens the door, takes Jeremy from his wife, who is stopped short by the grave expression on her husband's face.

The Soviet Union, Brian says. It's collapsing. It's on the news.

Alice has sometimes thought her marriage is verging on collapse, or her entire small world. The Soviet Union is too far away and too big to fit into her thinking. Then she remembers. Mia! she gasps. Mom and Dad! Where are they? She pictures a huge explosion, a vast land mass erupting like a volcano, flinging bits of itself—clods of earth, stones, boulders, bricks, ash—in every direction. Buildings come crashing down, sidewalks splinter, gardens are scattered, trees pummelled. Her parents and her sister are helpless to defend themselves. She sees the earth opening to suck them in. Oh God! Oh God!

That evening, as if someone has tricked them into re-enacting the Job story, Alice and Brian are informed of another event, a road accident that will register low on the world's scale compared to the collapse of the Soviet Union, but high on theirs.

Brian, seeing the anguish in his wife's face, has no choice. He takes Jeremy from her and rocks his sleeping son in one arm while he draws Alice in with the other. She sobs on his shoulder. Lucas clings to his father's leg, terrified. Brian wants to pull free of this upheaval but he finds himself standing quite still.

~

Mia wakes up in the half-darkness of a hospital room. An ache drives deep into her shoulder and her head pulses as if someone is hammering at it with mindless persistence. In her strangely muddled brain she thinks she hears GranMarie saying, You know Mia, I never did get to see the Dnieper River and now I never will. Mia remembers sailing up the wide Dnieper River, but where is that ship now?

And where are her parents? At the thought of her parents she tries to sit up but pain shoots into every crevice of her body. She closes her eyes. Something enormous stirs in her memory, straining to surface. Something chaotic and violent enough to bring about an end. A terrible weight pins her down. She is engulfed in darkness.

Are her parents somewhere in that darkness?

Then, as her mind clears, she remembers hearing the harsh buzz of foreign voices tearing through the confusion that surrounded her when she was lifted and carried and laid down, her body flaming with pain. She remembers the comforting, unintelligible words of a white-clad woman.

She raises her hand and sees that it is white. Bandaged. It is the hand that should be holding a small perfume bottle filled with ashes. Where is that bottle? Where are the ashes? Where is that brown folder that contained important information?

Where is the yellow journal Alice gave her?

Where is Adam?

Bracing against the pain Mia tries once more to pull herself upright in the narrow bed, but movement is excruciating and she gives up.

When she regains consciousness hours later, she edges a leg slowly, slowly toward the side of the bed. And then the other. Her feet search for the floor. She pulls the blanket around her to keep from shivering as she waits, wanting to call out for help. There must be someone in this alien place. With gargantuan effort she pulls herself up on her feet. In spite of the raging pain she is able to take a step. Then another. Inching forward she gropes her way past two or three beds—the sound of breathing rises from each—and stumbles her painful way toward a door. Keeping close to the wall for support, she struggles toward a dim light at the nursing station. It is unoccupied. Panic grips her, fear of abandonment, and she tries to shout, Is anybody there? Her voice is faint, no more than a whisper. She tries again—Help! help me! —but the words remain in her throat. All strength leaves her then and the nurse finds the Canadian teenager she admitted last night crumpled on the floor.

When Mia wakes once again, a new day has begun, another sweltering day, but though the hospital is not air conditioned, she is shivering. A nurse comes with a blanket, a cloth and a basin of water.

My father? Mia asks. My mother?

Ah, Papa, Mama, the nurse says. A volley of Russian words tumbles from her mouth and her eyes stream sympathy. She moves her head, but Mia can't tell whether she's nodding or shaking it. The nurse wrings out the cloth and places it on Mia's

forehead and mercifully it is warm. The nurse gestures toward
the door as if something or someone will enter through it. But
no one comes and the nurse who can't speak English leaves. She
returns after a seeming eternity, bringing a needle, and sleep
takes over.

When Mia wakes again, a doctor is standing at the foot of her
bed reading a chart. When he sees that she is awake he comes
close to her side. Ah, Miss Vittenberg. Good morning. His voice,
calm and restrained, is a breath of comfort.

Are they dead? Mia asks.

The doctor places a hand on Mia's forehead. Your parents,
they are alive, he says and Mia's face trembles and soon the
whole bed shakes with the trembling of her body. The doctor
takes her hands in his to steady them. He calls for the nurse who
comes with a syringe and a warm blanket.

They are here, the doctor says, his English sparse but clear.
They are in this place. This hospital. You are in Dniepro. Soon
you will see them.

Mia clings to the doctor's hands while the warm blanket and
the needle take effect.

~

After lying all night and most of next day unconscious Millicent
wakes to the sound of steady rain. Her bed is next to an open
window and her first words are: I smell rain.

Mia, in a hospital gown, a blanket around her shoulders, is
sitting at her bedside, keeping watch. She lets out a small gasp
and reaches a hand out to her mother.

Later Millicent will say the rain smelt like earth. I thought I
was coming up from the earth and I found myself surrounded
by light. She will tell Joseph her awakening was more than

coming out of sleep into consciousness. Everything looks different now, she'll say, and Joseph will be unable to take his eyes off her pale cheeks, her hair, her eyes, as if he cannot believe that she is not a fleeting vision.

Joseph has suffered the most serious injuries—his leg broken and his wrist shattered. But he is alive and his wife is alive too and now Mia is standing, alive, at his bedside. The wonder of it turns to gratitude. We're all going home, he tells Mia. Might have to ask you to dig up the carrots again this year.

Mia pulls up a chair and sits beside her father. The asters will be blooming when we get home, she says.

The doctor who speaks English assumes charge of the three foreigners. He orders casts fashioned for Joseph's wrist and leg. You are damaged, he tells him, but not kaput. Not like our Soviet Union. He grins as if he has made a joke. The attending nurse does not smile.

Once she has been assured her father and mother are not fatally injured, Mia recruits a nurse to help her find a telephone and calls Alice, who is frantic. Are you sure? Are you absolutely sure you are all right?

We're all coming home.

Thank God, Alice says, Thank God. She calls Lucas to the phone to say, I love you, Anniemie.

~

As if nothing in the country has changed, the *Dnieper Princess* has continued her steady course up the Dnieper River toward Dniepropetrovsk, a large city with several hospitals, including the one to which ambulances with sirens keening brought the Wittenbergs and their driver Vitaly.

Incredible! the passengers say. A putsch, and we are here to see it.

Gorbachev in Crimea! We were there! We visited Yalta just days ago.

What does it mean? What happens next? Will we get home?

The cruise ship passengers are at breakfast, where the events of the last days are on the menu, servings too large for the travellers to digest. They can't fully comprehend that the land of their ancestors has been rocked at its foundations, thrown into panic and instability. And, as if that is not tumult enough, the three Wittenbergs, their fellow travellers, have been in a road accident and will not rejoin the cruise. Wedged between these calamities, the travellers are stunned. And exhilarated. They demand assurance from Ludmila that the Wittenbergs will be safe, but she is more shocked than they are, and less inclined to speak. They look around for Adam Sudermann, their resident historian. Cool analyst of things cultural and political in this country.

But Adam has skipped breakfast and is standing alone on the deck, willing the ship to gain speed. How fortunate he is to be so close to history in the making. So close to a country's upheaval that he can feel its convulsions. Notebook in hand, he looks ready to waylay the staff and crew of the *Dnieper Princess,* who today move like zombies through their duties. What does it mean, this coup, for your family? he might ask. How do you imagine your future? Are you glad? Afraid?

But the questions uppermost in Adam's mind concern Mia. Is she badly hurt? Will she survive? Who is looking after her?

When the cruise ship arrives in Dniepro, where it will dock for several days, Ludmila and Adam disembark first, take a taxi to the hospital, where they demand to be led at once to where the Wittenbergs are kept. Mia wakes to see them seated on plastic chairs, watching her. They come to her bedside and Ludmila takes the girl's unbandaged hand in hers. Thanks God, she moans. Thanks God you live. She wipes her eyes. Tell me please what you need, she says. I will do for you everything. When she lets go Mia's hand, Adam is there to claim it

The next day Mia and Adam walk slowly along the poorly lit hospital corridor. In a few days the Heritage Cruise will leave Dniepro, taking Adam and leaving Mia behind. They stop in a deserted doorway and Mia doesn't resist when Adam pulls her toward him, carefully, because she is still bruised. Mia remembers how once, very long ago, she wanted Kurt to hold her like this. Now, she can feel the beating of Adam's heart and wonders if his body is the place to which she can bring everything that has ever happened to her. But Adam too would bring with him everything that has happened to him and she doesn't know if she is ready to contain all that. Doesn't know if he is someone with whom she would feel at home. Right now the word *home* conjures the white bungalow on Kildonan Drive. She has been saved from death, saved to return to that bungalow. Return to her life.

It's so incredible, Adam is saying. You're alive.

He releases her and they walk hand in hand back to Mia's room. He waits until she's settled in the bed, then bends to stroke her cheek. You're so lovely, Mia, and his words sound to her like, I love you, Mia.

She is exhausted, but wide awake. The words Pastor Heese spoke at her graduation come suddenly to mind: *the greatest of these is love.* Not so long ago GranMarie said on her death bed:

I ... love ... you ... Mia. She also said, Is this real or are we dreaming? At this moment, the quiet of the room interrupted by breathing from the other beds, her whole life seems like a dream to Mia.

~

Like the three Wittenbergs, Vitaly has suffered severe concussions. But more seriously, his spine is damaged, and the doctor does not sound confident when he says, I believe thirty percent Vitaly maybe again will walk. He will maybe not stay like a cripple. It will need much time.

Before the *Dnieper Princess* leaves Dniepro, Ludmila prepares the Wittenbergs for a meeting with their injured driver. Vitaly, he cannot remember everything, she warns. His brain, it has received such shock. She shakes her head at the severity of the shock. But the accident, it is really his fault. He cannot deny it. There are witnesses. She lowers her voice and tells Joseph apologetically, Vitaly, he has not much but he can give you maybe something.

Joseph understands then that in this country there is a certain way these matters can be settled. He shakes his head. No, he doesn't want Vitaly's money. But he wants justice. Properly administered justice.

The three Wittenbergs are ushered into the grey light of the ward where Vitaly's bed occupies the far corner. Mia pushes Joseph's wheelchair, Millicent trails behind. The sharp antiseptic odour of cleaning products pervades the room.

Ludmila joins the nurse and the English-speaking doctor who has tended the Wittenbergs through wearisome hours. The Russians stand together near Vitaly's bed, gesticulating while they talk, interrupting each other, agitated. The coup that threatened bloodshed and violence has failed as suddenly as it began and its uncertain aftermath is settling around them like a collapsed tent. The face of the doctor is radiant with relief, but Ludmila's is grave, as if she cannot trust the future. As if the upheaval has left them hanging at the edge of something so completely new she doesn't know whether it spells gain or loss.

The Russians fall silent and the two parties appraise each other, neither side willing to speak first.

Joseph gestures to Mia, who wheels him close to Vitaly's bed. Millicent follows and stands next to her husband. Hello, she says, addressing the man on the bed. Are you all right? Are you in great pain? At the sound of her voice, Vitaly opens his eyes and everyone can see the fear in them. Millicent bends down to the injured man, whose bloodless face is almost as white as the pillow. We want to know how you're feeling, Vitaly.

Joseph is sitting very straight and for a minute it appears to the others that he will pull himself even straighter, thrust back his shoulders and rise from the wheelchair. The Russians are watching him, the foreigner about to demonstrate his worth as a husband and as a man. Now is the time for him to speak. To denounce the man whose actions endangered his wife. And his daughter. He must demand restitution. He must ask Vitaly what in God's name possessed him to drive like a maniac. Now is the time to speak out loudly and clearly. For justice.

Vitaly lies on his bed, helpless, eyes fixed on the ceiling.

As if she can read her father's intentions, Mia places a restraining hand on his shoulder; he cannot shrug it off. Dad, she says quietly. Dad.

Millicent reaches for his good hand, holds it and doesn't let go. Joseph looks away from the driver to the woman with whom he walked—it seems so long ago—in a rose garden. In the rain. She is frail and slender and wears a summery floral-patterned housecoat—Ludmila brought it—over her hospital gown. Her dark hair, fluffed around her pale forehead, is flecked with light. Her cheeks are flushed, her face is animated, and the expression he sees in it is a plea. Or a warning.

Distracted, Joseph turns from her steadfast gaze to face Vitaly, who is now looking directly at him. In that instant Joseph knows that he has been granted another reprieve. Another narrow escape. The moral indignation that rose up so sharply, so self-righteously, is already weakening because it lacks justification. It is tainted. Joseph is embarrassed and weak with relief that his thoughts and intentions, so evident to everyone in the room, are left unspoken. He raises his hand, still held in Millicent's, in a salute to Vitaly. Then he answers Ludmila's questioning look with a shake of his head. No.

Mia, he says, I think your mother is tired. Let's go.

~

Joseph sleeps, and when he wakes, the pain is less acute and the room he is in less dingy: the sun must be out. Someone has placed flowers on his bedside table. His first thoughts are of Vitaly, about whom he knows little. Does he have a family? Will he walk again? Will he be able to make a living? Will his life be made better or worse by the political change? He doesn't want to remember the arrogant accusations he had been ready to direct at a helpless man. As if he is entitled to cast even one small stone. Joseph hoists himself up and sits on the edge of his bed. He thinks of the wooden bench waiting for him in his garden. He will sit on that bench, let the sun warm his injured body and wait while the healing takes its course. There will be no hurry because the school year at George Sutton Collegiate will begin and end without him.

~

Brian parks the car near the airport terminal building and unloads his equipment while Alice takes charge of the boys. Bring your camera, she reminded him this morning. We have to have pictures. Brian does not refer to the return of the Wittenbergs as a miracle the way Alice does, but he agrees that they are lucky to have come away from the accident alive. He had planned to zoom in on them coming down the escalator, but Alice reminded him that Joseph will be in a wheelchair. He sets up his tripod and video camera as near to the elevator as possible.

Alice is busy rocking Jeremy and restraining Lucas. Don't just fly at Opa and Oma, she warns. They had an accident.

Can I fly at Anniemie? Mom. Anniemie?

No, Brian says. She was in the accident too. He tries once again to explain "accident" to his older son. It's something bad happening, he says. Something nobody planned. Nobody wanted it. Nobody knew.

But God knew all about it, Alice objects. God was there. Right there.

Yeah, Lucas says. God did the bad. God.

Brian grins wryly at Alice and keeps on grinning until she smiles too.

A voice announces the arrival of the flight and after a wait that's too long for Lucas, the Wittenbergs emerge from the elevator to face Brian's camera. Joseph in a wheelchair is first. Alice rushes forward, holding Jeremy out like a welcome, and Joseph reaches with his good arm to receive the boy. Millicent looks tired, but she smiles as she manoeuvres Joseph's wheelchair. Mia is last to step from the elevator. She sees Lucas, who is speechless, his body rigid, his hands fluttering uncontrollably. She folds the boy tightly in her arms while Brian's camera records everything.

Brian has hammered together a wooden ramp to the Wittenberg bungalow to accommodate a wheelchair and Alice has ordered in pizza for a homecoming celebration. Lucas quickly spills pop over everything. Brian wipes it with a napkin. Careful, buddy, he says.

Alice settles Jeremy once more in his grandfather's good arm. I prayed for you, she says. Every day.

Brian turns to his mother-in-law. That was quite an adventure you had.

I've heard much worse, Millicent says. A woman in our tour group told me a story about rape and murder ... such a terrible story, you wouldn't believe it. But if life is crushed in one place, it springs up somewhere else, doesn't it? It's ... it's unstoppable. She pauses, surprised at what she has said.

I sure hope Vitaly springs to life, Mia says.

You're talking about the guy responsible for the accident, Brian says. In my opinion ...

But Alice interrupts. I'm so glad you got to all those places, Mia, to Barvenkovo. And that other place ... that village. What did you do with GranMarie's ashes?

We scattered them in a field of sunflowers, Mia says. Over there they've got this proverb: *Life is not as easy as crossing a field.*

Our Mia didn't just find a Russian proverb, Joseph says. She found a new friend.

Millicent sends him a warning look as if this is Mia's story to tell.

Alice doesn't ask whose story. That's so wonderful, she exults. Mia, I'm so excited for you. Tell me everything.

That notebook you gave me? Mia says. I had it with me the

day of the accident. I wanted to write down everything. About Barvenkovo. About the factory.

Are you suing him? Brian is still working at his pizza.

Who? Mia asks.

The driver, of course. He's bloody responsible. There's such a thing as law and order. Even in that country, I hope.

The returned travellers exchange glances. Who should answer? The uneasy pause that follows is brief: Lucas, reaching for more pizza, bumps into the pot of tea Alice has just set on the table. The women rise as one to rescue the boy. In Joseph's arm, Jeremy is whimpering softly. Brian's question is left unanswered.

~

On Mia's first weekend back from the Heritage Cruise she is seated on a log watching sausages sizzle and split open above the fire in front of her. The smell of roasting meat fills the air. Kurt opens a beer for her. Angela is peeling melted marshmallow away from a willow branch. The charred sweetness sticks to her fingers and she licks it greedily. Bev is passing around mustard and relish. She has organized this campfire reunion of a handful of GSC's latest graduates.

We're going camping, you have to come, she had told Mia.

Camping? Bev, you don't even like camping.

You've come back to us, Bev said. You're here. Alive. That's worth celebrating.

In the end Mia agreed and here she is, not in Bur Oak Park, where fires aren't allowed, but close enough to the city for its lights to be reflected against the sky. Mia is unsure how to bridge the gap between now and the seemingly long ago territory of high school. Her classmates are at university or launched into jobs. They are forming new friendships. Can old ones survive the reconfiguration?

The campers have exhausted themselves setting up their tents and flinging Frisbees and footballs in the open field. It's almost morning and they are mellow, sleepy, slightly drunk. They devour the last blackened marshmallows and trace patterns in the sky with glowing wiener sticks.

Someone asks, So Mia, you were in Russia? and this sets off a string of questions: Is it true you were in an accident? Is it true your dad nearly died? What's communism like? Were you in Moscow when that coup happened?

Mia realizes that her friends can't imagine what she experienced. She lifts a burning stick from the fire and holding it high, says: Want to hear what communists do? They kill! and rape! and torture! At each verb Mia stabs the air dramatically with her torch, then, laughing at the stunned faces around the fire, she says, And they grow the best watermelon in the world. That's all you need to know about Russia.

The campers are satisfied with that. Angela thrusts a branch into the embers and yells, Let's set the world on fire! She rushes through the darkness toward a clump of bushes where she shoves her burning branch into piles of dead, dry leaves. The others join in, hooting and laughing, as they fan the incipient fire into a genuine conflagration.

Mia doesn't move from her log. Kurt, who has jumped up with the others, comes back and sits beside her.

Having fun? he asks.

She smiles into the dark. Look at the sky, Kurt. See the Big Dipper? There's Cassiopeia.

There should be a moon, Kurt says. Or at least half a moon. At the mention of that heavenly body both of them drop their eyes to stare at the fire and when the silence has lasted long enough, both look up at the same time. Kurt shrugs, she grins and the awkwardness dissolves.

You don't have to stay, Kurt says. If you aren't having fun, that is.

I'll stay. Bev would be disappointed. She wants to ask Kurt about university. About the dark-haired girl she saw with him in summer. Tonight's gathering, cobbled together by Bev, does not guarantee anything. It holds no clue to the future. Mia feels alone. And free. Free to sit here beside Kurt, without uneasiness. Without expectation.

But now the dry bush has become a blaze; the flames dance eerily, creating grotesque patterns against the encroaching darkness, and the campers' excited laughter gains an edge of panic. Kurt jumps up, pulls Mia to her feet. They run to join the others around the burning bush.

It's out of control! someone yells.

Water! We need water!

Everyone runs for water, but their supply is small and will not avail. There is confusion instead of action.

Sleeping bags, Kurt shouts. Get your sleeping bags.

Mia and Bev drag theirs from the tent and along the grass to the escalating fire, where Kurt is already using his as a weapon. Working side by side with Kurt and Bev, Mia feels the warmth of a camaraderie. There is no wind to fan the flames and spread the sparks; the blaze, though spectacular in the darkness, is not beyond control after all, and everyone is relieved to see it abate and finally capitulate.

All notions of sleep squelched, the campers beat the sparks from their scorched sleeping bags and then return to sit around the dying embers of the campfire. Bev brings out a bag of apples to share and someone finds more wood to feed the campfire.

In the morning, when Mia wakes up, Bev's sleeping bag is empty. She lifts the tent flap and light pours in. She breathes in the fresh air and the silence that pervades everything. But even as she inhales, a wind springs up and the rustling of poplars replaces the stillness. A shrill blue jay makes its displeasure known, and somewhere Bev is singing, *Here comes the sun.*

~

On the first Sunday back from the Heritage Cruise, Joseph wakes to see light filtering through the curtains. He doesn't move. Beside him Millicent is sleeping. A mass of dark hair spread on the pillow and one splayed hand are all he can see of her. He listens to her scarcely audible breathing, feels her warmth and wants to wake her. Hold her. Love her. He moves his injured leg cautiously, gets out of bed and with the help of crutches makes his way to the kitchen, where he starts the coffee. This morning, if Mia hadn't taken the car to go camping, he might have asked Millicent to drive them to the Edison Avenue church to join the congregation. He longs to join in the singing of familiar hymns: *Holy God, we praise your name.*

He finds eggs in the fridge, breaks them into a bowl and, balancing on his good leg, begins whipping them with a fork. He knows without turning that Millicent has appeared in the doorway and is watching him. He drops the fork and, grasping at chair backs, makes his way clumsily toward her as she moves toward him. Millie, he whispers, takes her in his arms and they stand together, the morning light falling on them. Joseph wants to lead her back to the bedroom, to the sanctuary of their rumpled bed where love will become worship. Instead he releases her and returns to the eggs. Almost ready, he says.

Millicent sets the table and they eat.

Coming Home

On a frigid December evening Millicent is composing a letter to Susan Loeppky. So far she has written:

> Dear Susan: It was such a pleasant surprise to hear from you. It must be nice to be preparing for Christmas with your large family in Vancouver.

Millicent has not written many letters in recent years and she's not sure what to say after stating that her family has pretty much recovered from their injuries. She could mention the Wittenberg Christmas, but it will be a quiet celebration over which the ghost of last year's Christmas will hover. Alice will come on Christmas day with her family and everyone will say how much they miss GranMarie.

She could write that yesterday at the thrift store a man

pushing a walker had come in with frostbitten fingers and was given a free pair of woollen gloves. She had wanted to give him a parka too but there were none his size. Two women locked horns over who was actually first to lay claim to the glass-topped coffee table reduced to five dollars. Elaine had called in sick with flu and Millicent had to handle the till alone. She could tell that to Susan.

Or she could say that she is at her daughter's house, baby-sitting while her daughter is at the community centre singing with an a capella group she's joined. This is the first rehearsal and now Alice will have something besides Fragile X and the Church of Abundant Joy to talk about, and that's good. But it would take too much explaining.

She could write about Lucas and Jeremy. Susan's letter was full of her family. Her seven grandchildren are all, it seems, at the top of their class, or winning awards at ski competitions or gymnastics or flute. What can she say about Lucas and Jeremy?

In late fall Millicent got her driver's licence and last week, in spite of snow-covered streets, she drove her husband and her daughter to the airport. She could write about that. But it would be bragging and besides, Susan has probably been driving since she was a teenager.

She could end the letter by saying she looks forward to tomorrow, when Joseph and Mia will arrive home from Toronto. She wants to write "I can hardly wait"—it would make a pleasant ending. Whatever she writes, everything that's important will be left out.

Millicent hears stirring in the boys' bedroom, and when she turns on the light, Lucas opens his eyes and mutters, Oma, Oma. She smooths his hair, caresses his cheeks, and his eyes close once more. Her grandsons' motionless faces are small moons half buried in comforters, pale and pure and helpless. She wants to tell them she doesn't care if they'll never play a flute or score a winning goal, but that would not be true.

Headlights turn into the driveway. It's not Alice but Brian, back from wherever his job took him on such a cold evening. Millicent folds her letter and gets her brown fur-trimmed parka, a gift from Joseph—to keep you warm on your way to the thrift store, he said. But when Brian comes in he kicks off his boots and says, Tea, Millicent? and the suggestion, coming from him, is so unusual, so unexpected, she drops her parka and follows him into the kitchen, where he opens drawers and cupboard doors in a clumsy effort to find tea bags and cups and sugar.

On that cruise, Millicent, with all those Mennonites, did you always feel like you were the odd person out? Brian asks. Did you ever start feeling like you were one of them? Millicent is surprised at Brian's question. At this inkling that the two of them have something in common. She has to think a moment. You know, she says, I've always been an outsider. Everywhere. Even in my own family. Maybe all my life.

I think you're doing really well, Brian says quickly.

Does Brian mean she's doing well with Mennonites or doing well battling depression? It doesn't matter. His attention has edged close to kindness and she must hold on to it.

She asks, What about you, Brian? You married into a family that's half-Mennonite. What she really wants him to tell her is that he loves Alice and will never leave her. That he loves his two sons and always will, even when they must be placed in a special class and assigned a teaching assistant. Even when excitement causes saliva to drip from their mouths. And when they fail to make it onto a hockey team.

I'm still thinking about that non-retaliation, Brian says. Why did Joseph refuse to sue that driver? At least have him charged?

His words jolt Millicent back to that hospital room, Vitaly lying on his bed, Joseph ready to lay charges. She wants Brian to believe that the Wittenberg family acted as one and the relief on Vitaly's face was sufficient reward for all three of them. Joseph is a good man, she says.

They sip their tea, united in the silence and warmth of the kitchen.

Joseph told me something about Mennonites. Brian leans in toward Millicent as if he's divulging something he shouldn't. They formed some kind of army, even though they're supposed to be pacifists. They had guns and everything. They were defending their women and their property against bands of lawless murderers.

Millicent tries to recall the details of Adam Sudermann's lecture, but all she remembers is how she became nauseous and wanted to leave the auditorium.

Joseph says they actually shot and killed their enemies, Brian says, looking up to see if Millicent is shocked, and when she says nothing he adds, Sounds totally sensible to me. You don't turn the other cheek to bandits, for God's sake.

I don't understand it either, Millicent says, but I know it was right not to charge Vitaly. How else could I have faced him when we said good-bye just before leaving the hospital? And the country. And then, keeping her voice steady, she says, Can I ask you something, Brian? You don't have to say, but you and Alice, you have these two boys ... and you live with their condition, and that can't be easy ... and I wonder—and here she falters—I wonder how ...

Brian is stirring and stirring his tea. Finally he says, You know that equipment I've built in our basement for that program someone invented to stimulate young and less than perfect brains and limbs? And to give hope to desperate parents? There's a structure for Jeremy to crawl through and a table where he's helped to move his arms and legs in rhythm. When our boy is old enough, it'll be there, waiting for him. Brian's voice is near to breaking and, rising quickly, he takes the teapot to the kitchen.

Millicent has long wondered if Brian believes in this program. She realizes now that though his heart is broken, he has moved over to side with Alice and maybe that is a kind of healing.

Last Sunday I went to Joseph's church, she says when Brian returns with more tea.

Alone?

Yes. Alone.

Millicent had arrived late at the church and when the usher wanted to seat her near the front, she shook her head and slid into a pew near the back just as the scriptures were being read.

To everything there is a season

The reader, a middle-aged woman with a clear, pleasant voice, read as if she could taste the words on her tongue and relished their texture. She did not hurry and did not dramatize. She enumerated clearly: *a time to be born, a time to die; … a time to break down, and a time to build up; … a time to mourn, and a time to dance; … a time to embrace, and a time to refrain from embracing; …*

Listening, Millicent had felt the rhythm of the phrases seep into her and she relaxed. She'd wanted Joseph beside her, but even alone, she felt more at home in this place than she had ever done. When the reader came to the end of the litany—*a time to love and a time to hate, a time for war, and a time for peace*—the congregation sat perfectly still and Millicent wondered if everyone was trying to absorb the wealth and variety of options. The choices to be made. She wondered why the scriptures didn't include: A time to heal and a time to wait for healing.

Learn anything? Brian asks, interrupting her reverie.

Learn?

At church. Did you learn anything?

Yes. Millicent is about to say she learned it's a time to love, but that seems too revealing and so she says, I've learned that it's time to move on. And that's how I'll end my letter to Susan, she thinks. I'll say the Wittenbergs are moving on.

The two are still at the kitchen table when Alice arrives, bringing with her a cloud of crisp cold. She pulls off her toque and her dark mop of hair springs to life. She kicks off her boots, and holding her upturned hands in front of her like empty cups, she sings:

Above the tumult and the strife
I hear that music ringing
It sounds an echo in my life
How can I keep from singing?

There are tears in Brian's eyes and Millicent wants to comfort him. Alice, her face glowing from the cold, heads for the boys' room and when she returns announces, Everything's good. At the kitchen table, sheltered from the bitter December night, the trio is content to sip hot tea and listen to the comforting hum of the furnace fan. When Alice takes the cups back to the kitchen she sings again:

O healing river, send down your waters
Send down your waters upon this land.

In the bedroom the boys are asleep.

~

The flight to Winnipeg leaves Toronto on time and among its passengers are Joseph Wittenberg and his daughter. Mia has the window seat, and Joseph, no longer needing crutches though still accepting the security of a cane, sits beside her. They have stowed their winter jackets in the overhead bin.

In Toronto they stayed with Phil and Sue. When Taylor saw his uncle he burst out: Wise man! Wisewisewise man! His words burbled over each other delighting everyone—the boy had remembered last year's Christmas pageant.

Stretching his leg into the aisle, Joseph smiles at the words Taylor used. He knows the limits of his wisdom. A wise man would know how to think about Taylor and Lucas and Jeremy, three boys who could not refuse the heritage passed on to them. Phil and Sue were reluctant to speak of the affliction, as if it was shameful territory. As if allowing such talk would make them poor hosts and spoil the visit. Joseph didn't speak of it either until the last day at the supper table, after they'd finished the lasagne Sue and Mia had made, and silence waited to be broken.

I guess we should be tested, Phil. You and me.

Tested? Phil spoke as if this had never occurred to him.

For Fragile X. For the record.

Phil and Sue's faces registered embarrassment. Or weariness.

Thing is, Sue said. Thing is ... Taylor ... is he ... is Taylor likely to ever get married? Have children? Sue's grief was naked and raw and Joseph was sure his own face reflected it.

Some legacy our mother left us, Phil muttered bitterly. *She* should have been tested.

But she wasn't, Mia had broken in. You can't blame GranMarie.

The brothers were silent. It was true. There was no concrete proof that Marie Wittenberg had brought with her to Canada a secret and undesired legacy. It could have been their father, a man they had never really known.

GranMarie gave us a lovely inheritance, Mia said. She brought her memories with her to Canada and gave us our story.

When Millicent had driven them to the airport, she'd turned to Mia in the back seat. You have to visit Hedie Lodge, she said. And your father should go with you.

Joseph had been too startled to respond to his wife's words, which seemed a kind of permission. He'd dreaded the visit more than he cared to admit. He and Mia had found Hedie's apartment and she was not as he remembered her but a stranger, sitting straight and thin in a wheelchair that seemed much too large, her small hands motionless on her lap like two pale doves, her face narrower than he remembered. Her hair was cropped close to her head and he realized he'd never noticed what a fine head it was, perfectly formed, delicate. Her grey-green eyes appeared enormous, the sadness in them like an ocean.

Hedie smiled, extended her hands and he took them and bent to kiss her cheek. Mia watched. For a moment there were no words. Then Hedie turned to Mia. Did you see the Chekhov museum? And before Mia could reply she said, The Handi-Van will be here any minute. She looked apologetically at her watch. Rob and I are going to the movies. *Crocodile Dundee*— can you believe it? She smiled sardonically at Mia, but then her face turned thoughtful, her voice sombre. It's not my choice, exactly, but I can't be choosy, can I? About where I go, and with whom? And I must say Rob's been a good friend. Friendship, thank God, is still possible. It's undervalued, don't you think? She looked away as if to hide what she really felt.

Joseph and Mia had agreed not to talk about their accident unless Hedie mentioned it. And she did, addressing Joseph: How was the trip? Tell me about the accident ...

Just about healed, Joseph said and indicated his cane. Hedie did not look at it. Her face was empty of expression now, and a feeling of shame came over him. I know, he said. It's not fair. We all came out of it alive and we're all ... He'd wanted to say "well" or "mobile." When Hedie still had nothing to say, he added, I don't deserve to be so lucky, and after more silence, I'm on a leave of absence.

And so am I, Hedie said, though mine's more permanent in nature. She grinned up at him then. What's next for you? she asked. She didn't say his name.

We'll see what happens, Joseph said.

Mia had turned to examine two small watercolour paintings, matted but unframed, lying on a table. One showed a bowl of polished red apples, the other a winter street, the roofs and cars snow-covered, the sky metal grey.

Recognize it? Hedie called from her chair. It's Edison Avenue.

And then Mia read the signature scrawled in the snow. Danny did this? she asked, taking the street scene to the window.

The apples too, Hedie said. He sent them in spring, before he ... before ... you know ...

And then the door opened to admit a stranger in a wheelchair who announced that the HandiVan had arrived. This is Rob, Hedie said and her face brightened. Joseph and Mia bustled around, helping Hedie into her jacket, wrapping a scarf around her head. Gloves, they said. You'll need gloves. All four squeezed into the elevator and descended together.

Sorry to be cutting the visit short, Hedie apologized. These HandiVans are hard to book and you don't want to cancel.

Joseph and Mia watched as a ramp was lowered, the two wheelchairs lifted into the van and the doors closed. Hedie and Rob waved through steamed-up windows as the vehicle took them away, leaving the visitors alone on the sidewalk.

Looking past Mia, Joseph gazes at the clouds piled white as snow outside the small window. Above the clouds the sky is blue and dazzling except at the far edges, where the horizon is blurred. Like the future, Joseph thinks. The burning desire to claim Ab Solinsky's position and occupy his office is not as acute as it once

SARAH KLASSEN

was, but the thought of one day returning to George Sutton Collegiate brings with it a small frisson of joy. Almost like the joy of coming home. He checks his watch. Soon Millicent will start the Camaro, back out of the driveway and navigate the city's snowy streets to the airport to meet their flight. White flakes will settle on the dark swirl of her hair and on the soft brown fur of her parka. He will say, I love you, Millie, and hold her close. She will hand him the keys and he will drive home to the white bungalow with its backyard garden dormant under a blanket of snow.

In spring he will plant a rose bush and tend it so it will thrive. He will work the soil of his garden with diligence, like that distant ancestor who was a farmer. Who returned home one day from a journey that brought consequences no one had foreseen. But a homecoming does not have to be an ending, Joseph thinks. It could as well be a beginning. He adjusts his backrest and closes his eyes. He hopes the streets of Winnipeg are not too slick. He wants Millicent safe.

Mia is thinking of Adam Sudermann, who was, of course, the real reason for this flight to Toronto, though ostensibly it was the interview she'd requested with the counsellor at Ryerson University. Adam had recommended the University of Toronto, where he teaches a class. An excellent university, he'd written in fall. They offer creative writing—a really fine program. You should come, Mia. You deserve the best. Adam didn't know that Mr. Yakimchuk had given Mia a C as her final mark in English. She has to be realistic.

When she sees that her father is sleeping, Mia takes from her pocket Adam's latest letter, which she received a week before they flew to Toronto.

My dear Mia, the letter begins. She likes the greeting. "My darling Mia" would be going too far; "Dear Mia" not far enough. She has always addressed him as "Dear Adam."

She reads on, rereads how much he misses her, how impatient he is to see her, how she will love Toronto, he'll be at the airport to pick them up, and why must their visit be so short, etc., etc.

Mia, I've found the perfect place for you, he writes. It's near the university, lots of students live there. Nothing fancy, just a bachelor pad, a walk-up and mostly furnished. And available next fall if you decide to come.

Mia had let herself imagine walking up with Adam, the two of them holding hands, house hunting. A scene so domestic, so intimate, it triggered a fluttering inside her. They would stand together appraising the stove, fridge, cupboards. There would be gauzy curtains at the windows. They would be pleased with everything and Adam would lead her to the bed, which would be covered with a clean white sheet and they would lie down together.

Of course she'd expected none of that to happen. And it hadn't. Not just because her father was with them. She and Adam could not have held hands walking up to the third floor—the stairs were too narrow for anything but single file, the apartment dingy and dark, smelling of stale food and unwashed clothes. She thought she might throw up. Her father had looked around as if he was seriously appraising the rooms, but Mia knew he was pretending. Adam smiled encouragement.

I don't have to decide right this minute, do I? She hadn't looked at either of the two men, but she knew Adam's face had fallen and her father's brightened.

When Adam showed Mia his office the next day, Joseph was not with them. Alone with her, Adam spoke about the course on Eastern Europe he would be teaching, and his research on Mennonites in the former Soviet Union. Mia traced her finger along the spines of books on the shelves. She pulled out one about the Russian Revolution and said, We had this same book at my high school. She stepped close to show Adam, who took the book with one hand and with the other smoothed her hair back from her forehead. You are so lovely, Mia, he said, and once again she heard it as, I love you, Mia. Kurt had never said he loved her.

Adam put down the book and Mia thought that now he had both hands free to touch her cheeks, her breasts, her thighs. An adoration she was ready for. Adam held her by the shoulders and kissed her on the mouth. Lightly. We have to go, he said. I have a class.

When they said goodbye two days later, Adam once again had to rush. You'll write, won't you? he said to Mia.

As the flight nears Winnipeg, Mia closes her eyes and thinks of Taylor, his awkward movements, his unclear speech.

If you come here for university you could live with us, Aunt Sue said at the airport. Mia hadn't expected her aunt to see them off and this invitation surprised her even more. She had hugged Sue, who smiled and hugged her back and said, I mean it. We'd love to have you.

Mia didn't say no. The offer was an improvement over the apartment Adam had shown her.

Staring at the clouds outside the window Mia wonders whether she would learn to love Taylor if she moved in with Uncle Phil and Aunt Sue. And if one day a child like Taylor—or Lucas or Jeremy—should call her mother, would she know how to love that child?

Last September, when the doctor in Dniepro finally discharged Joseph, the Wittenbergs boarded the next flight home to Canada, Joseph in an aisle seat to accommodate his injured limbs. Somewhere over the Atlantic, with Millicent asleep, Joseph turned to Mia: What made you end GranMarie's stories when they left Russia? You didn't write anything about Edison Avenue.

We ran out of time, Mia said. The school year was over. She has never told her father that Mr. Yakimchuk refused to accept her last, late assignment.

And besides, Mia added, GranMarie claimed she couldn't remember much about when they arrived as immigrants on Edison Avenue. Did she speak to you about it? When you were a boy, did she tell you stories?

When I was a boy, Joseph said, I didn't listen, but I don't think she spoke about that. Not then. But more recently she did. Not long before she died.

What did she tell you?

A love story.

And then, surrounded by sleeping passengers and the hum of the aircraft, Joseph became the storyteller, giving Mia a missing chapter of GranMarie's life. A chapter in which "such great love" was offered her by a man who would become a permanent shadow in her memory. A man who would leave her with a secret she could never tell until her son was ready to be her confessor. And she his.

Mia closes her eyes. Tomorrow, first thing, she will make an appointment for the test that will determine whether somewhere within the mystery that is her body she carries a Fragile X chromosome, dormant and waiting to be passed on. She will be brave and go alone.

No. She will let Alice come with her. Alice, who lives with the evidence of what she carries in her genes. Evidence that fills her life, present and future.

Mia will continue at McDonald's, but her real work this winter will be to complete what she has begun: her family's story. Her father has filled in a missing chapter and their summer cruise provides a sequel. She will make out of what she has been given a narrative worthy of those who lived it. It will be good enough to support an application to any university. She will send it to Hedie Lodge, whose story has been cruelly altered. Will Hedie still be interested in hers? If Adam asks, she'll let him read it too.

The flight is approaching Winnipeg and the passengers are instructed to fasten their seat belts in preparation for landing. Joseph sets his backrest upright. Mia looks out the window as the aircraft plunges into cloud and suspends the travellers for a while in the uncertainty of darkness before breaking through into the low light of a winter afternoon. Below them the Red River is a wide white ribbon winding its frozen way to the heart of the ciy where it is joined by the Assiniboine River, then on past Bur Oak Park, past Kildonan Drive and the Wittenberg bungalow with its snow-covered garden.

This novel has become a receptacle for stories told me by my mother. Events and characters have been filtered through her memory of them and through my memory of her telling and retelling. In the process of embedding her memories in a work of fiction, events were further altered, sometimes pared down, sometimes embellished; characters were reimagined and reshaped; fresh details and new characters were invented. The core of my mother's stories remains, however, and I remain indebted to her.

Acknowledgements

Deep gratitude to the Turnstone team—Jamis Paulson, Sharon Caseburg and Sara Harms—for their interest in this manuscript and their diligence in seeing it through the stages of production; to Wayne Tefs for rigorous editorial guidance that made the story better; and to Heidi Harms for meticulous attention to every detail. Thanks to Sandra Birdsell who read the ms at an early stage and offered valuable advice and to Sally Ito for her response to a chunk of it. Thanks also to Becky Wood and Angeline Schellenberg for conversations regarding genetics; to Christine Longhurst and Dorothy Dyck for email exchanges about songs; to Dora Dueck for encouragement and wise words; and to the late Peter J. Froese whose unpublished memoir was a helpful source. Thanks to the Manitoba Arts Council for two productive summers at the Deep Bay log cabin artists' retreat at Riding Mountain National Park. Brief excerpts from this manuscript have appeared in *Rhubarb* magazine.